The
River
Hideaway

"Hearts have no color"

Billy Beasley

The
River
Hideaway

by

BILLY BEASLEY

Oak Tree Press Hanford, CA

Oak Tree Press
Publishers Since 1998

For information, address Oak Tree Press, 1820 W. Lacey Boulevard, Suite 220, Hanford, CA 93230.

Oak Tree Press books may be purchased for educational, business, or sales promotional purposes. Contact Publisher for quantity discounts.

First Edition, May 2014

ISBN 978-1-61009-136-7
LCCN 2014939235

≈≈≈≈

Author's Note:

This book is a work of fiction. The characters reside only in my heart and mind. And while Wilmington, NC was indeed a place of civil unrest at times in my youth, this book is in no way an attempt at historical fiction.

This book is dedicated to my mom, Beatrice Rogers Beasley. I hope that God allows you to peer over the balcony and see that your prayers have been answered in my life.

And to my grandmother, Ruth Rogers. Grandma, I based the character of Vicky on you but no fictional character could ever match who you were in real life to a little boy that knew his safe place was always with you.

PROLOGUE

Louie

Louie gazed out at the still lake and smiled at the tranquility that the early morning offered. The sun was scarcely up and the light filtering through the towering pine trees behind him soothed his skin with its gentle warmth. There were days past belonging to a much younger man when he could easily swim across this lake and back without being winded. He swam better than the white boys, and on those rare occasions when for a brief time skin color was forgotten they swam together in this same lake. Of course they had to make certain that no adults were around to segregate them if they were caught, or dole out a far worse punishment. He recalled his brief friendship with Nicky, a white boy who grew up on a struggling farm just down the dirt road. They spent virtually every late afternoon swimming this same lake during the summer they were ten years old. It was a sweltering hot day in mid August when Nicky's dad arrived without warning as they were playing and laughing in the lake. They never swam together again.

Louie was old now and his gait stiff as he leaned ever so slightly to his left to compensate for the pain in his right hip. Neither the pain nor the loss of younger days removed his smile. He was seventy-three and he was okay with his lot in life. There was more waiting for him and of that he was certain. He would one day go to a place where no one would look down on him. His thoughts drifted to his bride of over fifty years and he knew that he was not anxious to leave this world just yet. He loved her more now than ever. They still could not keep their hands off of each other but it was a softer, gentler touch now, and it did not lead to the way they once ravaged each other with love and laughter. He shook his head softly and smiled at this passage of time also. "I love you, Elma," he said softly as he watched a mallard glide effortlessly across the lake.

He sensed the presence of someone and his eyes were drawn to a figure seated on the bank across the lake. The man wore a purple robe streaked in the brightest color of white that he had ever witnessed. The man wore sandals that seemed as if they came from another era. That is a peculiar way to dress, he thought.

The man stood and stretched out his arms much wider than his body was created for. Louie's entire body immediately covered in goose bumps. He rubbed his arms vigorously trying to warm himself. Just as quickly as they appeared the goose bumps departed and he felt warm inside. His thoughts drifted to a soft glowing candle placed on a dinner table illuminating the room with soft, peaceful light.

The figure placed his left hand to his side but his right arm remained stretched out. Louie followed the direction of his arm and viewed a scene he failed to comprehend. There was a large group of people and they seemed divided evenly between black and white, male and female. He could see into the middle of the group and what he saw disturbed him greatly. Bret Marin and his little brother Alex were in the middle of the crowd holding dearly on to each other as the mob fought to tear them apart. His eyes moved to the top of the hill and he saw Walker Marin Sr. gazing smugly down at the scene without concern. In fact he seemed to have a look of triumph on his face and there was the slightest of smiles portrayed in the corners of his mouth. He was the richest man in town and their father. Louie tried to get along with everyone, even the white people at the Country Club, the place of his employment.

He never felt comfortable around Walker Marin. Mr. Marin was cordial enough but the truth was Louie felt the presence of evil permeate from the man.

He was startled by a gentle but firm clear voice. "The boys need you, Louie. Will you do this for me?"

He fell to the ground and with tears streaming down his face he cried softly. "Yes, Lord. Yes, Lord."

"Friend, tell no one until it is done, save Elma."

He rose to his knees. "Friend, Lord?" But he saw nothing. The lake was silent and only the mallard remained. He stood and turned toward home.

He woke abruptly. "You all right, honey," he heard Elma say so kindly.

She softly persuaded him to turn to her and she was concerned when she saw the tears on his face. "Louie, why are you crying?"

He failed to answer and the room remained silent as Elma smiled warmly, pulling him into her bosom and held him as if he were the greatest treasure life offered, because he truly was.

CHAPTER ONE

The Marin Family

The horn sounded, abruptly concluding the dream of a state basketball championship. Bret Marin stood motionless on the wooden floor in the New Hanover High School Gymnasium. He had played his last game for the New Hanover Wildcats. There was but one trip left and that was the short walk to the locker room. The *losers'* locker room that now seemed so far away. It was the same room that he emerged from two hours earlier never considering for one moment that this day could end in defeat. He took one step in the direction of the locker room and turned back. He gazed up at the scoreboard suspended over mid-court as if it might tell him something different than what he already knew. He had lost. The lights on the scoreboard seem to shine the numbers as brightly and pierce as lightning on a dark summer night. Visitors 72 New Hanover 65; He stared at the scoreboard as if he could somehow will it to show a different conclusion. The numbers glaring back at him thrust a searing, numbing pain throughout his entire body.

He lowered his eyes and surveyed the confines of the gymnasium where he spent so many years and poured so much perspiration into the game that he so dearly loved. At this moment his passion for the game was desolate. There was no comfort in the twenty-eight straight victories that led up to this night. The dream of a state championship was gone, cruelly, and without warning. His teammates were leaving now, making their way to the locker room where they would hear Coach Brown address the team for the final time.

Bret gazed toward the other end of the court. The Tigers from Williston were celebrating their advancement to the Eastern Regional. The all-black school had defeated the predominantly white school. There would be no arguments to last through the coming summer, as in past years, about who would win if the two teams were allowed to compete.

There would be two high schools the following September of 1967 in Wilmington, North Carolina, a small, sleepy, coastal city that comprised much of New Hanover County. The county was bordered by the Cape Fear River and the Atlantic Ocean.

A new high school would open its doors after the summer vacation, John T. Hoggard High School. The other school would be New Hanover or Williston. Next year would bring new school district lines and real integration to the schools of New Hanover County long after the passing of the Civil Rights Act.

There had never been a white student to attend Williston. There were a handful of black students who had fought to attend New Hanover. They went in hopes of achieving a better education. The harassment, the bigotry, and the cruelty forced most to return to Williston.

Bret never joined in the taunts, the name calling, or the mindless pranks the black students endured but he never tried to stop it either. He walked away from it without concern as he did nearly everything and everybody.

Two black girls were all that remained of the twenty black students who began the school year the previous September. Two from a student body of over two thousand students.

Next year, there would not be black teams vs. white teams. An era was ending. Things would never be the same. Change was finally coming to this region of the South so rooted in hatred over the difference of the color of one's skin.

The pain of losing was now joined by the fatigue that Bret felt throughout his 6'3", 180-pound body. His legs felt heavy and weariness consumed them. He felt the tightness and the ache especially in his calf muscles that now seem to bear most of the brunt of thirty-two minutes of intense running, sliding, and jumping. His calves cramped badly the last three minutes of the game, but he said nothing. He scored 33 points, pulled down eleven rebounds, dished out six assists, and stole the ball four times. None of it was enough. He had failed.

He looked across the floor at Money Wilkins. His nickname, "Money," was derived from fans that often said when his jump shot left his hand that it was as secure as money in the bank. Bret could not argue that point as he watched the fans swarm around the victors. Bret had chased Money's slim 6'5" frame with all the intensity he could muster, but to no avail. Money scored 41 points, including the last ten for Williston that sealed their victory.

Several Atlantic Coast Conference schools were recruiting him to play basketball with North Carolina State rumored to be the leader. He had a full ride scholarship just waiting for him. Bret envied his position.

Bret walked slowly toward the victorious group. The white bigots in the gym screamed the same tired racial taunts that they had for the entire game. They noticed Bret and the path he had chosen. They put down their crudely made signs that displayed pictures of watermelons, fried chicken, and monkeys. The group inched forward wanting to join in any fracas that arose despite the heavily guarded gym. There were two dozen policemen lined around the gym floor. It was the tightest security ever witnessed at an athletic event in the city.

The police primary focus was on the bleachers containing white supporters on one side and black supporters on the other that continued to jeer at each other as they had the entire night. They failed to notice Bret approaching the group of players and fans. Caught up in the euphoria of their celebration, the group from Williston on the floor was also slow to notice. He entered the group and continued his path toward Money. Puzzled eyes gazed first at him, then at the police who still had failed to observe the intruder.

In the midst of the suddenly quiet group, Bret approached Money. Money looked at him, his eyes turning from unbridled joy to the intense stare that was etched on his face throughout the game. It was his eyes that were the centerpiece of his handsome light brown face.

It was only at this moment as Bret felt the pressure of the mob surrounding him that he realized what a foolish act he committed.

Bret reached his hand out. Money hesitated at first, his face puzzled, but then he reached out to grasp the white hand stretched out in
front of him.

Neither man spoke. Bret's eyes met the dark eyes of Money's and
nodded once slightly. Money's eyes softened as he realized that for
the first time in his life, he was seeing respect in a white man's eyes,
and it was directed to him. The respect was returned. He knew what
it was like to give your all and still lose. He also knew that, white or
not, Bret was good, very good. And with one exception, he was better
than anyone else the court contained this night. He felt empathy for
this white guy that he had never previously seen and in all likelihood
never would again, and briefly he speculated as to why.

Bret let go of the hand that was dominated by long, skinny, fingers
that held a basketball as easily as others held an orange. He turned to
walk to the locker room. The lane that was open on the way in was
now firmly closed. He knew that he should be fearful but the truth
was he was just too tired to be afraid. He stared at the people blocking his way. He looked them in the eye and waited. A voice from behind him rose above the silence of the group. It was a voice that commanded respect, a voice that once it was in the air, could not be questioned on this night.

"Let him pass."

As the group made a path for him, he knew that the voice belonged to Money Wilkins. He walked across the floor, hearing the
slight squeak beneath his Converse high top shoes. It was a treasured
noise that he already missed.

He entered the silent locker room, greeted by the damp, musty
smell that seemed to breed in all locker rooms like a fungus refusing
to die. All eyes turned toward him, many of them containing the tears
of defeat. "Glad you could join us, superstar. What were you doing,
signing autographs?" Coach Brown's deep, husky voice pierced the
hush of the room.

Bret stared back at him without concern. He was very tempted to
tell this short, fat man just what he thought. He refrained. Their relationship had deteriorated over the years that began when Bret was a
sophomore. Even then, when he was the only sophomore on the var-

sity team he was also the best player. He was a needed commodity for Coach Brown, who would have preferred to win without him. The trouble was he couldn't, and as much as he disliked Bret, he disliked losing more.

Coach Brown intimidated the other boys on the team with his angry, often foolish words that rarely offered even a whisper of praise. He blamed the boys when they lost, though that was a mere five times on Bret's watch. He did, however, take full credit for each win. He loved the spotlight and would spend countless hours explaining to the local media the intricate details of his master game strategy and often how it was a miracle the team could win with the lack of desire and talent his players possessed.

Bret survived the past three years by communicating very little to Coach Brown. He listened to his insults and then went and did it his way. The only thing they shared was a thirst for winning. "Well, superstar, that nigger kicked your ass tonight."

The expression on Bret's face remained unchanged. His eyes gazed intently into the eyes of Coach Brown.

Finally Bret spoke, "I'm going to take a shower. I've got a date tonight." He grabbed his towel and walked to the shower.

He could barely hear the words that came from a startled and now embarrassed Coach Brown. "You get your ass back in here now."

He kept walking. He was through with the little tyrant. Coach Brown was one part that he surely would never miss about high school basketball.

He sat on the bench outside the showers and removed his shoes. He took off the uniform and removed his socks and tossed them in the basket in the corner. He could still hear his former coach cussing loudly as he entered the showers and turned the water on. The rest of the team soon joined him. Only six of them had removed their warm-up clothing to actually play in the game, but they all showered. It was a routine that never failed to amuse Bret.

He ignored the chatter of his teammates as he felt the hot, steaming water soothe his aching muscles. Eventually, he was alone again. The shower slowly brought relief to his exhausted body. He lingered for that reason and more in the hope that Coach Brown would be gone to spin his yarn with the local media. Coach Brown would probably blame him for the loss and that was okay. He accepted full responsibility for the defeat.

He emerged from the shower and walked to his locker. Coach Brown and part of the team were gone. He stood in front of his locker drying his short, thick, black hair, before parting it to the right. Beneath his hair was a face that was prettier than most of the girls at New Hanover High. His looks were just one of the reasons that made him the most adored, and the most hated guy in school. He was loved by the girls who had not yet had their chance with him, hated by the many who had. The guys resented him for simply having so much more than any of them possessed.

Bret's complexion was smooth, avoiding the acne that seemed to infest his schoolmates like the plague. His face curved delicately and there was a slight dimple at the bottom of his chin. His nose was slightly prominent, but in an enhancing way. His eyes varied from blue to green much like the colors of the nearby Atlantic Ocean.

Dan, the center, stood across the room from Bret. His 6'1, two hundred-pound frame that worked relentlessly for every rebound as if it were some priceless possession made him a favorite teammate of Bret's.

"They were lucky. They got all the calls. We're better than they are." Dan's voice was loud and angry.

Three other players spoke in unison, "That's right." Another player chimed in. "Nothing but a bunch of jungle bunnies. There is no difference between them and a bunch of apes."

Dan, growing angrier by the moment added, "And next year, we have to go to school with them. It's wrong. They need to stay with their own kind and we need to stay with ours."

Bret finished dressing and tossed his locker contents into his school gym bag. He looked at the rest of the group, knowing they wanted him to join in with their assessment of the game. He remained unemotional. "We played our best game. We lost. Accept it and move on."

The room was rendered silent as he eased out of the locker room back door into the clear cool March night. He gazed upwards for a moment at the multitude of stars. He paused for a moment and thought of someone he missed before continuing to his Rangoon Red 1965 Ford Mustang convertible. It was a present for his sixteenth birthday from his father. Brand new, the best of the line, just as everything was from his father. But it came with a precipitous price.

He slid into his car and turned the key. The roar of the powerful V8 289 horsepower engine greeted him. He drove the three miles to the country club for the planned dinner with his family and his latest girl, Bonnie.

He walked up the white concrete steps that led to the massive dining room. The doorman, Louie, an elderly, short black man had worked at the club as long as Bret could recall. Louie always seemed to be in a good mood. Bret tried to recall one time that Louie had failed to smile upon greeting him. There was no such time he decided. How could a man with so little be so happy?

"Good Friday evening to you, Mr. Marin, sir." Louie smiled cordially as he spoke.

"How about we make that Bret, Louie?" he replied sharply.

"You know the rules, sir."

Bret shook his head slightly, making no attempt to conceal his annoyance. "Well, we wouldn't wish to offend anyone, now would we, Mr. Louie?"

"Sir, you know that you are going to do just that. You know Mr. Charles is going to be some kind of mad about you not having a sports coat on. It is evening and that means your attire must be—"

"Jacket and tie," he interrupted. "I kind of forgot," he answered smugly. "Don't you think he might let it pass just this once? I mean, it is not like the universe is going to topple over if every single one of these pompous Country Club rules is not followed meticulously," he said bitterly. "Besides, it will free time up for Mr. Charles to do what he does best."

"And just what would that be, Mr. Marin, sir?" Louie asked, with a bright twinkle in his eyes.

"Kissing the butt of every hallowed member in this sacred club," he answered derisively.

Louie studied the young man for a moment. "I take it that you lost the game tonight, Mr. Marin, sir."

Bret closed his eyes and answered tersely, "Why, Louie, I think that you should quit your job here at the good ole country club and become an astronaut. You know something really important."

Louie eyed the young man in front of him without a trace of resentment.

Bret opened his eyes and looked at Louie. He thought he might see anger but only compassion mirrored his eyes. It was compassion that he knew he did not deserve. He shook his head softly and wished he could retrieve his harsh words aimed at a man who never failed to be anything but kind to him. He knew that the warmth and concern in Louie's eyes had nothing to do with the menial job he worked to make ends meet. "I'm sorry, Louie. I didn't mean..." he said so softly that his words were barely audible.

Louie looked at the young man in front of him and smiled broadly. His aged, but still smooth round face was hidden under hair that had passed gray and turned as white as freshly fallen snow. His light brown eyes twinkled with sincerity. If you watched and listened closely you would find the wisdom in this sweet genuine old man. But at the "Club" he was just an old uneducated black man who opened the door for the hierarchy of the city.

"Don't you fret none. The sun don't shine on one dog's behind all the time. Everybody loses something. Now wait right here and let's see if ole Louie can find you a spare coat." His voice lowered as he leaned in, "Maybe his majesty, Mr. Charles, will not die on the spot over you not wearing a tie." Louie winked as the words left his mouth. Bret knew that those very words if repeated could easily result in the loss of Louie's job. It made him feel slightly better that somehow this man trusted him and knew his words were in safe keeping.

Louie returned quickly with a navy blue blazer. He stretched it out allowing Bret to slide comfortably into it. "It's a good fit, sir."

"Thank you, Louie," he said as he turned to face him.

Delicately and efficiently the door man reached out and adjusted the lapels of the coat. "Your family is waiting for you at the..." he said as he began to point. "Oh, you know where your father sits," he said. Louie turned and walked back to his station.

Bret watched him leave, mustering a small smile before turning in the direction of the best table in the house. He walked across the floor passing through the elite families of Wilmington.

His father, the famous attorney, Walker Sr., sat at the head of the table flanked by Bret's two older brothers, Walker Jr. and William. Seated beside William was his little brother, Alex, and beside Walker Jr. was Bret's date, Bonnie. Bret gently touched Alex's soft brown hair as he sat down next to him, considering no other option.

His father spoke, his voice powerful and articulate. The air of his voice always sounded the same whether he was speaking in a courtroom or asking for the Kellogg's Corn Flakes. "It is customary for a gentleman to sit with his date."

His father's believed superiority led him to speak to nearly everyone as if they were beneath him. The utter condescension in his voice seemingly took on an even edgier tone when dealing with son number three. That didn't matter to Bret. He could tune his father out as well as he could anyone and perhaps better.

"Well, sir, I spoke earlier with Bonnie about it and she understands how Alex likes to sit beside me. Isn't that right, Bonnie?" he asked as he looked in her direction assuredly.

"Why, that is correct, sir." Bonnie's southern drawl filled the air. "I don't mind at all." A subject that had not been broached until this very moment failed to catch her off guard.

She was striking. Her auburn hair was long and her eyes were a light, vivid green that glowed from her milky white complexion that contained a few very discreet freckles. She was tall, with long slender legs that seemed to start at her neck. Her chest was generous and the light blue dress she wore accented that fact rather well.

Walker Sr. looked at Bret with disapproval. It was the appraisal that Bret was most familiar with in his dealings with his father.

Walker Sr. was a tall man, as were all of his three oldest sons. There was less than an inch of difference in any of their heights. He stayed in decent shape by playing tennis, though as he neared fifty, there was a slight belly developing. His hair was light brown. It was thinning noticeably and he tried frantically to make each hair serve its optimum purpose. His eyes were a deep ice blue that reminded Bret of a Husky dog he once saw. He was reasonably sure that the dog possessed a soul. Inside his father he was pretty certain there lay only a black vast hole of darkness.

The eldest two sons were skinnier than Bret. They looked more like the type to hang out at the local library than to be competing in athletic endeavors. Walker Jr. or *Wally* as the family called him, was twenty-six and worked with his father at the prestigious Marin law firm. William, twenty-four, was about to graduate from Duke Law School. He was set to join the firm full time in June. Wally and William constantly followed their father's instruction, never questioning him. Bret felt little of anything except contempt for his older brothers.

Alex, well, that was another story entirely. He was a late addition to the family and had just turned ten years old the previous month. Bret was certain that Alex was the one occurrence that Walker Sr. had not scripted precisely in a life that he had thoroughly planned out well in advance.

Alex's face was the adorable kind that old ladies insisted on pinching, much to his dismay. He was lean and was nearing the five-foot mark in height.

He fell off of the balcony at their home four years ago this summer while trying frantically to say one more thing to Bret before he left for a summer basketball camp at Campbell College. His left leg was so severely shattered that he still walked with a slight limp. It was a limp that he would not outgrow and that would prevent him from being like the basketball player and older brother that he idolized. There was but one person remaining in this world that Bret truly cared about, and that was Alex.

Their mother, Georgia, died three years after Alex was born. Bret recalled every intricate detail of that April day. He joyfully got off of the school bus, anxious to practice his basketball skills. He immediately noticed the ambulance parked awkwardly in the driveway, with its rear doors flung open. He started to enter the house but was interrupted by his father. His mother had died of a heart attack at the age of forty-five.

She was a graceful, charming woman, a southern beauty that Bret found difficult to picture as the years passed. He did, however, remember vividly her every word the morning that would prove to be her last on this earth.

She called Bret into the living room before he left for school that day. She beckoned to him to sit with her on the couch and she took his hand in hers. "This is important," she began softly. Her words in sharp contrast to his father's were always soft and gentle. He looked up and stared into her eyes. "What is it, mom?"

"You know little Alex lights up every time you come into the room?"

He nodded his head in agreement.

"He'll need you, son, as he grows up. Be different than Wally and William are with you. Always make time for him."

He answered his mom by saying he didn't care to be with his older brothers anyway.

"I know, son, but realize that Alex loves you above all in this world, even me. Treasure that, dear. I love you Bret." She hugged him tightly and then gave his hair a finishing part with a touch as delicate as a sparrow landing on a tree branch. She kissed him good-bye with a kiss that would need to endure a lifetime.

She was laid to rest on a beautiful sunny spring morning. The azaleas bloomed in various colors of white, pink, red and his mother's favorite, the brilliant purple color that the Formosa offered. The dogwood trees collaborated by offering huge white flowers. The birds sang brilliantly celebrating all that had come to life. His mother lay still in a brown oak casket adorned with flowers. Never again would she be present to talk with, to laugh with, and to love.

His father returned to work that same afternoon. He was a distant man before that day and yet he grew even harder and colder with each passing day.

Walker Sr. never considered marriage again. The talk among town was that he had a lady friend who lived at nearby Carolina Beach that he visited, but Bret had never met her.

Walker Sr. had grown up poor but determined. He worked and earned every scholarship possible and graduated as a lawyer from the University of North Carolina. Always independent, he opened his office alone and with no bank account to speak of. He methodically crafted a reputation as an astute courtroom tactician. He took on a murder case in 1947 that expedited his dreams of acquiring money and power.

He was appointed by the court to defend a house painter, Luther Hayes, a poor uneducated black man. Luther was the last person seen leaving the house of Cecil Arlington, a wealthy fifty-two-year-old man who owned all of the lumber business in town.

Inside the house was Diane Arlington, Cecil's young pretty wife who had sold her heart for wealth. She lay dead, crudely stretched diagonally across their bed. The right side of her head was caved in by the force of the iron fire poker that lay on the floor beside the bed.

The case was open and shut. It was a mere formality for Luther who was hired to paint the house and now would rue the day that he ever set foot on the Arlington property. No one cared about this black man and his destiny with the electric chair, not the least of all his young, aspiring attorney.

Walker Sr. did care, however, about creating a reputation that would bring him the riches he so desperately sought. He began to dig into the case even though initially he didn't believe his client's story, not that it would have mattered. What he discovered through neighborhood gossip was that young Mrs. Arlington liked men more her age and drive than her husband.

Walker Sr. discovered one man in particular, Roland Garrison, who was seduced by the wiles of Diane and then had taken it rather badly when he was dismissed. Roland's repeated attempts to contact Diane were met with no interest. Boldly he walked into her house late that afternoon and attempted to sway her into being with him. She coolly rejected his proposal and taunted him for thinking that she would leave a life of wealth for a man who worked loading lumber onto trucks for her husband.

Roland, his heart torn, his pride humiliated, slipped for one brief moment and went over the edge. In his fury, he grabbed the poker and struck her bluntly, killing her instantly.

Roland waited several minutes as darkness set in. He left through the back door and walked to his truck that was parked several blocks away. One person saw him enter the Arlington house that afternoon, an elderly black maid that worked next door. No one saw him leave.

Walker Sr. lured Roland into a sense of security on the witness stand initially with his smooth, soft-spoken authoritative voice. Why he practically apologized to Roland for his being questioned when there was a black man handy that surely was guilty. The all white jury could not conceal their smiles but then neither could Judge Brenner, a slight man, with a booming authoritative voice.

Walker Sr. asked Roland if he had ever been inside the home of his employer. Roland smiled easily now, being lured unknowingly by the charm of Walker Marin and responded,"Of course not," and suggested that the black maid next door needed to change her eye glasses. A remark met with laughter from nearly everyone in the courtroom.

"You never have been inside that house?"

"No," answered Roland, who suddenly did not feel quite as comfortable. His mouth grew dry and he wanted water but did not dare ask for it.

"Were you ever intimate with Diane Arlington?"

"No," he blurted out abruptly.

The door opened in the back of the courtroom interrupting the stillness of the courtroom. Walker Sr. turned toward the sound as nearly everyone did. A well built man of average height nodded to Walker Sr. confidently.

"A moment, your honor?" Walker Sr. requested.

"Make it quick, counselor," Judge Brenner responded with irritation.

Walker Sr. knew every eye was upon him as he strode with purpose toward the visitor. The man handed him a large envelope and Walker Sr. opened it and glanced inside as he chatted softly with the man.

"Counselor."

He closed the envelope and patted the man on the upper arm. The visitor turned and walked to the back of the courtroom and stood against the wall beside the door. "Forgive me, your honor," he said as he walked toward the witness.

"You have never been inside the Arlington home? Never been intimate with Mrs. Arlington?" he asked as he pulled a stack of 8x10 photographs from the envelope.

"Objection. Asked and answered." Mark Singer, the district attorney, said tersely.

"My apologies, your honor," Walker Sr. said before the judge could rule.

He turned his full attention back to the witness, locking his eyes in on the defendant. Roland's forehead was noticeably damp with perspiration.

"What if I told you that Mr. Arlington was suspicious of you and his wife, and hired a private detective?" he asked, as he turned and looked toward the man who had delivered this key piece of evidence.

Roland could stand the dryness in his throat no longer. "Could I please have some water, your honor?"

Judge Brenner motioned to the bailiff who quickly obliged the request.

Roland gulped the water hurriedly, spilling part of the contents down his chin on to his lap. He took a deep breath and tried in vain to calm his nerves. "No," he tried to say with conviction, but his voice seemed tiny and shrill to him.

Walker Sr. smiled shrewdly. "How would you explain pictures of you entering and leaving the Arlington home on several occasions and this one in particular," he said as he pulled it out the envelope and gazed at it. "The one with you and Mrs. Arlington kissing each other as you are exiting the house."

"I didn't mean to do it," he blurted out. Walker Sr. broke Roland Garrison down to a sniveling, confused, pathetic man. Roland tearfully sobbed out his full confession. He foolishly added how much he loved her, as if that justified his actions. He was still looking in disbelief at Walker Sr. as he was led in handcuffs out of the courtroom.

Walker Sr. walked back to his table and placed the envelope on the table as the judge dismissed the charges. Luther stood and shook Walker Sr.'s hand and thanked him profusely but he was barely acknowledged because none of this had been about him. He walked away greatly relieved but perplexed with the man that saved him from capital punishment.

As people filed out the courtroom, Walker Sr. gathered his material and began placing the items in his briefcase. Mr. Arlington appeared in front of him and took hold of the envelope. He opened it and to his dismay found one dozen similar pictures of the front of the Marin home. He shook his head and smiled slightly. "What if you would have had to produce these pictures?"

Walker Sr. retrieved the envelope and filed it away in his briefcase. He looked at Mr. Arlington. "But I didn't." He gathered his brief case and walked triumphantly out the courtroom.

The results of the trial stretched across the nation. Walker Sr. made certain of that when during the course of his research he discovered that another of Diane's suitors was the married son of the manager of the Wilmington newspaper. The victory expedited Walker Sr.'s career and in due time his reputation grew with each triumph. He received calls from as far away as Texas to take on murder cases, and he could name his price. He was cunning, and lacking of any moral fiber that would inhibit his conscience from turning guilty people free.

He also possessed an uncanny ability to know the exact moment to pull the trigger on a business deal. He was presently the largest landowner in town, and his stock portfolio rivaled a mutual fund, though with far greater success.

Walker Sr. was easily the richest, most powerful man in town if not the entire state. He had been approached to run for governor several times and his reply was always the same. "I couldn't stand the pay cut." He meant that statement with complete candor.

Predictably, dinner was already ordered for everyone. It was an easy choice because Friday night was prime rib night at the club. The chefs were the best the port city had to offer. The food was one perk of the hallowed club Bret thoroughly enjoyed.

Even better than the cuisine were the pretty young ladies the club contained. Girls like Bonnie. Bret knew that his looks were certainly not a detriment, but he also knew that it surely did not hurt that he came from wealth and even more awaited his future. He knew that many of these young ladies carried hopes that they might one day become a key component of the Marin clan and enjoy the wealth it contained. The things these delicate creatures would do behind closed doors. They displayed boldness and a willingness to satisfy that he was fairly certain they had not learned in charm school.

Bret felt little for any of them, including Bonnie. They were objects detached of anything real. They were to be enjoyed physically, and for nothing else. He grew tired of each one very quickly. Bonnie foolishly thought that she would be the one to change him, choosing to ignore the dozens of country club girls that had previously tried and failed.

The conversation at dinner consisted mostly of business between Walker Sr. and his two oldest sons. Bret was expected to follow in their footsteps. The path lay out by his father for Bret's career that he rarely questioned, though he was not so enthusiastic about it. Each son would finish near the top in his studies and each summer, beginning at age fifteen, they would work in the law firm. The job included running errands, researching cases, and as much courtroom observing as possible. All mandatory classes dictated by Walker Sr. By the time his sons were ready to join the firm full time he wanted them as seasoned as possible.

It helped that Bret didn't have a real desire to do anything different. That was good because, while many fathers threatened to cut their children off, Bret was certain his father could and would do it if any of them thought of deviating from his plan. Besides, who would be foolish enough to walk away from a lifestyle so luxurious?

Following the old man's rules did come with perks. There was the new car on your sixteenth birthday and with each graduation that followed. They were paid for working at the law firm. Initially $100 dollars weekly, paid year round for a summer job. Each year, the pay was increased an extra $50 till they passed the bar exam and joined the firm full time. Bret's pay, beginning in June, would rise to $250 weekly, while most working high school kids would be earning the minimum wage of $1.40 per hour.

Walker Sr.'s dignified voice filled the air. "Bonnie, has Bret told you that he has been accepted at Duke?"

"No, sir, he has not," she replied, as she smiled at Bret.

Bret smiled sarcastically. "That is if I don't get drafted and have to go to Vietnam."

"Could that happen, Bret?" Bonnie asked with such concern, foolishly thinking she would still be around in the occurrence of such an event.

Walker Sr. interrupted, "The draft board doesn't bother aspiring attorneys who are headed for Duke. Bret knows that." There was a forced smile as he stared at his rebellious son intently.

Bret looked beyond that and recognized the cold ice blue eyes that carried a warning. Do not dare challenge me in public. Bret's sour mood led him to disregard the look.

"So, Dad, you even have control of the draft board?" He smiled tightly at his dad. He was the only one of the boys to engage in any conversation that could be even slightly misconstrued as being disrespectful.

His father gazed at him for a moment before deciding to change the subject. "Coach Brown told me that you started an argument with him in the locker room after the game."

The silence overwhelmed the table. Bonnie shifted uneasily in her chair. Bret looked at his father and turned away, failing to reply.

Alex broke the silence, "Bret, are you going to play basketball anymore?"

"I'd like to, little man."

"Basketball is over. It's time for Bret to work as hard at being an attorney as he has being a basketball player," Walker Sr. said, the derision evident in his voice.

He knew it was fruitless to try but Bret couldn't resist one more attempt to sway his dad. "The coach from Campbell called and offered me a full scholarship. I could go there for my undergraduate work. It's a good school."

"That's nice, but a future member of my law firm is going to Duke. Do you know how badly I wanted to attend? Chapel Hill is a fine school, but it is public. I couldn't afford a fine private school like Duke. It is held in as high esteem as the Ivy League schools."

"Campbell is private."

"End of discussion, Bret."

Bret knew just how far he could push the old man. Still, he tried one more time. "I called Coach Bubas at Duke this week. I asked for a chance to play. He said that he will place me on the freshman team and give me a chance. And maybe if things work out I can get a scholarship down the road."

"Basketball is over for you as of tonight," his father replied, leaving no room for debate.

Alex asked, "Bret, why can't you get a scholarship to play at Duke?"

"They didn't offer me one. They aren't sure that I am good enough."

"They are wrong." Alex's voice rose defensively bringing with it the high shrill his father hated.

"Be quiet, young man, or at least till that voice changes." Walker Sr. said, his voice harsh and humiliating.

Alex's head dropped and tears welled up in his eyes.

"Aren't you ever going to outgrow crying about everything?" Wally asked sarcastically, trying as always to win favor with his father, even if that was produced by bullying a little brother who had done no wrong.

There were two reasons Wally had picked a poor time to gain favor with his father. First, Bret was tired and angry, and more pertinent than that, it was Alex who was the victim of his brother's cruelty.

Bret rose slowly from his seat. He placed both hands on the table and leaned forward. His eyes raged across the table to their intended destination. "Do not ever embarrass him in that way again? Do you understand?" he said evenly.

Wally stammered and started to speak.

"Save it. I can't do anything now about how you two wonderful brothers of mine treated me growing up," he said, drawing William into the subject.

William interjected, "I didn't say anything to your precious little Alex."

"No, but you have before. You two have a thing for ridiculing little brothers, and it stops, now."

There was something unnerving in his voice that made his two older brothers very uneasy about continuing the conversation.

"Sit down, Bret," his father said, uncomfortable that his table was now the focal point in the room. He made a halfhearted attempt to smile. "Why didn't you tell me about the scholarship offer before?" he asked, in hopes that the subject might soothe his young son.

"Because I knew what you would say," Bret replied as he sat down.

"But you tried anyway. That determination will make you a great attorney. It is in the genes, son."

"I have genes from my mom too, or have you forgotten her?"

"Don't be disrespectful about my wife."

He answered quickly, "I would never disrespect my mother."

Walker Sr. tried again to pacify his defiant son. "Were there scholarship offers from other schools?"

"Yes, but Campbell was the only school that I thought that you might approve of. Bonnie and I are going to go to the movies now, if that is okay?" He didn't wait for an answer as he stood up.

Bret looked at Bonnie who immediately got up, thanking Walker Sr. as she did for dinner.

Bret bent down, kissing Alex on top of the head, and whispered softly in his ear, "Don't let them get to you. You let me know if they pick on you, little man."

They left the table. Bonnie went to the powder room and Bret stopped at the door to return to Louie the loaned sports coat. "Thanks, Louie."

"You're welcome, sir. How was your dinner?"

"Better than tonight's game."

Louie looked around, insuring that they were alone. He smiled mischievously and softly said, "Mr. Marin, you should have known that you couldn't beat a bunch of colored boys in no basketball game. Don't you remember what happened in last year's college championship game? That coach from Texas Western put five black boys on the floor together and whipped them good ole boys from Kentucky. Times are a changing, Mr. Marin."

Bret returned Louie's engaging smile. "Well, Mr. Louie, sir, I'll tell you one thing, if my team would have had one more guy as good as me we would have kicked their behinds."

"Maybe so, young man," he nodded with a wink. "Maybe so."

Bonnie walked through the door as Louie held it opened. Bret and Louie exchanged one last smile as Bonnie and he walked toward his car.

Bret drove to the Holiday Inn at Wrightsville Beach where the night manager, Jeff Mason knew the value of a good customer and even more knew to be discreet.

Bret entered his usual hotel room, 444, for which he had his own key, courtesy of Jeff. He decided that this was Bonnie's last night. He'd tell her in the morning.

CHAPTER TWO

Vicky

Bret dropped Bonnie off at the esteemed country club at nine o'clock the following morning. She was meeting a friend who would drive her home. Bonnie's parents were away for the weekend, but still it was better that a female be the one seen dropping her off at home. There was no need to chance nosy neighbors seeing her driven home in Bret's Mustang.

Bret broke the news to her on the way that he was ready to move on. He gave her his standard line that he wasn't ready for anything serious right now, though the truth was he couldn't fathom a time in his life when he would be ready for such a relationship. He was diplomatic, but unyielding even as the tears flowed down her cheeks.

He never offered promises and he rationalized that it was her fault for not seeing him for exactly who he was, or even worse for thinking that somehow she could change him. There was a good reason that she had no chance with that endeavor. He didn't want or see any need to be changed.

He drove the two short blocks through the prestigious neighborhood toward home, though it had not seemed much like home since the day his mom died. The neighborhood was South Oleander and if you had money in Wilmington, this is where you lived.

The houses were predominantly two stories. Brick was the prevailing exterior among the houses, coming primarily in different shades and patterns of red, though a few of the neighbors had selected white brick. Sidewalks ran parallel with streets that were so abundantly lined with massive, gnarled live oak trees that the sunlight strived valiantly to whisper even the tiniest presence upon the ground.

He parked his car in the driveway underneath the basketball goal. The house was two stories. The brick was white and there were two huge white columns rising off of the front entrance with the front door centered between them. There was a large balcony with wrought black iron rails on the second floor in both the front and the rear of the house.

He entered the house where a large foyer presented you with three options. The hallway straight ahead led to the kitchen and dining area. To the right of the foyer was a huge great room, complete with a fireplace that was constructed with deep gray stone. The mantel was a huge uneven piece of marble where family pictures rested. The left of the foyer guided you to the living room. Adjacent to the living room was his father's office. The kitchen and the dining area seemed outlandishly large and empty, but there had been a time when it was habitually filled with dinner guests. The only part of wealth that he could recall that his mom seemed to revel in was the elaborate dinner parties she frequently hosted.

He heard the sound of cartoons filtering in from the living room and it produced a smile and an idea. He walked in finding Alex nestled on the couch. He sat down beside him.

"So, Alex, what do you think that coyote's chances are of catching that roadrunner today?"

Alex kept his eyes glued to the television and answered smartly, "Well, Bret, I think Wile E. Coyote has a pretty good plan today."

"Where is everybody?"

"Dad went to the office and his shadows went with him," Alex replied, borrowing one of Bret's frequent descriptions of his older brothers.

"Are you alone?"

"Barbara is on the way over."

Barbara was a young girl who attended the local college, Wilmington College. She enjoyed keeping Alex and was available practically anytime she was needed.

Walker Sr. had run off three live-in maids since their mom died. Alex was growing older and Barbara had become a better solution than the futile attempts of finding live-in maids that could tolerate Walker Sr.

"How do you feel about me calling her and telling her that you are going to hang out with me today?"

"All right," Alex said with a grin.

"Well, get your butt up those stairs and get dressed while I take a shower."

Alex hurriedly ran upstairs to his room. He put on a pair of jeans, a baseball undershirt with a white body and orange sleeves, and a dark green pull over hooded sweatshirt.

Bret emerged minutes later, wearing jeans, a baseball undershirt with black sleeves, and a black pullover hooded sweatshirt. He looked at Alex and remarked, "Who dresses you, anyway?"

"Well, we are not going to the club for dinner, so I didn't think a coat and tie were needed," he stated with a faked air of superiority.

Bret smiled. "Smart little guy, aren't you?"

Moments later, the cherished Mustang was roaring down the road. The warm, bright sunshine soothed the two boys, lending promises of spring. They rode in a comfortable silence for several miles before Alex broke the quietness.

"Where are we going?"

"I thought we might visit grandmother," Bret answered, and wondered why he felt the least inclined to visit someone he had not laid eyes on since their grandfather's funeral two years ago.

Victoria and Ralph Rogers were the parents of his mother. They lived a modest life in Castle Hayne, a rural area at the northwestern outskirts of the county. Bret used to visit his grandparents with his mother. The relationship he had with his grandparents was best described as cordial.

His grandfather filled his days toiling as a master carpenter and his nights with a bottle of Jack Daniels. Three years ago his liver began to shut down. He drank himself to death and no one ever offered a reason as to why.

Ralph was a quiet man, a loner. The last years of his life when age made it hard for him to find work building houses, he passed the time in his workshop, building bookcases, tables and chairs.

Bret always marveled at what a magician he was with a piece of a wood. He rarely, if ever, made a mistake. As a young boy, Bret enjoyed watching him work and it never bothered him that they seldom talked. Many days, Bret would sit and watch for hours with never a word, or even a glance exchanged. The puzzling thing as he reflected on that time was the realization that he was never bored.

Bret entered the long dirt road that wound its way through the woods that led to his grandmother's house. Both sides of the road were tightly bunched with trees. The tall longleaf pines towered over the plethora of laurel oaks. Mixed in were a few scarlet maples, magnolias, and an occasional cherry plum tree. The cherry trees would largely be unseen in a few weeks when new leaves would create a dense forest. But for now, they glistened with vivid white flowers.

Ralph and Victoria purchased the land over forty years ago and somehow managed to hang on to it through many hard times. The hardest of which was the great depression.

There was a brief opening in the woods, revealing the modest white wood frame house with dark green shutters. It sat on a slight hill near the front of a five-acre tract of land. Each time he saw this house he struggled to picture his mother growing up in a place so vastly different than the house she died in. He noticed that he was holding his breath and he shook his head slightly in annoyance.

Behind the unpretentious home was his grandfather's workshop, which was practically as big as the house. The land behind the buildings was wet, swampy, and dense. Three small creeks ran away from each other, winding their way amongst the river birch trees till they rendezvous again at the Cape Fear River.

Near the bank of the river, centered between two of the streams, lay the greatest mystery the Rogers land contained. There was an old A-Frame shell of a house nestled on top of pilings. It had never been completed. Bret recalled the day he innocently inquired about its origin.

He was about the age of Alex. His grandparents, mom, and he were eating lunch in the small worn kitchen. He asked why that old house down by the river just sat there unfinished.

His grandfather stopped eating and moments later walked outside leaving his dinner behind. His grandmother started to speak but thought better of it and rose and began to tend to chores in the kitchen.

The sadness that consumed his mom's face brought deep sorrow to him. She touched his face gently, smiled, and softly said, "You finish eating, okay?" She rose and walked to her mom, momentarily resting her hand on the old woman's shoulder, before walking outside in search of her father. Bret felt bad that one question brought such heartache. He never inquired about the origin of that incomplete house again.

Strangely, during the last year of Ralph's life he began to work on the old house. He was dying slowly and while his skill as a carpenter was still intact his stamina was not. He asked Bret for help, and Bret obliged. It was the only thing his grandfather ever asked of him.

Bret spent a good part of his last free summer, before his mandatory job would begin with his father, working alongside his grandfather. Bret enjoyed working with wood. He loved breathing in the various aromas that different types of wood produced as the saw eased through them.

He also discovered that he possessed a skill for woodworking. It seemed as if the talent his grandfather possessed had somehow been passed on to him. Bret did not understand it but the only way it made sense to him was that it came as natural to him as basketball always had. He seemed to be able to see what he was supposed to do with very little instruction needed.

He surely did not come by his woodworking skills by listening to his grandfather, being as he seldom spoke. Still, his grandfather always seemed to be able to stop Bret at times when he saw a mistake in the making. Ralph would gently show him the proper procedure, and most often without a word.

Bret never understood why the house became so important to his grandfather with death hovering over him like the early morning dense fog often did over the Cape Fear River. The last time that he saw his grandfather alive, he was weak, the life nearly drained out of him.

"You can finish the house," he said.

Bret protested that he didn't have the knowledge or the skill.

Ralph replied, "Yes, you do. People can't build because they choose too, or want too. They have to be born with that skill, and then that ability must be nurtured. My daddy had it and you have it, boy. I've seen it in you. You may work for your father as some big shot lawyer, but your eyes will never light up the way I've seen them when you mold a piece of wood that matches the picture that only you can see in your head."

It was the most Bret had ever heard his grandfather talk and all of it about a house that was destined to sit forsaken in the woods.

Victoria heard the sound of the car and walked out on the tiny porch to see what visitors the day had brought. She was a strong woman, proper, and dignified. She always walked with her head held high, a proud woman. Nothing ever took that from her, not a loveless marriage with an alcoholic, or a daughter that moved off to another world, forsaking all that she knew.

Wrinkles touched a face where unmistakable beauty once reigned. Her hair was white, but each one in its proper place. Her frame was highlighted by broad shoulders that knew the meaning of hard work.

Each spring, she worked a garden alone that helped bring food to the table. Each fall she made beautiful quilts. No two would ever be the same. The money they brought to help ends meet could never be the proper recognition for such artistry. The quilts were never art to her. They were work. It was a craft performed since she was a small child, learned at the side of her mother.

She had little in the way of friends and her only visitor for the most part was her sister, Ada, who lived in Dillon, South Carolina, and came each year on New Years Day and stayed for two weeks.

Victoria was glad to see the boys, though she refrained from showing it. She loved them and felt cheated that she had missed out on being any kind of grandmother to them. She blamed her daughter, but Walker Sr. more. She had no use for a man who grew up poor and then forgot where he came from. He never once visited after taking her only child away.

She never believed that Walker Sr. truly loved her daughter. She was certain that he only desired her because her beauty enhanced his standing in society. It pained her to think that her daughter spent a life in a marriage where love was merely a word.

Bret walked awkwardly to the porch, slightly ashamed that he had failed to visit in so long.

Victoria greeted them. "Dinner will be at eleven-thirty."

Dinner was always in the middle of the day at her house. It was always served at eleven-thirty sharp, even now when she ate alone.

"We're not hungry, Grandmother. Don't worry about feeding us."

Victoria eyed him sternly and Bret knew that he had said the wrong thing, and as usual with his grandmother it did not take very long to accomplish such a feat.

"Surely you didn't come out here just to insult me by not having dinner. You wouldn't want to teach that little boy with you bad manners, would you?"

Bret's head dropped slightly. His grandmother always seemed to be angry with him and he did not have a clue as to why. At this moment, he was wondering what idiotic thought possessed him to come here. "We'd be glad to eat dinner with you, Grandmother," he answered.

"That would be nice. Now," she paused, before adding, "never drop your head to anyone and stop with that formal sounding, Grandmother."

"What would you like for me to call you?"

"Vicky will do. But you knew that already."

Sheepishly, Alex offered, "Our father says that it isn't respectful to call adults by their first name."

Bret thought that he saw a faint glimpse of a smile emerge from her eyes.

"Well, I don't expect to see your father in these parts anytime soon. So while you are on my land, let's make it Vicky."

"Yes ma'am," Alex replied.

"Bret, go ahead and look in the workshop and that old house down by the river. You'll find everything just as it was. Alex, you can go with your brother, or stay here with me. I might be able to use some help feeding the chickens."

Alex drew closer to Bret and away from this woman he scarcely knew. "I'll go with Bret."

"Suit yourself." If she felt any disappointment, she hid it from view.

They entered the workshop. Each tool was properly put away in its place, just as his grandfather did after each day of work. The place was clean despite being unused in over two years. Bret wondered why his grandmother would go to such trouble to keep a building clean that was not in use.

As he touched the saws, he remembered the last things his grandfather had said. He waits till he is almost dead to try and talk with me. "Gibberish from a dying man," he muttered softly.

"What did you say, Bret?"

"Nothing," he said with a dismissive shake of his head.

"Let's go down by the river." Bret walked out with Alex on his heels.

They walked along the smallest creek till their destination was reached. Bret looked out over the murky waters of the river and thought of the end of those workdays with his grandfather. The sun would work its way down through the trees on the other side. The river would catch streams of orange light that flickered in the ripples of the slow moving water before disappearing out of sight.

There was something in those sunsets that stirred him in a way that he could not explain. He turned and looked back at the house that remained empty, unfinished. He wondered again why it was there and why it had meant so much to his grandfather. He looked down at Alex and was met with a huge smile. Bret smiled back as he studied the eyes that held such admiration. He thought back to last night and how he almost lost control when his brother's feelings were hurt. He remembered his mother's last words and for really the first time, he thought he understood what she meant. Alex was his. His and his alone. He didn't belong to his father and certainly not to Wally and William. He never would.

They approached the steps that were located to the left of the house, leading to the porch that extended ten feet from the house and ran the width of the house. "Let's go in, Alex."

Bret reached over the front door for the key, unlocked the door and walked in.

Suddenly, a large dog appeared. His body was mostly white with two huge spots of dark brown on each side of his body, and with ears that matched the spots. He eased past both of them to enter the house. He went to a corner and lay down to observe.

"Who's that?" Alex asked.

"That is Fred. I didn't expect him to still be around. The summer I spent with grandfather working on this house he showed up out of nowhere and decided to stay. He loved grandfather. He would sit and watch him work all day from that very spot."

"What kind of a dog is he?"

Bret chuckled. "According to your grandfather, he is a sooner."

"What's that?"

"It doesn't matter. I guess he is some type of bird dog that someone turned loose, though he never appeared to be real thrilled about birds or much of anything else, with the possible exception of food."

Alex walked over to Fred slowly and stuck out his hand. Fred wagged his tail and licked his hand.

"He's cool, Bret."

"I'm surprised that grandmother kept him around. She never did like him."

"She doesn't like anybody."

"I can't argue with you about that. She especially doesn't seem too fond of me."

"Why doesn't she like anyone?"

"There are some things that I just don't have an answer for, little man."

Bret surveyed the interior of the house. The downstairs was open and inviting. The oak floor that he and his grandfather installed remained unfinished. Stacked in the corner to the left were the yellow pine studs to be used to section off the kitchen. The adjacent corner contained the tongue and groove knotted ponderosa pine wood that was for the interior walls. There was a set of steps leading up over the kitchen to a loft that ran from one end of the house to the other, and jutted out to occupy one third of the length of the downstairs. There was a fireplace built of slate on the right hand side of the back wall. The chimney ran up to the master bedroom where another fireplace was found before the chimney finished its journey through the roof.

Alex started up the steps.

"Stop, Alex," Bret cautioned urgently. "There is no floor up there to walk on, just the joists are in."

"What's a joist?" Alex asked.

"The joists are what the floor is nailed to."

"What was going to be up there?"

He pointed up at the area and said, "Starting from the end above the kitchen, two bedrooms, and two bathrooms, followed by the master bedroom. The plan he had was for a walkway, or a hall on the front edge. There would be a wall three and a half feet high along the edge to keep little guys like you from falling."

"Why did grandfather build this?"

"I have no earthly idea."

"It's kind of neat, isn't it? Why is there so much glass on the front of the house?"

"So you would always be able to see the river."

They departed soon after and made their way back to the house. Vicky was in the process of putting out ham, cabbage, sweet potato casserole, and the ever-present biscuits that seemed to melt even before they touched your tongue. They enhanced the main meal and afterwards served the dual purpose of desert, when homemade jelly was smeared on them.

There was little talk during dinner. Alex finished first. "Can I go outside and play with Fred?"

Vicky started to tell him to clean his plate first but Bret cut her off. "Go ahead, Alex."

Bret and Vicky remained at the table. Two strangers with very little to say.

"I guess that fancy car was your sixteenth birthday present. You boys get anything you want." Her words were short and sharp.

"What is wrong with that?" he asked defensively.

"Oh, I guess there is nothing wrong with it, unless the price is too steep."

"Oh, I guess the answer is to live out here in the woods like you and Ralph did. It's such a proud accomplishment to be poor."

Her eyes bore into him. "I owe no one anything. I pay my own way. Fancy cars, clothes, and eating at the country club are not something everyone needs to survive."

"What is it with you? I come out here to visit and you don't even appreciate it."

"So, you've done your good deed. I guess you can leave now."

He felt the frustration filling every ounce of his body. "Thank you for dinner," he said, rising out of his chair. He was determined not to lose control with this angry, foolish, old woman.

He called Alex to the front porch and informed him they were leaving. "Thank your grandmother for dinner."

Alex thanked her and they walked toward the car. Her voice pierced the air, "Your grandfather said that you would be back."

Bret stopped and turned to her, but refrained from speaking as he waited for the explanation that he knew was coming.

"He said it after you left that day. The day on his deathbed when he asked you to finish the house because he knew he couldn't. You remember that day, don't you, Bret? It was the day that you told him, no."

"I never told him no," he shot back. "I told him I couldn't do it."

"Slice it anyway you like, but the answer you gave him was no."

"Maybe to you."

"No, to him."

"I was just a kid."

"You have never been a kid, young man."

He looked at her and wondered what if anything would appease her. He stood silently looking at her waiting for her to finish whatever it was she had on her mind.

"He liked you. Do you know that?"

"How could I tell? The man never talked. Except when he was dying and about some stupid ass house that no one was going to live in," he answered, unable to keep the frustration from his tense words.

"Do you use language like that in front of that boy very often?"

Bret swore softly to himself that he would never come here again. He motioned Alex to the car and drove down the dirt road leaving the dust of the country behind him along with a disappointed old woman standing in the drive.

Bret spent the remainder of the day with Alex. It would be an adjustment to not be occupied with school basketball for six days a week. But for today, it seemed a welcome break to have a free day.

They went downtown and visited a few of the shops in the area. Most of Wilmington's shopping was concentrated in the downtown area. There were two shopping centers a few miles down the road, but the finer stores, the bigger stores, were downtown near the river. Bret bought a baseball cap for each of them. He also helped his little brother's baseball collection along by purchasing several packs of 1967 Topps Major League Baseball Cards, which had just arrived in the stores.

Alex was fonder of baseball than Bret was. He loved to watch the Saturday afternoon games that would soon be starting. His favorite team was the Philadelphia Phillies.

They arrived home around seven just as Walker Sr. was heading out. "Barbara is on her way over. I assumed you were going to the team party at Dan's house. What did you boys do today?"

Bret answered. "We visited grandmother and went downtown."

"I see," he replied, with a slightly puzzled look on his face. "I'm on my way out," Walker Sr. said, declining to ask why Bret visited Victoria's. He preferred they have no contact with her but it wasn't worth discussing.

Alex had disappeared up the stairs. Bret asked a rare question of his father. "Why is that old house down by the river at Victoria's?"

Walker Sr. shifted uncomfortably by the door that he wished now he was already through. "It was nothing but a foolish old man's dream."

"That's not an answer."

"There is no answer, Bret. There's really not."

He watched his father leave and he wondered what secrets that old house contained. It was just an old house. It wasn't a living thing, but for reasons unknown it was treated as if it were just that.

"Maybe it is haunted," he said sarcastically as he made his way upstairs.

He showered and got ready for what everyone had hoped would be a celebration party at his teammate's house. He put on jeans and a red McGregor knit shirt, topped off with a red and white windbreaker. He got enough of dressing up in his father's world. Outside of the club and his father's office, he dressed for comfort.

Barbara was downstairs waiting. She was a short girl, barely over five feet tall. She was not what would be termed as pretty, but she took cuteness to its optimum peak. Her thick blonde hair was kept short with the exception of the bangs that she was constantly removing out of her big brown eyes that seemed to contain a hint of mischief. Her body was somewhat stocky, but athletic looking. Her shoulders, arms and her legs in particular were slightly thick, but every inch of her was solid.

Barbara was way past the maturity one would associate with a young lady of twenty. It did not bother her that many of the girls she went to high school with were married, on the way to being married, or away at some prestigious college, partying every weekend.

She wanted to be a teacher of young children like Alex. It was not easy for her to be able to afford attending Wilmington College. She loved her parents and they helped where they could. Her dad worked at the local city golf course. He loved the outdoors and his work. The job paid for food on the table and other necessities but little beyond that, and certainly not enough for college tuition. She didn't mind working her way through college. The way she looked at it her parents provided a roof over her head, a warm bed at night, food in her stomach, and unlimited love. The rest was up to her to manage. She knew that in this area of riches and prestige that she was thought poor, but she knew better.

"Hi, Bret. I'm sorry about the game," she said, reaching out to touch him on his arm.

"Thanks," he replied.

She was wearing a loose white sweater and jeans the color of bone.

Bret often was tempted to make a move on her. She surely wouldn't be his first college girl. There was something about her that made him want her in the worst way. But he had refrained because of the relationship that she had with Alex. He didn't want that spoiled, or lost when he was through with her. Alex really liked her and Bret felt confident that Alex was not only taken good care of, but happy when he wasn't around.

"Are you going to the party at Dan's?" she asked.

"Yes."

"Some of my girlfriends from school are going."

"Did dad mess up your plans?"

"It's okay. I don't really want to go. Too many high school kids, no offense intended. Besides your father pays me well, and I know that I have to be available."

"Yeah, he doesn't take no very well. It's a shame that you have to miss out on so much."

"My school work is more important than parties."

There was something about Barbara that he found refreshing. She was so different than the country club girls that he was accustomed too. He was tempted to ask her to come by the party later.

Alex bounded into the room and jumped into Barbara's arms. "Are you spending the night?"

"No, your father said that he would be home by eleven."

"Can I stay up until eleven?"

Barbara winked at Alex. "How about ten forty-five?" She knew how punctual Walker Sr. was and she didn't want to hear any complaints about Alex being up too late.

"Okay," answered Alex, who understood exactly what the fifteen minutes were for.

"I'm leaving, Alex," Bret said as he hugged him good-bye. He walked to the door to leave. He stopped and turned back to Alex. "Thanks for hanging out with me today. I had a great time."

Alex grinned at Bret. Bret had a magical way of making him feel like the most important person in the world. That was easy for Bret, because in every way that mattered to him Alex was the only person in the world.

Barbara walked to the door with Bret. She stepped out on the porch and touched his arm again, but this time she held it with a light grip. She was close enough now that her subtle perfume was gently making its way into his nostrils. He breathed it in. He was closer to her than he had ever been. She seemed friendlier than usual.

"I really am sorry about the game. I'm sure that state championship that everyone has been talking about was important to you." She rubbed his arm slightly and he thought she was going to turn it loose, but she gripped it again, firmer. She smiled at him and he didn't know what was harder to resist, her lips that he wanted so much to touch with his, or those gorgeous dark brown eyes that looked up at him far differently than he had ever noticed.

"I heard that you and Bonnie split."

Word traveled fast in this city. He was struggling for words and, even more to resist her now obvious flirtation.

She turned her head slightly as she looked up at him, gently massaging his arm. "I thought you were Mr. Cool with the women. You sure are quiet right now. You act like you are scared of me. Is it because I'm not one of those fragile little country club girls?"

"Barbara, I can't go out with you. Alex cares about you and you are great to him, and as for your comment about the girls at the club, I find you to be a breath of fresh air."

"Bret, you are a great looking guy, with a monstrous ego. I am different than those girls at the club. For one, I am not a high school girl. I also don't want to be your girlfriend. And I've no desire to be part of the Marin family on that day that you dub some lucky girl a fairy princess by making her Mrs. Marin."

Bret was slightly stunned. No girl had ever spoken to him in a manner such as this. He tried to recover. "Why don't we meet somewhere after my father comes home?"

She smiled mischievously at him. "You mean meet you at the Holiday Inn? Maybe in room 444?" she asked, her voice now low, oozing with sensuality, but firm, letting her intentions be known.

He wanted to speak, but for some reason no words emerged. He wasn't in control and it felt awkward, uncomfortable. How did she know about the Holiday Inn? And the room number?

She put her other hand on him and pulled him closer. He could feel her against his body. His heart rate quickened as he contemplated his next move.

"That is what you want, right?"

Finally, words found their way through the dryness in his mouth. "It won't change anything with Alex?"

"It might, if I were inclined to meet you there," she teased.

"And are you inclined to meet me?" He smiled smugly, his confidence growing as he was quite certain of the answer.

She gripped his other arm and pulled him close to her, pulling him down to her so that she could whisper in his ear. He smiled, the temporary lapse of confidence of a few moments ago now dissipated into the evening air.

She laughed slightly before asking, "But you know what?"

"What?" he asked, smiling at her, assured of what was in store for him later tonight.

She locked eyes with him smiling ever so mischievously before answering. Her voice remained soft as she said definitely, "I am not inclined to meet a jerk like you at the Holiday Inn or any other place, for that matter."

She had played him and he did not like the feeling. He searched for words to say but all he could muster was, "Why would you do this?"

She stepped back. Her face was hard and anger raged in her eyes. "Because Bonnie's older sister is one of my best friends. I went by their house this afternoon. Bonnie had been crying nonstop pretty much for the entire day. She looked like hell and felt worse because of a complete jerk like you."

"I never lied to her. I made no promises."

"You never told her the plan though, did you? You never told her that when you were tired of sleeping with her you would coldly drop her off one day at the club and tell her that it was over. People aren't cattle, Bret. She is a human being with a heart, and a soul, things I am fairly certain that you do not value."

"Like she didn't know what she was getting into. It's no secret who I am."

She shook her head at him and breathed deeply. "I know the story, Bret. You are the cold, egotistical, self centered, heartless person that people say you are, and that fits, except for..."

She paused, unsure if she wanted to say what she felt.

"Except for what?" he asked harshly.

"That little boy inside the house," she stated, motioning toward the house. "You've got a heart and he owns it."

Bret stood, digesting her words and had none to offer. She smiled warmly at him and he was confused by the sudden change.

She touched the side of his face lightly. "You always think that you are saving Alex. Saving him from your father and your brothers and maybe in some way that is true, but what is also true is that he is your hope too. And do you know what my hope is, Bret?"

He sighed and answered, "You haven't held anything else back. Why would you stop now?"

"I won't," she replied. "My hope, Bret, is that you save each other and find a way out of this jail."

"This jail provides you with money that you need."

"Oh, I am supposed to be worried about losing my job because of this?"

"Maybe," he answered smugly.

"I'm not worried, and do you know why?"

He looked at her and knew exactly why.

"You won't tell anyone about our conversation, Bret. And for once it is not about your ego, or even about me turning you down, which I did. It is because you know that Alex loves me. You also know that this is more than a job for me. It is true. I am a young woman from meager means and this job allows me, along with the help my parents can give, to attend college."

She looked him intently in the eyes and said, "You know that I love Alex. You also know that I will protect him in any way I can."

He nodded his head softly in resignation. "You are right."

"I need to go to the party now." He turned and began walking to his car.

He was almost to his car when he was certain that he heard her say softly, "I have hope for you, Bret Marin, even if no one else does."

He turned back and saw the door closing with her on the other side. He stood in the early evening crisp March air, wondering just what it was she meant by her last statement.

CHAPTER THREE

Money

It was almost noon the following Wednesday. Bret chose to skip his usual lunch at McDonalds and venture home for the cold cuts that the fridge always contained in ample supply.

The sky was massed in gray and the air was damp and cool. A slight mist fell as he turned off of the main road, Oleander Drive, to enter his neighborhood. The mist mixed with the layer of pollen on the windshield creating a putrid shade of yellow.

He wheeled his car into the driveway and was disturbed to see his father's Cadillac. "What is he doing here?" he mumbled.

It was times such as this that he realized just how little he enjoyed his father's company, especially if it meant being isolated with him.

He entered the kitchen quietly through the side door of the garage. He planned to make two sandwiches and take them upstairs to enjoy in the privacy of his room.

He peered into the living room attempting to locate his father so he would know just what part of the house to avoid. He noticed the door to the office was slightly ajar. Cigarette smoke eased out of the crack filtering upwards to the living room ceiling. His father smoked, 'Lucky Strike', but only when he was extremely agitated.

Bret started to turn back to the kitchen when he overheard his father's obviously irritated voice. "Don't call me at home again. Use the private line in my office."

Maybe it was his father's mystery woman. His curiosity piqued, he walked through the foyer and entered the living room where his father would not see him through the opening in the door.

"Jerry, I understand that the timing is crucial in these transactions. I still think that you could have waited until I return from Chicago on Saturday."

"Okay, okay, fill me in," Walker Sr. said, obviously annoyed.

Bret waited silently, debating whether to leave since his hunch had proven wrong.

"You're sure that Luxum will get the new fighter plane contracts? What's the stock at now?" he demanded.

Bret was somewhat knowledgeable of the stock market. His father educated his sons very early about the importance of Wall Street. They were encouraged to find an area in the market of interest to them and to invest a portion of their salary. Since Bret could not invest in basketball he chose computers. He was certain that the surface was just being scratched as far as the technology they would eventually offer. The ample salary that his father paid him to work in the summer easily allowed a young guy with no bills the luxury to purchase a few stocks.

"When will word leak out that they got the contract? I know how to dilute a transaction, Jerry," Walker Sr. added, his voice rising steadily. "How many times have we done this? Who else knows about this? Okay, I've got a plane to catch, and Jerry, do not call me at home again."

Feeling the conversation coming to an end Bret quickly and quietly went back through the garage to re-enter the house from the front door. He entered the house loudly pulling the door closed behind him. "Anyone home?" he hollered.

His father emerged from his office, his face in an ugly scowl. "Must you make so much noise?"

"Just came home for lunch," Bret cheerfully replied. He entered the kitchen and began preparing two huge roast beef sandwiches, comfortable that his father did not suspect his eavesdropping.

He heard the front door close. He walked to the living room window and peered out at the Cadillac as it backed out of the drive and disappeared down the street. "What are you up to, dear old Dad?" he softly asked.

Walker Sr. stopped at a gas station on the way to his office to use a pay phone. The call was placed to his broker, Jimmy Jones. Jimmy had served as his broker for many years and enjoyed the generous commissions that Walker Sr.'s account brought to him. He was somewhat suspicious of his client's shrewd timing in purchasing stocks, but he was not about to question him, especially not when he was very close to his dream of living in South Oleander.

He reached for the phone. "Jimmy Jones here."

"Jimmy, Walker Sr."

"Glad to hear from you, sir, how can I help you today?" he asked, getting right down to business as he knew Walker Sr. preferred, or rather demanded of him.

"I need you to purchase some stocks for me today."

Jimmy could see South Oleander getting closer by the minute. He had thought at times to try and expedite his climb to the top by suggesting some stocks to Walker Sr., but he feared he might alienate him and he certainly did not want to risk that. Besides the fact of the matter was that Walker Sr. picked stocks better than anyone he knew. Patience is a virtue, he had decided, especially when it came to Walker Sr.

"I've got my pencil ready, sir."

"Add a thousand shares each to my account of Pepsi, Coke, and Mobil. Two thousand more shares of Ford, and ten thousand shares of Luxum."

Jimmy started to question the last stock. He searched his mind frantically to remember a company called Luxum. He was not successful. He would find out later that it was a defense-related stock that was currently selling at twelve dollars a share, and generating very little interest.

"Okay, sir. Would you like to hold for verification?"

"No, I don't have time. You handle it anytime this afternoon. There's no rush."

* * *

Bret returned to the kitchen, picking up the sandwiches from the counter. He grabbed a bag of Wise barbecue potato chips, a huge glass of sweet tea, and sat at the kitchen table.

He picked up the local newspaper and scanned the headlines as he began to devour his lunch. There were the daily accounts of the war in Vietnam and beneath that there was a lengthy article about the coming school year.

The article contained a debate about which school would remain a high school next year, Williston or dear old New Hanover. The black leaders felt that since the new school would be in a white neighborhood that it would not be fair to close Williston. They wanted their tradition, their heritage, and they did not want to be the only ones bused away from their homes for the integration of the schools. There was a march planned for the coming Saturday. There were rumors that Dr. Martin Luther King might attend.

Bret knew that at his school the students felt just as strongly that their school should remain open. Dan, along with several students planned to be at the march on Saturday. They asked him to join, but he declined, using his father and his future as an attorney as an excuse. The truth was that he really didn't care. He wasn't going to be in high school next year so the matter did not concern him. He put down that section of the paper to get to his main read, the sports pages.

* * *

It was a beautiful Saturday morning. The cloudless sky centered with a brilliant sun that brought gentle warmth to your skin. There were roughly two hundred people that began to march on Third Street under the watchful eye of the statue of General Robert E. Lee. The peaceful group marched seven blocks to Williston, where they met more supporters assembled on the lawn in front of the school. The march went smoothly with the only nuisance being the occasional jeering from white people as they drove by.

There were five speakers planned for the rally. Dr. King was unable to attend but one of his top aides was present and scheduled to speak last. The third speaker, John McDowell, a retired teacher of Williston was speaking when the passive rally was brought to a halt.

A light blue GMC truck entered Tenth Street driven by a lone young white male. The truck slowed as it neared the outskirts of the crowd. Suddenly, six young men appeared from the bed of the truck, hurling as many bottles as possible before the truck sped away.

Most of the bottles fell harmlessly to the ground. One made it to the makeshift wooden platform, shattering at the feet of John McDowell. It was the last bottle thrown that did the damage, striking a six-year-old girl in the head, knocking her to the ground, rendering her unconscious.

A doctor in the crowd quickly moved to assist the little girl. A teacher ran in the school to call an ambulance and the police. The police that the group had asked to be present at the assembly were blocks away. By the time they arrived it was too late to catch the perpetrators not that they showed any interest in investigating the incident. The doctor worked on the little girl but when the ambulance took her away she remained unconscious.

The group splintered and many of them grew angry as they watched the ambulance drive away. Restraint was the message from the older members in the group. But retaliation ran rampant in the minds of the younger element of the group. They had no intentions of going along with the status quo that their predecessors had endured.

Tempers raged and by nightfall, Wilmington was a battle zone. John Lemon, a white man who operated a small grocery store in a predominantly black area of the city was trying to lock his store and get home to his family when an angry mob jumped him, knocking him to the ground, leaving him bruised and bloodied. He was relieved of his deposit bag of money and the store was looted by the fiercely incensed group.

John Lemon was known as a friend of the black community. He treated all people fairly regardless of their background. Now, in a violent turn of events, he was the enemy simply because he was white.

Outraged groups of black men roamed the streets looking for victims while white men drove around searching for the same. Both groups, full of bravado, engaged only when the numbers were decidedly in their favor. Skirmishes were reported all over town. The rumors, especially the ones with reports of gunplay, thankfully were far exaggerated from the actual happenings.

At nine p.m., the mayor of the city announced that the town was under curfew and that as of ten p.m. any person discovered off their property would be arrested. By midnight the town was finally quiet.

Traffic signals operated for dark, empty streets, with only patrol cars breaking the silence. The city jail contained thirty additional people, twenty-five of whom were black.

Sunday morning brought some good news to the troubled city. The little girl was fine and would be released from the hospital later that day.

The area churches did their part. Preachers scrapped mapped out sermons of repentance to speak from their hearts. They spoke of understanding and peace.

Bret was in church along with his family. His father thought it was proper to attend church, especially today.

As Bret listened to the preacher's pleas, he recalled a time a few years passed, when this same church had shown such compassion and understanding.

A gospel group from a church in Maryland was touring the area, and was invited by the pastor to sing one Sunday morning. The group was talented and inspirational but they had one tiny flaw in their assembly, a teenage black girl.

One of the deacons at the first sighting of her desecrating his all white church gathered his family and departed. Many others followed closely behind. Soon the church was half empty and later the preacher was told in no uncertain terms, that if he liked his job, particularly his salary, he had better inspect visiting groups with improved scrutiny in the future.

As Bret sat uncomfortably on the hard wooden pew, he speculated as to where this Christian love and understanding for that girl was on that day. A girl who continued to sing praises to her Jesus with tears flowing down her innocent face. The message that Bret was hearing annoyed him as it reeked of hypocrisy.

As the preacher droned on his mind drifted to someone he once cared a great deal about. Bessie came to work for his mother when he was seven years old. She was a large woman, nearing seventy years of age. Her face was round, chubby, and she had hair the color of burnt charcoal. Bret recalled best her dark eyes that always possessed unmistakable kindness.

Bret recalled a day he came home from school soon after Bessie had come to work at the Marin house. He repeated a joke to Bessie that he had heard at school. It was a racial joke that contained the word nigger. Bessie was as black as midnight and failed to join his laughter at his joke.

"Child, what is a nigger?" she asked patiently.

"I don't know."

"It's an ugly word used to describe people like me, by ignorant people who don't know any better."

Bret's laughter changed quickly to embarrassment and shame. "Oh, Bessie, I didn't know that it meant you. I love you, Bessie. You know that, don't you?" he asked, as he began to sob.

Bessie wrapped him up in her large black arms. "Yes, child, I know you do," she said as she rocked him gently.

"Would you make Bessie a promise?"

"Yes, ma'am."

"Don't ever use that word again."

"I won't, Bessie. I promise."

He kept that promise. Bessie died two years after his mother passed. Walker Sr. did not allow him to attend her funeral. Bret hated him more on that day than any other. It had been Bessie who comforted him after his mother died. She was the one who held him late at night when he missed his mother so much. She would tell him that his mother was in heaven with Jesus and the angels looking down on him. "Make her proud, child, you make her proud."

He could still hear her today. He cried most of that day his Bessie was laid to rest in Pine Forest Cemetery. His older brothers teased him for loving a 'nigger maid' so much. He had not cried since that day, and with the exception of Alex, he refused to care about anyone else. Loving people meant losing them, and the pain of that haunted him. He grew harder after that day, allowing very little of any kind of emotion to exist. Life was simpler that way.

* * *

It was Saturday morning and the Twentieth Azalea Festival was taking place. It was the biggest event of the year in Wilmington. The culmination of the festival was the majestic floats that would parade down Third Street, along with marching bands, clowns, and riders on horses.

Appropriately, and on cue, the azaleas were at their peak for the weekend. Bret took Alex downtown for the parade, and at his little brother's insistence, Barbara was invited too.

Barbara had been business as usual since their altercation. The night had not been mentioned.

The floats rolled by the crowds lined along the street. Alex looked as if he was about to be swallowed whole by the huge ball of pink cotton candy that he was attempting to put in his mouth.

The last float passed containing the queen of the parade. Melody Patterson waved cheerfully to the large, enthusiastic crowd.

Bret, Barbara, and Alex began the journey back to the car. They walked along Third Street and turned into an alley that separated several tall brick office buildings. They were discussing the events of the day when they noticed five guys who appeared to be gathered around something, or someone.

As they drew closer Bret recognized his teammate, Dan. "Hey Dan, what's going on?" It was then that he saw the person surrounded by the group, Money Wilkins.

"Well, Bret, look who we caught. He said something smart to us and we thought that we would teach him a lesson. Maybe even break a couple of his fingers on his shooting hand. Maybe we will just break everything he's got. Wonder how bad that coach at State will want him then?"

The rest of the group cackled. Bret didn't recognize any of them. They were a few years older and rough looking.

He looked at Money and was surprised not to see a hint of fear in his eyes. Concern yes, fear no. There was defiance in his eyes, even now.

"I guess they need a little more help. The odds are not quite good enough for these brave men. Your teammate, now he's a real man. He likes throwing bottles at helpless little girls, and I bet these good old boys were with him," Money said defiantly.

Dan raised his hand to hit him. "No, don't. Let me have first shot at him," Bret shouted.

"What about your daddy?" Dan asked sarcastically.

"I don't see him around," Bret said smugly.

Barbara tugged at Bret's arm. "Bret, you can't be part of this."

He turned to her, his back now to the group. He lowered his voice to a whisper, placing his car keys in her hand. "Turn around and get to my car as quickly as you can. Wait at the corner of Third and Orange Street. Leave the motor running and put the top down."

She started to speak. Bret said quietly but sternly, "Do it now. Do what I said." He looked briefly down at Alex, and then back to Barbara. "Please." Alex looked up at Bret, perplexed. He could not believe his brother would be part of something like this.

Bret looked down at him and smiled slightly. He winked at him and said softly, "Trust me."

Alex's face abruptly softened and though he was still afraid, he nodded gently to his brother.

Barbara took Alex by the hand and began walking down the alley. One of the others in the group said, "We ain't waiting all day."

Bret moved slowly toward Money, trying to allow Barbara and Alex as much time as possible to get out of the alley and nearer to the car.

Bret sized the group up and while the others were older, he was certain that Dan would be the most difficult to remove from his feet. The odds needed to get better in a hurry if he was going to survive this event. He didn't know why he was going to do this, but he was going to do it, or try at least.

He neared Money, and just as he got up to him, he winked, turned quickly and kicked Dan in the groin.

"Aw," Dan screamed at the top of his lungs as he dropped to his knees.

Simultaneously, Bret and Money delivered powerful right hand blows to two members of the stunned group. Another jumped on Bret's back, while another attacked him from the front. Bret tried frantically to whirl the guy attached to his back into the oncoming blow, but he failed, catching the blow on the side of his head, dazing him momentarily. Money shook one man loose and placed one hand on the guy in front of Bret, but only managed to slow him down before he was hit from behind.

Bret used that moment to move backwards as quickly as possible, hunting for the brick wall behind him that he could not see. A few steps later he found the wall, and as planned, the guy on his back was sandwiched between the wall and him.

"Oooh," the guy screamed as he met the wall, letting go of Bret, and sliding helplessly to the ground.

Dan was about to regain his feet as Bret was working his way back to Money. He placed another direct kick, this time on the back of his left knee. Dan screamed again and fell to the ground turning loose of his groin to clutch his knee.

Bret was back to Money now, the odds two against three were getting better. They stood side by side and worked the others to a standstill. Bret saw Dan out of the corner of his eyes, attempting to get up again. Money delivered a thundering right to the jaw of one. Bret rammed his forearm into another. "Money, let's go," Bret hollered as he pulled Money's shirt. They ran down the alley. The remnants of the gang gave chase briefly. Dan, the most determined of the group tried to keep going, but he was unable to hold his groin, and knee, and limp at the same time with any kind of speed.

Bret and Money turned left out of the alley, and met the car at the prescribed destination. They jumped into the back seat of the car as Barbara sped away. The two rednecks who pursued the longest were left thirty feet behind.

They were a block away when Bret and Money looked at each other. The intensity in Money's face was replaced by an easy, almost silly expression. He began to laugh. "Your buddy, I peeked back as we turned out of the alley. He, he, he was," by now Money was laughing so hard that he could barely speak. "He was trying to chase us but he couldn't make up his mind which part of him to hold. His knee, or his, his..." Money was now so delirious with laughter that he lost any ability to speak words that could be understood.

Barbara and Alex looked strangely at the tall thin black man the car contained. Bret began to join Money, laughing with him hysterically. "It's a good thing the season is over. He'd never set another pick for me, or pass me the ball." They laughed for blocks, loudly, foolishly and for no apparent reason other than the relief of survival.

Barbara pulled the car over. She saw the lump on the side of Bret's face. "Bret, your face is swollen."

Bret looked at Money, seriously, for one second. That was as long as he could muster. "Oh no, don't tell me I'm not still pretty. The girls, aw, they won't love me. Where's a mirror?"

The two of them began to giggle again, and then it built into a roaring laughter. They got out of the car and laughed so hard that they fell down on the strip of grass by the sidewalk holding their sides. Barbara and Alex just looked puzzled at the two of them laughing, and then looked at each other blankly.

Bret and Money quieted down finally. Alex looked at Money. "You're the basketball player."

"Yes, I am."

"You were lucky to win. My brother is better than you."

Money looked at Bret and the laughter began anew. They howled for another five minutes and each time Alex started to speak, they laughed even harder.

Finally they tired of laughing. By now, their sides hurt worse from laughter than any blows they had received in the fight.

Bret asked, "Where do you live? We'll give you a ride home."

"Castle Street."

Money told Barbara the directions and she drove to his house. It was small as were all the homes that lined up in a row so close together that you could talk to your neighbor by raising a window. This particular house stood out from the rest of the aged homes. There was a white picket fence in front of it. The porch was exactly as the other homes in terms of size, but not in the fancy decorative railing design. The front door was made of beautiful oak, lightly stained, with a large oval piece of glass in the middle of it.

Barbara kept the car running as Money got out. "Aren't you coming in?" he said as he looked at Bret. "There is a first aid kit inside and you can clean up," he said before adding, "I mean all of you, come in, please," he gestured with his hand as he looked to Alex and Barbara.

"Sure, we'll come in." Bret agreed.

Barbara looked uneasily at Bret and Money picked up on it. He smiled at Barbara. "Is this your girlfriend, Bret?"

"No, she is Alex's baby sitter."

"Oh, I'm sorry, in all the excitement I forgot to introduce you. This is Barbara and this is my little brother Alex."

Money smiled at Barbara and reached out his hand to her. "It's nice to meet you. Thank you for being a good and especially a fast driver."

He looked down at Alex, and then he knelt down, achieving the desired eye level contact. He reached his hand out to Alex who took it. Alex's tiny hand disappeared inside of the tall man's hand. "It's very nice to meet you." Money's warm smile put Alex at ease. "I wish

I had a little brother to hang out with," he said, chuckling softly.

"Do you have any brothers or sisters?" Alex shyly asked.

"I have a sister who is a year younger than me. She lives in Philadelphia with my mom. Her name is Ma-tek-a."

"Mateka," Alex tried to pronounce a name unlike any that he had ever heard.

Money smiled warmly again. "That's okay. We have trouble saying it too. That's why we call her Teke."

Alex said, "The Phillies are my favorite team."

"Mine too."

"Do you like baseball?"

"Yes, I do, but not as much as basketball. You know, your brother really is a good basketball player, but do you really think that he is as good as me?"

Alex was not quite as adamant this time, but still he answered, "Yes."

"Well, I'm not going to win this one, am I?"

Clarence Wilkins peered out of his window at the unfamiliar site of white people and a red Mustang convertible in his drive. The only time white people came in this area was if they were bill collectors. That did not include him. He paid his bills. He worked and did the best he could to keep his son out of trouble. He insisted that his grades be kept up if he wanted to play ball.

He was forty-two, tall, but a couple of inches shy of his son's height. He was in good shape from the hard work he had done in his lifetime. Muscles bulged out from his arms, and his forearms looked like they would give Popeye a run for his money. His face was somewhat rugged, but he was not an unattractive man.

He stepped out on his porch to investigate. "C.T., what's going on?"

Money turned and attempted to speak, but Clarence saw the mouse under his eye first. "What have you been doing boy, fighting? Boy, I'll..."

Money raised his hands up with his palms facing toward his dad. "Whoa, dad, give me a chance, okay? I didn't go looking for a fight. You know better than that."

It was then that Clarence noticed the swelling on Bret's face, which confused him all the more. If they had fought with each other, why were they so calm?

"Now, Dad, where are your manners? Are you going to invite my guests in? Haven't I taught you better?" Money's infectious charm spared no one, including his dad.

Clarence smiled. "Forgive me. I'm Clarence Wilkins. Please come inside. Welcome to our home."

The introductions were completed and they entered the house. Bret's first step in the door he noticed the beautiful oak floors below him.

Clarence left to get a first aid kit from the bathroom. Money went in the kitchen to get drinks for everyone.

Bret looked at the beautiful woodworking in the house. He was amazed to find the same ponderosa pine wood walls that were in the A-frame house on the river. There was a beautiful bar that divided the kitchen from the combination living and dining room. Bret ran his hand along the top of it, maple. It was beautiful.

Clarence walked out and noticed Bret rubbing the counter top. "Do you like that?"

"It's beautiful, sir. This is a beautiful piece of maple. The grain, the way this was curved, the design of the counter. A true craftsman did this work. I've only seen one person who could have done better."

"Better?" Clarence's voice rose with unmistakable pride.

"Who did this work?"

"You're looking at him."

"Oh, sir, I, I..."

Money began to laugh, watching Bret wiggle out of his apparent insult of his father. Clarence pretended to be indignant but he could not pretend for long. He began to laugh and Bret, now relieved, joined in the laughter.

"Now, young man, tell me just who it is, what god of carpentry is it who is better than me, and just how is it that you know so much about the subject?" Clarence asked deliberately.

"My grandfather, Ralph Rogers."

Clarence was taken aback. "Your grandfather was Ralph Rogers?"

"Yes, sir. Did you know him?"

"No, I didn't know him personally, but I do know of his work. I've seen it and now I am not offended by your comparison. In fact, I am honored to be included in such company. You obviously know a little yourself."

"I worked with him the last year he was alive. I guess I picked up a few things," Bret stated modestly. "Who do you work for?"

"Myself," Clarence said proudly.

"I've inserted my foot in my mouth again."

"Don't worry, son. I'm a small contractor. I struggle, but I do good work and I am my own boss. I don't work for people who know less and refuse to listen to me. C.T. here is quite good with wood also. Now sit in this chair and let me have a look at that face."

Barbara stepped forward. "I'll take care of him. I'm used to it. I've been caring for Alex for a while."

Clarence smiled, but refused to hand the items over to her outstretched hand. "No offense, young lady, but I've been mother and father to this boy," he said as he motioned to Money with his head, "since he was eight years old. Now you sit back down and drink that Pepsi," he said evenly, leaving no room for debate. "Now, C.T. how about you explain what happened to you boys, while I doctor your guest. I guess it is safe to presume you boys were not fighting each other."

Money began to tell the story as Clarence carefully cleaned Bret's face. He wiped it down with alcohol first and then applied merthiolate to the small cut under his left eye. He finished by handing an ice pack to him. "Hold that against your cheek. It will keep the swelling down. Okay, C.T., you're next."

Clarence finished doctoring his son and, by now, had taken in all of the account of the fight. "You boys were lucky."

"Lucky, Dad, we were good."

"Before you get too brave, or too full of yourself you need to think. What if one of those boys had a knife or a gun? I'm not criticizing either of you. Sometimes there is no way out but to fight, but know it can go down differently. Be aware, and if possible walk away. Remember the people who love you. How they would feel if something happened to you? Bret, that was a brave thing you did. Most people would have walked away. I am in your debt."

Clarence looked at his son. Bret saw the look they exchanged and he was sure they had something between them that he could not comprehend. He could also see their obvious similarities. The proud way they spoke, the confidence, and their easy going politeness.

Bret looked at Money. There was something about him. He thought of Bessie and of the day he promised not to use that word, but that didn't mean that he didn't have his preconceived ideas of black people. You grow up listening about how inferior people are that aren't like you, and it naturally becomes part of you. How they don't want to work, always looking for a free ride. How limited they are. But Money, there was something about him. He could play basketball with such intensity that you would swear that he would kill to win. But there was also a politeness, a kindness about him, and it was not groveling as the waiters at the club were forced to do to keep needed jobs. It came from someone that Bret knew would bow to no one. He saw that in the alley. Money was not only different than other black people that Bret encountered. He was just different period. And so was his father.

Clarence looked at Bret. "Thank you, son." He gazed back at his young man and said without reservation. "I am proud to call this boy my son," he said as he gestured toward Money. "And it is surely not because he can score forty points in a game, or because he might one day be as good a carpenter as me. No, it is because he's a good person. I've watched him carry groceries home for the older people who live around here and refuse to take a dime. That is what I am most proud of. If you ever need anything, Bret, you know where to find me. Thank you," he said again as he reached his hand out to Bret, who met it, feeling the power in his grip.

"You're welcome, sir."

Bret tried to pull away but Clarence refused to let go of his hand. Clarence waited until Bret was looking him in the eye. "Anything. You understand me, son?"

Bret nodded and Clarence allowed him to have his hand back.

Money walked his guests out to the car. Barbara climbed in the back seat, allowing Alex the front. Money and Bret turned to each other. Money spoke first, "Thanks for what you did. I was in some serious trouble. They would have hurt me bad."

"No one that shoots a basketball the way you do should have his hand broken." They shook hands and Bret got in the car. Money started back for his house when he stopped abruptly and turned back. "Why did you do it?"

Bret paused. "I don't really know. I can't give you a reason."

Money nodded, "My dad saw what you did at the gym that night. He said you were either brave or a fool, he didn't know which."

"Maybe both, I don't know, Money. I didn't think about it then and I didn't think about today."

"He said your dad is the biggest attorney in the area and the richest man in town."

Bret struggled for words, but none came out. He was strangely embarrassed by all of the wealth that he was accustomed to at this moment as he stood in such a poor section of town.

Money sensed the troubled look on Bret's face and quickly changed the subject. "Tomorrow, at one, the gym at the school is unlocked. Why don't you come and run with us some."

Bret hesitated to answer. Money, sensing his uneasiness, said, "It will be cool." His voice carried that same air that it had in the gym that night. "You can run with me. We can be on the same team instead of us trying to kill each other this time," he said with a smile.

"Maybe I will," Bret said, and he drove away.

"Quite a day, guys, huh?" he said to his companions. "Alex, today, the fight, it stays between us, okay?"

"Sure," Alex smiled, before adding sarcastically, "Gee, I wish that you would give me a little bit of credit."

"Are you going tomorrow?" Barbara asked.

"I don't know."

"I think you should."

"Why?"

"I can't put my finger on it, but you and Money. He brings out something different in you. I've never even heard you really laugh before today. Most of the time you seem like this machine with no emotion, or enjoyment of hardly anything."

Bret shook his head, annoyed. "That's a little too much for me to grasp, baby sitter," he replied in a condescending tone. He tuned out the conversation and turned up the volume of his tape deck. He listened to the Beatles as they sang, *We can work it out*, and thought about what lucky girl he might allow to accompany him to the Holiday Inn tonight.

CHAPTER FOUR

Clarence

Bret warily entered the Williston gymnasium. There were approximately ten men on each end of the court shooting at the respective baskets. Several girls and a few small boys sat on old wooden bleachers. The one person Bret didn't see was the person he needed to see the most, Money.

He stopped awkwardly at the bleachers by the nearest basket. It was at that moment that everyone seemed to notice the obviously misplaced white boy. Balls stopped dribbling. Lively conversations ceased. There was something about the quietness of a gym that he loved. Many days he practiced alone at New Hanover with the silence interrupted only by the echo of a ball being bounced, the gentle swish sound when a well-placed shot found its intended destination of ball meeting nylon. This silence was nothing like that.

A booming voice broke the silence, "Yo cracker, I think you just might be in the wrong neighborhood."

Bret looked a few feet to his side and located the source of the voice. The man appeared to be 6'7", and about two hundred forty pounds of chiseled rock. He also seemed annoyed, very annoyed at the unwelcome visitor. He was no high school student, not even college. He was much older, and intimidating.

Another voice chimed in. "Can the cracker speak?"

Bret mustered, "I'm looking for someone."

"Well your mama ain't here, little boy," he heard another voice say, followed by laughter. The players on the court drew closer to the oddity that dared to interrupt their pleasant Sunday afternoon.

Bret was contemplating whether he could run out the door and escape to his car quickly enough to continue living life as he knew it. He chose another course of action. "Well, that would be a miracle," he paused for effect, "considering she's dead."

The awkwardness now briefly was on the group in front of him. The big man spoke again, "So, your mama is not here. Who you looking for boy?"

Bret looked up into the coal black eyes of the biggest man that he had ever laid eyes on and one thought entered his mind. I'm going to die.

In the silence, he heard footsteps from the other end of the gym. He thought about sneaking a glance in hopes that the footsteps belonged to Money, but he was not about to take his eyes off of the belligerent man in front of him.

Money eased up beside Bret, possessing a smile that beamed as if he had just seen his long lost best friend. "Hey guys, thanks for welcoming my friend. I know that is what y'all are doing. I know you wouldn't be giving my buddy the feeling that he wasn't welcome."

The big man looked incredulously at Money. "He's with you?"

"Yes he is, Willie, and I tell you what. You pick your four guys to run with you, anyone you want and I will take what is left. Oh, and Willie, don't pick the cracker. He's running with me. Oh, and, one more thing, Willie, you don't have a chance of holding this court."

"You ain't that good." He snorted with disgust.

"Don't talk me to death, big man. Make your picks. Five on five half court, make it, take it."

Willie quickly made his picks opting to take nearly all the size the gym contained, along with one small man, who he called Lightning.

Money made his picks quickly. They gathered together to discuss the matchups. Money startled his three teammates when he said, "Bret, you guard Lightning and run the point." They looked at Money as if he had just turned white on the spot.

"Whoa, Money, that honky will get eaten alive."

"You let me worry about that."

"Warm up, Bret, and when you're ready, we'll run."

Bret asked someone in the group for one of the balls. Reluctantly, someone passed him the ball. He began to shoot at a side basket. Money walked up to him, grinned and said, "A man can't even go pee without trouble these days."

Bret smiled back nervously and said, "Oh, next time, don't rush. I probably had another minute before they beat me half to death."

A few minutes later Bret nodded assuredly at Money that he was ready. Money grabbed the ball, moved to the top of the key and looked at Willie. "For ball?"

Willie nodded.

Money let fly an arching, rainbow shot that seemed to drop from the heavens, delicately entering the hoop almost apologetically moving the twine as it passed.

Bret took the ball up top. Lightning stood in front of him, a slight grin etched upon his face. Bret started hard with one dribble to his right, before quickly spinning to his left, leaving Lightning clutching at air. The smirk removed from his face. Quickly, Bret was in the paint. Willie came off of his man to guard Bret. Once he committed, Bret bounced the ball around him to Money, who cut into the spot vacated by Willie. Money gathered the ball and exploded to the basket. Another player stepped in from the other side attempting to halt the sure basket. Money went up over him, soaring high above the rim and then slammed the ball so ferociously that for a moment you would swear that he was going to dunk both man and ball in the cylinder. The gym grew silent. Lightning stood puzzled and slightly embarrassed. "Enjoy that one, white boy."

Bret moved back up top. He looked at Lightning as he checked the ball, and then smiled devilishly. This was going to be fun.

Money's team held court for the next three hours. The teams rotated trying to defeat them. They tried different combinations, but to no avail. The games were played in a mostly empty gym, no coaches, no title at stake, but they were still as competitive as any game Bret had ever played in. Even when they were dead tired at the end, Money and Bret refused to allow defeat. There was chemistry on the court between them that would lead you to believe they had played together for years.

The last game ended and Bret noticed a different look in the eyes of those that had confronted him initially. They didn't befriend him. He had, however, grudgingly earned their respect.

Bret and Money walked out together into the afternoon sunshine. Money spoke first, "Man, that was fun."

Bret smiled, saying nothing.

"Let's go to my house and get something to eat," Money offered.

"That sounds good."

They arrived at Money's, where he quickly began to prepare sandwiches out of the chicken salad his dad made that morning before he went to catch up on an office he was remodeling.

Bret sank his teeth into the sandwich. "This is great."

"Yeah, my dad is really something. He meant it yesterday when he told Barbara that he had been mother and father. He is an amazing man. He made this early this morning before he went to work. He should be home resting on what should be his day off. I dream sometimes about playing professionally so he can have everything. He's given up so much for me. I hope to pay him back. But you know when I say that, he replies, You just be a good man C.T." Money paused, adding softly, "He's the best."

The ease of his words spoken about his father was one thing, but even more impressive was the obvious sincerity they held. Money was proving very intriguing to Bret. He magically handled any situation that was cast at him. There was an infectious charm that led you to think he could charm an Eskimo into believing he needed more snow in the dead of winter.

"Why does he call you C.T?"

Money chuckled. "He doesn't care much for my nickname."

"What does C.T. stand for?"

"I'll tell you but you can't laugh. You have to promise."

"I won't."

"Clarence Thomas."

Bret began to chuckle and then it built to roaring laughter. Money feigned anger before joining in. "You said that you wouldn't laugh."

Bret stopped laughing and responded, "I lied," and with that the giggling began once more.

Finally Bret stopped laughing. "You know it is not a bad name. I wouldn't have laughed but since I knew it bothered you."

"You couldn't resist," Money said with a smirk on his face. There was silence before he added, "I'm glad that you came today."

"Me too," Bret replied. "I had a lot of fun especially after the first few minutes."

"I heard that you handled yourself pretty well without me."

Bret said nothing as he looked at him, feeling that there was more that Money wanted to share.

Money for once seemed nervous. It was so out of place on someone that moved and spoke so gracefully. "One of the guys in the gym said that you lost your mother."

It was not a subject Bret spoke often about. He hesitated, but then replied, "Yeah, a long time ago."

"I'm sorry."

Bret surprised himself when he heard his own words, "Me too."

Money continued, "I guess in a different way, I lost my mom too."

In the silence that followed, Bret thought to ask, but he didn't want to pry. Money offered without being asked, "Mom was visiting from Philly. Dad and she met, fell in love and got married. The best I can understand is that she never adapted to the south. She hated the limited opportunities. She wanted more. She tried to get dad to move north, but he refused. He's lived here his entire life. He wouldn't leave and finally she did. My sister Teke went with her. I didn't want to leave so I convinced them to let me stay. Mom began working for a doctor once she got there. She went to night school and got her nursing degree. Now she works at the biggest hospital in Philly.

"I visit each summer and Teke comes back with me for a few weeks. My sister is something else. She's smart, talented, and a real head turner. She could be a model and I am not exaggerating." He paused for a moment before adding, "Mom, I love her, but there's distance between us, and not just in miles, you know?"

Bret nodded, slightly uncomfortable at such honest conversation. It was not something he was well versed in.

"She hurt my father so bad. He still loves her. Her picture remains in his wallet. He's never dated that I know of. He's just taken care of me. He just wouldn't consider leaving here, and he told me that initially he thought she would return. I guess I blame her. She shouldn't have left, but," he said, failing to finish the sentence. "Have you got more family, Bret?"

"Two older brothers that I don't have much in common with and as for my father, I..."

Money watched him struggle to explain and interceded. "What about the little guy? You guys are tight?"

"Yeah, Alex is something else."

"I can tell."

It was obvious that the conversation had become uncomfortable for Bret, so Money shrewdly changed it. "So, Bret, you don't like Alex's baby-sitter? She is fine."

Bret thought for a moment of how those words would go over in another place. A black man speaking of a white woman, but Bret could also tell that Money meant nothing disrespectful.

"She's a cool girl, but we rely on her so much to take care of Alex that it just wouldn't be a good idea."

Bret shifted the focus of the conversation onto Money. "What about you? That smooth way you talk yourself out of trouble. That probably works for the girls too."

"Yeah, I go out, Bret. I do all right." The answer flowed easily from Money, but without the teenage bravado that usually accompanied such words.

Money continued, "Bret, I wonder do they want to go out with me, or is it because I am the basketball player that's going to State, and may play professional one day?"

"And you care?" Bret asked in a puzzled tone.

"Sure I do, and not just with girls, but friends. Would they want to hang with me if I didn't play ball? I don't need someone around to help me feel cool."

Bret had never known anyone to talk about the things that Money was so easily conversing about. It stunned him. "I know what you mean about not needing anyone."

"I didn't say that. I like people and I love pretty girls. But yesterday after you guys left, dad and I went over to Greenfield Park and fished the lake till dark. Just fishing and talking. I had more fun doing that then when I went out last night and we didn't catch the first fish. He's my father and I respect him, but he is my friend too. If I never play ball again, nothing will change with us. I'm not sure about that with anyone else."

The seriousness faded as quickly as it came and Money once again reverted back to his captivating sense of humor. "I know you don't have any trouble with the girls, Bret," Money said smugly.

"Why is that?" Bret responded sharper than he would have liked.

"No, because at the gym, I heard a couple of the girls saying, That white boy is fine. He sure is pretty to look at. I'd hurt him if I had half a chance."

Bret's moment of indignation passed quickly and he joined the now high-pitched cackling of Money.

The door opened, interrupting their laughter. Clarence entered somewhat loudly and with a face void of any of the kindness displayed the previous day asked, "Is that all you boys have to do, sit around and laugh?"

Money's expression mirrored his dad's and for the second time this afternoon Bret felt unwelcome. He squirmed uneasily in his chair.

Clarence and Money looked at Bret, and then at each other for about two seconds, before erupting with laughter. Bret, realizing now that he was the victim of a performance, a great performance, joined in their laughter. Clarence walked over to Bret, shook hands. "How are you, Bret? Glad to see you again." He paused turning serious again, "Bret, could you do me a favor?"

"Yes sir."

"Park that sporty car of yours someplace else. What will the neighbors think?" And with that, the Wilkins began laughing again as Clarence poked Bret in the ribs. "Boy, you got to loosen up a little." Bret joined in on the laughter once again not minding at all that it was at his expense.

The laughter died again and Money asked, "Dad, why didn't you get me up this morning? I could have helped you."

"I knew that you asked Bret to play ball yesterday. You need to be playing ball. Besides what would Big Willie have done to Bret if he showed up and you weren't there?"

"Shoot, Mr. Wilkins, Willie is a creampuff compared to the guys in my neighborhood."

Clarence looked at Bret as if he had just grown another head. Then Bret began to roar with laughter, and Clarence and Money joined in.

Bret's eyes drifted to the woodworking again in the Wilkins' house. "Those ponderosa pine walls really look good. How long ago did you put them in?"

"About two years ago. C.T. and I did it. When work runs a little slow we tackle a project around here. I did some work for this big contractor who was subbing out most of the work. He liked my work so much he told me to take any of the leftover wood home. That's where all of the walls came from. Bret, how about coming out back with me? I'd like to show you something."

The three of them walked out back to a small but neatly organized workshop. There was an old door leaning against the wall just inside of the shop. Clarence stood the door up. "This is an antique, or at least it is to me. The job I was on last week, they were going to throw it out. I brought it home. What do you think?"

Bret ran his hand over the oak wood that was badly in need of re-finishing. The top part of it contained glass designed like the top half of the moon. Below the glass a design of a tree was etched into the wood. The doorknobs and handles were badly in need of replacing. Still, he saw the beauty in it. He envisioned what it could be as a craftsman may.

The door was solid and heavy. "Dad loves doors. He hates those light pine doors that people are beginning to use," Money interjected.

"What are you going to do with it, Mr. Wilkins?"

"I don't know. I got no use for it but I couldn't stand to see it thrown away."

Bret felt the wood again. "I like the one you have in front now, but this one, it won't offend you if I say I like this one better, will it, Mr. Wilkins?"

He rested his big hand on Bret's shoulder. "Son, the only offense I take is that 'Mr. Wilkins' stuff. Call me Clarence."

Bret smiled at the kindness in his face. "Yes sir."

Bret felt more relaxed and friendly then he had in ages. It was in that moment that Bret let his guard down, forgetting black and white, and his grandmother for that matter. "Clarence, I'd like to show you and Money something."

"Sure, what is it son?"

"It's just an old house."

"Where is it?" Clarence asked.

"Castle Hayne. Could you spare a couple of hours next weekend?"

"Sure, we can," Clarence, answered. "I'd be glad to. When do you want to go?"

"How about we go next Saturday afternoon?"

The Wilkins nodded their agreement.

The three of them walked out to Bret's car. Bret felt the eyes on him from the people seated on their porches on each side of the Wilkins's house as well as from the people across the street.

The Wilkins waved to their neighbors. Clarence looked at Bret. "Son, are you going to be all right at school tomorrow? C.T. told me one of those boys played ball with you that was in the fight."

"Don't worry," he said, winking at Money, "I'll just take out his other knee."

"You be careful. C.T., will you go check the workshop? I can't remember if I locked it." Clarence asked this knowing full well that he had indeed locked the workshop.

"Bret, I'll see you Saturday." Money waved, smiled, and walked away.

Clarence looked at Bret. "He's real worried that something will happen to you tomorrow. We talked about it yesterday when we were fishing. He feels responsible. He wants to be there for you if you need him, the way you were for him."

"Mr., ah, Clarence, I'll be okay. Tell him not to worry."

"Have you talked to your father about it?"

"No, we don't, ugh, we don't really talk much. It's not like with the two of you."

"Have you tried?"

"You don't understand, sir. Just tell Money that I'll be okay."

"Bret, if C.T. would have helped me today he would have told me that he had to be at the gym in case you came. He would never have left you in a bad situation. He's that kind of boy, maybe that kind of man. I want you to know that. He also really likes you and not because you saved him from getting hurt."

Bret nodded with understanding. "I'll be okay." He shook Clarence's hand and got in his car. As he drove away he thought of how Clarence also possessed an infectious charm about him. He smiled and the rare warm feeling inside him lasted about one block. Right up until the moment he realized that he had made two mistakes, big ones. He had sworn not to return to Vicky's, and now, to return with two black men. *I must have lost my mind.* His mind raced to different scenarios. I could cancel the visit. Lie and say that I am sick. He shook his head. I'll call Vicky and explain that they might do some work at the old house.

He was still thinking about the best way out of a potentially bad situation when he walked inside his house and discovered that his dad was home from his trip. Better yet, he was also waiting for him, evident by the Lucky Strike dangling from his mouth. "You've had quite a weekend, young man. I just got off of the phone with Dan's father. Are you completely insane?"

The tranquility of the day was shot. Walker Sr. stood there in front of him. He dragged intensely on his cigarette. "Do you have anything to say, or are you going to stand there and look stupid?"

Anger raged inside Bret and he thought of how much he would like to knock that condescending look right off his father's ugly mug. One good shot to that big nose, perhaps hard enough to enable it to meet his big ears. He felt his fists tighten, but then as always he thought of Alex. "I guess Dan is a hero."

"Dan's father told me that some black basketball player started a fight with Dan, and that you teamed up with the black guy. What in the hell were you thinking?"

"Thanks, Dad, for listening to me first, for asking me what happened before you believed someone else. Oh, and wasn't it a black man that launched your career?"

"You don't know what you're talking about."

"I read the transcripts. You pay me to learn law."

"Are you saying that Dan lied?"

"It is true that I helped a black man. That part is right. Two against one, though. It was more like two on five, and Dan is upset because I kicked his behind so badly that he never got a punch in. Did Dan tell his father that he was involved in throwing the bottle at that little girl, starting a small war in our city?"

"How could you know that? Did the black guy say so, and who the hell is this person that you attacked your friend for?"

"Friend, Dad? I'm like you. I don't have any friends."

"I have plenty of friends."

"No, you don't," he replied sarcastically.

"Who was he?" Walker Sr. demanded angrily.

"Money Wilkins."

"The hotshot basketball player?"

"Yes."

"I'm sure he would have helped you out if the situation was reversed."

"Yes, I'm sure he would have."

Walker Sr. looked mystified at his cantankerous son. "I don't understand you. I give you everything and this..."

Bret's mind flashed back to Castle Street. Yesterday he thought about how poor he thought that the Wilkins must be. Now he thought about the laughter, the trust, and the love that those two men shared. For the first time in his self-absorbed narrow life, he was envious of someone. He looked at his father and he could hear Clarence urging him to talk to his father. He had no idea.

"Young man, no fights at school tomorrow. It would be a good idea to apologize to Dan."

Bret thought briefly to ask his dad if he had asked Barbara, or even Alex what happened but he decided immediately not to involve them.

"Stay away from this black fella, Bret. Look at the trouble that he's gotten you into."

Bret gave no reply. "I'm going upstairs to my room," he said, leaving Walker Sr. to light yet another cigarette.

* * *

The week at school passed without any major alteration in Bret's life. He started the week with no friends, and if possible, ended it with less. He heard snide comments in the hallways. He was avoided as if he had some kind of infectious disease. Even the girls that usually flaunted themselves at him moved in opposite directions. His only show of support came from the school potheads. The people who had made the American Flag part of their wardrobe apparel. They supported any liberal idea that enhanced their sense of being cool. Their support he did not want.

Dan talked tough one day after PE class when his growing number of friends backed him up. Bret stared him down, saying nothing and walked away.

He put off calling Vicky until Friday afternoon. He wished that he were on another planet as he dialed her number.

"Hello."

"Vicky, this is Bret. Uh, uh..."

"Well, out with it, boy. It can't be all that bad."

"I want to come see the old house tomorrow."

"That will be fine."

"Uh, Vicky, I'm bringing someone, actually two people."

The silence on the phone did not make Bret feel any more comfortable.

Vicky broke the awkward quiet. "So?"

"They are black. They're carpenters, uh, I thought that I could get some ideas," Bret lied slightly.

"Are they going to work on the house?"

"Ah, no. They are just, ah..."

"Shoot, boy, just come on out. Tell me when you find your tongue."

"Thank you," he replied before realizing that she has already hung the phone up.

It was three o'clock, Saturday afternoon when a slightly dinged green Ford pickup truck entered Vicky's property. Clarence insisted on driving his truck. Bret filled them in on the house and his grandfather's wishes as they drove.

They passed by her house and Bret was ever so grateful to see no sign of her. They parked the truck and got out. They walked up the steps and entered the house. Clarence and Money walked around softly, taking note of the work that was completed. Clarence went a step further and envisioned what it would take to complete the project.

"This is superb work. You should be proud to be a part of it," Clarence stated.

"I just helped. It was my grandfather."

"He couldn't have done it alone. Are you going to finish it?"

"Why finish it?"

"I don't know, Bret. You say your grandfather worked on this house as he was dying. He had to have had a reason. Something made him want to see it completed."

"It didn't make any sense then, and it doesn't now."

"Bret, sometimes a man just has a feeling, something inside of him that feels right. It can't always be explained. You boys may not understand that now, but one day you will. It looks like there is enough wood to finish the job."

"I'm sure there is. He calculated the materials before he died."

"Do you have the tools that you need?" Money asked.

"Yes, but I don't have any plans to work on it again."

"I'll help you on weekends and this summer, if I'm here."

"Where are you going?"

"Dad might have a chance to do a big remodeling job for a doctor in D.C."

"D.C.?" Bret asked.

Clarence answered Bret, "A good friend of the man in D.C., Dr. Sampson, lives here. I did some work for him and Dr. Rowell visited him and saw the work. That was two years ago and he said that he was considering an extensive remodeling of his house and that he wanted me to do it when the time came. Dr. Rowell is black and has done quite well for himself. He is passionate about his house and he wants to hire the best. He also wants to hire a black man. He says it is his way of giving back. I didn't think much about it, but he called last week, and for what he is willing to pay for two months work, well, I may not be able to say no. If it works out, I'll probably need C.T. to go with me. Dr. Rowell says that he could find me some good help there but C.T. is used to working with me. I'd just feel better about having him. He could make some good spending money for school, and I think it would be a good learning experience for him. Who knows, one day when he's through with basketball, he may want to be partners with the old man.

"Say, Bret, what about you? Did you get scholarship offers to play ball?"

"Yes, but not to Duke. That is the only place my father will allow me to go." Bret stiffened his posture and began to mock his father, "Bret, any son in my law firm is going to be a graduate of Duke. My God, it is held in as high esteem as the Ivy League Schools."

Bret relaxed. "Actually I imitate him pretty well. I've fooled Barbara and Alex before on the telephone."

Clarence looked at Bret and thought how he would feel if his children mocked him in that way. "Bret, it's not my business, but I just don't think you should belittle your father."

"Why not? He loves doing it to me." Bret responded tersely.

Clarence decided against pursuing the subject any further, as it was easy to tell by the tone in Bret's voice that there was conflict between the two that his words would not alter.

Money steered the conversation elsewhere. "Bret, my sister is coming next month. Dad told Dr. Rowell that if he took the job, he had to have at least two weeks with his daughter. She's through with school in late May. I'd like for you to meet her. I am as proud of her as you are of that little guy you hang out with. She'll be finished with high school a year ahead of schedule. She's been offered an academic scholarship to Temple."

They walked around the house and Clarence stopped several times to offer suggestions. He seemed to understand precisely what Ralph's plans were. Clarence pulled his tape measure out and measured the front door.

"You know, Bret, that door at my house is a perfect fit for here. It sure would look good. You're welcome to have it."

"I really don't have plans to finish this house."

Clarence merely smiled, as if somehow he knew that would change. "Well, the offer remains."

CHAPTER FIVE

Alex

May arrived with scorching heat and humidity that area inhabitants associated far more with the months of July and August. The very first day of the month set a record when the temperature peaked at 101 degrees. The days that followed were nearly as relentless as the unusually high temperatures refused to yield. The humidity alone in a normal Wilmington summer left your clothes clinging to every part of your body, and that was before you moved. Triple digit temperatures were not unheard of but many summers passed without seeing one day with heat that intense and never in early May.

It was minutes shy of one o'clock when Bret left school for lunch with no intention of returning. Field day at Bradley Creek Elementary School would begin promptly at one p.m.

He arrived at the school playground and quickly spotted Alex. He was standing in line waiting for his turn to participate in the ball throw contest. The principal, Robert Oakley, saw Bret, and immediately walked toward him to inquire as to the nature of his visit.

Robert Oakley was a tall, gangly man, with thinning brown hair. He wore small eyeglasses that were perched on the tip of his nose. "And just why would you be at this school right at this moment, Bret?" he asked smugly, adjusting his glasses higher on his nose.

"I'm taking my dad's place."

"Where is he?"

"He's out of town."

"That's strange, especially since I spoke with him just this morning about the graduation plans in place for the last day of school and I found it most peculiar that he knew nothing of it."

"It wouldn't have mattered. He would have been too busy with work."

"It is not permissible for a student from another school to be on these grounds. You know that. I'll have to ask you to leave."

Bret looked over at Alex, who was watching and wondering why his brother was not beside him. "Principal Oakley, with all due respect, I can't leave. Can't you just once look the other way? What would it hurt?"

"You are not the boy's father. You had no right to withhold pertinent information from your father."

"I'm here because I am who Alex wants to be here," he stressed. "If he had desired my father to be present he would have asked him."

"That doesn't make it right. You seem to have such an attitude concerning your father. It must be so very difficult to be born into the wealthiest family in town. It seems to me that you would appreciate your good fortune a little more."

Bret looked again at Alex, who was waving frantically for him to come over. He looked back at Robert Oakley. The glasses had worked their way back down to the tip of his nose. "I don't think that it is your place to tell me what I should or should not appreciate. Now, my brother is waiting for me. You handle this however you see fit, but I am going to watch my brother participate in the ball throw, and it's beginning now."

The principal looked at him and he knew that there would be no backing down for this young man. He briefly thought to call the police. The spectacle of the police arresting a son of the most powerful man in town, well, that was one fight he quickly decided that he did not need. "Your father will know of your insubordinate behavior," he said sternly to Bret who was already moving toward Alex.

Bret stuck his right hand out beside his shoulder, giving a slight circular motion that indicated the depth of his concern.

The principal muttered something under his breath that Bret

could not hear as he continued to walk away.

Alex ran to him and hugged him tightly. "It's almost my turn. What were you doing?"

"Oh, nothing, the principal just wanted to chat. Now get in line and do your best."

There were nine boys participating in the ball throw. The contestants were allowed three throws each. Alex went fifth. He gave all the effort he could muster, but the weakness in his leg prevented him from pushing off the way the other boys did.

Bret watched as Alex finished a distant last in the contest. He wanted so badly to return to that day when he watched in horror as his little brother fell from the balcony. He wanted to go back to that moment in time and somehow make it end differently. Why should Alex be punished so severely for his enthusiasm, for his love for me?

The dejection on Alex's face told the story. His head hung low and he shuffled away slowly, as the top three finishers got the ribbons that he so desperately coveted.

The rest of the people walked to the site of the next event, the one hundred-yard dash. Alex walked away from everyone and sat down under a huge Laurel Oak tree. He rested his arms on his knees and buried his head.

Bret waited a few minutes debating on the proper course of action. He looked at the program that he had been holding in his hand. He walked over to Alex and sat down beside him. Never once had he been stern with him about anything. He had always softly encouraged him. This time he knew he had to be firm. And he hated the idea of it.

He touched the back of his neck and said, "Alex, look at me."

Alex merely shook his head, refusing to lift it.

"Alex, look at me."

Alex looked up and Bret saw the water in his eyes. It was hard, but he was not going to show sympathy for him, not this time. "Did you do your best? Did you try to throw that ball as hard as you could?"

Alex nodded. "But I wanted to win, and I finished last. I want to be like you. You're always the best."

Bret's tone softened. "Alex, when I played Little League baseball, my coach, Mr. Wilson told me something I never forgot. He said that win or lose, if you could go home and look in the mirror and say, 'I tried my very best', that was all that mattered. Everyone wants to win, but all we can do is try our best. You remember when we lost to Money's team?"

Alex looked up at his brother, "Yes."

"It felt bad to lose, but I knew that I played as hard as I could. They were better. Money was better."

"No, Bret, you're the best. You're always the best."

"You know something, buddy. I am good, but Money can do things on a basketball court that I can only dream of."

Alex gazed at him trying to imagine that anyone could be better than his big brother in anything. He thought about Money and asked a peculiar question. "Do you like him, Bret? Is he your friend?"

Bret thought for a few seconds about something that, to this point, had not been put into words. "Yes, I suppose we are friends. Now, Alex, I want you to do something for me. I want you to enter one more event today."

"No, I don't want to."

"Yes, you will, and all I want you to do is to have fun. Don't worry about winning. There is nothing to lose. The only way you could disappoint me is to not be willing to try." He touched him lightly on top of his soft dark hair. "I love you more than anything in this world."

Alex could never let his big brother down. "I'll try my best. What is the contest?"

"It's a free throw competition. You're good too. What's important to remember?"

"Follow the same routine each time. Never rush. Right hand straight to the basket, and in the basket."

"That's right. Now let's go."

There were ten boys in the event. They would each shoot ten free throws. The first boy made three. The second contestant made six, and the third hit eight. The next six boys took their turns and only one of them made as many as five.

It was Alex's turn. He toed the free throw line, bounced the ball deliberately three times, paused and shot. He missed it off the front of the rim. He repeated his procedure and shot again, this time striking the back rim. The ball bounced back to the front of the rim and then fell crudely away from the cylinder.

Bret looked at him and smiled. "It's just you and me shooting baskets in the driveway."

Alex smiled, followed his routine and shot, swish. Again he shot, another swish. Bret could see him relax now as he shot. He shot five more and made each one. Only the sixth one even touched the rim. One more shot, to tie. Calmly, confidently, now he bounced the ball, three times. He paused, breathed deeply, and located the rim and shot, swish. A very muffled, but slight "Yes," emerged from Bret's mouth. There would be a shoot off for first place.

The other boy was Ben. His hair was such a shade of reddish orange that it appeared to be on fire. His face contained freckles in such abundance that it seemed his face was added on almost as an afterthought.

They would shoot five shots each. Ben went first. His eyes squinted fiercely in absolute determination as he coolly sank his first three shots. His fourth attempt struck the back iron, bounced to the front and hung there tantalizingly for what seemed seconds, before falling harmlessly to the grimy asphalt below. One shot was left and then it seemed Ben's nerves came into play. The shot fell way short, barely drawing the front of the rim.

Alex stepped up to the line with complete poise and focus. He didn't hear the idle chitchat of mothers whose sons were not involved in the contest, or the shouts of encouragement from his classmates. Sweat was dripping off of him. He paused before his three dribbles and looked over at Bret.

Bret smiled at him and wiped his hands slow and hard on his pants. Alex understood. He sat the ball down at his feet and dried his hands on his shorts. He picked the ball up. He was ready. He hit his first three, before missing the fourth. Bret's heart raced. He had never been this nervous about anything, certainly not when he played. This was out of his control.

He watched Alex bounce the ball three times once again. He watched him pause, and then he watched the ball release out of his hands. Swish. Alex looked stunned for a moment. Only when his classmates surrounded him slapping him on the back did he realize what had taken place. "I won, I won, I won," he shouted. He made his way through his classmates to Bret. "I won, Bret. I won, can you believe it?"

Bret smiled as he hugged Alex. "I sure do believe it. I sure do, little man."

Moments later, he watched as the blue ribbon was pinned on Alex. There had never been a victory in Bret's life so complete and so treasured.

The ringing phone stirred Bret from his Saturday morning sleep. "Hey, Bret, let's go pound some nails today. I'm feeling industrious. I'm making dad take the weekend off so I can take the truck. He said for us to take that door that you like."

Bret managed to work his way into the conversation. "What time is it, Money?"

"It's eight. You're not still asleep are you?"

"Now that would be silly, considering there is no school, and I have no plans, not to mention that I was out late last night."

"And what was her name?"

"Becky."

"Who is she?"

"A girl from the club who refused to allow me to enjoy a simple dinner without offering dessert."

"It must be hard to be such a pretty boy," Money said as he began to cackle. "C'mon, lover boy, I'm ready to work. Do you want me to pick you up?"

Bret was thinking of how to get out of working on the house that he seemed to keep getting pressed toward. Money now presented a larger problem. The wrath of his dad if Money was seen in the vicinity of South Oleander, let alone his house.

"No, I'll come to your house, but I promised Alex that he could hang out with me today."

"Bring him," Money said.

"Do you think we could have some time for breakfast, sunshine?" Bret sarcastically asked.

"That is covered. Dad will be whipping up his famous pancakes shortly. The kitchen will be opened in thirty minutes. Now get moving. There are things to be done and you don't need to waste your life away sleeping."

"Money, you sound like a parent," he said dryly.

Money winked at his dad who was making his way to the kitchen. "Well, let's just say that you might be getting the same speech I received fifteen minutes ago."

"Tell your dad, thanks for passing on the legacy of being such a nuisance to his little ray of sunshine."

"I'll see you in a few minutes. Hey, we are on for ball tomorrow at one, right?"

"Well I would hate for you to spend any of your weekend without me. People might talk. They might assume we are not still going steady."

"Why Bret, sometimes I think that you don't want to be my friend. Could that be possible?" he countered, feigning hurt.

This was two days in a row that someone used the word friend in connection with Money. He hadn't missed a Sunday playing ball at Williston since the first weekend. He did know that he liked being around Money, but he had never really had a friend. The truth was that it had never been that important.

"I'll see you shortly." He hung up the phone and rolled to the edge of the bed, working his way into an upright position. He walked to the next room and stirred his little brother. Alex rubbed his eyes with each fist until he finally opened them and blinked at Bret.

He immediately got a startled look on his face and he reached immediately for the blue ribbon that dangled on the corner bedpost, as if to insure that the winning of it was not a dream.

Bret smiled at him. "Put some shorts on and a tee shirt, and wash your face and brush your teeth."

Alex promptly did as he was instructed.

Bret returned to his room and put on some cut off jeans and a navy blue Duke tee shirt. Next was the part he dreaded. Should he call Vicky and tell her that he was coming? How would he get past not coming to her house for dinner? Here he was with a black man that he didn't want to insult, and a grandmother that he felt certain would not allow a person of color in her house. He decided not to call and hope, maybe, just maybe, to slip by without being seen.

They entered the Wilkins's house, finding Clarence hovering over the stove wearing a white cooking apron. Across the front of it, embroidered in red were the words, DON'T KISS THE COOK.

Bret grinned as he eyed Clarence.

"What are you looking at, boy?" Clarence asked gruffly.

"Oh, c'mon, not even one little kiss?" Bret said as he puckered his lips.

Clarence laughed and tapped Money on the arm, "I think that boy is developing a sense of humor."

Clarence looked at the blue ribbon that was worn so proudly by Alex on his yellow tee shirt. "What have you got there, buddy?" he asked, as he pointed to the ribbon.

"I won the free throw competition at field day yesterday."

"Get out of town," Clarence roared in appreciation.

"Give me five, my man," Money exclaimed, holding out his hand. Alex slapped it enthusiastically.

"My little man here, he hit twelve of fifteen, and that was after he missed the first two."

"I had teammates that couldn't do that," Money said.

"He was cool. He was locked in. He made eight straight to force a shoot off." Bret proudly passed on the details of the event.

Clarence began serving the pancakes. The table was amply supplied with toppings. There was butter, maple syrup, and three jars of homemade jam, strawberry, raspberry, and blackberry. Clarence dished out the pancakes and the three boys devoured them hastily. They washed them down with the glasses of milk that Clarence kept filled before there was a chance of any becoming empty. The pancakes were so light and fluffy that only the toppings gave them weight. Money and Bret ate six, and Alex devoured four of them before slowing part way through the fifth. Finally, Clarence got to eat, sitting down to a stack of five pancakes, which he covered with strawberry jam and maple syrup.

"About time I got to eat. I thought maybe there wouldn't be any left," he said as he winked at Alex.

The boys rose to leave. "Don't forget to take the door, C.T.," Clarence said in between bites.

Bret started to argue with him, but decided against it. "Thank you for breakfast, Clarence. It has been a long time since I had a breakfast like that." Bret looked toward Alex and nodded.

"Thank you for breakfast, sir. It was great," Alex said with the politeness of a cultured gentleman, but with the earnestness only a small child could offer.

"You are certainly welcome, son, and you come back anytime."

"Yes sir."

The three boys walked to the door.

Money turned to his dad. "No work today."

"Well, son, you are taking my truck."

"Yes, but no working in the shop either. "

"C.T., get out of here and quit being so bossy," Clarence said with a stern look before giving way to a smile that dominated his rugged face.

"Dad, I'll be back by four and we are going fishing. I'm going to catch so many fish that you'll need two trips with the truck to haul them to the house."

"Boy, two things you can't do better than me, building and fishing. Oh, and add cooking to the list," he replied.

Bret looked back. "Oh, Clarence, could you do me one more favor?"

"Sure, Bret," Clarence answered sincerely.

"Find me an apron like that," Bret cackled. "Don't kiss the cook, oh boy."

"Get out of here, boy," Clarence said as he threw the apron, striking the closing door.

Money and Bret loaded the door into the back of the truck. Money got behind the wheel of the truck, noticing the picnic basket that was sitting in the middle of the seat. Alex got in from the passenger side. "How about holding these for me, buddy?" Money asked as he placed the basket on his lap.

"What's that?" Bret asked.

"Sandwiches, apples, and some cookies. I guess dad didn't want us to starve," Money said, smiling.

"Your dad really is something."

Clarence sat alone at the kitchen table with a slight smile frozen on his face. He listened as the truck drove away.

"Lord," he said, as he looked upward toward the ceiling while picturing the sky. "My son and a boy from the richest family in town. I know that I prayed for him to find real friends, but are you sure about this?" He shook his head as if the Lord was sitting at the table to eat pancakes with him.

"I sure do like that boy, Lord. Were you watching the way he looks after that boy and teaches him manners and everything?

"Of course you were," he answered his question.

"Yes sir, anyone that looks after a little brother as if he were his own child. Well, there has got to be something special about him. I'll just trust you, Lord, but excuse me if I worry."

He rose and began to clear the dishes from the table. He paused and gazed upwards to the ceiling once again. "One more thing, Lord, thank you for my son. I don't know what I would have done if he had gone to Philadelphia with his mother and sister. No sir, I don't know what in the world I would have done," he reiterated.

The boys rode several miles without conversation before Money interrupted the silence. "Bret, you know how we talked about whether people were sincere in wanting to be friends, or whether it was because of us being a basketball player, or a rich kid?"

"I'm the basketball player in this scenario, right?" he smiled before noticing the serious look on Money's face.

"Yes, I remember."

"I always wanted to know where I stood with people, even if they didn't like me. My dad has a saying, don't tickle my ears. Just tell me the truth."

"What's on your mind, Money?"

"I asked you this morning if you wanted me to pick you up, and you said no. Was it because you didn't want me at your home?"

Bret paused, thinking of a suitable answer. "I wish I could say that you are wrong, but you're not." He locked eyes with Money and he saw the ever present pride there, but mixed this time with something else, maybe a trace of hurt.

"But you're not all right either. First off, that is not my home. It's my father's house. I've seen what a home is. We just left one. Look, my father found out about the fight. The kid from the basketball team, Dan, his father called after the fight. My father told me not to have anything to do with you. So, if you ask me if you are welcome in my home, the answer is yes, if I had a home. But we are talking about my father's house, and that's another story."

Money nodded his head softly and they rode in quiet for a few miles.

"Are we friends, Bret?"

"If we're not, you're the closest thing to it." Bret paused a few seconds. "I'm not really comfortable talking about things, the way you do, the way your dad does. So, I hope that my answer is good enough."

Money looked at his friend, "I understand. Why did you come over and play ball, and come to my house after your father told you not to?"

"I just didn't know any better," he said with a chuckle.

They drove past Vicky's. Bret breathed a sigh of relief as he noticed that her Oldsmobile was gone. They carried tools into the house. "Where do you want to start?" Money asked.

"We could start on the downstairs, but maybe it would be best to go ahead with the upstairs floor. Alex, you need to stay downstairs until we make the upstairs safe. Go find Fred, and don't walk too close to the river."

The two boys with their inherent carpentry skills carried a bundle of the flooring upstairs, resting them on the plywood that was laid across the floor joists. They tacked one of the sheets of plywood to provide a safe foundation for them to begin attaching the three-inch wide strips of oak wood to the sturdy pine joists.

Two hours later, they had nearly managed to cover a quarter of the upstairs space. Bret suggested a break, though neither of them wanted one. They were enjoying the work, almost as much as the Sunday after-noon basketball game that would follow the next day. Still, Bret thought it would provide a good time to check on Alex. No sooner than the thought had entered his mind, Alex came bounding through the door with Fred, and unfortunately Vicky, who was carrying a glass pitcher of sweet tea.

Bret braced for the storm that always seemed to accompany his grandmother. "I spotted this little boy outside my house," she said, mo-tioning toward Alex. "I thought you boys might need something to drink. It is awfully hot. I haven't seen heat near this since 1937. It hardly rained that summer. We lost all the crops. But we survived."

"Thank you, Vicky," Bret replied.

"Thank you, ma'am," Money said.

Bret was slow to react as Vicky stared at him. "Oh, Vicky this is Money. He's helping me."

"It's nice to meet you, ma'am," Money said with his pleasant and captivating smile.

"You can drop that ma'am stuff. Vicky will do just fine. Well, I'll let you boys get back to work."

Bret exhaled deeply as he watched her walk down the stairs. She had offered no questions about Money, and he didn't think that Money would want to go along with the lie that he was working for him.

Money looked puzzled at Bret. "She's always like that, gruff to the point, no chit chat?"

"Oh, that was chit chat. Didn't you hear her going on and on about 1937?"

"She said like what, four sentences?"

"Yes, the old girl is especially talkative today. I didn't think she would ever stop."

"Oh, she talks all the time like you?" Money beamed.

"Give me a board," Bret replied sternly, and smiled when Money looked down to pick up the wood.

The boys worked until three and by that time, the floor was two thirds of the way finished. Their pace slowed later in the day to allow Alex to nail a few boards, but it was worth the time to see the delight he derived from it.

As they put away tools, Money turned to Bret. "So, you don't want to work on this house?"

Bret struggled for an answer. "It seems you arranged this pretty well."

"I can't take credit for that."

"Who? Oh, that leaves only the breakfast cook," he said as he shook his head.

"That would be correct."

Money paused before adding, "He said that if it was that important to your grandfather then there was a reason and just maybe you needed to be prodded a little to get your behind moving. Now tell me that you didn't enjoy this."

"Okay, I enjoyed it. Are you happy?"

"No, not until it's finished," Money said as he smiled broadly

CHAPTER SIX

Chicago

Bret stretched out comfortably on his bed resting from the now routine Sunday afternoon of playing basketball at Williston. The gang still did not exactly greet him with open arms, but at least they no longer looked at him as if Casper the friendly ghost swooped in for a visit. At one point today after he was knocked to the floor by a very solid pick, Big Willie stuck his hand out to help him up, and with a somewhat friendlier glare than was customary.

Alex accompanied him today. He played with the other little boys that were present at the vacant end of the basketball court. Bret watched as the kids blended together. Money sidled up to him and softly stated, "If you don't teach them that they are different, they will never know."

Bret was almost asleep when the abrupt rap at the door jarred him from his pleasant thoughts. "Come in."

Walker Sr. stood forebodingly in the doorway. He was angry, but what else was new? "We are having a family conference. Now," he demanded to cut off even a hint of debate.

Bret followed 'Dad the dictator' down the steps. The family conferences were run just like the family business.

The Marin sons sat at the dining room table that these days served more as a conference table than as a place to eat. Family dinners died along with Georgia Marin.

Walker Sr. hovered over the table, standing at the end as if he were General Patton surveying his troops before sending them out to wage war.

"I've been hired to defend a rape case in Chicago. It is a very complex case."

Complex, Bret wanted to say, that means some rich man's son is guilty. He knew that Walker Sr. would provide no details about the case he was taking. He'd learned long ago not to ask questions concerning such matters.

Lately he was finding it increasingly difficult to conceive being a member of his father's firm for a sustained period of time. Maybe he would make his money and escape. He could break from the family business and wave good-bye to the lot seated at this table save one.

Walker Sr. pressed on. "The case will begin in two weeks, and it could possibly take the entire summer."

Bret thought briefly to leap onto the table and do his very best Elvis imitation, because he sure felt like gyrating his hips in elation. Summer vacation is coming and no father in sight to monitor son number three's behavior. Now, he thought, please tell me that you will be taking both shadows, and not just Wally.

"Of course, Wally will be coming with me, and I think that William will benefit greatly from the experience."

Bret wondered if in addition to dancing on the family table, it would be considered sacrilege to throw in a few *thank you, Lords*.

"Barbara has agreed to live here and look after Alex."

His father's eyes narrowed as he turned his complete attention toward Bret. "Bret, you will, of course, begin work at the office immediately following graduation. You will be expected to assist my attorneys. Each morning at nine you will report to my personal secretary, Ruby. She will have a list of tasks that you are to accomplish. The list has been compiled by me and she will be in daily contact with me regarding your progress."

There was no way, Bret thought, that dear old dad could damper this moment. It was all he could do not to smile. He was wrong.

"Bret." The voice lowered but the tone became even graver. His eyes narrowed to mere slits that held rage and indignation. "You have been seen with this colored boy, Money Wilkins. You've played ball at Williston on Sunday afternoon the past few weeks. You have been to his house on several occasions and even taken Alex with you. I could go on, but I don't need to impress you with my knowledge of your activities. It is time for you to shape up. I have had enough of your adolescent behavior. I know that you want a Corvette for graduation. You can forget that. You have this summer to prove yourself. If I get favorable reports from Ruby and the rest of my staff, and if I don't hear anymore reports of you hanging out in colored town, maybe you can get your car before you leave for Duke."

His older brothers looked at him smugly, but said nothing. This was their father's time. They relished the moment.

Walker Sr.'s eyes were full of fury, dissatisfaction, as he spoke. "Do you wish to deny this?"

"What good would that do?" Bret offered.

"Would you like to know how I know all of this?"

"I have known for a long time that you have your finger on the pulse beat of the community. Some might go as far as to say that you have even stolen its heartbeat."

"It is not a good time for you to be smart with me, young man. My patience is used up with you. Your mother..."

Bret interrupted him before he could offer another word. "Don't," he paused. "Don't bring my mother into this. She went along with you, but that doesn't mean she agreed with you. Let's leave her out of our quarrels."

"Your mother supported me."

"That may be true, but it does not mean that she thought that you were right in the manner in which you rule this family with an iron fist." The emphasis he placed on the word rule caused his father to pause.

Walker Sr. studied the son in front of him that he was determined to break. "You have one summer to get that thick head of yours on straight or maybe you'll be happy living elsewhere. The world needs ditch diggers and you can make your living doing just that alongside your colored friends." He glared at him with such resentment that Bret felt certain that not only did his father not love him, but he believed the hate he felt for his father was indeed mutual.

"I find it amusing a man of your education and standing in society uses a word like colored," Bret said with disdain.

Bret was ready to leave. The hell with this tyrant and his future being planned with no conception of what he might want. He might not be rich but there were jobs better than ditch digging to be had and maybe having sports cars and filet mignon was not worth living under the rule of his oppressor. He was ready to walk out and he felt his legs brace to rise but then he felt the eyes of someone dear to him. One look in that direction quickly terminated his plans to abandon the family. Alex was terrified. Bret felt his legs settle back into the chair. He breathed deeply, swallowing his pride. It was as bitter a taste as he'd known. His mouth had a sour metallic taste. Mechanically, he offered, "Don't worry, sir, I'll toe the line."

His brothers smirked at him arrogantly. The defiant one was finally broken. They had waited a long time for this day.

"Is that all, sir?" he asked.

"Yes, that is all," answered Walker Sr., who obviously was pleased by reaching his son on what he assumed to be the most basic of items, his life of wealth, his desire for a new sports car, and most important of all, his future.

Bret retreated to his room. Walker Sr. said to his sons that remained at the table, "He will thank me one day." Two of the sons nodded in agreement, while the other sat still and afraid.

Bret lay in his bed contemplating the many ways he hated his father. It was a deep seated feeling that he felt certain he would carry with him for the remainder of his life.

A few minutes later, there was a knock on the door. Wally and William entered.

"What do you want?" Bret asked coldly.

Wally began, "He only wants what's best for you, for all of us."

"That's right," William chimed in.

"So, what's this, suddenly, my two wonderful brothers care about me?"

"Of course," Wally answered, mustering all the sincerity he could. "One day, the firm will be ours. We will need to work together."

Bret certainly found no comfort in a future that when his father was gone would leave him working with his two brothers. He looked at the two of them, standing in the doorway. "You are up here for one reason, because he sent you. You are pathetic. Get out of here."

Knowing that the charade was up, the brothers made the most of their exit. "Oh and what about your groveling?" William asked.

Bret remained on his bed. He didn't trust his control to stand up. He had to toe the line, for now. Calmly, he said, "We'll talk about this another time."

As they were leaving, Wally offered, "Our poor little brother, comes from the richest family in town, and the only friend he can manage is a colored boy. What do the two of you do, eat watermelons, chitlins, and sing Diana Ross songs?"

William threw in a parting shot as they turned to walk away. "Let's put a bow tie on him, paint him black and put him to work at the club like that ignorant old man, Louie. Yas sir, no sir. He'd probably shuffle real well and just as natural as they do."

Moments later the bedroom door swung softly open. "What?" Bret hastily demanded, before seeing that it was a very distraught little boy standing there.

He sat up quickly. "Oh, little man, I'm sorry. I didn't know that it was you."

Alex stood there with a look etched on his face that tore at Bret's heart. He was on the verge of tears but trying so hard to be brave.

"Come here, little man," Bret said as he stretched out his arms.

Alex walked over, burying his head into Bret's chest. Bret heard the sniffling of tears, and then felt the wetness through his shirt. "Talk to me, little man. What's got you so upset?"

"I'm scared dad will throw you out. I don't want to be without you. I don't want to live here without you."

Bret took his hands, and ever so gingerly, he placed one on each side of Alex's face. "Hey, look at me," he said with a voice even softer than the hands that held his brother's face.

Alex looked at his brother, his eyes a mixture of tears, confusion, and fear.

"I won't leave you. I promise. He won't throw me out. It's tough talk." He knew that he wasn't being completely honest. He knew that his father was indeed capable of evicting him, and would do so without losing a night of sleep over it. The white lie, however, was worth the assurance his little brother needed at this moment.

"Bret, are you going to stop being friends with Money?"

"Let me worry about that, okay?"

"I like him, Bret. I want to go back to his house and eat pancakes. His dad said that I could. Why is it wrong for him to be your friend?"

He rubbed the top of Alex's head. "It's not wrong."

"Then, why can't you be friends?"

Alex answered his own question. "It is because he is black."

"Yes."

"I don't care what color he is. I still like him and I like his dad too."

"So do I, little man, so do I," Bret softly said as he delicately pulled his brother's head to his chest and rocked gently. "Let's go to your room and watch some television."

They watched television together and talked. He didn't leave his brother's room until he was safely asleep, where fear would not reach him again on this night.

He returned to his room and tried to sleep. Each time he heard his own words, "I'll toe the line," the humiliation sent a searing pain through his body.

He thought about Money. Now that he realized he might have to cut the friendship loose, it dawned on him just how important it was. For the first time in his life, he had a friend, a true friend. Someone who didn't care who his father was, how much money he had, or even how good a basketball player he was.

Solutions ran through his mind, but at three a.m., he resigned himself to the only reasonable one. Money had to go. He could not risk losing Alex. His mother had left Alex to him. She knew that day that she was going to die. It was difficult to comprehend, but somehow his mom knew. He was certain of that now.

* * *

It was three days later. Bret spent another uneventful day in school. Little had changed, since the fight. Dan talked tough, but fortunately, never pushed the issue to violence. Bret had to stay out of trouble. Maybe one day, he could find a way out of this, but for now he had to keep his wits. Alex had at least eight more years in the Marin household. Then he could decide his own path in life. Hopefully, by then, Bret thought, I'll have enough money to get away from the family, and help my little brother go anywhere he wants.

He walked to the kitchen and grabbed a soft drink and some

chips. He stopped by the kitchen table and looked down at the newspaper. He picked it up and walked to his room.

He read the sports section first, as usual, and then he turned to the financial section to check his small portfolio. In the bottom right hand corner on page three a small headline caught his attention. **LUXUM IS AWARDED BID**.

His mind searched anxiously for the reason that word was familiar. "Luxum, Luxum, Luxum," he softly voiced his thoughts. And then it came to him. The day that he came home for lunch and his dad was in the office conducting what he thought was a private conversation. "Luxum," he mouthed, barely audible. He scanned the stock charts searching for the stock. He searched the New York Stock Exchange first, no luck. He found it under the American Stock Exchange. Luxum was trading at nineteen dollars a share, but that was yesterday. He needed more information.

He thought to call his stockbroker, but quickly decided against it. He went downstairs and located the telephone book. He picked a brokerage firm that he was not familiar with and dialed their number.

"Brown Brokerage", a perky sounding voice answered.

Bret's voice took on an air that defied his youth, sounding very much like his father. "I'd like to speak to one of your brokers, ma'am."

"Is there anyone in particular that you wish to speak with, sir?"

"No, ma'am."

"Who shall I say is calling?"

"Lee Albert," he answered, and wondered just where that name emerged from.

A few moments passed, and then a distinguished sounding gentleman answered, "My name is Richard Phipps. How can I help you, Mr. Albert?"

"I was thinking of opening an account with you and I would like some information about your company."

Bret was bored very quickly with the sales pitch the man offered about how marvelous the company was. He endured it patiently as he waited for the time to collect the information he desired.

Finally he ceased preaching the virtues of the company and asked, "Are there any stocks in particular that you might be interested in?"

"Well, there is a war going on, so I guess defense stocks are a good sector. For instance, this company in the paper today, Luxum, what could you tell me about it?"

"It's up over three points today. The last trade was at twenty-two and a quarter. There was a big announcement yesterday. They received a huge contract to build fighter planes. Unless peace interrupts the war, this is a good looking stock."

"What's the year high low on it?"

"The high is today and the low was nine, back in December."

"When did it start moving up?"

"Let me check, give me a minute here. It looks as if it was flat for quite a long time, and it started moving up about the end of March."

There was a pause in conversation, and Richard pressed for a new account, "Would you like to open an account with us and purchase shares of Luxum today, sir? I can also recommend some other defense stocks that look really good."

"Let me sleep on it and I'll call you tomorrow."

"Could I get your number, sir?"

"No, that won't be necessary. I'll speak with you tomorrow." Bret hung the phone up before the eager salesman could get in another sales pitch.

Bret thought back to the day he first heard of Luxum. He recalled the name of the man his dad was angry with that day. "My kingdom to know who this Jerry is," he said to the only person in the room.

* * *

It was early Saturday morning and from the moment Bret's eyes opened he was on the move. He didn't want to chance a conversation with Money. He had not decided how to handle the situation, but he was not ready to lie to Money at the moment, and he certainly was not ready to tell the truth.

He walked into Alex's room and stirred him from sleep. "Let's go, little man. Get dressed."

Alex was downstairs in five minutes, fully dressed, teeth brushed and hair combed.

They were in Bret's car before Alex offered a question of their destination, "Are we going to Money's?"

"No, we'll eat out for breakfast and then go work on the house."

He was relieved that Alex did not interrogate him further. He was weary of thinking about Money and his handling of the situation.

They stopped on the outskirts of Castle Hayne at an ancient looking pale gray cinder block building that stated Mabel's Diner in worn letters over the awning. They devoured a typical southern breakfast of bacon, scrambled eggs, grits and toast. Alex was unusually quiet and for once Bret was glad. He had a lot on his mind and he didn't want to have any conversations with his brother that might turn to questions that he did not want to answer.

Minutes later Bret parked beside the workshop to gather additional nails. He instructed Alex to go tell Vicky that they would be at her house for dinner at eleven-thirty.

He watched him walk away and wondered if his grandmother enjoyed his returning for the second weekend in a row to work on a house that held no apparent future. At the moment, he didn't care. Maybe hammering some nails would help him forget having to bow to his father demands, and the avoidance of his sole friend.

He resumed working on the upstairs floor. Alex returned a few minutes later and began handing each oak plank to Bret. He constantly reminded Alex to stay on the inside of him and to not venture near the edge. At one point Alex smiled and said softly, "Don't worry. I won't fall again." Bret looked at his little brother and did not know what to say. Alex had never mentioned falling that day as far as he could remember. Moments of silence passed before Alex placed his hand on the back of Bret's shoulder and added reassuringly, "It's alright Bret. It wasn't your fault." Bret stared at the wood floor below him as his eyes watered slightly. He held no idea of how to respond.

Fred entered through the open door interrupting the brief stoppage in work. He decided that if the work were upstairs, he would be also. He trotted up the steps as if he were in a hurry to reach his destination. He found a spot in the corner that had been the starting point the week before, and wasted no time in snoring in rhythm with the nails as they entered the oak.

The time got away from Bret in the solitude he found in working. He checked his watch, eleven-thirty five. He was almost to the master bedroom with the flooring. "Dinner, Alex. Let's go."

Vicky was already at the table eating, "You're late," she stated evenly.

"I know. The time got away from me." Bret said as he and Alex sat down to dinner.

"Where's the other boy?"

Bret looked at her blankly. "What boy?"

"The boy that came with you last week to work on the house," she said tersely.

"He's busy today."

"He must not be much of a worker if you can't depend on him to finish the job. I hope you weren't paying him much."

"It's not really like that, Vicky."

"How is it then?"

He struggled for an answer and Alex decided he would offer one, "He doesn't work for Bret. He's his..."

Before the word friend could fill the kitchen, Bret interrupted, "He owed me a favor, that's all. The roast beef is great," he added trying ever so succinctly to steer the conversation elsewhere. "Hey, I noticed your garden is looking good."

The old woman eyed her grandson curiously. She was certainly not fool enough to believe that she had been told the truth, or that he cared about the garden, particularly since the garden was suffering from the early heat wave. Reluctantly, she decided to indulge him in his game of secrecy and grant him an escape.

She had not lived almost three quarters of a century without learning things about people. She knew that the look on Bret's face meant he was troubled and he probably did not know that she was willing to help, but circumstances had dictated a wide berth between them. She looked in his eyes and saw the good looks of her daughter. The daughter she'd lost to Walker Sr. first and to a heart attack later.

"What's troubling you, boy?" she asked, attempting to keep the gruffness that had become too familiar for even her own tastes from her tone.

"Nothing, everything is great," Bret replied cheerfully.

Vicky hated being lied to by anyone, but she refrained from tearing his head off. "Sometimes, if you got troubles, it just helps to get it out. Speak your mind."

For a brief moment he was tempted to tell her. He was sure that she would enjoy hearing what an even bigger jerk his father had been of late. The part about Money, well, he surely didn't want to bring that subject up. He took a bite of the roast beef to aid in ending the conversation and turned his eyes to Alex.

Vicky looked at him for a few moments and decided to drop the subject matter for now. "How's the house coming?"

"I might finish with the floor today. I've got good help," he said as he looked at Alex, hoping that she would not press him as to whether he planned to continue working on the house.

Several minutes later, he was back at the house, hammering away on the nails. By five o'clock that afternoon the upstairs floor was finished. The two brothers surveyed their work. "Looks great," Alex offered. "What's next?"

"Do you like doing this work, Alex?"

"I love it, Bret," Alex replied, though the truth be known, he would enjoy doing anything with Bret.

"So what's next?" he persisted.

"See the edge that hangs out over the first floor?"

"Yes."

"The wall should be next, for safety sake, and other reasons."

"Can I help?"

"Maybe not with that part, little man. But I can find work for you. Don't you worry."

* * *

The next afternoon, Money stood in the Williston gym eyeing the door.

"Your boy is not coming. It's almost one-thirty. Let's play," Lightning said.

He called Bret early yesterday and today, both times hanging up when an unfamiliar voice answered. He tried to convince himself that something had come up, but he couldn't shake the feeling that he was being avoided. He turned to the court and began to play, but his mind would not allow the enthusiasm that he usually played with. He thought that he had found a real friend. Now he wasn't so sure. His team lost the first game sending him to the unusual position of sitting on the sidelines waiting for the next up. He didn't even care.

Bret nailed a pine board to the frame he had constructed for the three-foot high wall. He glanced at his watch, one-thirty. They were playing ball at Williston and he wanted to be there. He came alone to work today desiring complete solitude. Barbara took Alex to the pool at the Country Club to escape the heat. Of course he had to assure Alex that it was okay for him to go and not accompany him to work in the sweltering heat.

It was the first weekend that Money and he had not hung out together since the fight. He usually called Money by Friday each week to check about playing ball, but mainly to head off any possible phone contact between Money, his father, Wally or William. He was relatively certain that Money would hang up on anyone but him, but still he didn't trust the immense pride that Money possessed. He stood looking out at the river, noticing a small wooden boat easing through the near motionless waters. "Pride," he muttered with disgust. "Where's mine? I'm hiding from the only friend I have." He attempted to disregard his thoughts. He had to do this for Alex but he also knew that Money deserved the truth. He followed the boat with his eyes until it disappeared from view. It had not mattered to him in a very long time what anyone besides Alex thought. It mattered nothing to him if the entire world chose to hate him. He was surprised at this moment to realize how badly it disturbed him to disappoint not only Money, but Clarence as well. He sighed and returned to creating a wall.

The day of work exhausted Bret, but it eased his troubled mind somewhat. He collapsed in his bed at ten, quickly drifting off to sleep. He dreamed throughout the night. There were glimpses of his father, his three brothers, Money, and Clarence. He would recall little of the intertwining characters the next morning.

It was shortly before daybreak and he dreamed again, but this time quite vividly and with total recall. He was at the old house by the river standing on a pier. In the dream, he could recall thinking that there was no pier. The sun was low, resting on top of the tree line across the river. The orange light was dancing atop the ripples created by a passing boat.

He turned back and looked at the house. Standing on the porch, looking at him was his mother. Beside her was a young man that he didn't recognize, and his grandparents. They were smiling broadly and waving to him. He walked toward them. God, his mother was so beautiful and younger than he could ever recall. Her smile was happier, freer than he recalled. Vicky's face was not the stern one he knew all too well. It was pleasant, inviting. Ralph looked healthy, not drained by whiskey. The man beside his mom looked at him, smiling, and then he looked back at Bret's mom. He took her hand gently, producing another smile from her. Then, like a cut from a movie scene his mom stood alone. He was almost to her, wanting so badly to touch her. She smiled so tenderly at him. "There's a way, my precious son. Find the right path and you will be happy." She reached to touch him. "I'm so proud of what you have done with Alex. I love you, my dear child."

He reached to touch her but she was gone. He woke quickly and his heart raced as if he had run dozens of wind sprints. The dream was so real. He longed to go back to it. It didn't make sense. Who was that man with his mom? He rolled over and eventually found sleep again, but what he wished for was to find his mother again, if only in a dream.

* * *

It was the next Sunday, a few minutes past one. Money didn't expect Bret to show, but still he peeked each time the gym door opened.

The fifth time he looked was one time too many for Big Willie. "It's time for you to give up on that cracker. He's gone. It is time for you to be with your own kind."

His voice boomed angrily back at Willie. "Your own kind? What kind of crap is that, Willie? Every white person is the enemy. That's what you're trying to tell me?"

"You can't bank on them. That's all I'm saying."

Money felt the heat of anger running through his body. Willie's words angered him for two reasons. One reason was that Willie was wrong about his friend, and the other reason that troubled him even more was that he just might be right.

Bret spent the weekend just as he had the prior one, hiding out at Castle Hayne, spending time building a house that he had once refused a dying man's request to do just that.

The weekend was winding up better though. It was four p.m., and his father, Wally and William were on their way to the airport. Their plane would leave in an hour, bound for the windy city of Chicago. They may fly back for a surprise visit on the weekends was his fathers' parting threat. His father was the best attorney money could buy, and that certainly was not because he put his family first. Bret had observed him in the courtroom. It was not a fight for his client, but rather his own ego that drove him to win at all costs. He would not return until the trial was over.

As they drove away Bret felt his shoulders relax and he took a deep calming breath.

At six p.m., Barbara walked in the door. "Well, I guess this is my summer home." She mockingly looked around at the extravagance of the house. "I think this will do."

Bret called upstairs, "Alex, let's go. Barbara is here."

"Where are you going?" she asked.

"No, our new house guest. It is where are we going?"

"And where are we going?"

"Out for pizza, beer, and sarsaparilla for the little man." She tried to speak, but he refused to allow it. "Your exams are over, no excuses. We are going to celebrate."

"Celebrate? Maybe I am not all that happy to be staying here this summer. Did you and that monstrous ego of yours think of that? And since when did you start drinking beer?"

"Well, baby sitter, my monstrous ego has taken a little beating lately. Now, as far as you residing here this summer, I am certain that the old man has made it worth your while financially. I also don't think that you will be too put out by spending sunny days lounging at the country club pool with Alex. But I do have just one small request."

"And that would be?"

"The country club boys will be quite taken by you in a bikini. Please don't bring any of those boys home. It would prove most embarrassing."

She glared at him and feigned being mad. "You are a country club boy," she pointed out. "And who says that I even own a bikini?" she added, squinting her eyes for effect.

"I have to eat somewhere, and if you don't own a bikini with a body like yours, it would be, how should I say, not proper."

She smiled and shook her head slightly at him. "Do lines such as that work on the garden variety, country club, charm school girls?"

"No."

"I find that hard to believe. They are so gullible."

"It is not that. It is because they use the lines."

"They say you should own a bikini?" Barbara laughed.

Bret joined her laughter, offering no reply. It was the best that he had felt in two weeks.

"So, why are we celebrating, country club boy?"

"The celebration is for the departure of my dear old dad, and his two shadows. May their plane crash somewhere along the way."

"Bret, don't talk like that!" she exclaimed. "That is a terrible thing to say. What if that happened? You would feel guilty for the rest of your life."

He smiled slightly and said assuredly, "Or not."

She looked at him and shook her head softly before Alex came thundering down the stairs interrupting the brief skirmish.

Minutes later they were seated in the corner booth at the local Pizza parlor. Bret ordered a large pizza, covered in pepperoni and sausage, a beer, sweet tea, and a sarsaparilla.

"Bret, when did you start drinking beer?" she asked.

The beer was in front of him now and he lifted the mug to his lips, drinking it slowly. "Well, my basketball career is over, so why not?"

She looked at him with great annoyance. "Because you are Mr. Control at all times."

"Alex, why do you think Barbara dislikes me so much?" he asked, turning to him.

"Because you are a butthead," Alex replied, giggling as he looked at Barbara who joined his laughter.

"Boy, it's going to be a fun summer with you guys picking on me," he replied, pretending to be hurt.

Bret drank three mugs of beer with the pizza. The first tasted bitter, but by the last one, he thought he had acquired a taste. His head felt light and he laughed easily at his own jokes, or any others that were offered.

They walked out into the muggy night air. "Bret, let me see your keys," Barbara said.

"Why?"

"Well, it's probably not a good idea to begin drinking and driving with a buzz all in the same night."

He looked at her but kept the keys.

"You had three beers. I had none. End of discussion," she said as she gestured with her head toward Alex.

He looked at her and then at Alex. "Okay," he said, and handed her the keys. Alex rested happily in the back seat as Barbara drove into the wind. The breeze invigorated Bret. He felt as if he could escape almost everything, for the moment.

* * *

Money sat on the porch surveying the quietness of Castle Street on a Sunday night. The door opened and his father joined him, sitting in the rocker beside him.

"What's troubling you, boy?"

"Bret didn't show up to play ball today. I've called but he never is the one to answer the phone."

"So?"

"So, I hang up. You know his father told him not to be messing with me. Why cause trouble for him?"

Clarence studied his son. "Friendships aren't easy, son, especially this one."

"Maybe he wasn't much of a friend." he countered.

"Is that what you believe?"

"I don't know," he sighed. "I do know that it is not a case of being busy. He walked away and I want the truth."

"Can I ask you something, son?"

He knew his dad was just being polite and careful of his feelings at this moment, but still it touched him. He reached over and put his hand on his dad's large shoulder. It was hard as brick. He squeezed it. "There are no boundaries between us, Dad."

Clarence was touched and it showed when he lost the words to his train of thought. He blinked his eyes and looked out into the street.

Money looked out at the same street and though their eyes were different in some ways, in most ways they were the same. "Dad," he said softly.

"Yes, son."

"It is obvious how Bret feels about his dad. He doesn't exactly hide it." He paused, and then added, "He has never said it before but I get the feeling that he looks at you and I, and he thinks that maybe we are the rich people."

Clarence turned to his son and was moved by the words of his son. Money turned and looked him in the eyes, and then ever so gently nodded. "And he would be right."

Clarence often observed parents and their children struggle mightily, especially fathers with teenage sons. He felt so very blessed, so very rich. "Yes, son. He would be right. But only a man could see that, C.T."

Money nodded in agreement and gratitude.

Their eyes returned to the street. A young lady, still clothed in her blue floral Sunday dress pushed a child in the stroller. She waved to them and they returned the greeting with a smile and a polite nod.

"Do you believe in Bret, son?"

"I don't know."

"It's easy to believe in someone when times are good, but it's harder when there are obstacles in the way. And that just may be the time when people need you to believe in them the most."

"Maybe he is just a spoiled rich white boy that can't be seen hanging out with a black man."

Clarence smiled softly. "Oh, he is spoiled, son. It would be almost impossible not to be in his world. But you know something, C.T.? I believe in that boy. There might be a reason that you or I just can't see. Something we don't know and maybe he is not ready to tell just yet, even to a friend."

Money thought for a few moments. "What would you do, Dad?"

"I would find a way to talk to him. It's going to eat at you until you do. That much is certain. You think on it, son. You'll find the right way to go about it."

"Dad, why do you believe that he didn't decide to forget me and hang out with the boys at the club? That's what the guys at the gym say each Sunday when he doesn't show up."

Clarence shook his head. "He's like you. I think it's been a long time since he had a friend, someone who didn't want something from him. You guys have more in common than you think. C.T., you've always been the best player on every team, beginning with the first one. Everyone wanted to be on your team so they'd win. The girls lining up to date you. Well, people want Bret for the same reason. He is the star basketball player and because of his last name."

"I don't know, Dad. I feel silly, in a way that all of this bothers me so much."

"Friendships are sacred, son. Before you give up on your friend, I want you to remember something. What he did that day in that alley took courage. And what he endured in school since then couldn't have been easy."

"So I should believe in him is what you are saying."

"No, I am not saying any such thing. This is your decision. I told you that you are becoming a man and men make their own decisions."

"Does that mean I can't ask you?"

"You know better than that, son. I'll always be here to listen and if you mess up I will crack that head of yours. But I also will allow you to create your own path."

"I'll do that, Dad. But I want your eyes on this."

Clarence nodded his head softly one time. He paused and then began to speak with great deliberation. "He might have me fooled, son. But I look at the way he sees to Alex. I listened to you tell me how he takes care of him. Well, I say that there must be something special in him to take on such an awesome responsibility," he said as he rose from his chair, resting his strong hand on his son's shoulder. "He has taken on a task that I have seen many grown men fail at. He is for entire practical purposes, Alex's dad. Think about it. He does all the things a dad does. He loves, nurtures, and protects that boy. He would fight me, you, and a dozen more if we tried to hurt Alex."

Money thought of the words that his dad offered. "Maybe his dad found out about him playing ball with me. Maybe he threatened him with something I can't see."

Clarence's smile was concealed now by the darkness. "Now, son, you are reasoning like a wise man would." Clarence walked inside to retire for the evening, while Money sat longer, staring at the dark empty street.

CHAPTER SEVEN

Toe the line

Barbara parked her bright yellow 64 Volkswagen Bug in the Marin driveway. The day was brilliant with sunshine and the afternoon temperature was nearing ninety-five. The record heat of May continued with no reprieve.

She got out of the car worrying briefly that some of her skin might sear to the seat. The soft green tee shirt she wore was drenched with perspiration. She wished, no, she prayed for air conditioning.

Alex leaped from the passenger side showing little effect from the heat. "Let's shoot some ball."

"Let's go inside and get out of this heat," she replied quickly.

She unlocked the door and managed one step in when the phone rang. "Thank God for cool air," she exclaimed as she rushed to the phone. "Marin residence, this is Barbara."

She heard someone stammer briefly and then there was silence.

"Hello, is anybody there?"

"Barbara?"

"Yes, who is this?"

"Money. Is Bret around?"

"No, he said yesterday that he was going from school to work on that old house. I guess he doesn't have anything better to do. So, how are you? Have you been cutting through any alleys lately?" she joked.

"I'm okay, and I check the alleys real well."

"Bret told me that he had been playing ball at the school on Sundays."

"Yes, but he hasn't shown up the past couple of weeks."

"Maybe he will be there next Sunday."

Money thought to ask Barbara if she knew what was going on, but he decided against it. He doubted that Bret confided in her. Besides, he thought of a better way. "Barbara, it was nice talking to you. Good-bye," he said, ending the call abruptly.

He walked to the workshop where his father was running strips of wood through the table saw. He waited for him to stop, being careful as always not to startle him when machinery was running that could easily take a man's finger or worse. Clarence looked up briefly at him. He lowered his head and finished the strip of wood that he was cutting. He switched the motor off. "Hey, C.T., what do you need?"

"Are you going back to the job site today?"

"No."

"Can I borrow the truck?"

"Sure."

"Thanks, Dad."

Clarence watched him turn and leave. He realized there was no reason offered for why his son needed the truck all of a sudden. He smiled as he cut the saw back on. "He will tell me when he is ready, Lord," he said softly.

Money cranked the truck and pointed it in the direction of Castle Hayne. Minutes later, he parked the truck by Bret's Mustang. The sound of nails being driven echoed throughout the trees as he walked toward the house.

Fred lifted his head and offered a muffled bark. His work done for the day, he lowered his head to the floor and resumed sleeping.

Money entered the house. Bret was upstairs working on the wall at the edge of the walkway. Money looked up at him and said, "I thought that you were not going to finish this old house."

The unexpected noise that invaded the quietness of the country and the hammering of nails startled Bret. He looked down at the intruder and an uneasy feeling moved through his body.

After another moment of awkwardness passed, Bret answered, "I don't know about finishing it but it gives me something to do."

"You mean to get away from."

"That's not what I said."

"Where have you been?"

"Busy, you know school is winding down, final exams."

"So, this is studying?"

Bret did not like the conversation, especially where it might be heading. "I guess that you could say I'm taking a break."

Money shrugged and began walking up the stairs. He stopped a few feet away from Bret, resting his hand on the completed portion of the wall. He looked at his friend, his only real friend that he didn't want to lose.

"What's going on, man?"

"Nothing, what do you mean?"

"C'mon Bret, don't do that. Since the fight, we have hung out together every weekend, played ball every Sunday. You don't accept the help that you know I'd gladly give you to work on this place. This is where you have been the past two weekends, haven't you?"

"So what if I have," he replied sharply. "I didn't know that I was supposed to inform you of my every move in life."

"Why don't you stop being the rich kid that closes the world off and talk to me?" Money said firmly, refusing to back off.

"I am talking to you," he replied, refusing to follow the conversation to where Money desired it to go.

"No, you're talking at me. Something happened and all I want to know is what. Friends should be able to get that from one another."

"I've just been busy, Money. Don't make more of it than there is."

"So you'll be there to play ball next Sunday."

"Maybe," Bret replied, knowing better.

"Why wouldn't you be? School is over Friday," he pressed, the frustration at not garnering the truth evident in his voice.

"I don't know."

He shook his head at Bret's evasive tactics. "I guess the boys at the gym were right."

Bret feigned his best look of boredom.

"The white boy gone back to his own. Whitey can't be a real friend. Don't look good for the biggest man in town to have his son running around with some nigger boy."

Bret was shocked at his use of that word. He heard the other guys in the gym at Williston use it frequently to each other, but never had that word derived from Money's lips until this moment.

"Believe what you want to believe. I'm not here to worry about what you or any of your friends think."

"They are people I play ball with. None of them are my friends, but I thought you were. Teke is coming next Sunday. I hoped that you could come over and meet her. I've been telling her about you and Alex. We're having a cookout next Sunday at six. Dad told me to be sure and invite you. Last night I was ready to forget you. But dad says no, maybe something you can't see, son. Maybe his daddy threatened him. Maybe with something really important. So I am here trying to find out what it is."

Money caught a glimpse of reflex in Bret's eye, but it left as quickly as it came. His face returning to one void of expression.

Bret was tempted, for a moment to tell the truth. If he did, Money would understand. He wasn't so naive that he did not know why Money was standing in front of him in such an agitated state. It was because their friendship was very important to him. He wanted to keep it also, but the risk was so steep. His father could throw him out and forbid him to see Alex, and what would happen to Alex? What would happen to him? Everything between he and Alex had remained private since their mother died. A place no outsider was allowed to invade. There were two families in the Marin house. There was the one consisting of Walker Sr. and his shadows that ran like a corporation. The other one was composed of Alex and him. Bret knew that it didn't matter that Alex was only ten. Alex never would tell anything private between them. He could be trusted above all.

"Your dad is a nice man. You're lucky he is your father." Bret paused. "Maybe we can play ball again sometime, but give me some time to work things out."

Money knew the answer was going to remain hidden, at least for now. No amount of probing would change that. He extended his hand. "I'll always owe you one for the day in the alley. You remember that. There's no statute of limitation on it."

Bret took his friend's hand, slightly amused at Money using a legal term. "Good luck. I wish it was me going to State on a scholarship."

Money smiled, letting go of his friend's hand. His friend had said farewell, and no matter the reason he would accept it. He walked down the stairs and out the door leaving the old house and his friend behind.

It was nearing darkness and Bret was nearly finished with the wall. He pounded nail after nail in frustration. His life was changing and he didn't like it. He was changing. Things that never mattered to him, like having a friend, suddenly did. The problems that occupied his mind were the reason that four of the soft ponderosa pine boards were tossed to the side, damaged by an errant hammer strike. He finished nailing the last board. The low upstairs wall was complete. He walked outside onto the porch. The sun had disappeared in the trees that bordered the opposite side of the river. He had lost basketball, except for pickup games. He had found a friend and lost him as well. A small wooden shrimp boat passed by. The reflection of its lights knifing through the water, stopping short of the shore. For the first time in his self absorbed life it was as if he was seeing the reflection of his own life in the water. He didn't care very much for what we he saw.

Bret drove the lonely dark road of highway 133, which linked Castle Hayne with downtown Wilmington. He was tired, frustrated, and troubled. Nothing seemed clear at this moment.

The thought of spending eight more years under his father's manipulation seemed like a prison sentence at the moment. But what choice did he have? Right now, he almost felt like he could leave the lifestyle that his father's world granted him. He could go to Campbell or somewhere else on a basketball scholarship. He had a few stocks he could sell and over ten thousand dollars in a savings account. He could get by. Getting by, that had a hollow ring to it, especially when he was use to enjoying the best of everything. He didn't want to live like everyone else. He liked never having to worry about money, and even if he could leave the lifestyle behind, what about Alex?

He was on the narrow Smith Creek Bridge, which separated Castle Hayne from the north side of Wilmington when he noticed that the fuel gauge was past empty. He thought briefly to chance it, to avoid stopping on the north side of Wilmington, an area dominated by blacks. The racial tension had slowly dwindled since the march. Still, stopping farther in town would be safer. As he left the bridge in his rear view mirror his car made the decision for him. The car lurched slightly at first, followed by bigger, more frequent ones. He kept the car coasting as best he could, aided by a slight decline in the road. He spotted a homemade quick stop store to his right that bore no resemblance to a 7-Eleven, but it did have a gas pump out front. He popped the clutch one last time and revived the car just long enough to coast beside the pump where it appropriately died.

He was pumping gas into his car when a yellow work van pulled up on the other side. The side of it was painted crudely with a cheap logo. The attempt appeared to be a key broken off in a lock. Over the key in bright red letters was the word 'Bryant'. Under the key in equally hideous letters, made even worse by the color combination, was the word 'Locksmith'.

Bret looked around, once again, at the darkness that swallowed the area, and continued pumping gas. He heard the door close, followed by a voice, "Wrong side of town for you, white boy."

The voice was familiar. Bret looked up, somewhat in relief that it belonged to Big Willie. "Hey, Willie. What's up?"

Willie looked menacing as always. "What's up, you little rich cracker, is that you ditched my boy."

"What are you talking about?"

"Don't play dumb with me. Where you been the past two weeks?"

"Excuse me, I didn't know it was mandatory to be at Williston every Sunday for the rest of my life," Bret said with more freshness in his voice than was wise.

"That's good. Talk smart to me. You on my side of town and your friend is nowhere to be found. I guess being rich sure don't make you smart."

Bret finished pumping gas and returned the nozzle to its resting place. He walked toward the store, turning his back on Willie.

"I'm not through talking to you."

Bret turned abruptly. "What do you want, Willie? You want me to crawl because you're so big? I'm not going to."

"Good, pride, that will carry you a long way, especially now. What I want is for you to stay away from our boy. He don't need no white boy hanging out with him that's going to mess with his mind."

"You don't know anything. Did Money tell you something that you would like to enlighten me with?"

"No, but I've watched him looking at that door for the past two

Sundays waiting for your sorry cracker ass to show up. The boys ask where you are and he don't want to answer because he don't know. So, we tell him the truth, that you are just some sorry white boy pretending to be his friend. Money, he's so young, not knowing how things are, so he defends you. Tells us all that we are wrong. He won't listen to another bad word spoken about you, even told me to shut up, knowing I'd crush him in a second. He would have fought me over you." He shook his head in dismay. "Fought me over some sorry country club punk like you," he said in a manner more like a question that he could scarcely believe the answer.

Bret didn't know what Willie was hoping to accomplish with this dialogue, but he was tired of it. "It's late. I'm tired and I've heard enough. Think what you want." He turned toward the store.

"Hey, I told you, don't turn away from me when I'm talking to you," Willie said as he reached out and put his hand solidly on Bret's shoulder.

Bret had reached the point where common sense was overruled by the frustration of all that had happened. He turned quickly throwing the best right hand punch that he had to offer.

It was not enough. His punch fell short of the taller man's face, coming to rest just below Willie's right collarbone. The full force of Bret's blow created a thudding sound as it landed. Fear came over him immediately when he saw that the blow didn't move Willie one inch in any direction. He realized quickly the magnitude of his error. He thought to follow the punch up but he doubted it would do any good. He waited for Willie to lift his hands and crush him. Willie stood there, his hands down by his side, his face calm and empty of anger. "I'm going to let you have that one. Talk got around town about some white boy that helped Money out of a jam in this alley. Word is that white boy was you. I'll grant you that one punch. You won't ever get another one and you best not forget that. My interest in this is that Money has got a chance none of the rest of us in town had. I was good, but I had to play at an all-black school in South Carolina. He goes to State, maybe the NBA, in short, I want to see him get his best chance. Right now, he don't need anyone or anything to distract him. I don't know why you matter so much to him, and I don't care. But all of us want him to make it. You want to be his friend and prove all of us wrong that you're not some fair weather white boy pretending to be a friend, fine do it. Otherwise, leave him alone and don't distract him. You understand?"

Bret nodded slowly and stood frozen as Willie got back in the van and drove away. He wanted to move, but he wasn't sure that he could. He felt very fortunate to be able to stand or to be alive for that matter. What he didn't know, what he couldn't know, was that Willie wanted to be wrong about the unkind remarks he issued. Willie was perturbed, because he too had begun to believe that this white boy was not the enemy.

Bret escaped one problem to discover another. He reached in his pocket and realized he had no money. Normally, that was not a problem. His Shell gas card was always in the glove compartment. This, however, was not a Shell station.

Nervously, he opened the rickety screen door and entered the store. Behind the counter was Rich Mears, a struggling family man. He was twenty-five with a wife and three kids. He worked long hard days as a brick mason helper, and three evenings a week he earned extra cash working the little store. He was tired much of the time and the early heat wave only added to his fatigue.

Bret walked up to the counter. He looked at the man who clearly was not in a good mood. He was tall, slim, and veins popped from his forearms like cords of rope. He had a goatee that seemed to enhance the anger in his face. The store was stifling hot. Bret wiped the sweat off his forehead.

"Six dollars," Rich said curtly.

"I've got a problem," Bret stated, wishing he could crawl under a rock and hide at the moment.

"I'm here to take money not solve problems," Rich said, his voice giving the obvious impression that he wanted money and no conversation.

"That's the problem. I ran out of gas in front of your pump and then I discovered that I didn't have any money." Bret heard a screen door open in the rear of the store and then slap against the wood, but paid it little attention.

"Let me see if I got this right. You have no money, but you fill the tank up. You don't get a dollar's worth. You fill the tank," he reiterated.

"I have a Shell card."

"And what good is that?"

"I know that it's no good here. But that is what I always use. I wasn't planning on running out of gas. I swear I'll come by here tomorrow afternoon and pay you."

"I don't know you. Some white boy here in my part of town and he's going to come back tomorrow." He waved his right hand in the air. "Do you think I am that stupid?"

"No," he answered.

Bret was aware of slow soft footsteps behind him as he thought about his dilemma. The cashier was unwilling to budge and he had no money. He tried once again, "C'mon, I'll pay you ten dollars tomorrow. It's been a long day."

"You got that right. This is how we are going to solve the problem. You will call someone and they will bring the money now."

Bret figured that was the only solution that the angry man in front of him was going to accept. What were his options? He thought of Barbara but that gave him pause due to the location. Money would come, but he couldn't ask him under the present circumstances. Vicky, well that was a possibility but he did not want to do that either. He decided to try one more time.

"Look, I've got money. I don't want to steal your gas. Can't you just trust me for one day for the money?"

The footsteps were close now and Bret started to turn, when he heard a voice. "Mr. Marin, is that you?"

Bret turned to see a friendly face, Louie.

"What's the problem, Rich?" Louie asked.

"He pumped a full tank of gas without having any money. I told him to call somebody to bring the money. You know how the owner is about the till coming out right. This boy here wants me to trust him until tomorrow. He doesn't come back and I'm out of a job."

"How much does he owe?"

"Six dollars."

Louie reached into his pocket and pulled out the contents. His house key and thirteen dollars. He pulled out one of the five dollar bill along with one worn dollar bill. "Here, that settles that," he said with a smile.

Bret's favorite doorman in the entire universe had just doubled in stature, maybe tripled. "Thanks, Louie. I will come by the club tomorrow and pay you. I'll pay you ten for helping me out, or more if you want."

"No, you'll pay me six and not a penny more. You pay me the next time you see me. It don't need to be tomorrow."

"Thanks, Louie. Can I give you a ride home?"

"No, I don't live to far from here. This young man that was giving you such a hard time is my nephew," he said with a slightly admonishing tone. "I like to stroll up here in the evenings sometimes, stretch my old legs a bit, and sit and chew the fat with Rich. Gets me out of the house, you know," he added, offering another warm smile. "I will walk out with you, though."

They walked out into the muggy night air. There was a slight fog settling in the trees that bordered the river. The irony of the situation was not lost on Bret that here he was the kid from the richest family in town having to be bailed out by a doorman from the club.

"Mr. Marin, you look troubled lately when you visit the club. Don't mean to pry none, but a young lad like you don't need the weight of the world on his shoulders."

"First off, we are not at any club. I'm eighteen years old, please call me Bret."

Louie smiled. "Okay, Bret."

"Second, you just saved me from more trouble than you can know. You can pry all that you want too."

"I watched you boys grow up in the club. Hate to see you troubled. You and your little brother, always give me a good feeling watching how you look after him."

"Louie, can I ask you something?"

"Sure, go ahead. I got no secrets."

"How do you do it? I mean, how do you go to that club and be treated like a...like a servant?"

"Everyone is not so bad."

"But still, you hear the remarks. I know I've been rude to you at times. But you are above it all. It never rattles you. You remain nice no matter what, but yet you don't bow down to anyone."

"But I do bow down, just not to anyone at the club."

"I don't understand."

"I don't preach to people, don't try to be righteous, but my savior is Jesus and he don't see no color when he look on a man. He sees heart.

He sees what's inside of a man. So, when those people look down on me, treat me less than human, I just picture Jesus looking down on me and I know he sees different. He calls me his friend. That is why I begin each day on my knees before him."

Louie looked at him and offered perception that the young man had not yet gained, but that he hoped that he might one day. He had a feeling that it needed to be sooner rather than later. "Bret, usually there is a way out of bad times. Now, it may not be an easy way, or the way we want, still if we search, there is a way." And with that, Louie put a friendly hand on Bret's shoulder. "I think I will get on home after all. The wife wasn't feeling all that well." Louie smiled once more and shuffled ever so gracefully into the darkness. Bret watched him until he was out of sight as he attempted to decipher Louie's words. Bret believed that there was a God but the way Louie spoke it seemed so personal. That was something he could not understand. Still, he did not doubt it was real, at least to Louie. "Is that really why Louie's is so different?" he asked, realizing that his eyes had drifted to the sky. He shook his head briefly not understanding the mystery of Louie's friend. He got in his car and drove away. He shook his head once thinking of Louie, and his God, and his predicament. "God, if you are listening I sure could use a hand." He chuckled at the thought of someone like him receiving help from Louie's God.

Bret entered the Marin house. The grandfather clock chimed once, signaling that it was ten-thirty. It had been too long a day, with too many confrontations and too many problems. He walked up the stairs to Alex's room. He opened the door quietly, finding him sleeping soundly. A basketball book lay beside him. He picked up the book and thought again of the day his brother fell. He had played the scenario out a million times, but each time Alex came up lame. He bent down and kissed him goodnight, pulling the sheet over him. Ever so softly he whispered, "I love you, little man. You're all I got."

He started to leave but stopped and sat in the chair beside the bed. He was so drained but still restless inside. He sat there until he heard the clock chime eleven times, listening to the rhythmic breathing of his brother. He walked down the hall and tapped on the guest room door.

"Come in."

He entered Barbara's summer living quarters. "You look beat," she greeted him.

"It's been quite a day."

"What's wrong?"

"Nothing that can be fixed."

Barbara was trying to figure out what looked different about Bret. She searched her mind for the word. It came to her. Unsure, Bret Marin, actually looked unsure of himself.

"Did you eat?"

Bret thought for a moment, "No, actually I haven't."

"I cooked spaghetti. You go take a shower and I will heat the food for you."

"You don't have to do that."

"I realize that, but I will."

Bret emerged a few minutes later feeling somewhat better that the dust and grime of the day was washed away. He thought of how he wished troubles could be cleansed away that easily. Just watch them disappear down the drain along with the day of work and sweat. He sat at the counter and watched Barbara prepare his late meal. She was wearing a large red nightshirt. It revealed nothing of her body until it stopped at mid-thigh.

She turned and gave him an admonishing look, knowing what he was doing. There was silence between them for a few moments before she turned back to what she was doing. "Money called."

He nodded his head and said nothing.

"Did something happen between the two of you?"

"Not really."

She set the plate down, piled high with spaghetti and garlic bread lathered in butter, accompanied by a glass of sweet tea. "I thought that maybe you decided to have a friend."

"Not tonight, Barbara. Solve me another time," he said dismissively.

She studied him and contemplated allowing him off the hook before deciding against it. "Are you always going to be closed off from the world, unwilling to talk about anything personal?"

"If you only knew the day I had. I think I've had enough personal conversation to last me a lifetime."

"Money went to the house, didn't he?"

"Yes."

"So, what happened?"

Wearily he looked up from the plate of food in front of him. "It's a long story," he said sighing.

"I've got time," she pushed on.

He smiled. He was too drained to fight her. "My wonderful father does not want me hanging out with Money."

"I see. Does that bother you?"

"Does what bother me, my father? Is that a trick question?"

"You know what I mean. Do you want to be friends with Money?" she pressed on.

"Yes, but I can't."

"Because he threatened to throw you out and even worse you fear that he will not allow you to be around to raise Alex?"

He looked up again, stunned by her words. "What makes you think that?"

"I've never seen you worried. You love only one person in this world. So, do I have to be a brain surgeon to ascertain that it involves Alex?"

He continued eating, refusing to respond.

"Is it always going to be this way, you and Alex against the world? Do you want Alex to grow up as self centered, as selfish as you?"

He stopped eating. His voice remained calm, "Barbara, please leave me alone, and just what is it that you think that you know about my life?"

"Will you just talk to me?" she demanded angrily.

"How do I know that this is not another trick? Like the one you pulled when you led me to believe that you were going to the Holiday Inn with me."

"You deserved it, and even a callous person like you knows that," she said, willing herself to be calm, though the irritation inside of her was about to boil over.

He looked at the fury her face held and he started to say something smart, but he breathed deeply and spoke softly, "I didn't mean to upset you. I think you are great. Alex really likes you. You're so good to him. I know that he is in good hands when he is with you. And," he paused...

"And what?" she pushed.

"I meant what I said that day about you being a breath of fresh air. I know that you are different than the girls I go out with."

She studied him carefully and started to speak.

He cut her off. "No, that was not a line. It is the truth."

Right now she did not know what to think. What bothered her most was at this moment she was more attracted to him than she wanted to be. She wasn't blind. She saw how he looked at her and though it was difficult for her to admit it she was flattered. He was about the best looking man she had ever laid eyes on and if he were not such a jerk she might have been tempted.

She was lost in her thoughts when he interrupted. "I'll answer your question about Money."

He filled her in on the conversation that had taken place at the old house.

She listened intently, and when he finished, she thought for a few moments. Slowly she began. "So, is he your friend? I mean is it important to you, because I want for some crazy reason to believe that you are more than what people see."

"Yes, I would like to be friends. Yes, I like hanging out with him. I've never laughed so much in my entire life."

"It would be nice to find a way for you to go to that cookout on Sunday. You could surprise him and tell him the truth, that your father threatened you with Alex. Sooner or later, you will need to let someone else in your life and Alex's. I think that your friend will understand. He sounds like one really good guy. I can still picture you rolling around on the ground laughing till your sides hurt. A sight I never imagined. Would it be so bad for you to need something, or someone else in your life?"

Her words strangely added to the loneliness that he felt at this moment. It hadn't been this bad since he had lost his mother.

He stood up and said, "I don't know."

She rose also and they looked in each others eyes without words. She felt nervous inside at the way he looked at her. He was not arrogant at the moment. He was real. You could see it in his face. Was he actually changing?

He touched the side of her face and it felt so good. She wanted in this one moment to allow him freedom to do what he wanted to do from the first day she showed up for work. She leaned into kiss him and their lips touched, and at that moment her level-headed side of her brain came back to her. She pulled away abruptly. "I'm sorry. I can't."

"You wouldn't want to stay in my room tonight?" he said softly.

She stood and gently moved his ruffled hair to one side. "That's not the answer, Bret. But maybe, one day, you'll change enough where some woman will want you for more than the outside stuff."

He looked at her and she could see the disappointment. "I want you to know that I am not playing with you like I did when I was upset about what you did to Bonnie."

He smiled and touched her face again. "I know that."

She felt relieved that he knew she was being truthful. She touched his hand and took it in hers. "I want to ask you one more question."

"Okay."

"If I can find a safe way to get you to that cookout, would you go?"

"How?"

"Let a college girl think, okay?"

He started to persist, but she halted him, "I know what you are going to say, but unless I can come up with an idea that involves only the three of us in this house knowing, I won't do it. The people in that house, that's for you to decide if they can be trusted."

"Why is this so important to you?"

She looked at him intently, carefully choosing her words before she made them audible. "Maybe, because I think that it is fate that you and Money's lives crossed. I want to see where it goes. At least, you know that you can trust me if for no other reason than because I will lose this job if anyone finds out, and I need the cash because we know that I am a poor college girl."

He studied her closely and shocked her with what he said. "That is not why you won't tell. You won't tell because you are a really good person. And," he added succinctly, "there is nothing poor about you."

At first she waited for the punch line but there was none. He was sincere. He bent down to her height and kissed her softly on the cheek. They left the kitchen, retiring for the night, in different rooms.

CHAPTER EIGHT

Teke

Teke Wilkins sat on the edge of the bed in the apartment that she had shared with her mother for the past three years. She eyed herself in the mirror once again, and fresh tears added to her already tear stained face.

Graduation was three days away. She was leaving to visit her brother and father on Sunday. The week that was supposed to be so exhilarating was replaced with a terror unlike any she had ever known in her young life.

She completed her last exam for high school earlier that day. It was in Biology and she felt quite certain that she aced it. Her high school GPA was 4.0, and she had made the first honor roll every semester for three years running.

She was wearing a bold colorful halter dress that was purchased the previous weekend for tonight. The cotton fabric was dominated by a brilliant royal blue, streams of silver and white, with a circular pattern of vivid yellow added to the conglomeration of colors. Wild, exciting colors were in fashion and that trend was well in place in the city of Philadelphia.

The dress was sleeveless and open in the back, tied in a bow behind her neck to hold up her chest, though that was one thing that nature failed to bless her with.

She was 5'5", 117 lb. Her frame was slightly thin with wiry muscles not usually associated with young ladies. Her legs, which escaped the confines of her dress at mid thigh, were stunning. They were neither skinny nor the slightest bit too large, but perfect in their symmetry. There was a sleekness about them that made you long for summer to come to the city of brotherly love and never depart.

She glanced in the mirror for the third time in the past two minutes. She almost managed a small chuckle at the ruffles in her dark hair. Her hair consisted of a million tiny curls, granted her at birth. All of them cascading south before coming to rest on top of her slightly broad shoulders.

Her eyes were similar to those that her brother possessed, but softer. They were dark and usually framed beautifully in a cloud of bright white, however at this moment they were violated by the color of blood. Her skin was slightly darker than that of her brother. One thing they shared was a smile that could illuminate a room mired in perpetual darkness. At this moment she found nothing to smile about. She often was the recipient of compliments about her maturity. Right now, however, she felt like a little girl. A little girl who desperately needed her mom.

She touched her slender nose and drew her hand back from the pain it produced. Her lips, luscious looking most of the time, were puffed in places and there was a cut in the right hand corner of her mouth that bled until a few minutes ago.

Tonight she went on a date with Lawrence Tuttle, her boyfriend of two months. He had been the nicest guy that she had ever been out with, until tonight. Tonight was to be special because her last exam was over, and next year, she would be joining him at Temple.

Lawrence was a freshman at Temple. His father, a homicide detective, possessed the highest ranking ever achieved by a black man in the Philly PD.

Lawrence charmed everyone he came in contact with, including her mother, which was a difficult task to pull off. He was 6'3", with a powerful body that topped out at 230 pounds.

The scene from tonight played out in her head again. They were in his dorm room. He had been a perfect gentleman to her during their courtship. He was patient when she explained that she was not ready for sex.

He took her to a fancy Italian restaurant near the campus. Afterwards they went to his dorm room for privacy. Their usual making out was taking place when he tried to persuade her into bed. She was almost ready, almost. Still, she said no. This night he did not take her answer well. He had held her tight, too tight. He pinned her body underneath his weight, kissing her roughly, violating her with his hands. She kept telling him no, to get off of her, but he refused. "Tonight is the night, baby. You know you want it." His words contained none of the gentleness he previously displayed. He transformed from a young gentleman to a monster in the time it took a dark room to light when the switch is flipped.

She felt the terror fresh in reliving the nightmare. Her screams had scarcely made it out of the room, drowned out by the music blasting in the next room.

He stood up, blocking her escape route to the door. "I have been patient with you. I've treated you well, taking you places, bought you things. Now it's time, baby, you're going to love it. Just relax," he said.

She stood in the corner of the room searching for a way out of this terrifying evening. She thought of how special she desired her first time to be. This surely was not the scenario she envisioned. It was suppose to be a treasure to cherish with someone special. Now, at that moment, a back seat at a drive-in movie on a hot, sticky, mosquito-filled night seemed almost romantic.

He removed his shirt as he walked toward her. His eyes were wild, like some kind of a crazed rabid animal.

In her moment of weakness and vulnerability anger joined her fear. She was still terrified, but she vowed that she would not surrender. She devised a plan how a woman half the weight and strength of the beast in front of her might survive this night.

"Take those clothes off now," he said menacingly.

"Okay," she agreed. "Give me a moment, please."

"I've given you enough time."

She stood beside the bed and began to untie the bow on her dress as she moved slowly toward him. The eyes belonging to the monster in front of her grew in delight at the sight of her surrender. He began to undo his pants and when they were half way down and he in the most vulnerable state she struck.

She smiled softly and persuaded him to look her in the eye, and then she kicked him as hard as she could in the area she wanted no part of on this night or any other. The scream he let out would have brought rush-hour Philly traffic to a screeching halt. As he grabbed his crotch he began to fall, facilitated by the trousers around his knees. He lashed out as he was falling and found enough strength to slap her hard across the face. She ran down the hallway, screaming at the top of her lungs, while struggling to secure the bow on her dress and maintain some type of decency, on a night that contained only indecency. The last words she heard were. "I'll get you for this, bitch."

She heard the key in the door and walked to the living room. A graceful light-skinned woman entered. One look at her baby girl and the wounds, the fright in her eyes, the shivering of her body scared her so terribly that she was temporarily frozen in place. "Baby, what happened?" she asked, as she willed her legs to walk to her daughter.

Teke met her mother, Jacky, across the room, burying herself in her mother's arms, breaking down in torrents of tears. It was several minutes later, as her mother held her on the couch before Teke could muster the words to tell of her ordeal. Her words mixed with the steady sobbing of tears.

They went to the police station an hour later as Jacky insisted. Teke tried to persuade her not to but to no avail. Jacky wanted a warrant sworn out for Lawrence Tuttle and she wanted him hauled into jail. She would get neither. This was a boy of seemingly impeccable behavior. His daddy was a detective who was not only respected by black officers, but white as well.

Officially, they performed their duty to question Lawrence. They went to his dorm room while Jacky and Teke waited at the station. His story was that a few of his friends had come by his room. Teke had gone into a jealous rage at the mention of an old girlfriend that was back in town. He asked her to leave, which incensed her even more. She slapped and kicked him before leaving. The officers questioned the friends and asked people living in the dorm hall if they had witnessed anything. No one saw anything. The officers smiled, slapped Lawrence on the back and told him to enjoy the summer break from college.

Jacky Wilkins demanded justice at the police station. What she received was an invitation to leave or she would be arrested.

They returned home past midnight. The phone rang and Teke picked it up, hoping that it was Money who often called late at night. The voice on the other end was haunting.

"Tonight was just the beginning, you little teaser. I'll get you. I'll finish what I started tonight. Count on it. Look out your window. Look in your back seat. Look behind every tree and bush, because, baby, I'll be there."

Teke's face went blank. She felt as if she were watching an Alfred Hitchcock movie, but it was she who was being terrorized.

Her mother, who had gone to fix a cup of coffee, reentered the room. "Is that Money?" she asked, before noticing the look on Teke's face. She took the phone out of her silent daughter's hand.

"Hello."

"Good evening, Ms. Wilkins. I was just telling Teke that there are no hard feelings for what she did to me tonight. The embarrassment she caused me with her lies. Of course, I don't want to see her anymore." The coldness that came from the phone was now replaced with an eerie silence.

Jacky hung up the phone and deliberated briefly on how best to protect her daughter. She picked the phone up again.

Money was jolted awake by the ringing of the phone. He rose from the couch where he had fallen asleep while watching television. He cut the television off and answered the phone.

"Hi, honey. Let me speak to your dad."

"He's asleep, Mom. I'll tell him to call you tomorrow."

"You wake him right now," she said evenly.

Money was silenced by the tone of his mother's voice. He walked to his father's room. "Dad, Dad."

Clarence was dreaming of shorter workweeks and an easier life. "What?" He shook his head trying to wake.

"Dad, Mom is on the phone."

Clarence was awake now at the mention of the woman he loved still and always would love. He glanced at the clock beside him on the nightstand. This was trouble.

"Hello, Jacky."

"Clarence, I'm sending Teke home to you tomorrow," and with

that she filled him in on the events of the night.

It took thirty additional minutes for her to convince an angry father not to come to Philadelphia to handle the problem personally.

It was four the next afternoon when the plane touched down in Wilmington. The airport's lone runway was surrounded by large grassy fields and a forest of predominantly pine trees served as a distant border. The transition was usually difficult for Teke, leaving a metropolitan city for a small town. She came to visit her brother and father. That made it bearable. Like her mother, she preferred the bright lights of the city, and the north.

She walked along the ramp and through the door. Her eyes searched for several moments before they rested on her dad and brother. Her face lit up for the first time since the ordeal had taken place. As they exchanged hugs, she felt safe, finally.

* * *

It was the last morning of school and the auditorium was filled for the presentation of awards. Bret won two awards, one as the school's top basketball player. He was the obvious choice. He was a little surprised to win best overall athlete, considering that he only played one sport, while many boys played two and three.

On each occasion that he walked to the podium, there was faint applause, mixed with indifference, and even a few boos. Dan refused to let the day in the alley die and successfully used people's prejudices and misconceptions to turn them against Bret.

He would not attend the graduation ceremony that night. They could send his diploma in the mail. His father would find out, but he would tell him that he heard that Dan was planning trouble. Since he was toeing the line, he didn't want to risk a possible altercation.

It was five o'clock, Saturday afternoon. They, at the urging of his little brother, spent the day at Wrightsville Beach. The ocean was unseasonably warm already, due to the record heat. They spent hours playing in the water, swimming and riding the waves with the rented rubber rafts from Crystal Pier.

They were drained from the sun and the ocean. Both of them had been asleep for over an hour. Bret was on the couch. Alex was below him, curled up on the floor clutching a pillow.

Bret was stirred by the sound of the door opening. Barbara entered looking as confident as Dick Tracy.

"I've got it."

"Got what?" Bret sleepily mumbled.

"The plan," she proclaimed proudly.

The enthusiasm in her voice stirred Alex. He rubbed his eyes and then pretended to admonish Barbara. "Why are you so loud?" he uttered, trying to hide his slight grin.

"Because, I am a genius, you little squirt," she boastfully exclaimed as she pounced on top of him pinning him to the floor.

Alex screamed repeatedly, "Stop," as he giggled with delight.

The brief skirmish over and the victor declared, she began to share the details of her plan. She knew that it would be a tough sell but she was determined.

"I can get you to Money's for the cookout."

Bret sighed heavily. "I thought that you would give up. Why is this so important to you?"

"Why are you such a perpetual pain in the butt?" she teased.

"Stop acting ugly around little kids and don't use those college words," Alex said dryly.

She feinted toward him as if she was beginning a new attack on his ticklish ribs. He squealed without being touched.

Bret grinned sarcastically at her. "What's your plan, Sherlock?"

"Now keep in mind, first off, your father is not in town."

"That doesn't mean that his eyes and ears aren't around."

"Yes, but his main ears and eyes are with him, and that is who found out about you and Money."

"How do you know that?"

She grinned mischievously. "Can't give you all my secrets. First, I borrow my parents' car."

"They can't know anything," Bret interrupted.

"I thought we agreed that no one would know, ever, but the three of us," she said wearily, as Alex nodded in her direction, his facial expression serious, as if war was being contemplated and only they knew.

"But," Bret started again to protest.

"Bret, shut up." She paused and breathed deeply. "Please excuse that, Alex. It is not a nice thing to say to anyone," she said before lowering her voice even more. "Even to your brother who will not be quiet long enough to allow me to complete what I want to say." She breathed in deeply and paused gathering her words and trying to calm the agitation she felt. "Please don't interrupt."

He reluctantly nodded in agreement.

"Let's sit at the table," she commanded, moving as she spoke. The now more disciplined troops marched behind her, walking softly and not daring to speak.

She flipped the light on over the table and grabbed a yellow legal pad and pen off the counter. "Okay, here's the plan."

"First, I get my parents' car. I'll come up with an excuse. My parents trust me. I am the good child, hard working student and all. Your basic nose to the grindstone kind of girl."

Bret started to say something clever, but a quick glare from the general quickly throttled that thought.

"You, of course, will wear long pants. We need to hide as much of that white skin as possible. Wear a dark shirt with long sleeves and a hat. The collar of the shirt will hide the back of your neck. The only thing exposed is your hands and face. I have the answer for that as well, being the genius that I am."

Bret and Alex looked at each other but continued to follow orders and declined comment.

"She pulled a tube out of her purse. This is how we change the rest of you from white to black. It's grease paint. It has other uses but, since I'm dealing with a couple of dumb jocks, I will parlay this to something you can grasp. Baseball outfielders put it under their eyes to reduce the glare of the sun. I drop you near the house as soon as darkness arrives. There is a vacant lot on the street behind their house. You cut through the vacant lot and enter their back yard, where you of course, go to the back door.

"That gets you in. Getting you home is simpler." She reached for the marker and began to draw a map. "Call me when you get ready to leave Money's house. Have Money drive to the Municipal Golf Course, entering off of the Oleander Drive side. The golf course is obviously deserted at night. He will drop you off at the ninth green beside the clubhouse. There is a pay phone beside the club house. Call me."

She began to draw his route as she talked. "You walk across the course, not down the road. Walk diagonally across number nine, eighteen, ten, and one. There is a golf cart crossing that goes from the number one green to the number two tee, crossing over Pine Grove Road. It will take you five minutes to reach the designated point, approximately the same amount of time it will take me to drive there. I'll make sure to stop only if there are no cars coming in either direction. I'll put my turn signal on for two blinks. That is the signal that it is us. Stay by the number one green. You'll be off the road where no one can see you, but you will be able to see the cars."

She put her pen down, obviously proud of her plan. She braced for the rebuttal.

Bret was impressed. He thought that would work. Still, everything he held dear was at stake. "Alex, what do you think?"

"Do it, Bret. You like Money."

"But I love you. Do you realize what would happen if we got caught?"

"Father would throw you out."

"And?"

"We would lose each other."

Alex showed courage and wisdom that defied his years at this moment. "Bret, I'll see you wherever you are. What's he going to do, throw me out? That's what I would want, to be with you."

He looked at his little brother and smiled. "Are you sure?"

"Yes."

"We won't get caught," Barbara added. "This plan is foolproof. There is only one thing remaining, and you must solve that. You tell Money the truth. Trust him."

Bret looked down at the table and breathed deeply. He looked up at her. "It's like you expect me to change overnight."

"No," she said firmly. "What I want is for you to continue to change. You've already changed more so than you realize. I'm almost about to like you," she added

"Tell me again why this is so important to you?"

"How about things happen for a reason?"

"That's a cliché. I hate clichés," he stated with a little too much sarcasm in his voice.

She stared coldly at him. "Don't make fun of me. I'm putting my butt on the line for you. This is a path for you to have a friend, to trust someone, to not be the cold, spoiled, arrogant little country club boy that nearly everyone perceives you to be."

"You don't even know Money. Why do you think it's worth it?"

"The way you look when you come home from playing ball with him. The way you act when you talk about him. You are like a real person and not some machine. I was there that day in the alley. You could have walked away, but you chose not to. There is a reason. I don't know what that reason is but there is a reason. You want a simple explanation. Well, here is the same old one. He makes you laugh. No one ever sees you laugh but Alex. Maybe it's time for you to let the rest of the world in on what Alex already knows."

"What?"

"That you are not a complete horse's ass."

"Is that a compliment?"

She stared at him without expression and did not reply.

He nodded his head softly. "Let me think it through and I'll decide tomorrow."

The other two parts of the force nodded their approval.

"If I do it, I'll call and fill him in."

"No, Bret. Surprise him."

"Why?"

"Because I like surprises and this will be a good one. He thinks a lot of you. He's a lot like you. He could pick and choose his friends, but he is wary of why people want to be his friend. You are important to him, or he would not have chosen to go to Castle Hayne to talk to you."

"Do you have any other good reasons, General?"

"Yes, since you are the one raising this boy, then do it the right way. Teach him what is important. Teach him the value of a true friend. Teach him that there is more to life than money and country clubs."

He smiled at her. He admired her spirit and even more her determination.

* * *

It was well past eight when a gold station wagon slowed to a stop in the vacant lot behind the Wilkins's house. Bret chose to go along with the plan at the considerable urging of his two cohorts. They added three turns that the route did not call for. He didn't know if

Barbara was being extra careful or if playing the part of the general had gone to her head.

He put the grease paint on in the car. Right now, he felt secure that he would not get caught, but showing up at a home containing black people, a white face painted black. Well, that part made him a little nervous. Maybe it was overkill, but shouldn't every precaution be taken? Barbara reassured him that Money would understand and in all probability laugh. Bret looked at his two partners again. Barbara had spent so much time to pull this off, and Alex had shown such maturity. He never asked if he could go, though Bret knew that he desired too. He realized that it would increase the chances of getting caught. Bret looked at him once again and felt something in his heart he could not fully explain. *My little man is growing up.*

There were no cars or people in sight. The car stopped and he emerged from low in the back seat. He walked through the vacant lot, jumped the chain link fence gaining access to the Wilkins's back yard. He could smell the aftermath of the charcoal cooker in the yard. Pork, he thought, as the aroma permeated his nose. Better yet, ribs. He was late for dinner, but he was here.

He knocked on the door. He hoped for Money, he got Clarence.

"What the...?" Clarence said harshly.

"Let me in. I can explain."

Bret entered the kitchen hurriedly and when Clarence failed to close the door fast enough Bret intervened, closing it so hard the wall vibrated slightly.

Money and Teke eyed the suspicious character that stood in the kitchen. Money smiled broadly and just as Barbara predicted began to giggle. He was so happy to see his friend that he didn't care about the face. It was more than that, though, he was confident enough to realize that there was a reason for such outlandish behavior. Friends give each other the benefit of the doubt.

Teke was not the least bit amused. She placed her hands on her hips in disgust. "Well, boys," she said, trying with little success to reclaim the southern drawl that once was hers. "I left here when white people dressed black for Halloween, now I see that they do it for other occasions too. That's great. The south is a changing and for the worse."

Bret was not sure if she was serious, or joking. "Money, will you please get me an old rag?"

Money brought him the rag, and he went to the sink and washed his face and hands, once again becoming Caucasian. He looked at Money and Clarence, but his eyes fell on the person in the room that he did not know as he began to explain the story.

"It took a lot to get me here tonight and against my better judgment." He sighed, suddenly tired, and added, "What I am going to tell you must never leave this room." He looked at them again, especially at Teke. Money and Clarence nodded softly in agreement. Bret looked again at Teke, who continued to look curiously at the stranger who had arrived with a face painted in black.

Bret was silent, not finding the confidence in Teke's face that he needed to continue the story.

Money intervened, "Teke, not a word to anyone, ever."

She smiled sarcastically. "I haven't heard anything yet."

"Then leave the room," Money snapped at her.

She eyed him curiously. He seldom if ever raised a voice in her direction.

"That won't do any good," Bret offered. "She already knows I'm here."

"I won't say anything," she said in a low voice, speckled with grit.

Bret looked at Clarence. "Could we sit down at the table, Mr. Wilkins?"

Clarence nodded at him and smiled faintly. "It has been too long since you been to my house, young man."

"I'm sorry, Clarence, please," he said, motioning toward the table. They sat down at the table together in complete quietness.

Bret rubbed his hands together and looked at his friend. "Money, you were right the other day. He threatened me with Alex. I didn't tell you because Alex and I have always been just the two of us. No outsiders allowed in, ever. We protect each other. I guess it sounds silly, that I trust a ten year old above the whole world, heck, he's all I do trust."

Money started to speak, to reassure Bret that he could add him to the list of who could be trusted, but there was no need.

Bret looked at him and saw the understanding in his eyes. He shook his head slightly as he thought about Barbara and how much she told him he was changing. And at this moment it dawned on him just how right she was. He reached across the table with his hand toward Money. "That is until now," he said evenly.

Money extended his hand to him and the two young men gripped each other's hand firmly and held it for several seconds.

Teke watched with piqued curiosity. She knew that she was witnessing far more than a handshake, and she realized that there was something between them that went far deeper than she could know. But she did want to know. Curiosity was consuming her and she wanted to expedite what was happening but she knew she could not. This was something that had been brewing for a long time.

Bret released his friend's hand and began to talk slowly. "This is hard for me and to be honest with you, I wouldn't have attempted this if not for Barbara. It was her persistence, her planning on how to get me here safely. She says I'm changing from a self-centered, country club boy to something better. I don't know about that, but there are things happening that I don't really understand. I do know that she risked a lot over this night, this cookout."

Clarence, silent until now, drinking in every word spoken, asked, "Why?"

"She says that Money makes me laugh, makes me different. She said that it began that day in the alley. She thinks there is a reason for all of this. I don't know about all that stuff. I'm just a selfish rich boy who has always had everything and now I guess that I don't feel so sure about things I once was so certain of." He paused and realized his voice sounded strange as if he were watching someone else play his part. "I know it's harder for me to tell you about this than it was to sneak in here. Personal stuff, well, that is not exactly, how do you say it, my forte?"

He paused and looked down at the wooden table below him. "I do know that I respect the two of you. The way you talk to each other. The way you guys always support each other. It influences me, and Alex as well. He told me to come. He wants to come back for pancakes. He really likes the two of you. My little man is growing up," Bret added, as he sighed slightly.

Clarence smiled a comforting smile and reached across the table and held Bret's forearm for a second. "It's okay, son, and I can promise you this, no one, and I mean no one, will ever breathe a word of this to anyone," he stated, leaving no room for debate as his eyes fell upon his daughter.

She nodded in agreement. There was unity at the table. Gaining confidence and comfort as he spoke, Bret proceeded to tell the entire story. He finished and there was silence. The two men looked at him with respect and admiration. He looked up as he felt Teke's eyes upon him. The hardness in her face that he witnessed when he first entered the house was replaced now by softness and her eyes filled with water. She nodded gently at him and smiled slightly. What else should he have expected? She was the daughter and sister of the two men at the table.

Clarence looked at Bret and then at Money. "You flatter us with what we have, but you have something very special with Alex. He's not your son, but you have taken full responsibility for raising him. There is more to you than you give yourself credit for. Every Sunday you have a standing invitation to dinner. If you can get here safely, there will be a plate for you. And any other time you need anything you have more than my son that you can call on."

Bret smiled at the man he had grown quite fond of. He was worn out from sharing so much of what was inside of him. "So, where's my plate tonight? I think I smelled ribs. Please tell me that vacuum cleaner of a son has left me something to eat."

Clarence smiled and rose from the table.

"Fix me another plate too, Dad," Money said, though he had just finished eating two full plates less than an hour ago.

His dad eyed him with mock disbelief. "Can't let my best friend eat alone." Money smiled. "It just wouldn't be proper."

CHAPTER NINE

Terror in two cities

Bret was at the old house early Saturday morning accompanied by Alex. They walked in the house and to Bret's surprise discovered a new item. There was a white, Philmore refrigerator standing in the corner where the kitchen might one day be. He opened the box, discovering several bottles of Coke and Sun Drop. It wasn't new by any means but it surely worked. It was also identical to the one that was in Vicky's kitchen. He stood and contemplated the new addition.

He walked by the creek that was almost desiccated from the heat and lack of rain. The stream's murmur was faint. The width of the water was normally six feet, but now it narrowed to less than a foot in most places. The uninspired croak of one lone frog begging for rain briefly interrupted the stillness.

Alex cheerfully trotted ahead of him. His gait stifled somewhat by his leg, but overcome by the enthusiasm for life that derived from being with his brother.

Bret knocked on the door and quickly heard Vicky bellow. "Don't stand on ceremony. Come on in."

She stood in the small kitchen putting away dishes.

"Vicky, where did the refrigerator come from?"

"I needed a new one, and the other still had some life in it," she stated as she turned to face him.

He eyed her warily, thinking that times could not be easy for her. He doubted that she would buy anything in her no-frills life until it was compulsory.

She felt his gaze of suspicion, but she did not allow it to infiltrate her proud unflinching look. "I got a good deal and I thought you boys might be tired of drinking well water that isn't cold. I suppose you could also keep food in it if you so choose."

"Thank you, Vicky. We surely can use it," he said, deciding to press her no longer on the good deed that was clearly making her uncomfortable.

"You're welcome."

He remembered that Money called the previous night offering his help. There was no concern on his part that Vicky would ever tell anything that benefited Walker Sr. They shared a sustained dislike of each other and they did not exactly run in the same circles. He did worry that someone might follow Money. Walker Sr. had a long arm that he firmly believed reached easily from one end of the region to the other. The danger was great.

Money, however, was certain that he had a foolproof plan. He would borrow the boat his neighbor owned under the guise that he was taking his sister for a boat ride up the Cape Fear River. Being the good neighborhood boy who carried groceries for old folks he was told to keep the boat all day and to take it anytime he wanted.

"Vicky, I won't be able to make it to the house for dinner," he paused, struggling for the right words that probably didn't exist to appease this old woman.

"Alex will be glad to join you," he said, although Alex looked slightly uncomfortable at the thought of dinner with her.

Graciously, she did not ask for a reason. That was good because he wasn't sure that he could produce one. He was fairly certain that he couldn't bring Money with him, and he wouldn't leave him.

Bret and Alex returned to the old house. Bret began to gather the materials needed to frame in the kitchen and the bathroom. He often wondered why he kept being drawn back to this old house. It had served as a worthy escape from Money, but that was no longer the case. He could be at the beach or lounging by the pool at the club under much cooler conditions. The truth was Ralph was right. He did love building, shaping something with his bare hands. It gave him a good feeling, a sense of accomplishment that with basketball being over he could not derive elsewhere.

He gazed out at the river, drawn by the soft sound of a small motor boat. Through the haze that permeated off the river, he saw that the boat contained two figures. He could not see them clearly enough to tell for certain, but he was confident that it was Money and Teke. The boat passed by the house, disappearing down the river.

Money and Teke, after first pulling the boat to shore and sitting long enough to be certain that no one was following them, walked cautiously through the woods to the old home.

They entered the house and Money introduced Alex and Teke. Alex being the consummate gentleman, offered his hand. Teke smiled warmly at him. "I have heard a lot about you. My brother speaks often of you and your brother."

She reached into the paper bag that she was carrying and produced a bright red baseball cap with a white 'P' centered across the front. "My brother told me you were a Phillies fan. I thought that you might like this."

"Wow! A Phillies hat, look Bret," he said, putting it on.

"That's really nice of you, Teke," Bret said, enjoying the glow on his brother's face.

"Money insisted, every time we talked since he met Alex, he has reminded me to bring him a baseball hat."

"Do you ever go to the games?" Alex asked, his eyes wide with curiosity.

"I went last week. The Phillies won 7-3. Richie Allen hit a three-run homer in the eighth. You come to Philly one day and I'll take you myself."

"That would be great." The expression on his face showed for a certainty that, very quickly, he had found yet another member of the Wilkins family that he liked.

"Well, let's do some work," Money said as he tied a nail apron on.

"I'm glad that you came. There's no way I could manage to section off these rooms by myself."

"Alex, do you want to take Teke for a walk? Oh, and find Fred. He's late for work this morning," Bret added.

Alex tugged at her hand and started for the door. Teke graciously went without protest though she was not interested in a walk in the wilderness that seemed to envelop this place. *Who in their right mind would choose to live out here away from civilization?*

"Alex," Bret started.

"I know, stay out of sight of any people or Vicky."

Bret shrugged and looked at Money, uncertain of what to say.

Money smiled. "Don't worry, Bret. Teke understands, and I surely do. This is just how it is. Now, have you got the studs cut?" he asked, sparing Bret the intimate conversation that always led him to a place of uneasiness.

The boys began to work and catch up on their enjoyment at being together. Money shared some good news. He and his dad were going to D.C. in two weeks. The job was too good to pass up. Clarence would make more money in two months remodeling the doctor's house than he would make the rest of the year in Wilmington.

Alex and Teke returned a little while later with Fred in tow. Fred walked in, observed that the work would be going on downstairs this morning, and found his corner. He circled three times, grunted, lay down, and soon was snoring. No doubt dreaming of an even easier life than the one he already enjoyed.

"I hate for you to be bored, Teke," Bret said, though there was no apology in his voice for working on a house he was becoming attached to.

"It's okay. Money insisted that I not make a liar out of him about the boat ride. He promised to make it up to me later, but in this small town, I don't know how."

"Forgive my big city sister. The bright lights of the big city have fried her brain."

Bret callously offered, "Well, it's only for two weeks."

By dinnertime, the kitchen and the bathroom were framed in. Bret sent Alex to eat with Vicky and attempted an explanation, but once again, Money cut him off.

"So, Money, did you bring lunch?"

Money smiled at Bret. "A man works for nothing, and is expected to bring lunch," he said as he reached in the small blue cooler that he brought.

"Chicken salad?"

"You got it."

"It would be hard not to like that dad of yours."

The three of them ate lunch and swapped small talk. After lunch, it was to the upstairs to begin sectioning the bedrooms off. Teke joined in, handing lumber to the boys, as they needed it.

They were halfway through with the first bedroom, when Teke decided to let go of words she had clung to all day, in hopes of finding the perfect time that did not exist.

"Bret, I want to tell you that I was wrong last Sunday night."

"Wrong about what?"

"I judged you and I was mistaken. As bad as I hate to admit it in front of my brother I probably do behave with a jaded view of the south."

He smiled reassuringly at her. "Well, Teke, I did show up at a black family's house, wearing face paint," he chuckled, letting her off the hook easily.

"I know, but my dad and brother speak so highly of you. I should have had confidence in what they think. Maybe, my mom, who I love dearly, has jaded my objectivity of the south. I am a better person than that. I hope that you can believe that."

She looked down at the floor, hiding her face. A face that embarrassment and shame could not hide the beauty it portrayed. She heard him say gently, "I do believe that."

She looked up at Bret, and as their eyes locked she was momentarily taken back at just how good looking he was. "I am curious about something. Why are you so open to black people?" she asked admiringly, aiming for some meaningful in depth conversation.

Money rolled his eyes slightly and laughed under his breath.

"Whoa, don't make me into some kind of saint. Things happened and before I knew it, I was friends with this pain in the butt brother of yours. His being black had nothing to do with it."

"Yes, but you didn't turn away either," she responded as Money softly chuckled at Bret's analogy.

"Maybe I should have." He laughed, effectively escaping the conversation. They continued to work and chat. Alex joined them later after staying at Vicky's far longer then Bret expected.

Money and Teke left shortly after four, carefully walking through a small trail in the woods that concealed them as they made their way to the boat that lie in waiting, nestled in the river marsh.

* * *

The week that followed Bret began his work at the firm that he was destined to be a part of even before he was conceived. He spent most of the week in a small room that served as his office. There was barely enough room for the small desk that sat in the corner. And worse than that there was no window. He felt like a caged animal. He perused the legal documents that his father demanded he study knowing that he would be tested at some point.

He tried each day to leave. There was a slight problem, the reigning secretary, who resided outside of Walker Sr.'s office, insisted on keeping tabs on him.

Ruby was twenty-nine, divorced, with two small children. She tried very hard to be pretty but could only manage to be mildly attractive at best, and that was on her best days. Her hair was blonde, and after a good trip to the beauty parlor her dark roots were not quite as visible. She had brown eyes that were nearly hidden by the heavy mascara that she wore. Her long, slender nose curled slightly up at the tip. Her lips were thin and her chin came to an abrupt point. The money that she spent on makeup was a large part of her monthly expenditures, and it did little to enhance her sharp features. The only thing worse than the makeup was the perfume she bathed in, that overpowered not only the office she commandeered, but lingered well down the hall.

She was tall, with a large chest that seemed too much for her long skinny legs to support. She wore short skirts that hugged every inch of her and she took pride in the firmness it portrayed.

He tried on Wednesday to enter his father's office alone, but was rebuked firmly. She reached for the key that was locked in her desk, opened the door, and stood eyeing him as a prison guard would a member of a roadside gang minus the shotgun. She liked the pay her job provided and it was well known that she was the eyes and ears for Walker Sr. of all that went on in his firm.

He tried in vain to soften her up, but to no avail. He even suggested they meet for a drink after work one day in an attempt to assuage the situation but was firmly rebuffed.

Mercifully, Saturday came, providing Bret an escape to do work that made him feel alive. Money joined him and by the time he left late in the evening, all the walls were sectioned off and each door was hung. The house was coming alive. The pine boards would complete the walls and he could do that alone. He could envision being finished with the house by the end of the summer, and he had reached a point where he didn't look as hard for a reason why.

Alex visited Vicky that morning for dinner and she instructed him to go eat with his brother. Strangely she sent enough dinner for three, as well as three dinner plates and silverware. Money, once again, entered by boat so Bret was certain that she hadn't seen him.

She was still far from friendly, but lately she didn't seem as harsh either. It dawned on him that she liked her grandsons being around, though it remained hidden from view. He attributed it to the loneliness of old age, and maybe something else.

* * *

Jacky Wilkins was returning home after a long grueling shift at the hospital. It was Thursday night, a little past eleven. She parked her car and walked down the sidewalk leading to her place of refuge. She missed Teke, but knew that this time was important, and after the recent events she felt better knowing that her daughter was far away from Lawrence Tuttle. Every night this week, she had felt an eerie presence as she walked to her apartment. She saw no one, and thought to look behind the tall bushes that bordered the sidewalk, but was too frightened to explore the potential.

She fumbled for her keys, hands trembling in fear. She located the keys and entered her place of security quickly dead bolting the door. She turned the light off in the living area downstairs, and flipped the switch that lit the upstairs steps. Reaching the second floor she turned the light off for the stairs. She entered her bedroom and turned the light on, before swiftly returning downstairs. She moved slowly to the front window and opened the curtain just enough to peer outside. She watched for five minutes when a figure emerged from behind the bushes that she had just passed.

The lights that lined the sidewalks revealed the shadowy figure. It was Lawrence. He stood staring up at the window of the bedroom of her daughter.

She felt a wintry chill run through her body. The coldness contained an evil that she could not turn off or attribute to her imagination any longer. The figure had been present all week. She reached for the phone, before deciding that the police would not be worth the time, or the aggravation. This young man was dangerous, but seemingly he had everyone fooled. She continued to hold the phone and then she decided to call someone more reliable than the police.

Clarence answered the phone, his voice gruff from being awakened.

"Clarence, Teke needs to stay in Wilmington a little longer."

Wide awake now, Clarence responded, "You know that I would love that, but I took the job in D.C. She wouldn't want to stay there while we are working all day. Besides, the place I rented is a cracker box barely fit for two."

"Well, I'd rather her stay in Wilmington alone than here." She then filled him in on the night's events.

They discussed scenarios before agreeing that Teke would remain in Wilmington. Clarence knew that he had good neighbors and they would watch out for her. It also helped that Teke was a very mature, responsible young lady.

The next night at ten o'clock, Teke was sitting on the front porch watching the sparse traffic venture down Castle Street. She missed her home. Now she was stuck here and soon without the comfort of being with her family.

She rubbed the plane ticket that she held in her hand. The ticket she had planned to use for her return to civilization on Sunday. Her father and brother would leave Monday morning for D.C.

Clarence walked out to the porch and sat in the rocking chair beside her. He waited, looking for the correct words for the daughter that he prayed each day he could know better.

"Teke, your mama is worried. I know that you don't want to be here under the best of circumstances. I could try and get another place when we get to D.C."

"Daddy, even with that, you guys will be working all the time. You'll work long and hard to get back here as quickly as humanly possible. If you didn't love this backwater town so much, we'd still be a family. So, whether it's here or D.C., I'll be alone," she said with an angry edge to her voice.

Clarence studied his daughter, admiring the beauty in her face that was illuminated by the nearby streetlights. She looked more like her mother everyday as she was leaving childhood behind and becoming a beautiful young woman.

"Maybe you're right. Maybe I should have left here to follow your mother. I guess I thought that she would come back, and by the time I realized that she wasn't, it was too late. I loved your mother very much. I guess it's no secret that I still do. But, there is nothing that can be done about it now."

He reached over, placing his rough, callused hand on her forearm. "Teke, we all lost a lot. I lost watching a beautiful daughter grow up. A daughter I am very proud of. I'm sorry that you are stuck here in this rotten backward town. It's my home and I wish that it were yours. I'd also like to go to Philly and take care of this young man myself. Your mother, she always was more practical than me. She made me promise not to come. She said that our children needed a father and that it is a no win situation if I go to Philly. I'd fix all of this if I could. I hope that you know that."

He rose to go back inside. He opened the door, but stopped when he heard the sniffling of tears from his little girl. "Daddy, I'm sorry for criticizing your home. I'm scared and I feel so alone. Don't be mad at me, please."

He turned back to the porch and the little girl it contained. He dropped to one knee beside the rocking chair and pulled her ever so gently toward him, cradling her to his chest. "I'm not mad at you. I love you. I think about you every day of my life. I want to be your father, your friend, but the distance keeps me from so much, but you always live right here," he said as he touched his heart.

Her tears grew stronger as she buried her head deeper into his chest. "I love you, too, Daddy. I'm sorry, please forgive me."

"It's okay, child. It's okay. There's nothing that needs forgiving," he said as he held his daughter, blinking back the tears emerging from his eyes.

* * *

Wilmington returned to a peaceful, sleepy, southern city after the riots that were triggered the day of the march. That was about to change, quickly and violently.

It was a Saturday morning in June when the newspaper reported what some already knew. The decision by the school board had been made in an extended private meeting the previous night. The newspaper headlines were bold, in large black letters, WILLISTON NO

LONGER A HIGH SCHOOL. The article below explained the decision made by the seven member all white-school board. None of the answers would prove suitable to the black community.

Leaders in the community spent the morning organizing the protest that would accomplish little except to vent rage that was bottled up inside people who were weary of promised equality that passed them by yet again.

As the street outside the Wilkins's home began to line with black people, there was rage in the air that rivaled the intensity of the spring riots. Clarence watched the street in front of his home fill with protesters as he packed for the trip to D.C. Money was riled by the situation, but Clarence didn't worry about him joining in. Peaceful demonstrations were one thing, but this day would contain little harmony. He was positive of that. He was glad to be leaving with his son, but how could he leave his daughter?

He debated momentarily before deciding to call Dr. Rowell. He was hoping to persuade the doctor to allow him to postpone the trip for a few days. Dr. Rowell was understanding but insisted that the work begin as scheduled. There were many events scheduled in his house late that summer. The timetable must be adhered to. Clarence understood. After the conversation he debated on canceling the trip and he mentioned that to his children.

Teke and Money both knew that financial opportunity as this one didn't come along for their father on a daily basis. Teke was the most vocal and she assured her father that she could tolerate her situation, no matter how deplorable the town may be. She encouraged him to go, reminding him that this was also a job that would provide Money with much needed spending money during the coming school year.

The phone rang, interrupting the persuasion by the two thoughtful, considerate, and mature children that Clarence felt so blessed to call his.

"Clarence, forgive me for calling but your call has me a bit unsettled. I need to know for sure. Are you coming Monday? I will understand if you need to back out for your family. I hate to sound selfish or uncaring, but I will need to know now if you can't come. I would need to find someone else to do the job. Please understand. These meetings are far more than cocktail parties. Some of the most renowned civil rights leaders in the country will be present. It is important that things go well for our race."

Clarence looked at his children, "Don't worry, Dr. Rowell, you have my word. I'll be there on Monday."

Wilmington was like a keg of dynamite and the explosion was merely waiting for a lit match. That was provided late that afternoon.

Fifty Klansmen, complete in the white robes that concealed their cowardice began to walk down Castle Street. Clarence heard the rumbling in the street rise and moved to the front porch to investigate. "Oh, my God," he mumbled.

The group made it five blocks before colliding with the black protesters marching toward them. All hell broke loose quickly. The first blow struck was by a young black teenager. He ran up to the front of the line armed with a Louisville Slugger and tried to decapitate the grand wizard himself, one Luther Lynch.

Luther operated as the head Klansman of the area out of his hometown of Angier, NC, a small town in the piedmont area of the state. Ignorance abounded in him and throughout his family. He was passing on his narrow beliefs to his two sons, ages six and three, just as his father before him.

Luther ducked just as the bat neared his head and quickly plowed his long hunting knife into the rib cage of the boy. The events quickly escalated. The street was a melee of combat. Men beat each other with any weapon that they held. The Klansmen were outnumbered and the tide turned against them. One member in the back after watching a comrade fall into the street decided to take a more serious approach. From under his robe, he pulled the pistol out that was strapped to his leg. He aimed carefully and fired. The bullet found a young black man, barely old enough to drive. He fell into the street, the life out of him before he touched the asphalt.

The shot brought a temporary silence to the mob. Sirens blasted as the police finally appeared on the scene. They were greatly outnumbered and had arrived slowly in hopes that the two groups would exhaust their energy fighting each other.

The enemies began attacking each other anew with a hatred that brought no fear of the approaching police. Two patrol cars arrived first and at the sight of the violence, decided wisely to wait for back-ups, many backups. It would be an hour before peace was restored to Castle Street. Multiple arrests were made from both groups.

Clarence watched as the sheet was pulled over the young boy's head and he was loaded into an ambulance. He looked at his children. "Teke, I can't leave you here, alone."

"And I can't go home, Daddy."

"I know, I just gave the doctor my word, but you are more important than that, than the job."

"I don't want you to give up that job."

"It looks as if I have no choice," he said as he reached for the phone.

It was at that moment that Money came up with an idea that he felt certain would work. He just needed a friend's help. "Dad, I have an idea. Teke, come with me."

"Where are you going, son?"

"I'll explain later. I need the truck."

"You want the truck with all that is going on around us?" Clarence asked. "Are you..."

"Trust me, Dad. There will be no riots where I'm going."

Clarence nodded gently, once again placing his belief in his son over his fears.

They got into the pickup and left the bloody streets of Castle Street for the serenity of the country. On the way Money began to fill his sister in on his plan. "Teke, I do not want to see dad lose this job. You haven't watched him work day in and day out the way I have to keep a roof over our heads, to send money to mom for you. I want you to go along with my plan, and I want you to assure him that you don't mind. So no complaining about it, okay?"

"What is the plan and where are we going?"

"I'm counting on Bret being at the old house."

"That's your plan?"

"You can stay there. No one will know and he'll look after you."

"You're putting a lot of faith in this white boy."

"I sure am putting a lot of faith in my *friend*," he said very deliberately.

They drove past the entrance to Vicky's house and saw an old road that led to the river. They drove part way down and parked the truck on the side of the road.

Fifteen minutes later, they were at the old house. Money was happy to hear the saw running as they approached. They entered the house slowly and Money motioned for Teke to wait with him. Bret sensed their presence, looked over at them and cut the saw off.

Bret knew right away that something was wrong by the look on his friend's face. He waited in silence for his friend to explain.

Money filled him in on the events that left his sister vulnerable in two cities.

He then got to the point of his trip. "Bret, I need a huge favor from you. Maybe I got no right to ask, but I don't know where else to turn. I hate for dad to lose this job and he won't leave if Teke is not protected. I want you to keep Teke here at this house. I'll get you money to buy beds or whatever you need to make this livable for a while. I know that I'm asking a lot, but she will stay here, no coming and going. I don't believe that it will jeopardize your situation with Alex. No one comes back here and at worst, if your grandmother found out, she might force you to move Teke out but from everything you've told me, she would never help your father with anything."

Bret debated briefly. It was indeed a huge favor, but if the roles were reversed and he needed help for Alex, he knew the friend in front of him would not let him down. He knew now that friendship was important. He valued the person asking this favor too much to let him down. He also wanted to help Clarence, who was the type father he often wished that he had.

"I'll do it. Teke, you will be alone during the day, when I'm at work, and you'll need to hide if Vicky comes around. I'll come back every night so you won't be alone. You will be bored, but safe."

Teke was resigned to her fate, "I won't say that I'm excited about this, but my brother has convinced me that this is a time for sacrifice, for family sake. Now, please tell me that someone has a television, stereo, something so I won't go nuts out here in the wilderness."

"I have both in my room that I'll bring," Bret answered. "Money, I'll get beds. I was planning on it anyway. I thought that if nothing else, this house could serve as a hideaway for Alex and me."

Money looked at Bret, his face showing appreciation as well as respect for his friend. "You keep bailing me out of jams. Look, hopefully, it won't be for long. Maybe we can find another place when we get to D.C., or things will calm down in Philly."

"If they do," Teke answered sadly. "I'm beginning to question if I'll ever get home."

"I need one more favor," Money said. "I need for you to help me with dad. You could call, but could Barbara sneak you in tomorrow night? It's our last cookout and dad wants you there anyway. That is if there is not more blood in the streets tomorrow. If there is, don't come near town. Today was something I could barely believe and I was watching it with my own eyes. It was like watching television, but it was people I know out there fighting. Maybe I should have been out there. I don't know."

"Why, so you could die in the street, or lose your scholarship to State? Big Willie told me once that you were the one with the opportunity that so many others wanted. None of them would have wanted you in that street fighting."

"Bret is right, Money. Besides, who are you kidding? Dad would have clobbered you before you made it off the porch."

Money chuckled. "Yeah, you're right about that. Bret, we need to go. He will be worried about us with all that is going on. Thank you, if there is any..."

Bret extended the same hand that he had that March night in the gym. Much had changed since that night. "I know. I'll see you tomorrow for dinner if it's possible. You tell your dad not to worry. I'll take care of Teke. I know what it is like to have someone that you would do anything to see that they are taken care of."

Bret's words soothed not only Money, but also Teke. She would be staying with someone who was practically a stranger, and white to top it off, but his words, his mannerisms had calmed her. She felt safe.

For the moment...

CHAPTER TEN

The favor

The city was tranquil Sunday night in stark contrast to the previous day. A hardware store, owned by a white man, was burned to the ground shortly after midnight. Before the sun greeted a new day, a black church that stood for seventy years was reduced to ashes.

The National Guard arrived in force at the breaking of the day. By nine that morning, they were present on nearly every street corner in downtown Wilmington. The show of power curtailed the hostility. The city was placed under mandatory curfew. No one was allowed to leave their property after eight p.m. All of these events and the curfew made it impractical for Bret to attempt a visit to Money's house.

Bret called Clarence and assured him that he would do as Money requested. He would watch over Teke.

Clarence was reluctant to go along with the plan, but he wanted to keep his word to Dr. Rowell. Money spent the better part of the day convincing him that Bret and this plan was the best answer to a complex problem.

The following afternoon, Bret left work the moment Ruby turned her back. He left a note that he was doing research at the courthouse and by the time she received the note he was well on his way to Castle Hayne.

He stopped at a small furniture store and negotiated with the elderly gentleman who owned the store. He bought two basic beds, nothing like what he was accustomed to, but that was okay by him. Besides, they seemed to mesh better with life in the country. He purchased a second hand couch that would serve as both furniture for the downstairs and a bed for Alex.

He was almost out of the store when he remembered the need for other basics, towels, bed linens, and a shower curtain. The man agreed to deliver all the items that afternoon. Bret paid in cash, shook hands with the gentleman and left.

The next stop was Vicky's where he hoped to explain what he was doing, or at least the version that he desired she believe.

He was thinking of what he would say as he walked up the steps to her door. She opened it before he could knock.

"Vicky, there is a furniture truck coming here this afternoon. I ordered some things so Alex and I can stay at the house some this summer. I've been working so late in the evenings that it makes sense. I hope you don't mind."

She studied him momentarily. "No, I don't mind. You do as you please. Put anything in the house you want."

"I need to go. Would you please direct them to the house? I've explained to them where everything goes."

She nodded in agreement, saying nothing.

"Thanks, Vicky. I'll see you later. I'll probably stay tonight, so don't worry if you see a car come through tonight."

"Did you think of curtains?" Vicky suddenly asked.

Bret stopped from his walk to his car and turned back to face her. He breathed deeply, perturbed that he seemed so inadequate at this moment. "No, I didn't." He had been taken care of, spoiled his entire life. Everything provided for him without any thought on his part. This was going to be a challenge.

"I have some old ones that will do. You stop by the house later and I'll have them for you. I'll throw in some other items that you may have forgotten."

"That sounds good. Thank you, Vicky."

He was almost certain that he saw a smile surface from her lips, but it departed so quickly that he could not be certain. He drove away contemplating the other things he had to do, grocery shopping, and an explanation for Alex. The more important task of picking up Teke he would conduct as soon as darkness fell.

Thankfully the curfew had been lifted. Teke would catch a cab to the same store that he had purchased gas at the night he had no money.

It was eight thirty and the sun exhausted its last effort to prolong the day. Bret drove by the store twice and was on his way by again when he spotted a yellow taxicab preparing to turn into the store parking lot. He drove to the gas tanks and began to fuel his car.

Teke emerged from the cab, paid the driver, and walked to the right of the entrance, never once glancing in Bret's direction. She sat her two suitcases down against the exterior store wall. She walked to the front door, carefully studying the area to make sure that no one was near before entering.

Bret finished pumping the gas and walked in, with money this time. The clerk was a middle aged man, and just as the last time that Bret was here, he drew a puzzled look from the cashier who was not accustomed to a white customer frequenting the store. Bret saw Teke, who was in the back of the store getting a Coke out of the long red ice box.

He paid the clerk as Teke walked up behind him. He returned to his car and looked around to assure that there was no traffic coming in. He backed his car from the gas pump to the same side of the building where Teke placed her suitcases. Hidden from the eyes of the clerk he casually got out of the car and grabbed the two suitcases. He returned to his car, opened the trunk and placed the suitcases inside. Teke's timing was impeccable and she walked out of the store to her left, the prearranged rendezvous point. Bret popped the passenger door open and Teke climbed in behind the seat and quickly lay down on the back seat. He pulled away hurriedly, just as the store clerk walked outside to observe just where the beautiful lady went. He saw no sign of her, only the rear of Bret's Mustang pulling out onto the dark highway. He gave it no more thought and returned to the loneliness of the store.

"Are you okay, Teke?"

"Yes."

There was awkwardness between two people who scarcely knew each other, but who would be living together. Bret endured a few minutes of the uneasy quiet before attempting to break the ice. "So, are you all excited about your move to the country?"

His attempt at humor failed miserably with Teke. "Oh, yes," she answered sarcastically, "This is proving to be a summer to remember. It was supposed to be so good."

The rest of the drive was spent in silence. Bret drove past Vicky's house. "You can get up now."

She rose awkwardly. In his rear view mirror he saw her attempt a smile but it was forced, and her eyes filled with sadness.

He tried again. "I got the television from my room. I set it up yesterday."

"Thanks, and the great thing is that your big city has all of two stations."

"Hey, I didn't ask for this job, but I'm doing it. Maybe, Miss Big City, you haven't thought that perhaps I had a different summer planned than babysitting some snotty Yankee, who feels the need to constantly remind us of how backwards we are. Poor dumb southerners, with our warm winters, our prettier country, and our lower crime rate. Do you want me to go on? Oh, excuse me, we don't have twenty television stations. Oh, and what else do we not have? Oh, the opera. Well, thank God for something."

"You've never even been up north, or to the opera," she countered angrily.

"Oh, really! So, New York City, Boston, even your precious Philadelphia, they aren't up north? I've heard the opera in New York and I've seen the grime in your streets of Philadelphia. And our beaches are slightly cleaner," he added sarcastically. "You are right. The north has it all. We poor southerners, excuse me, poor dumb southerners have it so bad."

"You could be a little nicer," Teke offered.

"Yeah, and you could stop being such a spoiled brat."

They were at the old house now. He cut the engine off and lifted the suitcases from the trunk and placed them on the ground. Next he began to gather the groceries.

Teke was silent as she squirmed out from the back of the car. She picked her suitcases up and walked toward her new home. Bret put away the groceries and then drove to Vicky's to get the curtains. Teke began putting up the shower curtain and making the beds.

At ten o'clock, Bret went to the smaller bedroom and shut the door, leaving Teke the master bedroom. His act was comical considering that there were no walls constructed at this point. Only the studs that Money had helped him frame in separated the rooms. Not one word was spoken between them inside the house they would share together on this long hot, June night.

By the following day they were once again speaking to each other out of necessity if nothing else. She gave Bret a list of books she wished to read, some for pleasure, and some to give her a head start on the coming college year. He obliged her request, going to the local library where he found nearly all of the books that she requested.

As she read the books to prep her for college, she questioned whether she would even be at Temple. Would she have to pass up a full scholarship, something that she had dreamed of and worked so hard for, because of one lunatic in the school? How could she not have seen earlier what Lawrence was like? She prided herself on her intelligence and now she questioned that.

She watched television, both stations, on occasion. But mostly she passed the day reading and making the old house livable.

The heat of the summer and the absence of air conditioning drove her from the house at times during the day. She would walk down to the river and sit in the shade that the towering river birch tree granted. She strategically placed a lawn chair in place where it allowed a view of the river through the smaller brush, but made seeing her from the river virtually impossible.

She sat studying the river, but more her life. She missed her mother, their apartment, but mostly she missed their life in Philadelphia. The river's leisurely moving current seemed to embody freedom, as well as the slow pace of the south. She felt as if she were a prisoner. Life reduced to hiding out in fear.

She thought about Bret's arrival that Tuesday afternoon when she asked him a very simple question. "How can we eat without a stove to cook on, or is cereal and sandwiches going to be the main course every day?"

Bret smiled at the question. "I guess I hadn't given that any thought. Can you cook?"

"If you can get a stove in this place, we will see. Also, would you buy some chicken? Dad said that he would take care of any expenses you had to incur, and I would like to pay for the chicken," she said, reaching for her purse.

He quickly cut her off. "I'll get everything, but I don't want your dad's money, or yours."

"Why, because you are a rich man's son?" she snapped.

"Is that what you think?" he asked, mystified, not waiting for a response as he departed to purchase a stove.

One hour later, as Teke hid down by the river, a young man delivered a stove, a small maple dinner table, a charcoal grill, in case Teke couldn't really cook, and fans to aid sleep during the hot miserable nights of summer.

Bret began enclosing the most important room for privacy, the bathroom upstairs. The wood replaced the sheets that Teke draped over the studs the night before, providing temporary walls. Thankfully, Ralph installed the plumbing and fixtures many years ago and that part of the house was operational.

At eight, Teke called Bret for supper. She served a chicken and rice dish that she learned long ago. Life with a mother who worked shift work necessitated the need to cook.

He began to devour the tasty dish, stopping momentarily to marvel. "You really can cook. What is this?"

She smiled at him. "It's too long a word for a southerner to articulate. You just go ahead and consume it. By the way, do you always eat without stopping to breathe?"

He looked up from his plate and searched for the harshness that often accompanied her words but saw only a smile that signaled a possible truce between north and south, black and white, and maybe even man and woman.

He did manage to mumble, "I'm sorry. I was starving."

"Oh, don't worry. I take it as a compliment. Now, if you will take a grocery list and the money my father left me I think that I can do even better."

"I'll take your list, but not your money."

She felt the anger rise that he so easily seemed to draw from her. "Why?" she asked, her dignity ruffled once again. "My father did not expect charity."

"You think it's because it's my father's money, don't you?"

There was no answer and he continued. "That would be wrong.

Everything spent on this house is my money, from my bank account. Now, it does come from my father, but I work for it, and what I have to endure does not come without cost. I earn this money. I know my salary is high for a kid just out of high school, but I earn it, believe me."

"Do you mean by how hard you work?"

"Partially, but more so for what I have to sacrifice."

"That doesn't change the fact that my father does not want charity."

"I will not take your father's money."

"Why, he's not poor. He's not rich like your father, but he makes a living."

"This argument you insist on is not about money," he answered, a slight anger in his voice.

"What is it about then?"

"Would your father take my money if the situation was reversed?"

"Of course he would."

"Well, then, you don't know your father."

"And you do?"

"Yes, I do."

She slowed, deliberating over the words she wanted to voice. She took a long breath and said, "Bret, you act as though you owe something to my father, to Money, but you are the one risking so much right now. You are the one who jumped into that fight in the alley. We owe you."

He shook his head and closed his eyes, unable to believe how wrong she was. "Look, I won't take your money, or your father's."

"But, Bret—"

"Please, just let it go," he snapped, before continuing with a weary exasperation in his voice. "Let's enjoy this really good meal." He looked across the table and saw hurt etched on her face.

"I didn't mean to hurt your feelings. I apologize. I'm not exactly an open book with my feelings. I'm a cold, selfish, rich white boy, and I know that. I prefer it that way. But your brother is my only friend in this world and I can't think of anyone I respect more than your father. I know that if things were reversed and it was Alex, they would do everything they could and never ask to be compensated." He paused, before smiling slightly as he added, "Why don't you just allow me to do the right thing just once?" He chucked slightly. "Trust me, it does not occur all that often."

She studied him, the softness in his voice and face. Who was he really? She was convinced of one thing. He cared about her brother and father. He might dance around the subject but it was apparent.

They finished eating. Bret rose from the table. "I know you hate this place and the south, and maybe me, but I want to show you something. Please," he added, as he extended his hand, a simple southern gentleman gesture. She placed her hand in his without thinking as she rose from her chair.

His hand was tough and callused from all of the construction work. He held her hand softly but securely. Her hand felt good, warm, intertwined in his, she thought briefly, before wondering what possessed her to have such a foolish thought.

"Where are we going?" she asked.

He let go of her hand and said, "Down to the river," as he began walking toward the door.

She followed him down to the trail that led to the river. The remaining light enabled easy and swift negotiation of the path. The tide was low, providing a wide shore to walk on. Low tide in the heat of summer brought an unpleasant stench to Teke's nostrils, while Bret breathed the air in as if it were the cleansing smell of fall. The only sounds she could hear were the cicadas singing with fevered pitch, and in the distance an owl hooted.

"See how the sunlight filters through the trees, and sits on top of the ripples in the water. I know it's not the bright lights of the city, but I've always liked the way the river looks this time of day. It's so quiet, so..."

Teke watched him and saw the glow in his eyes when he spoke of the river and the sun's last rays setting down on top of it. She could not see the magnitude of the beauty the sunset on the river contained, but she did see the magnitude it held for him.

"My grandfather used to talk about building a pier after the house was complete. That was to be the finishing touch to an old house that I still know so little about. The pier would be a nice addition. It could be a place to fish from, maybe dock a boat, or maybe even better a place to just sit and watch the river."

They sat on the sand and watched as the sun slowly abated. There were a few scattered clouds and the streams of orange lit them up in a magnificent display of color. They sat quietly studying the river until darkness enveloped all that was around them. Nothing else was said and their worlds, for a moment, did not seem quite so distant.

He stood first and turned to her and offered his hands. She grasped them and he easily pulled her up. She tumbled slightly forward and her head fell into his chest. She smiled up at him. "I don't hate you."

"What?"

"You said inside that I maybe I hated you. I don't."

"That's good to know." He smiled gently and faintly nodded. "Let's go back inside."

The dark was full now. "Let me go first," he said.

"Lead the way," she offered, before adding, "I do know the way."

"Not at night you don't. There are a couple of uneven places that could trip you up." He was in front of her now and she saw his hand reach back. She frowned for a second and did not know why. She took his hand and he led her on the path back to their temporary home.

* * *

The remainder of the week fell into a routine that proved much smoother than their initial night together. Teke was lonely and bored, but she tried to make the best of things. She was glad when he came home at the end of the day, if for no other reason than to see another human being. Her meals continued to surprise and please him. He had not tasted home cooking this good on a regular basis since Bessie died.

He still made time for the top priority in his life, Alex. He usually went to his father's house right after work. The two of them would shoot baskets, or go to the club for a late afternoon swim. Bret always made it to the river house before darkness.

It was nearing the end of June and the total rainfall for the previous six weeks was barely one inch. Crops were withering in the field and the dirt road through Vicky's property was so dusty that he had given up on washing his cherished Mustang.

Vicky's garden that she relied heavily on was at the brink of death. She watered with the garden hose, and a sprinkler set on top of a homemade tripod, but the fear of burning out her old water pump, or the well running dry kept her from being overzealous in any attempts to salvage the produce.

It was Friday afternoon and Bret was stuck laying the foundation of the law career that awaited him. He was in the office library when he looked out and noticed some of the cars crossing the Cape Fear Memorial Bridge with their headlights on. A closer look at the sky behind the cars showed why. The ominous sky was forebodingly black.

He walked closer to the large window that allowed such a picturesque view of the river, though he failed to understand why. Any employee of the firm of Walker Marin, Sr. caught gazing out at the river would surely be asked if they enjoyed their job. That was just like his father to have something that you were not allowed to enjoy.

His eyes trailed north along the river. Would Teke be okay? He was debating the scenario when he heard the first long muffled roar of thunder build slowly for seconds before popping so loud that the glass in front of him shook. This was no ordinary afternoon thunderstorm. He saw the lightening, pure white in its appearance dance slightly ahead of the darkest clouds. His next thought was Money. He promised to watch over his sister and he guessed that meant making sure she wasn't afraid. He cursed the responsibility under his breath as he reached for the phone to call Alex to explain why he couldn't make it to the house today.

As he returned to his office to close the door with Alex on his mind he recalled a similar thunderstorm many years ago and smiled warmly.

It was Alex's first year without their mother. Many times, Bret would awake in the middle of the night to find Alex beside him, safely sleeping. This particular night, a similar roar of thunder awakened Bret. The first clap of thunder stirred him from his sleep. The second roar began to build and he heard little footsteps moving hurriedly across the floor. As the rumbling thunder climaxed in an explosion, he could hear his little brother's feet leave the floor, coinciding with the boom, from what seemed several feet away. As the clap ended, Alex dove gracefully into the bed, where he quickly went to sleep, never offering a word.

Bret closed his office and walked briskly toward freedom. He gave

Ruby a halfhearted explanation as he passed her on the way to the elevator. She said something, but he refused to slow down to listen. He had been working hard at a job he hated. Maybe the old man wouldn't call at four fifty-five p.m., as he was apt to do, especially on Friday.

He reached the bottom floor and proceeded to his car. Once again, he heard the low roar of thunder building before it exploded. Three bolts of lightning flashed, a split second apart. He felt the first drops of rain as he trotted to his car. The rain felt cool as it splashed across the back of his neck, providing a welcome relief from the near one hundred degree heat. He drove north, and as he crossed the Smith Creek Bridge, he saw the first wave of rain come, accompanied by hail. He couldn't recall the last time that he had witnessed hail in Wilmington.

A few minutes later, he roared past Vicky's. The hail had ceased, but the rain was falling so hard now that visibility was just beyond the front of the car. His familiarity with the winding dirt road was the only thing that spared him from driving into the woods that lined the road.

He entered the house finding darkness. The power was out.

"Teke," he called out.

He was walking to the foot of the stairs when he noticed her sitting at the table. He walked to her. "Are you all right?"

"Of course, why wouldn't I be?"

"I thought the storm, uh..."

"Might scare me?"

"Yes."

"We have storms up north," she offered coolly. She smiled again and held it for a few seconds before she finally gave up the charade, and laughed nervously.

"Bret, I haven't ever seen a storm like this. I was scared to death."

He looked at her, somewhat perturbed, but more amused. "I should have left you here alone," he said, but he didn't mean it.

"You should go check on your grandmother."

"Why?"

"She might need something."

"You don't know Vicky."

"Vicky, why do you call your grandmother Vicky?"

"It is at her request. She will be fine. Besides, you should understand that she doesn't really like me."

"Who could blame her for that?" she answered with a grin.

"That's cute."

"Go check on her. It won't hurt. And if she doesn't like you, why does she let you stay here? Why does she do things to encourage you to stay?"

"Like what?"

"You sure are dumb for someone who is going to be an attorney. The curtains, the dinnerware, the fridge," she said, motioning with her hand at the items.

He offered no rebuttal. He had contemplated her actions as well, but the complete answer escaped him.

Teke refused to budge on the topic. "Go," she reiterated.

Bret, seeing that he would derive no peace until he went, gave in. "Okay, I'll go. The wooden box in the corner has some candles and matches in it."

Moments later he knocked on Vicky's door.

Vicky opened the door. "Don't you know enough to get in out of the rain? You are going to ruin that expensive suit."

He cursed Teke under his breath as he entered the house. "I just wanted to make sure that you were okay."

"Why wouldn't I be? It's just a storm. It's surely not my first."

Her house was lit from candles and two kerosene lanterns. Vicky had been self-sufficient her entire adult life but then, she was probably born as an adult. As he looked around the house, and then her, he surmised that a hurricane could strike and she would be able to ride it out for months.

"I'll be going."

"Are you staying at the house tonight?"

"Yes. That is okay, isn't it?"

"Of course it is. I don't guess you can cook tonight. No telling when the power will be back on. I fried some chicken before the storm. I'll fix you a plate, with some potatoes, green beans, and biscuits."

"I guess you heard the weather report about the storm."

"I heard the weather. They didn't mention any storm, or rain for that matter."

"But you cooked chicken in the afternoon. You don't cook in the afternoon. How?"

"My rheumatism in my right knee acted up. Now take this food," she said as she handed him a cardboard box loaded with enough food for four. Efficient as always, she inserted another box over the first, protecting it from the rain.

"Now go eat, and quit bothering an old helpless woman."

He wasn't sure if that was an attempt at humor, or a lashing out at him for checking on her. And why didn't she invite him to eat here?

"Thank you."

"You're welcome. That little brother of yours, will he be here to-morrow?"

"Yes."

"Tell him that I will expect him at dinner time."

"I'll do that."

"11:30 sharp," she added.

"Yes, ma'am." He turned and sprinted to his car.

Vicky sat down at the table and disgustedly muttered, "Ma'am."

Bret drove down the slick road to the house. He walked in and found the downstairs lit with candles.

Teke's back was turned to him as she plundered through the makeshift cabinets that had not been completed. "I don't know what we will eat tonight, and I'm starving."

He watched her explore the cabinets for a few moments before saying, "How about this?"

She turned and looked at the box he was holding.

"Where did you get that?" she asked, as the favorable aroma of the food reached her nostrils.

"Vicky, and thanks so much for her needing any help. She insulted me when I asked if she was okay."

"So, she sent food for you. Are you going to share?"

"Considering she sent enough for a small army, I think so. Of course, it's nasty southern cooking."

"Let me see that box," she said as she took it from him. "I was born in the south, remember."

"It's a miracle that you admit to it."

"I'll set the table. Why don't you get out of those clothes? You're soaked."

"I'm not that easy," he sarcastically replied.

"That's not what Money said."

Bret struggled for a moment. "You're making that up. He wouldn't."

She interrupted him, "Yes, he told me. Girls fall all over the rich pretty white boy. I guess I'm getting in the way of your weekend activities. From what I hear, it's a different girl every weekend."

He stood there not knowing what to say.

"Go, change clothes. Don't worry, I'm too hungry to sneak a peek at your beautiful body," she feigned.

He went upstairs to his room and changed into some shorts and a tee shirt. They were a welcome relief from the suit. He ran his hand over his wet hair.

As he went back downstairs, he couldn't help but notice that his guest was still quite pleased for how obviously uncomfortable she had made him. It was all too evident from the slight grin that refused to leave her face.

They feasted on the chicken and all that accompanied it. The bottom of the box provided one additional container, two slices of pecan pie. It was an extraordinary meal by candlelight and the two of them enjoyed the dinner in mostly quietness, while watching the storm perform a majestic dance over the Cape Fear River.

CHAPTER ELEVEN

Roommates

The intense storms ended by midnight, but the clouds that moved into the area lingered throughout the following day, bringing a much needed gentle soaking rain to the area.

Bret rose early to pick up Alex. He brought him back to the old house where he promptly put him to work, much to his delight.

The bathroom was sectioned off now with the beautiful pine boards that his grandfather selected before he died. By the conclusion of the day the master bedroom walls were up and they made it partially through the bedroom Bret was sleeping in.

It would not be too far in the future that the construction would be complete. He wanted to see the house finished and the satisfaction derived from a task completed. Another part of him enjoyed working, breathing, and shaping the wood so much that he wanted the project to never end.

It felt good that his grandfather's confidence in him was not misplaced. He could not only finish this house, but build it to a standard high enough that even his grandfather might approve.

At the moment he took comfort in knowing that there was still much work ahead. Once all the walls were completed, there would be the finishing work, cabinets to be installed, and all of the wood to varnish.

Alex and Teke both contributed to the effort. Alex was showing the initial skills that led Bret to believe that woodworking proficiency might flow through his veins as well. Teke did it out of the happiness of not being alone, and to stave off boredom. When the time reached eleven-thirty, it was Teke who insisted that not only Alex go eat dinner with Vicky, but Bret as well. She refused to take no for an answer, eventually wearing Bret down.

It was just past six, as Bret was returning from taking Alex home. The rain stopped around three o'clock but it began again on the drive home. The sky was blanketed in darkness. By now, even the weather forecasters seemed to know what Vicky knew yesterday. They were predicting rain for the entire night. The skies were expected to clear tomorrow, sometime in the middle of morning. Bret wasn't sure about that since he hadn't heard Vicky's forecast yet.

He purchased two steaks on his way back from driving Alex home. Teke had worked diligently all day, and actually did it without being disagreeable. He knew that she was bored and feeling as well as he did over today's work he decided a reward was in line for his crew member.

He was underneath the house setting up the new charcoal grill. He heard her descending down the steps.

"What are you doing?" she asked.

"I bought steaks and thought I would try out the new charcoal grill. Yankees do eat steak, don't they?"

"They...we do," she answered.

"I'll cook the steaks and you throw together something to go with it."

"That sounds like a good deal."

She turned to go back to the house. Suddenly, she stopped. "Bret, why don't you go out tonight? Go see one of your girlfriends," she said with a hint of sarcasm. "There is no need for both of us to be stuck here. I'll be fine."

"Actually, I had another idea."

"You with an idea, stop right now, you're scaring me."

He smiled at her. "Well, I was thinking that since you worked so well all day and without your normal amount of complaining, I might add, that maybe compensation would be the proper southern thing to do. We southerners pride ourselves on that kind of thing, you know."

She looked at him, her face void of any expression. "Does this idea have a point to it, or is it like most of your ideas, really slow to take off before fizzling out all together?"

"You, my little Yankee roommate, will not ruin my good mood over the day of work accomplished."

He paused once again, irritating her even more, if that were possible. "It looks as if the rain has set in for good. I thought we could go to a drive-in movie."

"No one goes to a drive-in movie in the rain," she quickly replied.

"That is correct."

She waited for him to finish, but he just stood looking at her with a mischievous smile etched on his face. What was it he knew that she didn't? And then her eyes sparkled as she gained understanding.

"Glad you could finally keep up with the conversation. I'll hide you on the way in, and, hopefully, you can sit up for the entire movie without having to dive in the back. Of course, if you'd rather stay..."

"No, no. We can go. I would love to go," she stated emphatically.

They sat underneath the house and ate dinner on a weathered gray picnic table enjoying the steaks that were grilled to perfection. The meat was so tender and moist that it could almost be cut with a fork. Teke cooked French fries and prepared a tossed salad to compliment the meal.

There was a different feeling between them as they enjoyed dinner. They sat looking out as the rain met the river. The normal strained bantering between them was not present. Maybe it was Bret's feeling of accomplishment over the work of the day, or maybe it was Teke knowing she was going to be free from containment for a few hours. Whatever the reason, there was a peace, a truce that had not been present since the storms of life forced this hand upon them.

Bret was sitting on the couch watching television. He heard her coming down the stairs, but paid no attention. She walked to him. "Bret."

He turned his head toward her and his eyes fell on the figure standing before him. She was wearing a black skirt with a white sleeveless top. He said nothing, but the shocked look on his face said everything. "Teke," he mumbled, but that was as far as he got.

"I know it's silly. I know this is not a date, but I've been stuck here and I just wanted to dress up. If you want, I'll change, but please, just don't laugh at me. I know that I'm this hard Yankee to you, but with everything that has happened, I suddenly don't feel so tough."

The sadness in her eyes enhanced her beauty all the more. She was afraid that he would make fun of her at a time when she felt very vulnerable. He said nothing as he looked at her, unsure of his choice of words.

The silence unnerved her and she was on the verge of tears. "I'm sorry. This was dumb. I'll change." She turned to the stairs.

He finally woke from his stupor and called to her, rising quickly, catching her at the bottom of the stairs. "Teke, wait."

She stopped, but refused to turn, not wanting to give him the satisfaction of seeing the tears that she was trying desperately to hold back.

He reached for her, catching her on her left elbow. "Teke," he said, in such a gentle voice that it seem foreign to her. He persuaded her to turn to him.

It was then that he saw the first lonely tear that was falling down her cheek. "Teke, you got it all wrong. I didn't say anything, because," he paused, unsure of what he wanted to say. He decided on the truth.

"I didn't say anything because you look great."

"You don't mean that. I'm not a charity case. Boys want to go out with me. You probably don't believe that, but they do."

She felt foolish and childish for the words that escaped her mouth, and for the tears that refused to stop.

He looked at her differently, or maybe it was the situation thrust upon her that he saw more clearly. He had thought mainly of himself as usual. This was always about his plans being disrupted to keep a promise to a friend. She had been through hell, and she was alone.

"Teke, I mean it. I swear. You came down those stairs and I was not prepared for this," he said as he gestured with his hand toward her. "Please, don't change."

"It's not like this was a date, or anything. I just wanted to feel, to look pretty, because there is nothing real pretty in my life right now, and why am I crying?" she angrily announced, the frustration mounting in her voice.

Without thinking about it, Bret reached toward her, surrounding her with his arms, pulling her close to him. She resisted for a moment but then relaxed, allowing him to pull her close to him. She cried in his chest briefly, but pulled away hurriedly and walked away.

She was halfway up the steps when Bret thought of another method. "If you change, I won't take you to the movies."

"What?" she said, turning to him.

"You heard me. Don't change. You look fantastic. I don't want you to change. If you do, I won't take you."

"You don't mean that."

"Well, there is one way to find out," he said as he turned away from her, and walked back to the couch, and resumed watching television as if she did not exist.

She looked at him perplexed, not certain what to do. She continued upstairs.

She returned several minutes later, wearing the same outfit.

"What is playing?"

"*You Only Live Twice*. It began playing yesterday."

She almost suggested an alternative to a James Bond movie but she refrained when she realized this was not Philadelphia, and this was probably the only choice. Besides, he was trying to be nice, to be kind, and she would allow that.

They walked out to the car and she stood staring at the trunk. "I guess to sneak in the movies I need to be in the trunk."

He stopped her. "Don't, it's rainy and dark. Sit real low in the back seat and when we go by Vicky's just lean down. If she comes out, which I doubt she will, I'll just drive by and pretend not to see her."

"What about at the movie?"

"Rainy night like this they won't be checking that closely. At the movies just lie down and pull that blanket on the back seat over you."

She stood by the car, the rain falling gently on her, "Are you sure?"

"Yes, get in before you get soaked," he said, grinning.

They drove to the movie. The spoiled, rich, selfish white boy, who on this night was not so spoiled and selfish, but kind and thoughtful, and the northern black girl who had so many emotions running through her that she wasn't sure of anything.

The movie attendant eyed him warily as he drove in alone. Smuggling others into a drive-in movie was a southern heritage, a rite of passage. The attendant started to quiz him, but decided against it, though he suspected that someone was in the trunk. It was then that ne noticed the lump in the back seat. He eyed Bret and said deliberately, "Nice try."

Bret was prepared. He gave the man a twenty and said, "You may keep the change."

The attendant debated for about two seconds about a $17 tip. "Enjoy the movie."

There were two other cars in the huge lot at the Oleander Drive-In Movie Theater. Bret planned well and arrived just a little late to pick out a secluded spot away from everyone else.

"That was smooth," Teke said from under the blanket. "May I get up now?"

Bret looked around one more time and said, "Yes."

"May I come up front with you?"

He chuckled softly. "I did not envision you remaining in the back."

She worked her way to the front seat as Bugs Bunny played on the big screen. "What if someone comes by?"

"It is raining, so I doubt that will be an issue but if they do just lean over and I will wrap you up and people will just think we are making out."

"Talk about low standards," she said with a smirk.

He smiled back at her and said, "Low for whom?"

"Good one, southern boy."

"I have my moments."

"Yes, you do," she said sincerely before adding, "I guess by wrap up you mean hide my dark skin."

He eyed her so he could see if this was a debate in which an incorrect answer would lead to confrontation. He was weary of dispute.

She shook her head slightly. "I don't want to fight." She hesitated before adding, "May I ask a question of a philosophical nature?"

"Yes."

"Do you think a day will come when none of this matters?"

"Maybe," he answered honestly.

"Be nice to think so, right?"

"Yes."

"Okay, enough with the one word answers."

He chuckled softly. "Yes, ma'am."

She punched him in the arm.

He frowned at her. "What are you, twelve years old?"

She punched him again. The movie began and they focused on the film. Several minutes passed and then she said, "It will change."

"How do you know?"

"Alex."

He looked at her perplexed.

"He doesn't see color. He sees people. You won't teach him different."

He raised his eyes at her and then nodded softly. They returned to watching the movie.

The movie ended and he drove to the same golf course that served as his rendezvous point with Barbara. As they entered the dark secluded road, she asked, "Where are we?"

"It's a golf course. Do you see the pay phone at the side of the building?"

"Yes."

He handed her a small brown bag with several quarters in it. "Here, take this. The number where Money and your dad can be reached is written on the side of the bag. Go call them."

"Bret, that is so nice," she beamed. The look on her face told him that she appreciated his kindness, and it felt good to him.

"Go ahead and call. I'll stand by the road and watch for anyone. If I whistle, get off the phone and duck behind the bushes."

"Thank you so much," she said happily as she walked away, leaving him to watch the road.

Minutes later she emerged with a smile. Her hair was wet from the relentless light rain. "Dad and Money say hi and thanks for all that you are doing."

He nodded and shuffled uncomfortably. He noticed the way the rain seemed to hug the curls in her hair to the last possible moment before surrendering and falling to the pavement below.

"We'd better get out of here," he said, and without a thought, he reached out and touched her hair. "Your hair is so soft. It feels like a pillow."

The tenderness of the moment left as abruptly as it came. "What did you expect, a brillo pad?" she replied angrily.

"No," he stammered.

"You're no different, are you?" she quickly judged.

"Different than what?" he exclaimed.

"All this for my brother, but I bet you sit around and tell racist jokes with the rest of the good old boys. Tell me that you don't use that word."

"I don't."

"Since when?"

"We'd better go. It's not very wise to argue here. Someone might drive by."

"Not until you answer me."

"Get in the car," he demanded.

Suddenly, headlights surprised them both. Bret quickly pinned her against the wall. "Kiss me."

"What?" she stated in total disbelief.

"Shut up and kiss me." He put his lips to hers and held her tightly, hoping that his body was shielding the darkness of her skin.

Her anger temporarily subsided as she realized what he was doing. The car drove slowly by, looking, but not stopping.

He released her. "Now get in the car. If I lose my little brother over your stubborn stupid behavior..." He failed to finish his threat.

She was embarrassed that she almost caused them to be seen in public together, but still angry at what she was convinced was a bigoted suggestion on his part. She stood still refusing to budge, the rain falling even heavier now. She didn't care.

"You could have just answered the question, Bret."

"Why should I have to answer your accusations? Your mind is already made up."

"Well, prove me wrong."

"Why should I? Who cares what you think. You're just another Yankee who thinks the south needs your northern guidance. Well, I don't."

"You could have just answered my question. When is the last time you used the word?"

He remained silent.

"When?" she reiterated angrily.

His temper was rising, but still he refused to reply.

"Why do you hold everything in so tight? Why can't you just talk, Bret?"

He erupted, "Why in the hell do you want me to share my feelings? So you can make fun of me," he said in a mocking voice. "Barbara pulls this same crap. Maybe there is nothing inside of me and the two of you refuse to accept it. You know that is one thing I really like about your brother. He's not so damn nosy."

"Did you quit using the word when you met him?" she asked, not deterred from her question. "Bret..."

He quickly interrupted her. "You want to paint me a bigot, go ahead. I don't care. Of course, my only friend is black. I respect your father more than any man I know. But I'm a bigot. Well, I'm not a bigot. For the most part, I don't dislike blacks. I dislike everyone, all colors, all people. All right, I was surprised at how soft your hair is. I don't even know why I touched it. I was looking at you and you were so cute standing, smiling, in the rain with your hair all wet." He tired of talking and moved toward her suddenly. Before she knew it, he was kissing her and she was responding.

When they stopped, Bret backed away. "I'm sorry. I shouldn't have done that." He was struggling for words, any words that might make sense out of what had just taken place.

She watched him, astonished at the moment passed, and she felt sympathy for him. The stoic one was confused, even bewildered. She could see it all in the same face that hid so many emotions. She was confused as well. Why had she allowed him to kiss her?

She watched his face torn in anguish until she could take it no more. She tried to lighten the situation. "Hey, where do you get off kissing me, when there is not a car in sight?"

Her feeble attempt at humor did not bring a laugh from Bret. "Please just get in the car." he asked wearily.

They got in the car, quietness enveloping them.

"So, when was the last time you used the word, Bret?" she asked delicately.

"I was a little boy," he sighed in defeat as he recalled that day with Bessie. "And for the love of God, don't ask any more questions," he said as he drove away.

They drove to his father's house with Teke once again hidden from view in the back. He stopped in the driveway just short of the garage door.

"Stay down, okay?"

"Where are we?" Teke mumbled from her hidden position.

"Just stay low and please be quiet," he said wearily.

He got out of the car and pushed the button to the electronic door and got back in. He drove into the garage and got out of the car warning her once again to stay down. He shut the door and cut the lights out. He peered outside through the windows in the garage door.

Satisfied that no one was near, he said, "Okay, you can get out."

"Where are we?" she asked.

"It's my father's house. Come inside, hurry," he urged her.

They entered the house. Teke looked at the surroundings and exclaimed, "This is some home you have."

"It belongs to my father," he said firmly.

Barbara and Alex emerged from the living room to inspect their unexpected company. Alex bolted to Bret jumping into his arms.

"Are you going to stay tonight, Bret?"

"We sure are. Barbara, is the guest bedroom ready?" Bret asked, before adding, "Oh, my fault, this is Teke, Money's sister."

"It's nice to meet you," Barbara said, offering her hand warmly. "I'll go up and get the bed ready for you."

"I'll help you," Teke offered.

"No, I'll do it. You go with this little guy and watch television with him."

Teke looked at Bret. "You planned quite a bit today, didn't you?"

He shrugged his shoulders. "I tried," he answered honestly.

Before the words were completed, Alex grabbed her hand, urging her to the living room.

Bret inspected the living room, making certain that all the curtains were drawn. Satisfied, he returned to the kitchen and began popping popcorn.

Barbara returned as Bret was carrying the bowls of popcorn to the living room. The four of them watched television, ate popcorn, and talked. The two girls hit it off and discussed fashions, music, and the latest movies, including one that was premiering in August, *In the Heat of the Night*. Both girls were interested in the social aspects of the movie, which produced large yawns from Bret.

After midnight, all adjourned for bed. The two of them that had not enjoyed air conditioning of late looked forward to a night of cool slumber.

Bret carried Alex, who had fallen asleep earlier. He tucked him in and kissed him good night on top of his head. Teke watched him from outside the door and was moved by such tenderness.

Barbara walked Teke to the guest room after observing Teke watching Bret put Alex to bed. "Here's your room, Teke," Barbara said as she flipped on the light. "There is a bathroom that should have everything that you need."

"Thank you, Barbara. Could I ask you something?"

"Sure."

"Why does he trust you when he doesn't trust anyone but Alex?"

"Maybe because he knows that I have a lot to lose also."

"Why do you take the risk?"

"I don't know, maybe because he is not as big a jerk as he wants people to think," she said adding a slight chuckle.

"Are you sure about that?" Teke laughed. "He has his moments."

"Yes, but he is changing, more than he realizes. There was a time, not so long ago, that all he cared about in this world, all he trusted was Alex. He trusts Money, and your dad, and you."

"I wouldn't go that far. I think he trusts that I won't cross my family, but he doesn't really trust me."

"He laughs at me when I say it, but I believe that Money and he crossed paths for a reason."

"Yes, he would laugh at anything that contained a hint of depth to it, wouldn't he?" she laughed softly, before adding, "I do know this, my brother loves him and I think my dad does too. The two of them don't allow many people to get close either."

"He loves them too. He just doesn't know how to say it. He probably doesn't realize it himself. Things are changing for him and he is more uncertain these days than I have ever seen him."

"Let me guess. Alex is the only one that hears him say how he feels."

"Bingo," she replied, with a warm smile.

"Teke, I'm going to bed. Can I get you anything?"

"No, I'm fine. Thank you for your hospitality."

"No problem. You deserve it, living with him."

Barbara left and Teke went to the bathroom to wash her face. She realized as she returned to the bedroom that she had nothing to sleep in. She walked down the hall and tapped on Bret's room.

"Come in."

Teke opened the door and walked in finding Bret already in bed. "I'm sorry to bother you. Do you have a tee shirt that I could sleep in? I don't have anything."

"I guess I should have told you my plan for the night so you could have prepared better."

"No, that's okay. I like surprises and you were full of them tonight. Thank you. What you did tonight, the movie, the phone call, and bringing me to air conditioning, all of it was really sweet."

He cringed visibly at the word sweet, but said nothing.

He got out of bed and walked to his chest of drawers, pulling the middle drawer out. He tossed her an orange shirt that read 'New Hanover' across the front in big black letters. "This should be good for you. A shirt from a basically all white school."

She tried not to look at him, or acknowledge that there was a stirring inside her that both excited and frightened her. It probably did not help matters that he was clad only in red gym shorts. "Thanks for this," she said, motioning to the shirt, surprising him that she failed to respond to his all white school comment. She stood and closed her eyes and suddenly felt exhaustion consume every component of her being.

He returned to bed and crawled under the covers when he realized that she had not left. He rolled over and looked at her standing over his bed, clutching the tee shirt and looking at it strangely.

"Turn around," she said.

He looked at her and she just nodded softly to him. He turned around. She removed her skirt and top and put on the tee shirt that went almost to her knees.

She sat on the edge of the bed and looked away from him. Her voice was distant. "There are times that I think I am just too young to feel so worn out," she said wearily. Her voice scarcely above a whisper.

"Can I turn around?"

"Yes," she answered.

Bret fluffed his pillow and rose up slightly looking at the back of her. He touched her back gently. "You've been through a lot, Teke. Everyone gets tired."

She turned to him and rested a hand on his arm. "Bret, can we talk?"

"It's late," he said, before chuckling softly. "I know that you are a little slow sometimes, but we are talking"

"I'm sorry for how I acted. One minute I am telling you that Alex will not see color because of you and then I lash out and call you a bigot. I know better than that. I don't know what is wrong with me."

He did not know what to say and he chose the path he was most comfortable with, silence.

"You're sorry that you kissed me, aren't you?" she asked.

"It was a mistake. It won't happen again."

"Is it because I am black?"

He said nothing.

"Are you ashamed?" There was no anger in her voice. He said nothing so she charged on. "Don't worry, Bret. Dad says that they may get a place by next weekend and I can fly away and get out of your hair. You can go back to your routine. You can kiss girls that you don't have to be ashamed of, and sleep with them, too, like you did Barbara."

"No, I never slept with Barbara," he quickly corrected her. "She is too good to Alex."

"Aw, Alex, your one redeeming quality."

"That's right. The only redeeming quality," he agreed.

"So, why would it hurt Alex?"

"Because I am all you think that I am. I don't last long with one girl, any girl."

"Maybe you met your match in Barbara. She doesn't seem to fall at your feet so easily."

"Does any of this have a point? I kissed you, I'm sorry. As for Barbara, if it will make you feel better, I tried and she shot me down."

"Maybe I'm not sorry."

"About what?"

"That you kissed me."

"You should be."

"Why?"

"I think you know."

"Because you are white and I am black?"

"It was just wrong," he said, declining to elaborate.

"I thought you meant all those things you said about me tonight, how good I looked."

"I did."

"Then why do you regret it?"

"No, it's because I was trusted with your care, not to romance you."

"I wouldn't call it romance. It was one kiss, and it wasn't all that special," she said, forcing a slight smile.

She felt so drained at the moment and lightheaded. She lifted the light cover and lay down, facing away from him.

He listened to her labored breathing unsure of what to do. There were parts of him that wanted to wrap his arms around her and feel the softness of her skin meshed against his. There was no denying that. But he knew where it would end, because he knew who he was. He thought of Money and then Clarence. He wanted just once to do the right thing with a girl.

"Teke, you need to go to your room," he said gently.

"Will you do one thing for me before I do that?"

"Yes," he answered quickly, without realizing what it might be.

"Hold me for just a few minutes. I won't turn around. I just feel so alone right now. I can't explain it. I don't want to try too." She waited and was about to rise and leave as he wanted when she felt his arm pull her close to his chest.

She breathed in deeply and whispered, "Thank you."

They lay there a few minutes in the silence. "I'm tired of everything being black and white, Bret. We're all just people. All God's creation," she offered wearily. She waited for him to speak but he remained silent. She continued, "I don't mean that directed to just you. I am just as guilty. And I don't want to be that way. I just don't."

"Is all of this because I kissed you?"

"What do you think?"

"No," he sighed. "I think that what you are struggling with is far bigger than a kiss from someone you don't like."

"Yeah, that is just what I do all the time. I lie in bed and ask boys to hold me that I don't like."

"Did you just say yeah?"

"I guess I did. Even my language is failing me."

"Don't worry. I won't tell."

"Can we just forget that it happened? The kiss and all," he elaborated.

"We can try."

Moments later, he heard her relaxed breathing and he knew that she was asleep.

He rose from the bed and walked to the other side. He watched her as she slept peacefully. She was beautiful, even while wearing a tee shirt three sizes too large. He wanted to undress and remove the shirt she wore. He wondered if she would allow it.

He pulled the covers up around her shoulders and gently tucked her in. He sighed heavily, turned and walked down the hall to the guest room.

Doing what was right sure was difficult, he thought as he lay down in bed.

CHAPTER TWELVE

Fog

Bret drove past Vicky's, after another grueling day dealing with Ruby. Each day she seemed determined to dish out torment and she accomplished this feat with a seemingly wicked gleam in her eye. The best he could ascertain the main focus of her job for the summer of 1967 was to make his life at the Walker Marin & Sons firm as wretched as humanly possible. And she was doing a bang up job.

It was five o'clock and Teke was sitting in her spot watching the river. She survived the week by reading books to prep her for school. She had a plan in place for her life, and that included attending Temple University. She would reconcile herself that all of the misery in her life caused by Lawrence Tuttle would resolve itself. It had to. She longed to return home and get away from the city and the boy that slept a few feet away each night.

She failed miserably in her attempts to persuade him to talk about the one moment from the previous weekend that now seemed to hang over them like a huge weight. The week was far worse than their initial week together. She preferred arguing to the aloof conversations favored by Bret. He abruptly cut off any suggestion of a conversation that entailed more than what was for dinner that night. He was particularly adept at firing up the table saw, skill saw, or whatever happened to be the most handy power tool to drown out potential dialogue.

She wanted to be angry with him, but for some peculiar reason she found it difficult. She was captive living out in the country, but she knew that one day she would escape. Bret was held hostage by something far greater. Something keeping him from being what she believed he could be. She now believed in the good that her brother and father saw. Still, there was no denying that he was trapped in what he was raised in, and though she knew he wanted to break away, she doubted it possible. Maybe somehow he could be courageous enough to leave the wealth, but never would he leave Alex.

She watched the river and the wake created by the large dinghy white shrimp boat passing by. The boat was going out for the night. Bret had taught her that by the direction it was taking.

The river seemed a tranquil place for her to sort through her troubles. There was a certain peace, a certain beauty it contained that became clearer to her each day. The sun was far around to the west now, and slowly was beginning its descent.

"Why can't I just hate him?" she asked herself softly. It seemed so natural in the beginning, from the first night that he showed up at her father's house painted as a black man.

She thought of how he felt about her father. How he respected him. Bret reminded her of what a good man her father was. She felt guilty for the years that she had looked down on him for remaining in the south, blaming him for not leaving this place of misery for her mother and her. She missed out on having a father. Money missed out on having a mother.

She thought again of the past week. She attempted to close herself off from him, but she was not as proficient in that area as he was. The part that she could not escape was how one kiss seemingly produced such feelings. How could it have happened so easily and how could she not have seen it coming? She admonished herself with her less than truthful observation. It was time to come clean. She had been trying to look away from him but the truth was she had stolen a thousand glances at him. How many times had he turned around and she pretended to look the other way? Too numerous to count.

The kiss brought to light something she was oblivious to. She had fallen, in some twisted way, for someone that she could never have.

She wanted to return to her previous hostility, but found it impossible to rekindle.

The shrimp boat disappeared from of view. She asked herself again, quietly, "Why can't I just dislike someone who is so different than me?"

Moments later, she said, even softer, "Because I love him," answering her own question. She buried her head in her arms and cried softly, and wondered why her heart would betray her in such a manner.

She heard the bushes nearby rattle and looked up to see Fred sitting obediently like the perfect gentleman that he was not. Fred avoided her the first week of her stay. But this week he had accompanied her to the river on every excursion, providing her with some much needed company.

She heard the roar of the Mustang's engine and she buried her head once again into her arms. Fred sauntered closer, and with his long cold nose, tried to lift her head up.

She looked at her new friend. "Fred, why does he run so fast from me, over one kiss?"

Fred looked puzzled at a question that involved more than food and a nap. He offered no answers, only an unwanted lick.

Bret, unable to find her in the house, walked down to the river. He saw her sitting looking out over the river. The thoughts of the previous weekend rose again and he willed them away. He had told her the truth. He felt that he betrayed his only friend. Still, there was more that he wasn't telling her.

"Teke," he called softly to her.

"Yes."

"I just wanted to see if you were okay."

"I know, just doing your job for my brother."

"Yes," he said callously, though he didn't mean it to sound that way.

"I didn't cook. Just go to the club, go out. Fred will watch me."

"No, that's okay."

"No, it's not okay. I want you to go. Go to your country club girls. I'm sure they miss you by now, and you them."

He made a noise but nothing audible came from it.

"Go away," she demanded. "I want to be alone. I don't want you here. Just go. Tomorrow, please take me to a phone and let me call dad. Maybe I can fly out of here Sunday and you'll be relieved of your duty."

"What exactly is it that you want from me, Teke?"

"Obviously nothing that you are able to give," she answered tersely. "Now, go to the club and eat. Take one of the girls to a hotel, or home, or wherever it is you take them."

"I won't leave you alone."

"I don't want you here. Don't you understand?" she said, her voice sounding as if she was angry, though she wasn't. Thirty minutes later she walked to the house and he was gone. She sat on the couch and began to weep.

Minutes later she gathered enough composure and walked to the kitchen. She thought of cooking but the truth was her heart was in her stomach and there was no room left for anything else. Moving to the refrigerator for something to drink she noticed a white book on top that was partially leaning off to the right side. She reached up and retrieved it only to find to her surprise that it was a Bible.

As she studied the soft leather cover she opened it and her eyes seemed drawn to a particular verse. Isaiah 41:10 *Fear thou not; for I am with thee: be not dismayed; for I am thy God; I will strengthen thee; yea, I will help thee; yea, I will uphold thee with the right hand of my righteousness.*

She read the verse again and thought about it. What did it mean exactly and where did this Bible come from?

* * *

As instructed, Bret went to the country club. He parked the car, and as he got out he noticed a third of the ruling Country Club board coming out of the front door of the establishment for the very rich. They were indeed societies finest, or at least that is how they viewed things. He watched their staggered steps and knew that once again their dinners were more liquid than solid. It was the way they lived.

Underneath this air of dignity lay a far different group of people. There were alcoholics throughout the club. Men, who thought it pertinent to have a mistress to go with a wife. The club was filled with women that chose to marry for the big house on the hill. Once in place they found the house to be beautiful only from the outside. Inside, it contained lives that were ugly and overrun with despair.

The president of the club, Avery Boyer, was a typical member. He drank too much, smoked too many expensive cigars, and at one point nearly gambled away the family shipping business that he inherited. He was forty-seven. His mistress was twenty-eight. His wife enjoyed her first drink of the day usually by ten a.m. The young college boy, Stan, who cleaned the pool at their house, was rumored to be paid very well by her. But then, he was providing more than service on the pool.

They had two children, Anthony and Priscilla. Anthony, nineteen, was following in his father's footsteps but with a slight variation. His choice of drug to get through the day was any barbiturate he could lay his hands on.

Priscilla was sixteen. She had slept with most of the young men in the club, including Bret. Now, she was venturing outside of the club for fresh material. Of late, she fancied poor rough boys. She also deliberately chose not to be discreet and that infuriated her father far more than the actual acts she committed.

The Boyer's were like most of the club. They looked down on people throughout the city, while conveniently excusing their own little troubled paradise. They would pull out all measures to protect an image that actually fooled no one.

Bret walked to the entrance. He basically disliked everyone here. He looked down on the phoniness and the snobbery, while comforting himself with his reasons for being here, food and girls.

He spotted the one person that he did like but not even Louie could bring light to his bleak thoughts.

"Mr. Marin, it is good to see you tonight. Where have you been keeping yourself?"

"Working at my father's office."

"That's good," Louie cheerfully offered.

"No, Louie. It is a bad thing, a very bad thing," he said, declining to elaborate. The silence that hung in the air after his statement created a moment of awkwardness.

"Sir, it's not like you to dine alone," he said, as he held the door open for him.

"I can't bring who I would like to bring, Louie. I guess that's why."

Puzzled, Louie said, "I don't understand, sir. You always come through these doors with all sorts of pretty girls."

"It's a long story."

Once inside, he walked to a table in the corner. A young waiter appeared and Bret ordered the prime rib without glancing at a menu.

He was there ten minutes when Sandra, a pretty girl with long dark hair and skin to match, appeared at his table. She was sixteen and had just decided how she planned to spend her evening in a house void of any family.

"Are you alone, Bret?"

"Yes, I am," he answered, gesturing toward an empty chair.

The waiter reappeared and Sandra ordered a chef's salad. He nodded politely and departed.

"So, Bret, do you have any plans tonight?"

"No, not really," he answered.

"My parents are gone for the weekend. You can come over to my house if you want to. We can hang out and raid the liquor cabinet. There's no one else there. They took my little sister with them," she added, touching his arm delicately.

Bret's mind was back at the old house by the river momentarily. Sandra was smiling at him and that took his mind back to present company. He looked at her. Beauty had found her quickly, rescuing her from, awkward, less glamorous teen-age years.

A year earlier, she was a little overweight, with shorter hair, and the looks of a girl too young. That had changed drastically since last summer. She was stunning, and the red flowered sundress she wore did nothing to diminish that. It clung to her every curve, and the cleavage that it opened up for the world to see was causing the men in the dining room to look with eyes that could not conceal lust, much to the dismay of the women seated with them.

"Do you want to come over?" she asked, reiterating her question, her dark brown eyes looking at him, seeking a favorable reply.

Moments passed before he finally answered, "Yes, I'll come over."

Why not? Why shouldn't I go over? Teke wants to be alone. She can be alone for the entire evening. What do I care anyway? Hopefully, she is leaving tomorrow and I can return to my life, the way I want it to be. He tried to convince himself that he meant every word of the thoughts that flowed through his mind.

He caught the waiter's attention. He moved quickly to the table.

"What can I get you, sir?"

Sir, I'm eighteen and I get called sir and all because of the supposed royal blood that flows through my veins. Half of that blood coming from a man I despise. I wish there was a way to cut out that half from inside me. The darkness of his thoughts startled him back to reality and he looked up at the waiter who had been patiently waiting for his request.

"I'd like a Heineken."

"Sir, may I see some ID?"

Coldly, Bret looked at the waiter, who was barely older than him, if that. "No, you may not see an ID. I think that I am aware of how old I am, and though I am not an attorney yet, I do believe that the law in this fine state is that anyone eighteen can drink beer. Now, can I get that beer, while I'm still young?"

The now embarrassed waiter said nothing and returned quickly with the requested beer.

"Thank you," Bret said smugly.

One hour later, only the remnants of dinner remained on the table. Bret was on his fifth beer and for the moment was in slightly better humor.

Sandra tugged lightly on his arm. "Can we go now?"

He nodded in agreement.

They walked to the door, which Louie was holding open for them. Sandra walked through the door, looking back at Bret. "Wait here and I'll pick you up, okay?" He watched briefly as she walked to her black Mercedes.

He stood watching her walk to the car. Her back side moved the red dress from side to side, gently, and smoothly. She felt his eyes on her as she intended. She glanced back and smiled in a way to insure that he knew all of what was in store for him this night.

How many girls, now? It was easily over fifty now, but probably shy of a hundred. Then again, maybe not, he smiled.

Louie observed Bret as these thoughts played out in his mind. "Sir, have you been drinking?"

"Just a few beers, Louie"

"Be careful, sir, and make sure that the young lady does the driving tonight."

"Why should you care about what happens to me?" he snapped,

"I'm spoiled, arrogant and rich. I'm everything you are not."

"Something troubling you, sir?" Louie asked softly, choosing to ignore Bret's ugly tone.

"Yes, there is a lot troubling me, but I think that young lady will fix it, don't you?"

"No, I do not," he answered evenly.

"How would you know, Louie?"

"I was not born an old man." He looked away for a moment before looking back at Bret. His eyes soft and generous. "You know that I'd help if you ever needed it, don't you?"

Bret looked away from him and said tersely, "Why? I'm not worth it."

"Don't get down on yourself. You got plenty of good in you, what about..."

"Yes, I know Alex, right?" he barked. "Did anybody ever think that maybe the reason that I am good to him is because he is all I've got? Maybe it's me that needs him. Maybe I'm selfish about that just like I am everything else in this world."

Louie spoke softly, "No, Bret, I never thought that. You take care of that boy because you love him. That's a fact, plain and simple."

Bret looked back at Louie, his surly demeanor somewhat diminished. "You like me, Louie. Why?"

"That's not important. What is important is that you like yourself. Find the good that is in you and let it grow. Turn it loose."

"And if there is no good?"

"I won't hear that kind of talk. Now go home son, go home."

The blaring of the horn startled Bret. An anxious female motioned for him to join her. He had little intention of going home. He turned back to speak to Louie, but he was already on the other side of the door. Slowly he began walking to the car not with any excitement over what his night was to be, but rather a dread, a darkness, that he could not explain. What did Louie mean when he said "go home, son"? Home to South Oleander or home to the river house? Louie did not know about the river house. His mind wearied at the debate taking place.

He looked again at Sandra and tried to focus on the eager beautiful girl awaiting him. Maybe I will feel better after a night with her. Feel more like myself.

But there was darkness that hung over him like a black cloud that he could not shake or understand. He walked toward the girl in the car and got inside.

* * *

It was nine-thirty, and Bret was driving toward the river house. He was half way there when a light rain began to fall. He slowed down and drove on to the shoulder of the road. He stopped and put the top up, which of late had proven stubborn. Minutes later and with a little guidance the top was up.

He began driving again, reflecting on a night that held no precedent in his life. He had walked away from a beautiful and very eager girl. They entered the house and she had quickly pulled him to the couch, kissing him, and making her intentions known. And then he suddenly stopped.

She had asked what was wrong, and all he could muster was, "I need to go."

He left a stunning young girl behind and ran a mile to the country club to retrieve his car.

As he drove, he thought of Louie and their conversation. Louie always stood and watched him walk away, not wanting to miss any opportunity at possible extended conversation. Tonight, he turned and walked away. He was probably disgusted with me. Who could blame him? He passed the old convenience store where Louie assisted him that night, the same one where he picked up Teke to bring her to the country and safeguard her. She was alone now and though she wouldn't admit it, she was afraid. The fact that she had run him away was not an excuse and he knew it. He had let her down, and more importantly, he had let Money down. "What in the hell is wrong with me?" he screamed furiously into the night air.

Thoughts of Louie came again. He wasn't mean to him earlier, but he wasn't nice. The man has never been anything but good to me. Bret tried to find him when he returned to the club for his car to make amends, but he was gone for the evening.

He attempted to ease his mind by just writing it off as an old man that didn't matter. He wasn't successful because Louie did matter. Louie walked away out of disappointment in him, and the reason that it mattered was that Louie was one of the few people in this world that actually believed in him.

His mind raced back to Teke. Why did she run him away? Why was she so angry with him, but crying at the same time? He thought back to the previous Saturday night. The kiss, one kiss, seemed to have realigned everything.

He could still see the hurt in her eyes from when he left her earlier down by the river. Two girls, two weekends in a row that he ran from. Why did I run tonight? Last weekend was easier to understand. She was the sister of the only friend that I have in this entire world, or is it more than that? Is it because she is black?

He drove past the entrance to Vicky's in his state of confusion. He saw an access off to his left. He turned into it, remembering that it led all the way to the river.

He drove to the end of it and shut the engine off. The rain had stopped and he got out and sat on top of his car, peering out at the river in the darkness. Somehow, he wanted to make some sort of sense out of what was happening.

He had tried not to think about it, but he knew that she was not offended by the kiss, even if it had startled her, as it had him. Did she have feelings for him, despite all of the harsh things that she had said about him?

He returned to his car and cranked the engine. I kissed a girl that I was not trying to sleep with, and I felt something, something different. Why?

As he drove back to the highway, he thought again of how he had left her alone. He wondered if she had eaten anything. He looked at his watch. It was five after ten. Everything in Castle Hayne was closed, but in Rocky Point, there was a bustling hot dog place in the middle of nowhere that stayed open to eleven. The least he could do was take Teke a late dinner. He felt better at the thought of doing something nice as he drove toward Rocky Point.

It was a good deed that could prove tragic on a night when he should have never left Teke alone.

CHAPTER THIRTEEN

Terror in the night

Teke sat on the couch watching a movie about aliens invading earth and destroying nearly everything in their path. She found the entire concept of the movie silly, but it was passing time better then reading, which on this night took more concentration than she was capable of.

Fred, after graciously assisting with finishing off a batch of Jiffy Pop Popcorn, snored peacefully at her feet. She eyed the clock on the wall. It was almost ten. By now she assumed Bret was with some girl from the club. Well, that is what I sent him to do, she thought, as she slightly shrugged her shoulders.

She walked to the front of the house and looked out into the darkness. The rain began again, falling steadily, obscuring her vision. She felt the tears building but this time she willed them away. She returned to watching television with Fred. She heard a thumping sound. Fred poked his head up and growled menacingly. His snarl made her skin crawl.

She decided to overcome her fears and walked cautiously out on the front deck. The rain was light, and the coolness it provided felt good on her skin. Hearing nothing, she relaxed somewhat, feeling no desire to continue. Fred pawed at the door wanting to join her. She opened the door and he ran outside hastily. He barked without stopping as he took off around the side of the house.

"Fred, stop!" she called.

"Stupid dog, there is nothing out here." She stood for minutes listening to him bark and then suddenly his yelping ceased. "Fred," she called out. She heard nothing but the stillness offered on a country night.

She feigned being courageous and set off walking in the direction that Fred took. She walked to where Bret normally parked his car. There was no sign of Fred. She continued walking away from the house in the direction of Vicky's place. It was so difficult to see with the cloud cover and the slight rain that was falling.

"Fred," she called again angrily. "Come boy, come."

She grew more fearful with each stride. She passed a large laurel oak tree. Her anger at Fred was more of an attempt to cover the trepidation she felt. She felt like she was being watched. She took a few more steps and stopped by a pine tree. She tried to relax and tell herself that there was nothing to be afraid of.

Suddenly, a large hand grabbed her throat and tossed her roughly to the ground. She looked up and what she saw sent waves of terror throughout her body. They stood in front of her. Seven figures robed in white. Their eyes glowing with sadistic evil.

She started to speak, but was slapped hard across her mouth. She tasted the blood that trickled across her lips.

"You speak and I'll cut your tongue out," the lead figure said, holding the back of her hair roughly with his left hand. He pulled a large hunting knife out of its sheath with his right hand.

"Do you understand me, one word, one noise, one cry for help?" he stated calmly, as he pointed the knife at her. He touched the steel blade against her cheek. "Do we have an understanding?"

She looked up and nodded slowly, trying with all her might not to cry, or make any noise that would give the man in front of her a reason to use the weapon that he pressed against her.

"Stand up," he ordered.

She slowly rose to her feet. The group quietly and efficiently formed a circle around her. Two of them lit the torches that they carried. Black smoke rose into the night air and disappeared in the trees. The smell of kerosene permeated her nostrils. She heard a loud pounding noise that she could not place until she recognized it as her heart.

She noticed a crudely constructed cross behind the evil men. One man walked to it and touched his torch to the wood. The Christian symbol of hope was immediately engulfed in flames.

The light provided by the cross enabled Teke to see her attackers clearer. Illuminated eyes peered out of the white robes that covered them. This was the one place that she was thought to be safe.

She debated as to how they discovered her. Had she gotten too close to the river? Was it the bold trip to the movies? It didn't matter. They were here. All she could hope for now was that they wanted a mild demonstration of a cross burning. Silently she recalled the Bible verse she read earlier and she prayed to God for help. I will not be dismayed for your righteous right hand will uphold me.

They were quiet. Was it her imagination or was the night growing darker? No one spoke, save the man directly in front of her, who was clearly the leader.

He observed her closely. "You ain't bad looking for your kind," he crudely remarked. He moved closer to her, his face just inches from hers. She was tempted to spit in his ignorant face, but feared the repercussion of such an act. He shoved her toward the tree that he had hidden behind. "Turn around and put your arms around the tree," he commanded.

She did as she was told. The leader nodded at another member of the group, who pulled her hands around the tree tightly, banging her head slightly into it. He pulled out a rope and tied her wrists together securely.

"Please don't hurt me," she mumbled, as she noticed the rest of the group tighten the circle around her.

"What did I say to you? No talking." He moved to the other side of the tree where she could see him. He moved his knife up higher near her face.

"First we are going to have a little fun with you. Being as you are such a pretty Yankee nigger. After that, we are going to kill you and bury your dead carcass so deep in the woods that no one will ever find it. Now, we can make this as slow and painful as you like, or you can be a good girl, and maybe we will finish with you quickly. We got all night. Last word was your keeper was heading home with a fine looking white girl. She is one of God's creatures, not an animal like you."

Teke's mind raced from fear to wondering how he could possess so much information. They obviously had planned quite well for their excursion. Why did I send Bret away? She thought, before reconciling that he might have been hurt trying to save her. She didn't want that. She loved him. That feeling was never clearer then it was at this very moment. She wished that she could tell him that, not that it would be reciprocated. She still wanted him to know. She wasn't even angry if he did go home with someone. She drove him to it, and she knew that she could never have him.

The man walked around behind her. She felt his knife move slowly down her back, beginning at the base of her neck. She wasn't sure if he had cut her, but she heard the cutting away of her white button down cotton shirt.

Her whole body shook, but she didn't mutter a whisper. Next, she felt him press the knife against her light blue sweatpants that long ago had been made into shorts.

She saw the enjoyment grow in the eyes of the robed men in front of her as she stood trembling tied to a tree. I will not be dismayed. I will not be dismayed.

"Ever had a white man before?" he asked, not caring for an answer.

"I never thought an animal like your kind could look so good, but you are fine looking from head to toe," he said, laughing loudly.

She had no knowledge of what the devil's laugh might be like, but she was convinced that it sounded much like the sinister noise emitted from this man. Please God rescue me. I will not be dismayed. I will not be dismayed.

He handed his robe to one of the men as if the cloak of hatred was too sacred to be laid on the ground. He stood crudely behind her his hands on her shoulders. She prayed to God to let her die. Once again she recalled the verse and she whispered quietly, "I will not be dismayed. Your righteous right hand will uphold me."

The rain suddenly stopped. The woods were still, save the occasional popping from the flaming cross. She heard the heavy breathing of the man behind her. Felt his hot putrid breath on her neck. She caught a glimpse of something white in the brush in front of her. She stared until she saw clearly. Fred lie still in the edge of the bushes. She knew that he was dead. He had tried to protect her and they had killed him. She wept softly for Fred and for herself. She felt her heart pound even louder and hoped that it might burst inside her chest and deny the evil men their pleasure.

Suddenly, a voice disturbed the still night. "I don't think that you want to do that."

Teke listened closely. It was the voice of an old woman. Vicky, it had to be Vicky, though she had never heard or seen her.

The leader turned to face the unwelcome intruder. She appeared frail to him in every way, except for the Remington rifle that she was pointing at him with purpose.

"Old woman, you best go back to where it is you came from. I don't want to hurt a white woman, but I will."

Vicky eyed him, while keeping a close eye on the rest of the group. "You are on my property and you're poorly dressed. I suggest that you leave and take the rest of these trespassers with you."

"I doubt that you even know how to fire that rifle."

"That would be a mistake on your part, now wouldn't it? My husband taught me a long time ago how to use a rifle, but you don't have to believe me. You can try your luck. You might want to keep this in mind. Since I am roughly eight feet away from you maybe you should think the damage it will do from this close range. One thing is for certain. I won't miss," she said confidently. "And you won't live. Out of the corner of her eye, she noticed one of the other members inching slowly away from the group. "I assume you are the leader of this group of cowards, so I suggest that you tell that man of yours to move back to where he was. In fact, I want all of them to place their hands on top of their heads and stand still."

"And if they don't, old woman?"

She stepped closer. The rifle pointed directly at his chest.

"You're crazy, old woman."

"I might be." She noticed one of the members in the center of the group began slowly bending down.

"Tell that man of yours that plans to reach under his robe that if he stops right this moment, I won't shoot you." The man froze bent over with his hand at the bottom of the robe.

"And if he doesn't?" the leader smartly answered.

"I'll shoot you before he gets the chance to do harm. He may well get me, but you won't know about it. You will be in hell by then."

The man thought better of his action and stood up.

"Now, I'm getting a little impatient at being ignored by a bunch of trespassers. I want each one of you to take those robes off, and I want you to do it one at a time. I want all the weapons tossed on top of them." She moved closer to the leader.

"Are you ready to die, old woman?"

She pointed the rifle mere inches from his head. "You do as I say, or so help me God, I'll blow your empty head clear to the river. Drop that knife on the ground right now."

He debated her demand for a few seconds before deciding the knife was not the equal of the rifle pointed at him.

Teke still could not see the woman who was trying to save her. Her voice was calm, and if there was a trace of fear she could not detect it.

The leader looked at Vicky and then at his group. He calculated rightly that this old woman would indeed shoot him.

"Do as she says, boys," he commanded.

A small discussion broke out among the group. Vicky moved the gun closer, resting it against his left temple. "I guess we will find out just how respected a leader you are. Me, I've lived a long life, but you aren't more than forty I bet, maybe less."

"Get the robes off now and put the weapons down just as she said." His voice contained a new found urgency. The discussion ceased and the men did as directed.

"Now one more thing," Vicky stated. "I want all of them to strip to their underwear."

The group murmured its disapproval of her latest suggestion. She gently pushed the gun firmer against his head.

"Do as she says," the leader sighed.

"Now, you walk over there with your buddies."

He began to zip his pants up.

"Forget that. You strip too."

He complied without a word.

"Now move."

She watched him walk over to his group. "Now, all of you turn around." The men turned their backs to her.

"Kneel down and put your hands on top of your head."

One man, his voiced pitched in fear, shouted, "Are you going to shoot us in the back?"

"Maybe, if you don't move quicker."

She watched them do as instructed. She bent down to retrieve the knife on the ground, keeping the rifle pointed at them with her other arm. She cut the rope from Teke's hands with her left hand.

She picked the rifle back up. "Are you okay, child?" she asked quietly.

Teke looked at the old woman and nodded.

"Take one of those robes and stretch it out. Pile all the weapons in the middle of it, and then wrap them up. Tie a good strong knot. You can do that, can't you, child?"

"Yes, ma'am."

"That's good. Go ahead now."

Teke wrapped the three pistols and the seven knives in the sheet, and tied a good strong knot as instructed.

Vicky turned her attention back to the men. "Boys, I want you to walk down to the river in single file, nice and slow. I'll be right behind you. Now, move."

She looked at Teke. "What's your name, honey?"

"Teke, ma'am."

"You stay here and I'll be right back."

"I don't want to be alone," Teke whispered, her voice sounding to her as if she were a small child.

She smiled at her compassionately. "Okay, Teke. Stay behind me."

"Okay boys. Let's move and I want the leader in the back of the line. If one of you makes a false move you will need to elect a new leader."

The men did as they were told without offering a word. They walked down to the edge of the river where they stopped short of the water.

"I want you boys to start swimming for the other side."

The leader spoke first, "We can't do that. It's near a half mile."

"More like three hundred yards. Now start swimming."

"What about him?" he said, motioning to the man beside him. "He can't swim."

"You boys are a tight knit group, brotherhood and all that, right?"

"That's right."

"Well, then I suggest that you don't let him drown. Now, move. One move towards this shore and my charming disposition will be gone. I'll shoot the first man that turns back this way."

The men cursed silently as they entered the water. They began swimming in utter humiliation across the river.

They were twenty yards out when Vicky reminded them to swim straight across.

She looked at Teke. "Sit down, child."

They watched the figures slowly make progress toward the other side. They were half way across when Vicky fired three shots over their heads, increasing their pace.

"We can go now, child. Let's go to my house and get you cleaned up."

"But, what..."

"Don't worry, they got no clothes, no weapons, and they are tired."

They began to walk and when they reached the area of the ordeal Teke walked to Fred. She knelt down and touched his still-warm body. His throat had been cut and there was blood all down his white chest.

"He tried to help me and they killed him," she said as she sobbed.

Vicky laid the rifle down on the ground. She put her arms around Teke and held her strongly. "You cry all you want, child."

When Teke's crying subsided, Vicky looked into her eyes and smiled. "Now, child, I think that you owe me some back rent, don't you?"

Teke looked into the kindness of the old woman's eyes. "You knew, but how, since when?"

"Since the first night that he brought you here. You live as long as me, you get a feel for things. That boy, I don't know why he just didn't ask me."

"You wouldn't have said no."

"Of course not," she exclaimed gruffly. "My guess is that he had a good reason for hiding you. You look a lot like that boy that was out here with him before working on the house. Now would you two be related?"

"That's my brother."

"I thought as much. He's a fine looking boy. Now let's get you cleaned up."

"You don't seem anything like how Bret described you."

"A mean old cantankerous woman, you mean, that doesn't like him."

"Yes," Teke said sheepishly.

"I am mean, and there are things about Bret that I don't like. But he's my grandson, and..."

"You love him," Teke said, finishing her sentence.

Vicky snorted something that was not to be deciphered by the human ear. "Let's get to my house."

"What about Fred?" Teke asked.

"Let's get to the house. We'll bury him later."

She followed the old woman carrying the rifle.

They walked the rest of the way to Vicky's in silence. They entered the house. "You sit down, child, and I'll get some medicine and take a look at you."

Teke had forgotten her wounds in the aftermath of her rescue. She felt the dried blood on her lip and the stinging of the air on her back.

Vicky led her to the kitchen table and sat her down in a chair. She left the room and returned with a warm rag and medicine.

She began cleaning Teke's face. "He cut my back," Teke said, calmly.

Vicky said nothing and finished cleaning her face. "Lean in and let me look at it."

She examined Teke's back. "It's okay. It just did cut the skin, kind of a slit like an oyster cut. It will be sore, but you don't need stitches."

"Did they hurt you any other way?" Vicky asked.

"No, ma'am."

"That's good, honey. Now my name is Vicky. It's not ma'am."

"Yes, Vicky."

"I could have been assaulted twice in less than two months and I am still a virgin," Teke blurted out. She then proceeded to tell this stranger about the event in Philadelphia that started the chain of events that drove her to hide out here. The old woman listened intently without offering a word.

Moments passed quietly before Teke asked, "Why did Bret think that you would be mad about me staying here?"

"He doesn't know me for one reason. For another, I guess you grow up in the south and, maybe you assume everyone looks down on someone because of the color of their skin. I've always thought that it was what was inside someone that mattered."

The clock chimed eleven times. Vicky finished cleaning the wounds.

"You go take a bath and clean all the grime off of you. You will be fine. After your bath, I'll put some medicine on your cuts to make sure you don't get any infection. You stay here tonight. I have a spare room." She paused for a moment before asking, "Why did that boy leave you alone tonight?"

"I sent him away. We had an argument. I know he's tired of watching over me."

Vicky looked at the young girl who had been through pure hell on this night. She was defending her grandson despite what she had been through. There was more to the look in this young girl's eyes than an argument about a boy's obligation to protect her. Of that she was certain.

CHAPTER FOURTEEN

Light of morning

It was past eleven when Bret drove past Vicky's in route to the river house. He was surprised to see lights, but gave the matter little thought.

He didn't see the smoldering cross, or the dog that lay still. He got out of the car and walked up the steps, carrying a box containing hot dogs and chips.

"Teke," he called, as he reached the deck. He approached the door and found it slightly ajar. An uneasy feeling swept over him as he cautiously proceeded inside.

"Teke," he called again. Receiving no response he walked upstairs to check her bedroom. The bed was untouched.

He paused to think things through. A dreadful feeling swept over him that he tried to fight off. His mind played out different scenarios. Was she down by the river? No, she would be too afraid, he thought, answering his own question.

Maybe she got mad enough to leave, but where would she go? He walked back down the stairs. He sat the box of food down on the kitchen table and searched the room for a flashlight, finding one on top of the refrigerator.

Slowly, he walked back outside. He decided to check her hiding place down by the river anyway. She was not there. He retraced his steps back to the house, and then walked behind it.

He smelled smoke and followed in the direction of the smell. His throat tightened and he could hear the hammering of his heart when he discovered the smoldering cross. There was a pile of clothes, which only served to confuse him more. He searched for more clues and discovered Fred lying still in the brush.

Slowly, he walked over to him. He knelt down and touched him. He was dead. He looked closer, discovering that his throat was slit. Everything in him wanted to panic but he fought the temptation. I have to be cool. First, where is Teke? She's got to be all right. She's my responsibility. He rarely ever spoke to God, but he did now. "God, please let Teke be okay."

He continued walking, searching for clues but finding none. He was outside Vicky's. He had no choice.

He knocked on the door. Vicky walked to the door with rifle in hand and peered cautiously through the small glass opening. Seeing it was Bret, she opened the door. She stood the rifle in the corner.

He walked in not knowing where to begin, which questions to ask first. She saw the look on his face and felt such compassion. He was not the calm cool boy he normally was. He was scared.

"Vicky, have you seen anything tonight, or heard anything? Someone killed Fred and there is..."

She interrupted him, wanting to remove the torment that was raging through him. "I know son, but everything is okay."

"No, it's not okay. Nothing is okay. I've deceived you." He rubbed his hands furiously through his hair as if he were trying to rub all the bad thoughts.

Vicky tried again to tell him that she knew, and that everything was okay. But he kept rambling on about deceiving her and letting his friend down. He was somewhere else and right now he didn't seem to hear anything that she said.

Teke, hearing the voices inside the bathroom wrapped the navy blue bath towel around her body snuggly and opened the door to investigate. She peered around the corner.

He saw the figure out of the corner of his eye. He was frozen for a moment. He noticed the bruise on her face and the swollen lip.

Relief filled his body. She was okay. His feet seemed to float over the floor as he walked toward her. He would never be able to recall walking to her and he would barely remember what he did next. He embraced her, holding her tightly, apologizing repeatedly. "I'm so sorry for leaving you. I'm so sorry." He held her tightly, refusing to let go, as he continued to apologize.

He held her so firmly that it brought pain to the wound on her back, but she said nothing.

She tried to reassure him, "Bret, I'm okay. It's not your fault. I ran you off. I'm sorry. I wasn't really mad at you today. I was just hurt, and I reacted foolishly."

He refused to let go of her, unaware of Vicky, or that Teke was wearing only a towel that was struggling to remain in place.

"I promised your brother, your father, and I left you."

"Bret," she said sternly. "Listen to me. It is okay. Now, I am wearing only a towel in case you haven't noticed. Maybe you'd better turn me loose."

He let go of her. She smiled warmly at him. He backed away awkwardly as he remembered that Vicky was in the room. Questions flowed through his mind but he didn't know where to begin.

"Bret, your grandmother saved my life tonight."

Bret looked at Vicky astonished. "But how, and why?"

"First of all, I am a lady, despite what I have been put through tonight. Would you please go to the house and bring me some clothes, then we'll tell you what happened," Teke said evenly.

"Yes," he stammered. "I'll be right back." He walked to the door, stopping at Vicky. His eyes searched hers with a plethora of questions.

Before he could speak, she said, "Your mom would be proud of you."

The words pierced his heart. She found a tender spot in him that had been stored away for far too long.

"Do you really mean that?" he asked gently.

She smiled at him and softly said, "Have you ever known this tough old bird to say anything that she didn't mean?"

It wasn't clear who moved first, but suddenly they were embracing each other. Teke watched and began to cry. Somehow, this terrible night had broken down an icy barrier between a grandmother and her grandson, and she found such warmth in that. It was a tender moment that seemed out of place on such a horror-filled night, but yet it was also perfect in its timing.

They pulled away from each other and Vicky smiled warmly at him. "Don't you think that it's about time for your friend to get a little more than that towel to wear?"

Bret returned the smile. "Yes, ma'am, I do."

"You know what you can do with that ma'am stuff, don't you?"

Her statement lacked its usual gruffness because the warm smile never once left her face as she looked at the boy in front of her. The boy that she had wanted for so very long to have in her life.

Before he made it to the door, Teke stopped him. "Why did you come home?"

"To bring you dinner," he said.

She smiled slightly. "So, where were you getting dinner from this late?"

"A hot dog place down the road."

"How many hot dogs did you buy?" Vicky asked.

"Eight."

"Good, bring them. I've worked up an appetite. I'll get the soft drinks out."

He opened the door when she called to him. "Bret, did you see that pile of clothes in between our houses?"

"Yes."

"Be a good idea to grab those and bring those with you."

"Okay," he answered softly.

Bret retrieved all the requested items and drove his car back to Vicky's. He walked in and placed the robes and all they contained on the floor. He put the food on the kitchen table and then walked to the bathroom. He tapped lightly on the door. "Teke," he called out. She opened the door slightly and he gave her the clothes she requested.

He walked back to the kitchen. Vicky was mixing a drink.

"What have you got there, Vicky?" he asked, slightly amused.

"It's bourbon and coke. Yes, once in a while I have a drink. I just never let it get the best of me like it did Ralph."

Bret smiled at the memory of his grandfather, his mentor.

"Do you want one?" she asked.

"Sure."

"Promise me, boy, that it will never become a daily thing."

"I promise."

She handed him a drink, and took a swallow of hers.

Bret thought back to the day he had returned to this land, never dreaming of where it would lead. He thought of Vicky saying that Ralph liked him.

"Vicky, did Granddad really like me?"

She looked at him with unmistaken tenderness in her eyes. "He loved you, son. It just wasn't his way to say it."

He mumbled, "Seems that way for more than just him."

"I think you were a last chance for him. You reminded him of someone he once lost."

Teke entered the room and looked at the Coke they were having and innocently requested her own.

Bret winked at Vicky, and she smiled mischievously. She walked to the counter and with her back turned she innocently mixed another bourbon and coke. She handed it to her and was amused when Teke asked why the glasses were so small.

Teke took one swallow and quickly discovered why. She choked as they laughed at her.

"Okay, what is this?"

"Bourbon and coke," Bret offered.

"After the night I've had, I think I'll keep it," Teke said as she took another swallow that went down only slightly smoother this time.

The three of them ate lukewarm hot dogs and potato chips. Teke surprised herself by discovering an appetite on such a horrid night.

The two women filled Bret in on the night's events. The story seemed unbelievable to him as he listened to every detail.

The story completed, he asked if the men used any names among themselves, but they had not.

He deliberated a few moments before speaking what he wished not to be true. "The men knew that I was at the club, and they knew when and who I left with. My dear old father is connected to this."

"No, Bret," Teke said in disbelief.

He shook his head, dismissing her argument. "There is no mistake about who set this in motion."

Teke's heart seemingly stopped when she remembered the most vulnerable area that Bret's father could attack him with. "No, Bret, Alex. Oh, my God. I'm so sorry. God, you can't lose him over me, for helping my family."

Now it was Teke who felt the burden of guilt, but he reassured her. "I've got time. He's still in Chicago for at least a month, and he won't act quickly."

"Why?" Teke asked.

"He won't want any chance of being tied to the Klan, and he won't suspect that I know that he was behind all of this. He'll cut me out, at the latest, right before school begins in late August, but not before the trial ends."

"How do you know that, son?" Vicky quizzed him.

"The trial is what's most important now. He won't leave Chicago until it's finished. Also, he will want the satisfaction of personally evicting me from the house, family, and Alex."

"You can't mean that, Bret," Teke said, not believing a father could enjoy being so cruel to his own flesh and blood.

"We are not talking about a dad like you have," Bret said softly, but with such tenderness that it brought a tear to her eye.

"Bret, you might lose Alex. I can't stand that. I am so sorry. Can't you reason with him? I'll leave for D.C. tomorrow. Tell him anything to keep Alex."

He touched her arm, trying to reassure her. "Don't worry I won't lose him."

She tried to interrupt but he stopped her. "Trust me, okay. You stay here as long as you need. It won't do any good for you to leave now, unless you want to. He knows, and this was my last chance to be his son, to toe the line, and follow in the family footsteps. That's okay, because after what he has done on this night I can no longer be a part of him, in anyway. Not for school. Not for wealth. Not for any-thing. I've been doing some thinking and I believe that I may have a way to break free from him and take my little brother with me."

"But how?" Teke asked.

"I don't have the details all ironed out. Up until now it was just a dream, but now I believe I can beat him. Maybe it is because now I have to. There is no other way."

Vicky spoke. "Do you think that Walker ordered her killed? I can't believe that he would be a part of that, and you know how little re-gard I hold of him."

"First of all, his hands were not near the direct order. He is not foolish enough to deal with the Klan. He had someone set all of this up. My guess is that the Klan was not supposed to do anything but scare her. Get her out of town before he gets embarrassed over the situation, but I guess when you deal with the Klan, well, plans aren't always carried out the way they're supposed to."

"I can't believe any of this," Teke said, shaking her head.

"Well, believe it," Bret said, unflinching.

"How can you beat such a man?"

He wanted to answer no more questions. He would do this with as little involvement from others as possible.

"Trust me," he said sternly. "Do either of you think that I would leave my little brother to be raised by that man and my brothers? It's late, Teke, let's go," he said, rising from his chair, before issuing one more statement. "Not a word of any of this to Alex. He gets upset anytime that he thinks there is a chance that we will be separated."

The women nodded in agreement. Bret and Teke started for the door.

"Wait one minute," Vicky requested. She grabbed the rifle. "Take this." "I don't believe they will try again. I really don't, but just in case. You know how to use it, don't you Bret?"

"You know that Granddad taught me. What about you, for your protection?"

"You don't think I'd give my last gun away do you? Ralph had a collection."

He remembered the earlier conversation that had been cut short. "You said that I reminded Granddad of someone."

Vicky thought about the subject that started Ralph's affair with a bottle. It proved to be an affair that ultimately killed him.

"There was a boy who grew up down the road, Jackson Humphrey. He and your mother were friends from the time they were old enough to walk. The two of them were inseparable. They were in the ninth grade when romance entered the picture.

"They dated all through high school, and a couple of years after graduation they were engaged. Ralph loved that boy like he was his own son. He worked for Ralph when he wasn't in school. They were going to be partners. They began the house that you are finishing a long time ago. Your mother and Jackson went to the mountains once. He had kinfolk up near Boone. Your mom saw an A-frame house built on top of a mountain and she decided that she wanted a house like that. Ralph and Jackson tried to tell her that an A-frame was out of place here, but she wouldn't hear of it. Next thing you know they were building it. It's the only one in the area that I know of.

"Your father met your mother one day. Her car had run out of gas in town. He saw her and stopped to help. She was such a beautiful girl, and she became a prize your father had to have. I guess it was like winning another court case to him. She resisted initially, but he won her over eventually with all of his big show and promises of riches. They were married a short time later. It nearly killed Ralph, but fate chose a long lingering death for him. He saw Walker for what he was. He knew that she was about to make the mistake of a lifetime. Maybe, if he had given her time to see. Well, she resented him telling her what to do, and she married Walker, probably out of spite. It's hard to blame her. We were always struggling and here comes this smooth talker with promises of a big house and trips around the world. She fell for the package, if not for him."

"What happened to Jackson?"

"He couldn't take it. He enlisted in the service. He died in a training accident six months later."

"Was he about Mom's height, medium build, with light brown hair?"

"Yes, but how in the world could you possibly know that?"

Bret was recalling the dream in which he saw Vicky and Ralph, his mother and a man he did not recognize waving to him from the deck of the old house.

"I saw him in a dream," he softly said. "So, it was like I was a second chance for Granddad to finish the house."

"He did love you. You gave him life when he was dying. You added time to his life, good time."

He smiled at her and took the rifle. "Thank you for everything."

She turned to Teke. "Dinner is at eleven-thirty every day. I will expect you here and don't be late. You come here anytime you want, you hear me?"

"Thank you, Vicky," Teke said as she hugged her.

They drove the short drive that knifed through the woods. They got out of the car and Bret wanting to spare her the ordeal of watching Fred be buried suggested she go inside and he would be right in.

She was not fooled in the least. "No, Fred died trying to save me. I want to help."

"Okay," Bret said, and he went under the house to obtain shovels.

Together they dug in silence through the rich black wet dirt. They finished the hole and Teke asked Bret to wait. She went inside for one of her oversized nightshirts.

"I want him buried in this, so he'll be warm," she said as the tears flowed down her face, finding the dark soil below.

Bret merely nodded, and then worked the shirt underneath him. He tied the shirt around him and positioned him gently into the grave.

"He tried to save me, Bret. You should have heard him growl. Why would anyone kill a sweet old dog like Fred?"

Bret remained silent as he finished the grave, knowing there could be no answer to her question.

"Bret, will you make a marker for his grave?"

"Yes, I will, tomorrow. Now, let's call it a night, okay?"

"Okay," she said as she accepted the hand he offered to her. He pulled her to her feet and they walked inside. "I am going to shower, okay?"

He looked at her strangely and said, "You took one at Vicky's."

She blinked back tears and muttered, "I can still feel his hands on me."

He nodded gently with understanding. "I will wait right outside the door. Okay?"

She started to speak and he gently put a finger to her lip. "No arguments. Go ahead and shower."

She showered for thirty minutes till the hot water turned lukewarm. She opened the door and he was sitting on the floor by the door his head on top of his knees. She placed her hand on his head and gently rubbed his hair. "Thank you," she said. He rose and looked at her. He breathed out so hard that he actually whistled.

He touched her wet hair delicately. "You're beautiful, Teke, you know that? Even on a night when you have been through hell, you are still beautiful. All this tonight is my fault." He hugged her gently, aware now of the cut on her back. "I am so glad you are safe."

She let go of him and cupped his face in her hands. "Listen to me, okay?"

He closed his eyes and gave the tiniest shake of agreement.

"I forgive you. Now let that be the end of any guilt. Focus on what you need to do to protect Alex." She let go of him and he opened his eyes and smiled softly.

Teke looked at the clock on the wall as they went toward their separate bedrooms. It was past one.

"Bret."

He turned to her. "Yes."

"That girl you left with tonight. Was she pretty?"

"Yes, she was."

"I know that it is not any of my business, but did you go home with her?"

"Yes."

"Oh."

"I didn't sleep with her, Teke, if that is what you want to know."

"You didn't? Did she say no?"

"No, she said yes. I said no."

"But why?"

He sighed audibly. "I had hot dogs to pick up. Now, let's go to bed, okay. Try and get some sleep. If you get scared, just call for me."

It was an hour later. Bret was soundly asleep, while Teke lay awake in her bed thinking about the boy in the next room. During her ordeal, she was certain that she would tell Bret the truth, plain and simple. She loved him. It wasn't that she felt the love would be reciprocated. That would be nice, but it was not what was important.

She made a decision, as she lay there unable to sleep. She rose from the bed and went to the bathroom. Her bruise was the first thing that caught her attention in the mirror, followed by her slightly swollen lip.

She released her hair from the small ponytail that it was in. She brushed it away from her face, letting it fall naturally on her shoulders.

She took off the tee shirt and replaced it with a long sleeve, soft pink, button-down shirt. She removed the gym shorts that Bret retrieved for her earlier in the evening. She stood there gazing at the girl the mirror contained. She trembled at her reflection but another part of her, the part that was dominating her thoughts now, was calm, assured about what she wanted to do. It was her heart. She easily could have died tonight. She did not want to die afraid or be held captive by what she could not have.

She walked to his bedroom. The door was open. She entered quietly, and stopped by his bed. The moonlight filtered through the glass behind his bed and she could see him sleeping so peacefully. Why this had come to be she didn't know. She only knew, as she looked at him, one thing for certain, and that was that as improbable as it was she loved him.

"Bret," she said softly. "Bret."

He woke, thinking that he was dreaming. He saw the girl standing over him. His eyes rested on the legs that he had secretly watched countless times as they moved so eloquently across a room.

"Teke, are you all right?" he asked, rising quickly.

She placed her hand gently on his chest, persuading him to lie down as she sat down on the side of the bed. "I'm fine. Don't worry. I have something to tell you and I want you to please promise me that you'll let me finish before you answer."

"But—"

"Promise me, please."

"Okay, Teke. I promise."

She shuddered quickly.

"Are you cold?" he asked

"Just a chill."

He lifted the covers up and moved to the far side of the bed. "Knowing how long-winded you are you might as well lie down."

She stood over him and looked at him intently.

"I didn't mean anything was going to happen, okay?" he said.

She nodded softly and lay down beside him. She turned on her side and faced him, and slowly she began to talk. "Bret, I could have lost my virginity twice in a very short time and the hell of it is that both times were by an ugly violence. I know I am supposed to wait for marriage and all that."

Bret shifted uncomfortably in his bed wondering just where this conversation was going.

"I've been lying in my bed and thinking that I want to give myself to my first love. Who knows if I'll have another? Look at my father. He has loved my mother and that is all. I'm not asking you to return anything. What I'm asking is that you allow me to give myself to the man I love," she said, placing her hand on his chest, rubbing him slightly.

Bret sat straight up. "You mean me?" he asked foolishly.

"Who else do you think I've been talking about?"

"But—"

She placed her hand gently over his mouth. "But you are white and I'm black?"

"No, it's not that."

"What then?"

"How? I don't understand. You didn't even like me to begin with."

She chuckled softly. "That changed. I love you, Bret. I have never been surer of anything in my seventeen years of living. I may not be able to have you, and you may not feel the same toward me. None of that changes how I feel about you. I know this. I want you tonight. I want to love you for one night, even if that is all I can ever have. I don't want to wait and think about this any longer."

"And if you regret it later?" he asked.

"I'll never regret it. I'll only regret it if I lie in the next room alone and let our moment, our time together pass."

"Teke, I don't know. Your brother, I..."

"He never has to know. I've seen you look at me. I've seen tenderness in your eyes for me. Maybe it's not love, but there is feeling there. You can't deny that."

Moments passed before Bret responded, "I won't deny it."

She smiled at him and rubbed his chest softly. "I have seen you look at me, especially my legs. But you like the rest also, don't you? I know you said that I was beautiful. I know I am okay but I know I am not that. "

She waited for a witty remark, but what she got was the truth. "You are far more than okay. Don't say that about yourself." He closed his eyes. "It would be impossible for any man to look at you and not be attracted to you. You are as pretty as any woman I have ever seen." His smile contained a hint of mischief as he added, "And your legs are off the charts. I've stared at them a million times."

"Then, let's have this one night. Let me give myself to you for one night, with no thought of tomorrow."

She kissed him, barely touching his lips before rising slightly to look into his eyes, and then she began kissing him passionately, ignoring her swollen lip. She rose and stood beside the bed, smiling as she looked at him in the moonlight. Slowly, she unbuttoned her shirt, dropping it to the floor below, before removing her panties.

She stood there for a moment, completely at ease in her nakedness. She smiled at the boy below her.

He thought to say no, but he couldn't. He took her hand and gently guided her to his bed.

* * *

It was early the next morning. Wally hesitantly joined his father for breakfast.

"Things didn't go so well at home last night."

"What do you mean?" Walker Sr. answered gruffly.

Wally repeated the story as it had been told to him early that morning by his contact.

"I tell you to see that they are scared away from each other and you involve the Klan. Are you crazy? I wanted some of the good old boys to visit her, not the damn Klan dressed to rape and kill."

"It got out of hand, but they'll finish the job now. They are anxious to get the old woman too."

"Are you nuts? You make sure that no one goes near that property again? She took their clothes, and probably the dumb sons of bitches had their wallets complete with ID. If they got arrested the next thing you know they'll want us to represent them. We don't need any ties to the Klan. Damn, boy. You fix it now. I'll deal with that ungrateful son of mine when I return home. It's sure as hell obvious that you can't handle this."

Wally left in search of a phone, while Walker Sr. lit his first cigarette of the day. "God almighty," he sighed as he drew heavily on his cigarette. The smoke lifted toward the ceiling. "God almighty," he repeated.

* * *

Elma reached across the bed seeking comfort as she had a million times before. There was no one there. "Louie," she called out.

Hearing no reply, she rose, and walked to the front door. She pushed the screen door open and found Louie asleep in the rocker, with his worn tattered Bible in his lap. She gave him that same Bible on the night of their wedding. Many times she offered to buy him a new one and he refused every time. "Louie," she whispered.

He woke and looked at her warmly.

"You never came to bed? You been out here all night? Why?"

"You went to bed last night and I came in a few minutes later. You were already asleep. I was standing and looking at you. You always so beautiful to me, Elma. But then I got this horrible feeling come over me. I knew it was Bret and something was wrong. I saw him earlier at the club. He was upset. God give me this dream or vision and I don't want to fail."

"You won't," she said sweetly. "Maybe things got better after Bret left the club."

"No they got much worse. Somehow I just know it. I could feel evil. It worried me so bad I looked up his phone number and a girl answered and said he was not home. So I sat and prayed here all night till I fell asleep just before dawn."

Elma was no stranger to spiritual revelation. She believed every word Louie told her about that vision weeks ago. The man never told her a lie about anything. She looked at the Bible opened in his lap. "What were you reading?"

He looked up at her and then back down at the words that he could recite by heart. "I opened the Bible to this page and my eyes went to this scripture. Here, you read it."

She took the Bible from him. "Where do I begin?"

"It is just one scripture and I read it bout a million times last night and this morning. Isaiah 41:10."

She spoke the words. *"Fear thou not; for I am with thee: be not dismayed; for I am thy God; I will strengthen thee; yea, I will help thee; yea, I will uphold thee with the right hand of my righteousness."*

She finished and placed her hand on his shoulder. God, how she loved this man. He was as kind and decent a man as she had ever known and he was hers. Hers and God's. "Louie, Bret is okay. You hear me. He is okay."

"How you know?"

"That is why you were directed to that scripture. He is okay. You will not fail him or God. I will hear no more talk of that."

"You always believe in me, Elma."

"You always give me good reason to," she answered quickly.

"Give me that Bible and go to bed. You have to work this evening. I will cook breakfast for you when you wake up."

"Even if it is lunch time?" Louie asked, like a small child.

She grinned at him. Breakfast food was always his favorite. He considered it a big treat to have breakfast fare for a meal other than the early morning.

"What you gonna do?" he asked.

"I am going to sit here and pray for Bret. He is going to need wisdom to do what he has to do."

"What does he have to do?"

"I did not get that instruction."

CHAPTER FIFTEEN

The plan

Bret woke shortly after ten from a few hours of very sound sleep. He felt the girl next to him and guilt promptly consumed him along with other thoughts that puzzled him deeply.

Sex had been a ritual for him since the first time. That was when he was fourteen. The girl was Allison. She was sixteen and Alex's baby sitter. Last night was no ritual. He didn't understand what he had felt, but he had felt, and that was definitely unchartered waters.

His thoughts drifted to Alex and he knew that he had to foolproof his plan. There was one distinct advantage that he held over his father in the battle that was to be waged. He hoped that his father's arrogance would prove his downfall. There was no way the old man would think that he or anyone else for that matter could prove a worthy adversary.

He looked at his best friend's sister, asleep in his bed, and remorse swept over him. There was no way that Money would ever understand this. How could he, when I don't? He turned away from her as if that could make what transpired disappear.

"Don't do it. Do not make last night anything less beautiful then it was. Please, do that for me, if you never do anything else. You did not betray anyone."

He turned to her and forced a smile. "You know, Teke, a few weeks ago, I could have cared less what anyone in this world besides Alex thought. Now, I'm thinking of Money and your dad and how I would hate it if they were disappointed in me."

"It will be okay. They don't need to know. I'll call them tomorrow and explain that I have to go to D.C. Your father knows and I think that it would be easier on you if I'm gone. He may change his mind and give you another chance."

"And if I don't want another chance?"

"You have to try, for Alex first, and because you don't want to live poor, Bret."

"Maybe being poor is not part of my plan," he responded, with a playful twinkle in his eye. He continued, "How can I take care of my little brother if I'm poor?"

"I can't take that chance. I have to go. I'll always have last night. And it is a memory I will always cherish."

Bret had thought for so long of how he wanted her to leave, but now the idea of that left him with an aching emptiness.

He rose from the bed. "I need to go pick up Alex," he said, looking at his watch, noticing the time was ten-thirty. "I'll meet you at Vicky's for dinner."

He was back at Vicky's with five minutes to spare. He entered with Alex, who had been told only that Vicky had joined the tight knit group that knew of Teke's hide out, and that it was okay.

The meal prepared by Vicky consisted of roast beef, butter beans, rice and gravy, and biscuits. The mood that accompanied the meal was the most festive that Vicky's house had seen in far too many years to recall.

There was a glow in Vicky's eyes as she watched the two boys eat. She had made some progress with Alex, and now with the distance between Bret and her narrowed considerably, Alex would follow suit. She was as happy as she had been in a long time. She still maintained her gruff demeanor, but a smile hidden away for far too long was difficult to suppress.

At one point, Bret insisted on calling her ma'am, trying to rile her. She acted angry, but her performance was not authentic. Alex sensing the playfulness took things a step further and began calling her grandmother.

Dinner was finished and Bret left with Alex to begin working on the house. The cabinet work in the kitchen was proving quite tedious, and at one point, Bret thought about hiring a professional cabinet-maker. He quickly decided against it. He would build them.

Teke remained behind, insisting on helping Vicky with the dishes. Teke was drying the last dish when Vicky asked her how long she planned to stay.

"I'm going to call my father tomorrow and see if I can fly to D.C."

"Well, if that is what you want, child, but this is my land and you are welcome to stay."

Teke nodded slightly, appreciative, "Thank you, but if I leave things will be easier for him."

"And for you?"

"Oh, I'll get by. I can be bored in D.C. as easy as here. At least I can get out, go places, you know?"

Vicky nodded, and then her directness floored Teke. "And what will you do about being in love with my grandson?"

"Ah, but..." Teke stammered, unable to coax any words from her mouth.

Vicky continued, "I saw the way you looked at him last night. It had to hurt when he held you so tightly with that fresh wound on your back. Don't fret about it. I don't condemn you. He's good looking, takes after his grandmother," she said without a smile.

Teke knew that it was useless to pretend. "Do you think that it is wrong?"

"It's difficult, child. There is no mistaking that. But wrong, I prefer to let God be the judge of that."

"You believe that, don't you? A God who is fair and impartial who really doesn't care about..."

"He sees the heart, child. The rest is just window dressing."

"And he does not mind that I love a white man."

"I don't think that it is on the top of his to do list."

"I prayed for help last night. Why is it that it is so easy to pray when we need help but so much of the other times we just go our way?"

There was silence for a few moments as Vicky looked at the young lady in front of her who had dropped her head. She reached out delicately and placed her hand under Teke's chin, lifting it gently. What a beautiful face and too much sadness in it. "Do not drop your head to anyone," she said evenly, but with warmth that Teke felt in her soul. Teke returned the gesture with a slight smile.

"I was dead asleep last night and I woke abruptly and I felt a horrible evilness. That is why I showed up with a rifle."

Teke nodded and understood. She thought of the scripture she read and wondered if that was her warning or her assurance.

"I didn't plan any of this with Bret. I couldn't stand him initially."

"That's easy to understand," Vicky replied crisply.

"It just happened, Vicky. I don't know how to explain it."

"Don't try. Love can't be explained. It's a feeling between people that someone on the outside looking in can never truly understand."

"He doesn't love me, Vicky."

"Maybe, maybe not. I won't pretend to know that. He cares though. You could see that in his eyes last night. There is more at stake for him than an obligation."

Her words soothed Teke. "And you are not against Bret and me? I mean, if it could be," she quickly added, searching Vicky's eyes.

"Oh, I'm not for it, child. Black and white together in the south. You would have to be a fool to be for that. That's trouble for sure, and maybe one day, it will be okay, but not now. You're asking for ridicule and scorn. Who would choose that? You do what you think is best, Teke. Now, do you think that my grandson would mind if I walked down with you and looked at the house?" she asked, changing the subject.

"I think that he would like that very much," she said with a smile.

As they departed for the short walk to the river house, Teke said with a chuckle, "Thank you, Vicky. You're nothing like Bret said you were."

"Oh, don't kid yourself. I am a mean, old, cantankerous woman," she said, never breaking stride.

Teke called out as they entered the house. "We have company."

Bret and Alex looked up, seeing Vicky. Bret watched her as she walked around observing all that had taken place.

Finally, she spoke. "I'm not sure Ralph could have done much better. He sure would be pleased with your work."

Bret savored her high praise. "What do you think that you will do with it, Vicky? You could sell it."

She frowned at him. "We hung on to this land through the depression and other hard times. It will never be sold while I am alive, not one parcel."

"Maybe you could rent it out as a fishing camp. It would provide extra income."

"Strangers coming and going on my land," she huffed with indignation. "No, I don't think so." She eyed the surroundings once again and added, "Yes, Ralph would be quite pleased with the carpenter he taught."

"I wish he was here right now. The cabinets—I want them to be just right. He was so good at that, his specialty among specialties."

Vicky left minutes later and the boys continued working on the kitchen cabinets. Teke walked down to the river and sat in the chair that awaited her in her hiding place. It did not seem the same without Fred.

She sat there deliberating about last night. She wished for a different time, a different place, where they would be free to explore each other, without hiding, without hatred. She knew that such a world did not exist. Maybe it would one day. Her people, just a few short years ago, could not even drink from the same water fountain as a white person. There were still schools that had yet to really integrate and that was not only true in the south but the north as well. She wished right now that she felt more passionate about all of this, but what she felt the most fervor for was the man she could not have. She heard footsteps coming down the path. She knew they belonged to Alex.

He walked to her and smiled slightly, with a hint of sadness in his eyes.

"Bret wants me to ask if you wanted to stay at the big house tonight, or here. He said that he would get lots of pizza for us if that is what you wanted." He was struggling with his words. "I mean he will get pizza wherever we stay tonight."

"I would like to stay here and I hope you will stay and eat with us."

"I want to. And the pizza, is that okay?"

She was touched by his thoughtfulness, and the charm offered by a small southern boy. "That would be great."

He hesitated, and she could tell that there was something else he wanted to say. "Are you okay, Alex?"

"Yeah, I'm okay." He took a couple of steps toward the house, before turning back to her. "Are you leaving tomorrow?"

"I'm not sure yet. I have to call tonight."

The small child in front of her kicked slightly at the ground. "I don't want you to go."

She refused to cry in front of the sweet child in front of her, though it took every ounce of her strength not to.

"Let's have a good time tonight and not worry about me leaving. Will you do that for me?"

Alex nodded. "I'll try."

"Will you do one other thing for me?"

"Yes."

"When I do leave, will you take really good care of Bret?"

"Yes. You like him, don't you?" he added.

"Of course, I do, and I like his little brother, too. Do you think that I could have a hug?"

The precious little boy in front of her said nothing as he stepped closer and wrapped his arms around her. She held him tightly in return as one lone tear escaped and landed on the little boy's shoulder.

* * *

Darkness had fallen. Bret dropped Alex at Vicky's, with plans to drive Teke to an isolated pay phone.

Vicky, hearing of their plan, insisted that they use her phone. Bret was wary of that. He thought paranoia might be getting the best of him, but he respected his father's ability enough to not risk the phone being compromised.

He drove Teke to a phone booth that he spotted the previous night on his way to get the hot dogs. The phone booth was around the side of a hardware store that closed hours earlier.

As Teke got out, he said, "I need to speak with Money."

"You're not going to tell him?"

"And lose the only friend I have? No, I need a favor from him."

He sat in his car as Teke talked for several minutes before she summoned him to the phone. He tried to read her eyes as he took the phone, but he could decipher little.

"Money, what's up?"

"Not much, buddy. I'm ready to come home."

"How much longer will it be?"

"At least a month. I guess you are glad to be getting Teke out of your hair."

Bret said nothing for a few moments, as the numbness that he was not prepared for surged through his body. Slowly, he recovered, "Well, I won't have to hear repeatedly about how terrible the south is and how great the north is."

Money laughed and then he asked, "Teke said something about a favor. I don't know what I can do for you from here, but shoot."

"Money, there is a lot going on with my father. It's gotten worse since you left. We don't have time for all the details, but he's going to try and take Alex from me."

Money's tone was instantly serious. "What is it I can do to help you?"

"Everything about this has to be kept between us. Anyone else involved, we have to be sure of their ability to remain silent, or we don't risk it."

"I hear you."

"It involves Big Willie."

"Yeah, your buddy that wanted to kill you in the gym that day."

"Well, he really wanted to kill me one day at a gas station when I was avoiding you."

"Really?"

"Yes, I never told you about it, but anyway, what is important is that he is a locksmith."

"I take it that the services required might be a little on the shady side."

"You would be correct. I know that he thinks a lot of you. Now, he won't do squat for me, but for you."

"I can handle that. Bret, you call me tomorrow at nine. That will give me time to get up with him. I'll have an answer by then. Now, is there a phone book there?"

"Yes."

"Look up W. Malloy, on Red Cross Street, and give me the number."

Bret thumbed through the tattered pages of the book. "763-3465."

"Okay, I got it."

"Money."

"Don't you worry about my things on my end. You be smart."

Bret hung the phone up and walked to the car. Teke was leaning on the hood. "I need to call the airport."

He shrugged as if he did not care.

She made flight reservations to fly out of Wilmington on Monday morning. She would be leaving behind all the misery of the south, along with the boy she loved.

It was past midnight. Alex was sleeping peacefully on the couch. Bret sat out on the deck, staring out at the stars that hovered over the river. He had spoken little since Teke told him that she was leaving. It was always easier for him to draw everything inside him and leave it in a secure place.

Teke walked out on the deck and sat down in the chair beside him. "You've been awfully quiet tonight, even with Alex. Tomorrow is my last day and I don't want it to be like this. If I did anything to hurt you in any way, I am sorry."

Bret sat quietly continuing his silence.

"Are you upset with me, Bret?"

Moments passed before he answered, "No."

"Bret."

"Teke," he interrupted. "Let's not talk about it. I'm not mad at you, and I am struggling with what happened last night, but it is not all what you may think." He turned away and looked into some place she could not see.

Teke respected his not wanting to talk, and his obvious need to be alone. She stood up, and touched his right shoulder as she walked inside and went to her room.

* * *

It was fifteen minutes before nine the following night. Bret had spent a futile day trying to construct the kitchen cabinets. He finally gave up that afternoon and began to coat the wood walls downstairs with a clear sealer.

The little brother he'd taken to Barbara an hour earlier was what was important. He had to save him. But his mind was also occupied with someone who was preparing to leave. Someone he wanted to stay.

In his mind, he had debated all day. He tried to convince himself that she was no different than all the other girls that he had been with, other than the small fact of skin color.

He tired of every girl that he dated and he was sure that he would be weary of Teke if she stayed. That analogy ran through his mind, along with the remembrance of that night with her. He knew that it was different than ever before. She was not just a conquest, a night of fun. There was something he had never experienced but he didn't understand just what that was.

As the battle lines formed in his mind the conclusion that he was resigned to was that while he didn't want her to go he could not make her stay.

He called to her, "Teke, it's time."

She descended down the stairs. They walked to Bret's car and drove in silence to the same pay phone outside the hardware store.

Bret sat in the car and watched her walk to the phone booth. She began dialing the number. He smiled as he observed her. She was dressed in black shorts and a white top. The irony of the black and white color combination gave him pause. "This is so crazy," he mumbled. It was not the color of her clothes or even the difference in skin color that was at the forefront of his thoughts. It was how he loved to watch her move. Every movement from her was such a portrait of grace, of beauty.

"God help me," he exclaimed, as he got out of the car quickly, walking to the phone booth.

"You are killing me," he said through gritted teeth as he took the phone from her hand and hung it up rudely.

"What are you doing?" she asked irately.

"Be quiet and listen."

She started to speak, but he put his finger over her mouth shushing her as one might a small child.

"No. Don't talk. You always want me to talk, right? Well, I can't if your big mouth is open."

He paused as he searched for words. She looked at him and several wise comments emerged but she held on to them, remaining silent. It was slightly amusing to see him boldly declare his intention to speak and then be silent. She waited and kept her big mouth closed as instructed.

Finally he spoke, his words coming in a rush. "I don't want you to go, not now. You said Friday night for me to give you one night. I want you to give me one month until your family returns. I want you to listen and stop thinking that you know the situation better than I do. This is it for my father and me. Your leaving will not help me in anyway. I'm disappointed in you," he exclaimed, with a shake of his head.

"Why?"

"Because you don't believe that I can beat him. You say you love me, and maybe you do, but right now what I need is for you is to have faith in me. I will not lose Alex. It will not happen."

The tone of his voice was strong, confident, and though Teke searched for any trace of doubt in his words she found none. "What is it that you are asking of me?"

His voice softened, "I'm asking you not to go."

"Why?" she asked, searching his eyes as if they might explain this rapid turn of events.

He breathed in deeply. "I don't know," he said wearily. "Maybe because I would miss you."

She studied his face, and then smiled at him. "That's enough for now. Stay right here."

He stood beside her as she dialed the number and listened as she explained to her father that she had decided to stay in Wilmington.

When Money got on the phone, she explained briefly about not wanting to interfere with their work. This way, dad could concentrate on work solely and return home sooner to the place that he loved. Money accepted her change of decision, though he was confused about a sister who hated the south and now was choosing to remain.

Bret took the phone.

"How is it my sister can tolerate the south better than D.C. all of a sudden? What did you do to her?"

Moments passed before Bret's nervousness gave way to the realization that Money was merely making light of his sister's inability to make up her mind.

"I don't know. She's your sister, and she is from the north. Isn't that reason enough for someone to be a little strange?"

Money chuckled slightly at Bret's analogy. "I got in touch with Big Willie. He will provide the services that you need. Before you ask I have no problem trusting him. I told him that this has to remain between the two of you."

"What did he say?"

Money laughed. "He said, 'I don't really like that white boy, and I don't understand why you do, but for you I'll do whatever he wants.'"

"Did you have to use your charm to persuade him?"

"I told him that it was a family thing. There is something that you don't know about Big Willie. What you know is he would break anyone in half that looked at him the wrong way. What you don't know is that he has a real soft spot for family. His mother is single. Always has been. He doesn't know anything about his dad. She raised him alone. She lives a block away from him and every morning before work he goes by to check on her. Well, I asked him, what means would he use if someone tried to take his mother away from him?

"Of course he said, any means possible. I explained to him that you loved Alex as much as he loved his mother, and that someone was trying to take him away from you."

"What did he say?"

"He snorted, and said, that's a cute little kid. I'll do whatever it takes to keep him with his brother. You have my word on that. Then he added, I still don't like Bret. That's about it. I told him cooperation was imperative. That this was too big for him to carry that boulder of a chip on his shoulder toward you."

"You mean he might not act like he's going to kill me at any second. How did you pull that off?"

"Let's just say that when State plays Carolina, my first varsity year, that Willie and his mom will be sitting behind the bench. Turns out she is a real basketball junkie."

"Seriously, Bret, he would have done it anyway. He's not as tough as he wants people to think. He's just a big old mama's boy."

Bret laughed heartily. "Money, thanks."

"I owe you."

"No you don't owe me anything. We're friends."

"That we are. Good luck. Talk to you soon."

Bret and Teke returned to the house by the river. As they prepared for bed, Teke smiled at him. "What are we doing? This is crazy."

"It sure is. Now where are you sleeping tonight?"

She giggled as she joined him in his bed.

CHAPTER SIXTEEN

Uncovering the moon

The following Friday was the last day of June. It was late morning as Teke walked outside, soothed by the sound of the creek flowing to the river. The temperature was again in the mid-nineties, but even the stifling heat of a Wilmington summer failed to dampen her light mood.

She knew that come early evening, Bret would be home. The pretense was over and she embellished every possible minute with him. He arrived home to special dinners, illuminated with candles. Later each evening they would be drawn to the bedroom where they would explore each other for hours until exhaustion finally won out and they would fall asleep in each other's arms.

She tried not to think of the time when she would leave. She desired only to enjoy this captivating ride until it ceased. She forced away any thoughts of reality that invaded her thoughts. The reality that this glorious feeling of wonderment would come to an end with nothing to fill the void.

The week proved easier also because of Vicky. She arrived early for dinner each morning and often spent the remainder of the day with her.

She won Vicky's favor with her willingness to work. She worked beside her in the garden and the two of them shelled butter beans together for two entire afternoons.

Teke reached down to pick some of the yellow flowers that grew near the creek. She took them to Fred's grave and delicately laid them on top. "You silly brave dog," she said. "I'll never forget you."

She left the memorial behind and began the walk to Vicky's house. Minutes later, she tapped on the screen door, and was immediately welcomed in.

Smiling as she walked in with a glow that warmed Vicky and saddened her at the same time. She knew that soon Teke would leave, and even if she could stay she would not be able to have what her heart desired.

The look reminded Vicky of the early years with Ralph, before a whiskey bottle became his lover. She knew that life hardened her, but still she had not forgotten the entrancing feeling of love.

"Child, how are things at the old house?"

"They're good," Teke beamed.

"Child," Vicky said softly with a slight shake of her head.

"What?" Teke asked, the tone of Vicky's voice penetrating the exhilaration that she desperately wanted to cling to.

"You know that this cannot be. I hate to see you hurt and you will be when this is over. That's the downside of love you know. The awful pain left in its wake."

The glow left her face abruptly. The thoughts she had tried to refrain from having swept across her mind. A few moments of silence passed before she offered, "I know that, Vicky, but the way I look at it is it's going to hurt if it ends today, why shouldn't I enjoy it for as long as I can?"

The old woman smiled at her. "That's a good point. Forgive my meddling. Let's eat."

"That's okay. You have earned the right to meddle," Teke said, her smile partially returning.

Bret spent much of his time at work planning his escape. He had stored away in his mind the conversation that Walker Sr. had with Jerry that spring day he came home for lunch.

On Thursday, he received some possible help with his plan. The Wall Street Journal contained an article about the defense department possibly changing to another type computer in the coming fiscal year. There was an expected announcement sometime in the next month.

Bret knew that the company that was awarded the contract would see a rather significant boost to its bottom line. If he could buy that stock ahead of time, he could walk out of the Marin household not only a free man, but a not-so-poor man as well. This Jerry, whoever he may be, could bring his plan together nicely and neatly.

It was almost six when he drove to the old house on the river, accompanied by Alex. The sound of the engine outside the door brought a smile to Teke.

She walked out onto the deck to greet the two Marin men. She caught the brief wince in Bret's face as he watched Alex limp as he climbed the steps.

Alex reached her and hugged her. "I'm glad that you didn't go."

"I am too, Alex."

Alex romped into the house as his brother reached Teke. She looked in his eyes and smiled. She could swear that she felt the pain he felt at watching Alex limp. She touched his face delicately and cradled it ever so softly in her hand. "That little brother of yours, he sure is lucky. Most people go their whole lives and don't have anyone love them as much as you love him."

He looked at her and knew that she had seen the hurt in his face. He studied her eyes and saw her compassion, her tenderness, and it soothed the ache inside him.

"You never know, Bret. Medicine is getting better all the time. Maybe one day, some doctor will find a way to fix that leg like brand new."

"I'd give..." his words trailed off.

"I know," she said, taking his hand in hers for a moment. "Now boys, let's eat. Dinner is on the table."

As the lasagna was being enjoyed, Alex asked about the work to be done on the house.

"Tomorrow, we are going to seal the walls. You, my little man, will get the boards from the top of your head to the floor. Teke picks up where you stop and goes as high as she can. I'll work off the ladder and do the high stuff. It has to be done right with no drips or runs on the walls. Maybe we can finish this weekend. Next I sand the floor and we seal that. The job will be near completion."

"At least until we find a cabinet builder," Teke slyly suggested.

"That's funny. I built the ones in the bathrooms, didn't I?"

"Yes, but you are struggling with the kitchen cabinets."

"I was distracted last weekend."

"So, build them this weekend."

Bret looked at Alex first, pretending to be angry, before quickly giving up. "I would if I could figure out what I wanted to do, and how to do it," he said humbly.

Teke looked at Alex. "You know, that brother of yours is getting to where he is not quite so conceited. I think I like it."

"Yeah, he's not so much of a butthead," Alex giggled.

Sunday night came and the smell of sealer permeated through the house, driving Bret and Teke outside onto the deck. Bret had driven Alex home an hour earlier. The project of the weekend was not finished completely, but it was close. Vicky visited both days after serving dinner and insisted on helping. When patronized by Bret somewhat, she countered by saying, "Who do you think helped Ralph before you came along?"

Bret and Teke sat quietly looking out at the river. It was the river that he loved and the river that had gently carved its path into her soul as well. They were both tired from the day's work, but satisfied with the accomplishments.

She took her eyes off of the river and looked at him. "Bret, you've had a lot of girls, right?"

He fidgeted in the wicker rocking chair, not wanting to engage in conversation of his sexual history. "Teke, let's not do this."

"Just one question, please?"

"It's never one question with you," he replied wearily.

"I promise."

"Okay, go ahead, but don't ask me about how many."

"I want the truth. Don't worry about hurting my feelings, okay?"

"Okay."

"Do I please you like the other girls, or..." her words trailing off as embarrassment took over.

He continued gazing out at the river, before softly speaking. "Beyond compare, Teke, beyond compare. Now, please be quiet and let's go to bed."

They rose, but stopped when they heard footsteps coming up the steps. "Why don't you get a phone? You wear an old woman out."

"Vicky," they both said simultaneously. "What are you doing out here at night?" Teke asked. Their eyes fell on the rifle attached to her arms.

"Is anything wrong?" Bret asked.

"No, I'm just being careful. Teke, I forgot to tell you that Tuesday there will be surveyors here. I'll bring dinner here."

"You don't need to do that."

"Bret, tell this Yankee it is not polite to argue with a tired helpless old woman."

Bret smiled at Teke. "Don't argue with Vicky." Looking back at Vicky, he asked, "Why the surveyors?"

Vicky turned to leave, "Oh, probably just rechecking the acreage to make sure the county is getting enough taxes."

"You don't have to go," Teke said.

Vicky paused on the top step and turned for her descent. "Yes, I do, you two are ready for bed," she said looking back.

The two of them stammered for an answer and an escape from what Vicky must have heard. She looked back once again before leaving. Her eyes sparkled. "I wasn't born this old, you know."

The two of them looked at each other, momentarily stunned, before bursting into laughter as Vicky vanished into the darkness.

"Wouldn't it be nice to celebrate the fourth of July like normal people? I wish we could go to the beach."

He looked at her and arched his eyebrows.

"I know, but I wish we could. Are you working?"

"I have a special project to take care of, but it won't take all day."

She started to ask, but was cut off. "Don't ask. Now, let's go to bed."

"Race you," she said as she ran for the door and up the steps.

The alarm clock rang annoyingly. Bret reached over and quickly turned it off. He fell back into the bed but didn't dare shut his eyes. He was exhausted, but it was Independence Day and the office was empty. There was a very important meeting that had been planned down to the most intricate detail. He hoped. He looked at the clock, three-thirty. Teke stirred and snuggled closer to him. The moonlight allowed enough light for him to see her stretched out, wearing a white tee shirt that stopped at her navel. The covers were of no need on the hot sticky nights of summer. Her legs flowed to the bottom of the bed. He smiled as he looked at his favorite body part. This girl had legs that were unsurpassed by any that he had felt, by any that he had seen. His eyes worked their way up her body and found her face, partially covered by her hair that had managed now to leave the top of her shoulders and inch gently down her back. Her face glowed with innocence and grew prettier with each day that passed. Her skin, as smooth as velvet, was more comforting than anything he had ever known. He had never studied a girl before, not every inch of her as he was doing now.

His pleasant thoughts were interrupted with thoughts of her brother. One day, he would know. How would Money feel? Would he lose his only friend? How would he convince Money that this was not planned? He laughed with him about his reputation, all the girls. But this was not just a girl. This was his sister. As he studied her he wondered how this all came to be? He still didn't understand. He only knew that she was not like any other girl. Teke made him feel things. He didn't always close the world out when she was near. She stirred and turned away from him. He moved closer and kissed her softly on the back of the neck. He rose from the bed and slipped into a pair of jeans and black knit shirt. There was an important job to complete today, July fourth, the day he hoped would begin his freedom.

At ten past four, he parked his car in the parking deck in downtown Wilmington. He waited precisely five minutes and walked the two blocks along the river northward to Market Street. He reached Market Street and walked up the steepest incline that the city had to offer. He arrived at Front Street where the pavement leveled off and turned left. Slowly, he moved to the fourteen- story building, the tallest building in the downtown area. He was forty feet from the building when he spotted the only other pedestrian on the street. He relaxed. It was Big Willie.

They said nothing as Bret inserted the key into the burglar alarm first and then into the glass door that greeted all the occupants each day. They entered quickly. Bret locked the door behind them. They walked to the stairs and began the fourteen flights up as scheduled. Bret was reasonably confident that the building was completely empty on this early holiday morning, but if there was anyone here they would be using the elevator. They walked quietly, the only sound the slight echo from their footsteps. Reaching the top, they exited onto the fourteenth floor and into the lobby. Bret stopped, opened his briefcase and took out the flashlight. They moved to the central entrance and he unlocked the door. He moved past the receptionist's desk and down the hall to Ruby's office.

He broke the silence of the early morning. "This is the door. Get me in."

Willie knelt down and eyed the lock as Bret provided the light needed. He opened his duffel bag and sat three large rings of keys and a small machine out on the floor. He proceeded to go through the rings of keys. He was on the seventh key of the second ring, when he stopped. He took the key off and inserted it into a small devise, producing a grinding noise.

The noise sounded as loud as a jackhammer busting through concrete in the otherwise still building. Nervous sweat ran down Bret's side.

Willie took a file and gave the key a finishing touch. He inserted the key in the door and turned, bingo, one down.

They moved to Ruby's desk. Bret shined the light to the right drawer on her desk. "There."

Willie pulled a ring out with smaller keys on it. He was in the desk drawer in less than a minute. He smiled as the drawer slid open.

Bret reached in and pulled the magic keys. He hoped to find keys to the files in his father's office, but there were none.

He walked to his father's door and inserted the key. They entered the sacred exclusive office of Walker Sr. "The files over there, Willie," he said, pointing out the direction with his light. I need keys to those file doors."

There were five rows of files. A keyhole was found in each top file that opened that file and the four below. Twenty file drawers, and in them, hopefully enough dirt to bury his old man, if need be.

He glanced at his watch. It was four-thirty as Willie went to work on the file locks. Willie had been a locksmith for seven years and he was good. It took four minutes and he was into the first file. Willie took that key and checked to make sure the other file cabinets were keyed alike. They were. Bret wanted to search the files right then, but time was too precious.

He whispered to Willie. "Let's go."

Willie nodded, packed up his tools and the two men retraced their steps, but not before Willie produced a small towel and wiped the cabinets cleaned. "Just in case," he said, his voice barely above a whisper.

They entered the stairs and began their descent. They reached the first floor and Bret motioned at Willie to remain. He walked out into the first floor. The building was empty. He returned to the stairs. "It's clear." He held out five one hundred-dollar bills.

Willie raised his hand to object. "No, I did this for Money."

"The risk was for me. We don't have time to argue. Buy your mama something nice."

Willie looked at Bret, making sure that there was no disrespect meant in his gesture. Bret smiled. "Take it, and get out of here."

"I will have the keys ready today. Tonight they will be hidden under the trash can at the gas pump where we met before."

Bret extended his hand and Willie grasped it, almost causing Bret's hand to disappear from sight.

"You know," the big man began.

"I know. You still don't like me."

"That's right," Willie replied, but his voice was not so convincing. "I do hope that you hold on tight to that little brother of yours."

Bret nodded. "I'll check the front door again and wave you on if it's clear. I'll leave later."

A few seconds later, the sidewalk contained only one man. A proud, strong black man, who was contemplating the many ways to spoil his number one girl, his mama, with the unexpected windfall he received.

Bret rode the elevator back up and this time when he reached the fourteenth floor, he turned the lights on. He wanted to give the place one last inspection to insure that there was nothing to suggest that two intruders had been there.

Minutes later, he was back at the river house. The sun was up and he saw a surveyor's truck parked a few hundred feet from the house and three men were taking their instruments off. Bret slowed to a stop.

One of the men approached him. "I hope you don't mind the early start, but we would like to be out of here by noon, and have at least half the day off."

"That's no problem," Bret answered. He drove away leaving the men to their work.

He walked quietly up the stairs to the bedroom and found the same legs he had admired earlier still uncovered. He stripped and returned to the bed.

"Where have you been? I woke once and you were gone."

"I went to work."

"In the middle of the night?"

He ignored her question. "The surveyors are here and I have an idea how we can pass the time away."

She smiled broadly and said, "I bet that you do." Gazing into his eyes she said, "I guess that it is a good thing that I will leave before you get tired of me."

"Maybe I wouldn't get tired of you," he said as he pinned her down, "And maybe I won't let you leave."

"Stay here in this little town, with some spoiled rich white boy like you. I can't see that."

"Well, I sure would not go to Philadelphia."

"Who asked you?"

"You can't resist me."

"You are so cocky."

Teke looked at the smile on Bret's face. She could not believe or comprehend the feelings he produced in her. "Bret, I wish sometimes that things were different. I wish that we could have each other, or at least have the chance to try."

He smiled at her. "I know," he said gently.

* * *

Vicky arrived with dinner at eleven twenty-eight. The surveyors were gone, but that didn't matter to her. She said she would bring dinner and she always kept her word.

As they enthusiastically devoured the breakfast of chicken and pastry, Bret asked Vicky for the loan of her car that night. He explained that he wanted to get Teke out and that the Oldsmobile was less conspicuous than the Mustang.

As dark arrived, Bret and Teke headed out in Vicky's car. "It's not as classy as the Mustang, but safer," he remarked, stating the obvious.

"Who cares?" Teke answered, before adding, "Where are we going?"

"First, a little errand, then the beach, and we'll pick up dinner on the way." He pulled into the store parking lot.

"There are keys under that trash can."

Teke got out of the car and found the keys. She returned to the car, handing them to Bret.

"What is this for?"

"Pay dirt, I hope."

Minutes later, they entered the Marin house through the garage, surprising Barbara and Alex. Bret raided the fridge making huge club sandwiches piled high with turkey, roast beef and ham. Barbara assisted him. She produced an old picnic basket to carry the items in. She placed it on the counter and began wiping it with a dishcloth.

"Where did you find that?" Bret asked, motioning to the basket with a slight nod of his head.

"I saw it in the attic one day and decided to bring it down and clean it up. Why?"

"Oh, no reason," he lied. He had not seen the picnic basket in years but he remembered it. It was the one his mom used when she took him for outings to the beach or the park. It was a memory of good times. It had been a long time since he had allowed himself to think just how much he missed his mom.

Barbara saw the look on his face and started to press but refrained.

Bret and Teke left a few minutes later and drove toward Wrightsville Beach.

"Where are we going, Bret?"

"It's the fourth and you wanted to go to the beach."

Bret drove toward the south end of the beach, hoping for seclusion. The inlet at the most southern end seemed to draw out numerous night guests. He decided on parking four blocks north of Crystal Pier, one of two piers on the beach that jutted out over two hundred feet into the ocean. The other pier, Johnnie Mercer's, was the most populated area of the beach, be it night or day. Crystal Pier saw its share of daytime traffic but at night only a few fishermen ventured out on the pier.

He parked the car as far from any houses as possible. They walked down a path that wound through sand dunes six feet high, held together by the sea oats that rustled in the evening breeze.

Bret surveyed the beach and was relieved to find the area empty. He stretched the blanket out on the sand, just past the dunes that would serve as cover if needed.

"You know that it is a full moon tonight," Teke said as she looked at the clouds in the sky that were holding the moonlight hostage.

"I know, why do you think I brought you here?"

"It doesn't look like it will show, but who cares?"

They were seated on the blanket now and Bret was distributing the food from of the basket. He had hidden a bottle of wine and two glasses that he now uncovered in the bottom of the basket. He handed her the glasses and fished for the corkscrew. He found it and tried to open the wine, but was only proving successful in butchering the cork.

"Give me that," she demanded. She took the corkscrew and opened it easily. As he stared at her eloquence with an instrument that unlike a saw or a hammer refused to be brought under his mastery, she said, "Mom likes wine. She even shares at times. She just doesn't know it. Wine, food, a night on the beach. You are really something."

"Don't forget the full moon."

"But it's hidden."

"Do you think that I would bring you here and not bring the moon out?"

"This is perfect without it."

They began to eat, watching the brilliant white capped waves illuminated in the darkness by the distant lights of the pier as they raced to shore.

They were looking at the sky when the clouds began to move. They were both in awe, though Bret would never admit it, when the clouds suddenly seemed to move horizontally in separate directions revealing a brilliant orange moon in its center.

"What a sight, Bret."

"You have to like a man who can move the clouds out of the way of the moon," he said coolly.

She smiled and reached over to hold his hand. They said nothing and minutes later the lights on the pier suddenly went out. He leaned over and whispered, "You have to really like a man who can turn the lights off on the pier," before kissing her as the moon hung majestically over the dark waters of the Atlantic.

The kiss ended and Teke looked in his eyes and said, "You can do anything, can't you?"

He didn't bother to answer. He didn't need to. She looked back at the fullness of the moon suspended over the ocean. She knew that no matter where life took her, anytime she saw the moon full in its brilliance, her thoughts, her heart would drift to a night of magic at Wrightsville Beach.

CHAPTER SEVENTEEN

Two weeks

Each morning at four o'clock for the next four days Bret arrived at his summer job. He didn't like leaving Teke alone while it was still dark, even though there had been no suspicious activities since the night the Klan came calling. She assured him that she was not fearful, only lying slightly. She knew that he needed the time and any worries that she had were not going to be voiced. Besides, she didn't feel as frightened, knowing that Vicky, and her ever present watchful eyes were near. Still, as a precaution, Vicky spent an afternoon teaching her how to fire the rifle that rest in the corner of the bedroom.

Bret anticipated needing one hour to thoroughly search each file cabinet, hoping for one that would lead him to Jerry. By five each morning he was back at his desk. Hard work was naturally encouraged at the Marin firm and it was not unusual to see employees arriving as early as five-thirty. The earliest arrival of the week besides his own was a young attorney, Douglas Johnson, at five-fifteen on Wednesday.

He debated about removing the files. He couldn't know for certain whether Ruby was trusted with access to the files but in case she did he was hesitant to risk her noticing anything missing.

Friday afternoon his father called, naturally at five o'clock. Bret was almost out the door when Ruby called out to him. The good news was that the conversation lasted only two minutes. The bad news was they expected to be home in two weeks. The time to find all the answers drew perilously near.

Despite the long hours spent at work he still managed to finish sealing the walls at the old house, thanks largely in part to Teke who worked each day while he was at work.

He rented a floor sander from the hardware store. He picked it up Thursday afternoon and played with it enough to feel confident that he could sand the entire floor on Saturday.

He left the office Friday afternoon with the arrival of his father engulfing his mind. He picked up Alex and drove toward the old house. Even the youthful chatter of Alex failed to break his mind free from Walker Sr. He was coming home in two weeks to take Alex away, and banish him from the house.

They arrived, parked the car, and were scarcely out of it when they heard a loud crashing sound followed by a scream coming from the house. Bret raced up the steps and entered the house with Alex trailing behind him.

At the bottom of the stairs he saw Teke clutching her ankle. A few feet away lay the floor sander turned up on its side, and still running.

Bret cut the machine off and moved to her. "Are you okay?" he asked, as he knelt down to her.

"Yes, no, I twisted my ankle."

"What were you doing?"

"I was sanding the floor."

"That was pretty dumb."

"Shut up, Bret. Shut up right now. I was trying to help you. If you'll notice, the bottom floor is done. I watched you yesterday and it didn't appear to be too hard."

"Good thing it wasn't any harder. You might have broken your neck," he teased.

"Don't say anything else."

Alex had stood by watching and listening to the exchange between the two. He looked at Teke who appeared to be covered in sawdust from head to toe. Her hair was no longer black, but a pale yellow color, as was her skin and clothes.

Hiding the slightest of smiles he said disgustedly, "Teke, I think you need a bath, or a swim in the river. You look awful."

She looked up at him with frozen eyes. "So, now it's you. First, it's your ungrateful butthead brother and now you. Wait till I get up from here and maybe I'll drown your skinny behind in the river."

Alex began to giggle, joined by Bret. Teke tried to refrain from joining the laughter, but it proved impossible.

The laughter died moments later and Bret asked as he helped her up, "So, what happened?"

"I found out that sanding the steps is a little harder than doing an open floor. The machine got away from me and ..."

Bret eyed the machine, ignoring her, and said, "You better not have hurt that machine. I won't get my deposit back."

She whacked him on top of the head with her open hand, producing only a slight sarcastic smile from him.

Later that night, Bret dropped Alex by Vicky's house while he and Teke went to use the phone outside the hardware store. First, she called her mom, who told her that she had seen no more of Lawrence. The word was that he was dating a young lady quite heavily that was giving him what Teke refused to. Jacky was a little concerned but still felt like it was time for her to return home as soon as she could get a flight.

Teke's response was that she would call later in the week but that she thought she might wait until her dad and Money returned home.

Jacky found it difficult to believe what she had heard. She started to press the issue but decided against it. She thought that maybe Teke was still apprehensive about Lawrence, and for that she could not blame her.

Next, Teke called Clarence, who informed her that he and Money planned to be home in two weeks. Money talked to Teke and then asked for Bret. Teke motioned him to the phone. Bret hesitantly took it.

"Hello, Money."

"What exactly are you doing to my sister, converting her to being a southerner?"

Bret paused and then offered, "I don't think that there is much probability of that."

"So, are you two still at each other's throats?"

Images of how they were physically embellishing each other

flashed through his mind, rendering him very uncomfortable. "No, we manage to get along okay."

Teke and Bret managed a slight smile at each other.

"So, are things quiet in town? Have there been any more disturbances?"

"You hear talk once in a while. You know how that is. But I think things are relatively quiet."

"Is it safe for Teke to stay at our house?"

"I guess so. But I think that she is okay here."

There were moments of an awkward silence before Money spoke again. "Bret, what is going on? What is it that the two of you are not telling me?"

"What do you mean?" Bret asked hesitantly.

"I talked to Mom last night and she thinks it is safe and Teke hates the south so..."

"I guess she just wants to stay and see you guys and maybe she is not as confident about Philadelphia as her mom. Money, we need to leave before we are seen. I'll see you in two weeks."

"Sure Bret, two weeks. See you then."

Money put the phone down. He had grown used to Bret closing him off, but his sister had been reserved as well. Something was not adding up. He wondered what it could be. There was one thing that he was certain of. He had not been told the entire truth.

Bret placed the phone back on its hook. "Two weeks, everyone is coming home in two weeks. My family, your family. Are you sure that you want to stick around?"

"Do you want me here?"

"You have to go home sooner or later."

She nodded. His words hurt her, but she did not respond.

"Besides, you hate the south. It has to end sometime. Maybe it's better if I do this alone. I'm going to be disowned. Why should you hang around and have trouble with your family?"

"Does it really have to end?" she asked, the one part of her daring not to believe, but still holding out the slightest of hope.

He looked into her eyes. He could see the hurt and the glimmer of hope they contained. Slowly and softly he spoke, "We've known that it couldn't last. We never spoke of a future because we knew better. We're young and different colors."

"I hadn't noticed that as much lately."

"You know what I mean, Teke. It's easy out here but you know what it would be like if we go out in the world with what we feel and think about each other."

"And what is it that we think and feel about each other?"

"Please, not now, Teke."

"When would be a good time to discuss just what it is we feel?" she said curtly.

He looked away and refused to answer.

"What's the longest that you have ever dated anyone?"

"I don't know. Six weeks, I guess," he answered.

"I guess my time is up."

He felt his frustration level rise. "It's not that. I've never spent as much time with any girl as I have you. We live together. Obviously, I've never done that. I hate leaving you in the morning and I can't wait until I get home to see you in the evening. Don't compare this to anything. It's not fair, but we have to face reality. This isn't the movies. We can't play *Guess Who's Coming to Dinner*. This is real life."

"And what would you do if I was white?"

"That's not a fair question, Teke," he answered exasperated.

"Why?"

"Look," he answered as he held her hand next to his. "There is a difference. We have to accept that. We may not like it, but we have no choice. Maybe one day, it will be different, but not now."

"I don't care whether this will be possible in twenty years. I've only got one life, right here, right now. I love you, Bret. Tell me that you don't feel the same. I've seen your heart, Bret, and it is the same color as mine. It's what's inside of us. That is what is real. Nothing else really matters."

"You say that now, but being stared at in public all the time... Not being able to enjoy a decent dinner out."

"Why do you care? You only have one friend, and he's black, remember?"

"And do you think that he won't mind? You don't think that the black community won't frown on us being together? Are you so misguided that you think that they will accept us? I walked in that gym at Williston and I was called a cracker. The only reason I got to stay, and the only reason they didn't beat my ass is because of your brother. Prejudice runs along both sides of the street. If you think that your daddy, or mom, or even Money will embrace this, you're wrong."

"Tell me that you don't love me, Bret."

"I can't."

"But you can't tell me that you do either."

The silence hung mercilessly between them and the words that Teke's heart desired so strongly to hear did not interrupt the stillness of the humid night.

"Damn you, Bret Marin. Damn you for being such a coward."

"I'm not a coward," he answered, his voice strained. "A few months ago, I was in a world where I only cared about two people, and one of them was me. It was so simple. Now it's you, Money, your dad, Vicky. Does everything have to change so fast?" he added wearily.

"Maybe you should be afraid, just once."

"You think that I'm not afraid!" he exclaimed, his voice rising exponentially. "I may lose Alex. Don't you think that sometimes I doubt that I can pull this off? I'm talking about beating Walker Marin Sr., the shrewdest most corrupt evil man that I know. What happens to Alex if I lose? He's left with my father and two brothers to torment him because he is weak."

"He's not weak," she shouted. "He just has a weak leg. He is a wonderful little boy and you have raised him well. He idolizes you."

"I'm tired, Teke. I'm so tired. Can't we go home, please, now? No more talking, not now." Bret's voice was weary as exhaustion consumed him.

"I'll stay until my dad and Money get back. I want this time for us, and I want to finish the house. Is that okay?"

"If that is what you want."

"No, what I want is you, but this will have to suffice."

"And in two weeks?"

"I'll leave you and go home. I'll go to school. I'll try to forget the rich spoiled southern white boy that stole my heart."

"Will you be able to?"

"Not a chance of it," she answered tersely.

"I'm sorry. I don't know how to fix all of this." He handed her the car keys. "Will you drive? I am so tired."

She drove to Vicky's to pick up a little boy that she had fallen in love with as well. Bret slumped against the car door, his eyes were closed, and his breathing heavy and deliberate.

Alex got in the car and sat quietly, his eyes fixated on his brother as Teke drove easily through the woods on the dark dirt road.

"Bret, are you okay?" he gently asked.

"Sure, little man, I'm just real tired."

"They are coming home?" Alex asked.

"Yes, in two weeks."

There was silence for a few moments as Alex pondered the arrival of his family. "I don't want them to come back. You'll go away to school and I'll be left with them. You won't be here to look after me. They're awful when you are not around to protect me. I wish we could just live out here away from them? Vicky will let us."

"You like her, don't you?" Bret asked, in an attempt to change the conversation.

"Yes, she is neat. Do you know that she has peanuts growing in her garden? When it's time for them to be picked, she is going to show me how. Next year, she said that I could help her plant them."

Bret smiled through his weariness and chuckled ever so slightly. "I've grown kind of fond of the old girl myself."

* * *

It was past midnight. Alex was asleep on the couch. Teke lie awake in her bed. She rose and walked downstairs, peering through the glass out onto the deck. Bret was still there, unmoved from when they came home. He rocked slightly and though she could not see his eyes, she knew that they were fixed on the river. She wanted to go to him, to hold him, to love him, to remove his fear, and the hurt that tormented him. She would do it if she could. She would do anything to help, even leave him. She returned to her bed and stood over it, ready to lie down and maybe sleep some of the ache away, but she had another thought. She knelt beside her bed and began to pour her heart out. "God I need your help. I know there has to be a way. Would you please help us?"

Moments later, she heard the door open. She listened to his footsteps as they stopped by Alex. He knelt down beside his bed, resting his head on top of the small sleeping body of a little boy. She could hear the sniffling of tears and it tore into her as if someone had reached inside and gouged out a piece of her heart. She grasped her pillow and cried softly into it.

It was shortly before daybreak when Bret awoke. He was on the floor beside the couch. Alex slept with the gentle breathing that blended perfectly with the first song of the day offered by the birds nestled in their trees.

He rose to his knees and looked at the boy sleeping so peacefully on the couch. It had been a long night. Strangely, his thoughts drifted to basketball. He thought about how he reacted in close games, when the seconds were precious few and people on both sides were nervous, many even afraid.

He was always able to relax during that time, so much so that the game seemed to be almost in slow motion. He was fearless. He could focus regardless of the situation. The stakes here were so much larger than a game but the lesson remained the same. He lost his focus last night, allowing the situation to confuse, even frighten him. He could not allow that to happen again. He had two weeks. He recalled what his first basketball coach, Rob Oates, said after he had lost his temper at an official and was ejected from the game. "Focus on what you can control and waste no time or energy on what you can't." He never forgot that lesson. He realized that part of what was making him crazy was that Teke would be leaving. He tried to expedite the process the night before. She would stay two weeks. He could not think about that now. Right now there was a boy in front of him that he had loved longer, and more than anyone in this world. He could not fail.

He walked out onto the deck and breathed in the first smells of morning. Two weeks, focus on what is at hand. He had a plan that needed to be carried out precisely, one step at a time. Focus on each step. Don't look at the two weeks.

He walked toward Vicky's. He kept going over his plan in his mind again and again. Tweaking it as the need arose. He knocked on her door knowing that the sunrise would not find her sleeping.

She opened the door. "Come in, the coffee is ready."

He entered a house with the smell that settles into old homes mixed with the aroma of fresh brewed coffee. There was an open Bible on the table and she obviously had been reading. He wondered if she did that often, and he wondered about God. About how real he was and if he would help. His thoughts surprised him and he failed to understand why they surfaced.

"You're up early. Got something on your mind?" she asked, pouring coffee for both of them.

"Yes."

She looked at him and waited for him to speak but he looked away and said nothing. Things had changed for her and she smiled as she realized that her first inclination was not to rip his head off.

"Look at me, son."

He turned to face her.

"You have changed quite a bit since you drove here with Alex back in early March. You have grown into a man. But maybe there is something else you should know. You have caused a miserable, grouchy old woman to grow, to change also."

He smiled at her warmly and he thought how things between them had changed since that day he left in March vowing never to return. "You're not that old," he said.

She smiled back at him. "Now talk to me before I have to hurt you."

"That's what I came here for, to talk to you. I wanted to talk to my grandmother."

She didn't even feel the need to correct him for saying grandmother. And she waited as he looked away again and gathered his thoughts.

"Everyone is coming home in two weeks."

"By that you mean your father and brothers."

"Yes, and also Money and his father."

Bret accepted the black coffee that was placed in front of him. "My dear father. It appears the showdown is upon us."

"What is it that you need, child, when all this is said and done?"

"Alex. I need to be free to take care of him and protect him from being hurt by my father and brothers."

"Walker Sr. is wicked. I knew that from the very beginning. I still can't believe the fool sent the Klan here."

"I am certain that was Wally's call. My father is too smart to use the Klan. He told someone to take care of the matter and maybe it was Wally, or maybe Wally just overheard something. He tried to score points with the old man, and Wally, much like a lot of academic geniuses that I have known lack common sense." He paused and wrinkled his brow. "What was that thing Granddad said concerning that?"

She smiled and said with a chuckle. "Man has got a Ph.D. and doesn't have the common sense to pour piss out of a boot with the directions on the heel."

Bret began to laugh and could not stop for several moments. He looked at Vicky who just smiled warmly at him, enjoying seeing his troubles lift momentarily. "Now finish what you were saying before we got diverted with analogies."

He breathed in deeply and began again. "Wally sent the order and when dad found out he blew a gasket. He also told him to keep the Klan away from here. That is why we have not seen them again."

He paused collecting his thoughts. "He knows that I'm hiding Teke. I wonder if he knows that we have been..."

"Sharing more than a few meals and an old house," she said, finishing the sentence.

Vicky sipped her coffee as the steam rose up toward her eyes. He noticed how much softer she looked these days.

She sat her coffee mug down on the table. "Is she going to leave?"

"In two weeks."

"You'll let her?"

"I can't stop her."

"Boy, that girl would follow you to the ends of the earth. All it would take is a word."

He said nothing as he lifted the coffee to his lips.

"Let's say you beat your dad with whatever plan it is that you have."

He interrupted her. "Do you think I can, beat him, that is?"

"No one else has before, but you have the advantage of knowing him very well, and also you have so much at stake." She sipped her coffee again. "Yes, I think you can bring that miserable man to his knees. Now, if you win where will you stay?"

"That depends on how much money I come away with."

She studied him as the room grew silent. "You're not going to tell me how you plan to get this money, are you?"

"No. I will tell you that it's nothing my father has not gotten away with for a long time."

"And you plan on having enough dirt to somehow keep him away from Alex?"

He nodded.

She continued, "Well I don't know what I can do to help you beat your father but I can do one thing. As far as a place to stay I have something for you."

She walked to her bedroom and emerged moments later, gently placing a green document on the table in front of him. "I don't know if you want to stay here, but this is the deed to the house on the river, along with two acres of land."

"The surveyors," Bret said.

"Yes, that's right. I fibbed a little."

"Why?"

She softened her voice, "Because I hope that you will stay. You need a place, and besides, you did all the work. Ralph would want you to have it. I want you to have it, with no obligation. You like it, and you aren't going to be able to stay with your family no matter how this turns out. Regardless, it's yours whether you decide to live there or not."

"I love that house, Vicky, and where it is. I have a little brother to look after. We accept. But there's one thing that you are wrong about."

"What's that?"

"We will be with family."

The old woman smiled at her grandson and reached across the table touching his arm. "Be careful, and one more thing, that deed means that it is yours. Don't ask my permission about anything, and when I am gone a long time from now, the rest of it will be yours as well. Let me guess, you plan on being a builder."

"The thought has crossed my mind."

"Ralph said that you had the gift."

He smiled at her. "I need to go."

"Don't underestimate your father," she warned.

"I won't. And do you know what his downfall is going to be?"

"What, son?"

"His underestimation of me," he answered softly. "Teke still can't believe that he is the way I describe him. I know I'm a selfish rich boy, but..." his words trailed off as he searched for some meaning, some understanding.

She looked at her grandson with much pride. "Bret, some people, they got nothing inside of them worthwhile. That's just how it is. Don't waste time trying to understand them. There are too many good people who care about family, friends, and neighbors."

"I know," he said as he nodded in agreement. He rose and walked to the door and back out into the morning.

* * *

One week later, the floor was complete. Bret and Teke sat out on the deck in silence as Alex slept peacefully.

Teke had worked hard varnishing the floor during the week while Bret was at work. He was amazed that she could do such work and do it as proficiently as she did. She surprised him continually with how gifted she was. She was intelligent, pretty, bordering on glamorous when she dressed up. Still, she could wear cut off jeans and a tee shirt, tie her hair back and work with her hands. She could do that and be no less alluring. She was perfect in conceivably every way. His opinion of her and how he felt never failed to amaze him. He had never even had a serious thought about a girl and now his mind was overrun with thoughts of her. He searched his mind for the right words to explain all of this to her. Even though she would leave, he wanted to somehow tell her what she meant to him. But the words always failed to leave his heart and escape through his mouth.

His thoughts left her momentarily and drifted to the file searching that so far had only turned up files on clients. He had looked in every file drawer, hoping to find one that contained damaging information. His time was dwindling and he needed to know about Jerry. He thought of other possible places that the information he sought could be. The house had long ago been searched diligently.

The previous day at work he read an article in the *Wall Street Journal* about the defense department upgrading their computer system. The article strongly stated that the existing contract would not be extended.

There were four companies in the running to supply the new contract. All had seen modest increases in their stock prices of late as the speculation soared. Brown Technology was thought to be the leading candidate on Wall Street. The other three were Mac, Lindell, and Maxwell. The victor would formally be announced soon. The decision no doubt had already been made and only a private few people in the government knew.

He was disturbed from his thinking by the gentle touch of the hand that came to rest on top of his hand. She rubbed his hand lightly before holding it firmly.

"Bret, sometimes this seems as if it is just one big dream. I've always been the smart one, top of my class. I've read more and studied more than my peers. And all of that will be useful. I want to teach and be the best teacher that any kid will ever have."

"I have no doubts that you will be. You're not only smart. You're so gifted. No kid will do better than you for a teacher."

"But all those books could never teach me what I've learned this summer with you. Books are great but I've learned life with you. I became a woman this summer. I see things so differently."

"And is that good?"

She smiled at him, "Yes."

"Even..."

"Even, if it hurts when it's over I would never wish to give up this time with you. You've taught me."

Startled, he replied, "Me, teach you. I'm the shallow, arrogant rich boy."

"You never really were that, not really. Money saw that, my dad too, and I saw it in time. You had a lot of good in you. It was just hidden away, saved for Alex. It's good that it is not only the two of you anymore. Both of you need more than each other."

"I'm sorry that things can't be different. I hate that any of this will hurt you. I hurt a lot of girls, and I did it without ever giving it a thought. Now, the thought of you hurting over me attacks me in places that I didn't know existed."

Bret paused, and then asked, "Teke, you asked me once if things would be different if you were white."

"Don't do that, Bret. It's no good. Hearts have eyes of their own. That's what you've taught me. You've taught me about heart."

"More likely it's the other way around," he said with a light chuckle.

"Teke, I need to spend all night at the office. I'm running out of time."

"What if you get caught? You couldn't pass it off as coming to work early. No one would believe that."

"I know, but I'll just have to be careful. I'll sneak in and work by flashlight. Will you look after Alex?"

"What do you think?" She chuckled softly. "He knows about us."

"How?"

"Just because we don't share the same bed when he's here does not mean that he is fooled. He's a smart little kid and very insightful."

"What did he say?"

"That he wished that all three of us could live together forever and that you and I would get married."

"What did you say?"

"I asked him what would make him think that we should get married and he said, because we have fun together."

She giggled and then added, "And because he said he saw us kissing down by the river one day when we thought that he was at Vicky's."

"Little snoop," Bret laughed. "He doesn't miss much."

Teke rose from her chair, moving in front of Bret. She bent down slightly, kissing him lightly on the cheek.

"I know that this is strange. I'm almost eighteen but I know in my heart I'll never love this way again."

"You can't know that for sure."

"Dad once said that sometimes you just know something in your heart. A feeling that can't be explained, but still you know."

"I think I got that speech about this house. He said that there was a reason that my grandfather wanted to finish it even though he was dying."

"Do you know the reason?"

"For him, I guess I was a reminder of the happier times of his life. He wanted to give me something, I guess, to teach me. I would have never been a builder without him."

"What about you, didn't you feel that there was a reason to finish this house?"

"Not really, it just happened gradually. Money pushed me with some encouragement from your dad. Then it became a hideout from Money, something to do. It progressed and I got caught up in it and then I wanted to finish it for me. Vicky gave it to me? I never expected that."

"I knew. She told me. You've done a lot of good with her. She may be a tough old woman, but she was lonely. She had no one to love. You two are much alike."

"What?"

"Come on, Bret, don't be dumb. Tough exterior, very little emotion, difficult to share your feelings, but underneath it all, you are both as soft as marshmallows."

"Got it all figured out, don't you?"

"It's not too hard to figure you out, besides you're from the south," she said before adding, "And you are not through with this house because most houses come with kitchen cabinets."

"In time."

"Don't take forever."

Bret got up from his chair. He wondered if she was really talking about cabinets. "I'm going to search files."

Teke cupped his face with her hands, before gently moving his hair to the side. "I love you, Bret. I love you with all that is within me."

He struggled to speak. Teke moved her hand down touching his mouth. "Don't say anything. When I leave next weekend, I want you to remember something. If you ever change your mind and decide that you want me, call me, and I will be on the next plane out. But don't ever call unless I can have all of you, and you are willing to say the hell with what anyone thinks about us being together." She kissed him gently and walked inside.

CHAPTER EIGHTEEN

Jerry

It was two-thirty in the morning. The city streets were dark and void of movement. Bret stretched his tired muscles as he peered out the window in his father's office. He looked south and studied the lights of the high rise bridge. One lone car was driving west. He watched the tail lights until they disappeared into Brunswick County.

He sighed and returned to the task at hand. He began the search of file cabinet number seventeen. He was tired, so much so that he almost passed by a row of large brown envelopes located in the midst of the pale yellow file folders. He looked through the packet expecting more legal records. The first pages differed from the boring legal files. They became boring personal records, with property deeds and numerous bills that had long ago been paid.

He was opening the third envelope when he noticed something written on the inner top flap. It was a phone number, 232-698-1200, extension 349. He jotted the number down and continued his search.

Twenty minutes passed. He rose from the chair and stood, stretching his fatigued body once again before walking to his father's private restroom. He looked in the mirror at the figure before him. The dark circles under his bloodshot eyes looked wearily back at him. He pulled the phone number from his pocket.

He walked to his father's desk and opened the telephone book. He thumbed through the pages searching for a list of area codes. The area code 232 was in the D.C. area. "D.C., politicians and the Defense Department, among other things," he said softly.

He reached for the telephone and dialed the operator.

"Operator," a lady answered lazily.

"Would you connect me to an operator in Washington D.C.?"

"How can I help you?" the lady asked, speaking with a shrill nasally tone.

"I have an unusual request. I met this girl that was visiting here and she gave me her number. She was a beauty. I can't make out her name on the paper. Can I give you the number and you tell me who it is listed to?"

"She must not have left too much of an impression if you can't remember her name," the lady snootily suggested.

"No, she was a beauty, but, well, I'm a little embarrassed to say it, but maybe I had a little too much to drink that night. Can you help me? This might turn out to be my future wife."

"I doubt that, but if it's a listed number, I guess there is no harm."

There were a few moments of silence and then the operator said admonishingly, "Sir the number belongs to an office in the Defense Department."

"I'm sorry. I must have written the number down incorrectly. Thank you for your time."

He placed the phone down on the desk gently. Had he caught his first break? Maybe this was the mysterious Jerry. But even if that were true it was only a start. Still...

He propped his feet up on the mahogany desk. "If only I could find this Jerry." He thought of his plan as he absentmindedly made a paper football. He placed a pointed end on the desk and thumped it across the room. "Good," he said wearily.

He rose and walked across the room to retrieve it. It was time to take a bigger risk. Time was running out. He removed all of the brown envelopes from the cabinet. There were twenty-three of them. He walked to his office for a large box. He walked back to his father's office and loaded the envelopes into the box. If there were anything in these files other than legal records, it would be in these envelopes. He had searched through numerous file folders finding nothing but clients' records. These files were the first to have anything personal in them, even if it was just some old bills. He would still search every file, but with his time dwindling he needed help. He carried the box of files to his office. He began packing them into his brief case. The envelopes were too bulky to fit more than half of the contents into his briefcase. He would make two trips. He didn't want to risk police officers observing him carrying a large box on the city sidewalks at three in the morning. The briefcase was more natural, even if the hours of work were not. He made the two trips to his car in twenty minutes total. He was exhausted. Sleep had become a luxury that he could only sparingly afford, but right now, he was dead on his feet. He decided to go home and return for his normal workday. He was home before four. He quietly entered the master bedroom. His eyes fell on the woman in the bed. The one good thing in all of the madness of late was that he had so little time to think about how much he would miss her when she left.

He stripped to his boxer shorts and climbed quietly in the bed, trying not to disturb her. He stretched out on his back and began trying to turn his mind off so that he could sleep a precious few hours. He had been lying there for a few minutes staring up at the ceiling when she awoke, feeling his presence in the bed. She moved closer to him, placing her hand on his chest. "Are you asleep?"

"Yes, be quiet," he answered.

"I didn't expect to see you before tonight."

"I'm exhausted," he sighed. "I need to sleep, but I can't stop thinking."

"Can I help?"

"No, well, yes. Today I need you to help me very much. Downstairs, there are twenty-three files. I need for you to search each one thoroughly for anything personal. Make notes of any stock records or phone records. No matter how insignificant that you may think they are. Keep the exact order of all the files. Nothing can be out of place."

"I'll do that."

"Teke, I really need for you to finish today. I know that it is a lot of work, but I need to get the files back in the office tonight. I'm counting on Ruby not having a reason to look in that file cabinet today. I don't want to chance more than that."

"Okay," she agreed. She touched the side of his face delicately.

"Now you need some rest."

"I'm so tired but so restless. I can't seem to find a quiet moment. Does that make sense?"

"It's the sixties and there is a word that has passed you by. Peace."

He mockingly waved the peace sign. "Well, burn the flag and pass me a joint."

She smiled at his feeble attempt at humor. "Peace in your mind. Everyone gets restless, but everyone searches for moments of peace when they can turn the world off and enjoy the stillness, the calm of where they are. Let me put it another way. It's what you find late in the evening when you watch the sun dip down into the river completing another day."

He smiled at her and said, "How come you know so much?"

"I didn't shut things out, like the world."

"You mean like I have."

"That's exactly what I mean. A world of only you and Alex may be safer for the two of you, but that does not mean that it is a better world."

"I think even I am aware of that now."

"Now, I want you to relax. You need to quit thinking about all of this right now."

"I wish it were that easy."

"I'm going to help you. Now, be quiet. No more talking, okay?"

He nodded.

She pulled his shorts off and tossed them to the floor. She rose over him and gently touched his lips with her own. "I want you to relax and don't worry about anything."

His mind began to ease as her slow beautiful motion delicately began to cast his anxieties to another world. His mind drifted to the ocean. The rhythmic movement reminded him of the waves as they approached the shore before running back to the sea, only to return, again and again. He thought of the night on the beach with her. The magic that made the moon break free from the clouds and turned the lights off on the pier. He wished he really could do magic such as that. He realized that he might never see anything such as this again. He doubted there would ever be a time for him where the girls would not be available and willing to give him whatever he desired. He could walk over the top of them if he so chose.

This woman was not like that. She was strong, even headstrong at times, defiant maybe, but he doubted anyone would ever truly love him as she did. She had shown him a world that he had never desired or even contemplated. She also would love him if he had no Marin name. She would love him if he were penniless. Their closeness reached a crescendo and out of him flowed all of the worries that enslaved his mind. Seconds later he was dreaming. He was on a small boat in the ocean and the sea was serene as it gently rocked him to sleep.

She rose from the bed and kissed him lightly. He looked peaceful. She had taken care of him. She only wished that she could be the one to do that for him for the rest of their lives. She walked downstairs and began to peruse the documents.

It was eight-thirty when Teke went to wake him. He awoke slowly. "What time is it?"

"It's eight-thirty."

He sat up quickly. "I'll be late. Why did you wait so late?"

"Calm down, you needed the rest and what is he going to do, fire you? That job is history after Friday."

"I know but I don't want to arouse any suspicions."

"Take a shower and dress. I'll have an egg sandwich ready for you. You can eat on the way."

He mumbled a quick "Thanks," and walked briskly to the bathroom. He emerged ten minutes later fully dressed in a blue suit. "I hate wearing suits."

She kissed him lightly. "But you look so handsome." She gave him a sandwich wrapped in tinfoil and a bottle of Sun-Drop as he made his way to the door. He noticed the files out of the corner of his eye lying on the floor. "You already started, when?"

"As soon as I watched you fall asleep."

He looked at her as he searched for words, but all he could mutter was, "Thanks, Teke."

During the first hour at the firm, Bret's thoughts focused on what transpired at home. She gave him so much and all he could mutter was an inadequate thanks. He wanted to do something that might show his appreciation.

He walked to the lobby and informed Ruby that he was going to the courthouse to observe a case. She requested details and he mumbled something incoherent as he made his escape.

He walked a block before stopping at a pay phone to call someone wiser than he was.

"Hello."

"Vicky, aw, aw..."

Her patience had grown along with her love for her grandson. She chuckled softly, "Son, we can't begin a conversation until you speak clearly. Now use your words."

"I need some advice and you're the only person I can think of that I can ask."

"Thanks for the vote of confidence."

"Aw, uh, I didn't mean it like that."

"Out with it boy," she said sternly.

"Teke has done so many nice things for me. I try to tell her but I just can't."

Vicky was amused at his plea for help but she kept that to herself. He was obviously embarrassed. She need not heap coals on the fire that was torching him.

"Son, go to the drug store and pick out a nice card. It doesn't have to be all mushy. A blank one will be fine. Go sit somewhere and think of something nice to write. Don't worry about writing too much. Just something simple that says how you feel. Seal the card and walk to the florist at Fourth and Market. Pick out some flowers and have them delivered to my house along with the card. Put your card into another envelope with my name on it have them delivered to my house. Tell them that you want delivery at noon. You may have to slide them some extra cash, but they'll do it."

"I've never sent flowers before."

"That's because you never cared about a girl before. It's a whole new world, isn't it, son?"

"Well, Grandmother, Teke says that you and I are just alike."

"What does she know? Just do what I said and stop bothering me."

"Bye, Grandmother."

"You know what you can do with that grandmother stuff," Vicky said before realizing he had hung the phone up part way through her reply. "Just like me", she said to herself. "Huh," and then she smiled broadly.

He went to the drug store and picked out a card with a picture of the ocean on the front. He sat on a sidewalk bench and started to write.

Dear Teke:

This morning when I left, I wanted to say thanks for all you did for me, but I could not find the right words. I know what you are thinking, but it is not because I am a dumb southerner.

I made fun of you for using a word such as peace, but that is what you gave me. You told me once that you wanted to teach so that you could make a difference. I want you to know that you have made me different.

Bret

* * *

The deliveryman gave the flowers to Vicky at noon as Teke hid in the hallway unaware that they were for her. She emerged as the man returned to his van. She saw a dozen roses centered on the kitchen table. "Wow, Vicky, you got flowers."

"No, child. You did."

"But..."

"Open it."

Teke opened the large envelope only to find another smaller envelope inside. She pulled it out. In bold black letters she saw her name.

She opened the card and read it. The tears gently flowed when she reached the part about how she had changed him.

"Bret sent those?" Vicky asked.

"Yes," she said, choking on her tears.

"Well, I didn't think the boy had it in him."

"The flowers are nice, but the words on the card I'll treasure forever. I can't believe he did this. What do you think persuaded him to do this?"

The old woman's voice turned crusty. "I have no idea."

"I guess this was his way of telling me that he loves me. Sometimes, I think that he is about to tell me, but then he turns away."

"It's hard for some people to say the words. Now, the last thing I'd do is defend that grandson of mine, but he knows that you are leaving. Maybe he thinks that it might hurt you more to hear them. He doesn't want you to return to Philadelphia and grieve over him. He certainly cares about you. You can see the tenderness held in his eyes for you. Sometimes too, Teke, it's easier for people to write about how they feel. There are no interruptions. No words to get tongue-tied over. In the long run, the written word I think is more special, more binding than the words that come from our mouths."

Teke nodded, understanding.

Vicky was near the table now. She looked at the young woman seated in the chair and gently placed her hand on Teke's shoulder. "I just hope, child, that the tenderness, the hope that is in you never fades away. Don't become hard and cynical."

Teke gazed into her eyes seeing a lifetime run through them. She smiled at her. "You're not hard at all."

* * *

Shortly after five, the Mustang roared to a stop outside the river house. Bret walked inside.

Teke stood at the bottom of the stairs dressed in faded cut off blue jeans and a white cotton blouse. She smiled broadly. "Somebody sent me flowers."

"Do I know him?"

"That's cute, especially for a southern boy with half a brain."

"Such charm you possess. Makes one wonder how you could get any man."

"Maybe it is my legs that you stare at all the time."

"Umm, or for what you did to me this morning?"

"That as well, and maybe my unmistakable beauty."

He smiled and did not reply.

"So which is it, Bret Marin, that makes me so irresistible to you?"

He had several answers running through his mind but he chose simplicity. "It is everything."

She sprinted across the floor, leaping into his arms. She wrapped her legs around his waist, her arms around his shoulders. "That's a good enough answer. Now, it's my turn. Take me to bed, you king of romance, you."

"What about the files? Did you find anything?"

"Maybe."

"What?"

"Listen closely, southern boy, bed first, talk later, understand?"

she said very slowly, mimicking his drawl. "Now, later I may just di-vulge the information."

He sighed deeply. "Well, if that is the only way," he said as he car-ried her up the stairs to the bedroom.

They swept each other away to another world. It was a world where the color of one's skin mattered not, only the tenderness of hearts. A place that could exist in this room, hidden away from the narrow viewpoint the world outside held.

It was eight o'clock when Bret woke. The sun nearly surrendered its fight to extend the day, and only faint flickers of light entered the room. Teke was asleep beside him. His first thoughts darted quickly to the files. He eased out of bed and walked downstairs.

He began to look at the bundle of files that lay on the floor in front of the couch.

She woke as he left the room. She retrieved his white dress shirt from the floor and put it on. She buttoned all but the top two and walked down the stairs. "There is a file on the kitchen table. I believe that is what you are looking for."

His heart quickened as he moved to the table. He pulled out a chair and sat down. He began to search the papers that contained Walker Sr.'s portfolio of stocks and bonds.

"Now, I need to know which ones are defense related."

"The ones with a star beside them."

He looked up, surprised, "How do you know?"

"Vicky loaned me her car to go to the library this afternoon. I re-searched every stock mentioned in those papers. I also made copies. Everything is in the files in order. You can return those tonight. I no-ticed that stock Luxum. That phone call you told me about. If Jerry made it from his office, then it will be in the phone records."

"If we make it to court, which I have no plans to do, but it could be ammunition."

She moved to his side and picked up her legal pad. "He has pur-chased twenty-four stocks over the past six years that derive a sub-stantial amount of their business from selling to the Pentagon. Each one of them has made a tidy profit to say the least."

Bret shook his head slowly. "You did good, real good," he added. "Now, I need to find Jerry."

"Have you tried the number you found?"

"Yes, but no answer. It's probably a private line that bypasses the secretary, much like one my father has."

"Don't you have enough with these papers? All of these stocks moved up shortly after he purchased them and all of them had some type of contract awarded to them within six months of his purchase date. The information he obtained was obviously illegal. I don't think that he will want any of this to become a matter of public record."

"It's still not enough. I've got to find Jerry."

She stood behind him and began to rub out the tension that was finding its way back into his body. "You will find a way, but today has been a good day. You've made a lot of progress. You'll get Jerry and complete this plan that you won't tell me about. Now, in the meantime, why don't you sneak those files back inside now and not at four a.m.? That way, you can get a full night's sleep"

"Good idea," he agreed.

"I've got another one. Pick up some pizza and go see your little brother. Stay the night there. You haven't seen him since you carried him back Sunday night."

"You're coming aren't you?"

"There is nothing else I would rather do," she smiled, as she reached around his neck and hugged him tightly.

CHAPTER NINETEEN

The visitor

It was four-forty, Friday afternoon. Bret dialed the number in Washington for at least the tenth time of the day. Once again, he was greeted with the annoying sound of endless telephone rings. He still couldn't be sure that the number even belonged to Jerry, but he had no other options for finding him at this point. He was running out of time. He knew the stock records were incriminating to his father, but that wasn't sufficient enough to complete his plan.

His thoughts were disrupted by a knock on the door.

"Come in."

The door opened revealing his least favorite sight of the job, Ruby. She had gone a little heavy with the blue eye shadow today, even by her standards. She apparently applied it with a two-inch paintbrush.

"I just got off the phone with your father. The closing arguments have been made. The jury will begin deliberating in the morning. Your father expects to be back in the office Monday morning. He wants to see you first thing. So, keep your calendar clear, sweetie," she said smugly.

She made no attempt to hide the smirk on her face. He knew that his father had confided his intention to dismiss Bret from the firm, and the family. It was obvious that the witch was eagerly anticipating witnessing his removal from everything that she assumed he held dear.

"Is there anything else, Ruby dear?"

"No, that about covers it," she replied with a sarcastic smile.

"Thank you, Ruby, for the good news, and of course I can't wait to see him."

She glared at him, hating the cocky smile painted on his face. She knew that she was being patronized and it infuriated her. She started to say something in rebuttal, but thought better of it. Monday she would have the satisfaction of seeing him brought to his knees once he learned that he was left out of the Marin fortune. Coldly she remarked, "I'll see you Monday."

She was two steps out the door when he said, "And please, Ruby, would you wear that same perfume? It gives off such a delicate aroma and yet it fills every office on the floor. It is so thoughtful of you to share."

"Little bastard," she mumbled under her breath as she returned to her domain.

"Heard that," he called out.

Her step paused but she continued walking without additional comment. She would see the boy on his knees groveling to his father Monday morning, but no amount of pleading would save him. The life he knew was over. She might even get a bonus for her good work.

Bret left the office and drove to the Marin house to see Alex. Alex ran out the front door upon hearing the Mustang.

"Hey, my little man. How's it going?"

"Good. I'm packed for the weekend."

Bret paused, hating to diminish the pleasure from Alex's face but it was his last weekend with Teke. "I haven't been able to see you much this week, have I?" He continued, not waiting for an answer. "I need to ask you for a big favor."

"What?"

"This weekend, I'm going to be real busy working on stuff to keep us together. I need you to stay with Barbara."

"Aw, Bret," he said as he slightly dropped his head.

"What's Vicky say?"

Alex looked Bret in the eye. "She says, never drop your head to anyone and always look people in the eye."

"Okay, Bret, but I want to see her before she leaves."

"Hey, did I get dumb overnight? I know how much you like her and she feels the same way about you."

"She's so cool, Bret. Will she come back next summer and stay with us?"

"I don't know about that."

"We will see her again, won't we?"

"Look, I won't lie to you so I won't promise you that we will see her again."

"Do you want her to leave?"

"It doesn't matter what I want. This is how things are."

"I want her to stay," Alex persisted.

"Well, she can't," Bret snapped, immediately sorry for the harsh tone he used.

"Alex, I'm sorry. I didn't mean to sound like that. Just give me some time and I'll try to explain everything later."

"You mean the part about black and white."

Bret sighed deeply. The ten-year-old in front of him was relentless in his pursuit of the truth. It was a truth that he could not share with him because he did not know.

Barbara watched the conversation through the window in the great room. She couldn't hear what was being said but she could tell that someone was in dire need of help.

She walked outside onto the front porch. "Alex, please go straighten your room."

"I did it already."

"Well, do it again. Move," she said firmly.

He looked at Bret hoping for an over rule of the decision, but none was granted. He trudged into the house.

Bret walked to Barbara and smiled faintly.

"It appears that you were losing that discussion. I thought you could use some help."

"Thanks, he doesn't understand."

"Do you?"

"What do you mean?"

As usual Barbara minced no words. "Do you understand why you fall for no one, but you fall in love with a black girl?"

"In love," he scoffed.

Barbara stood there shaking her head in dismay. "Yes, moron, you love her. Anyone with half a brain could see that. She's leaving and the people you detest the most are coming. It's kind of comical, isn't it?"

"That would depend on your perspective I guess."

"As far as Alex goes, he is upset. He's had nightmares twice this week." He wakes up screaming, "Bret, don't go. I don't want to stay here."

"Why didn't you call me?"

"Because you are busy and because I can handle it. How is your plan going?"

"It's not complete. I've got things on the old man, but I can't find this contact of his to finish things."

"Maybe you need a different perspective."

"Barbara, I trust you, but this you don't need to know about."

"I'd like to help."

"You know that if I win you are out of a job, don't you?"

"I know that and you know that I love Alex. I don't want him to go through what you have. He's better off with you. Now, let me help. Maybe I can't, but you've got nothing to lose," she implored.

He pondered for a moment before she interrupted. "Isn't it worth exploring every possible scenario when it comes to Alex and his well being?"

It was an easy question to answer. "Maybe you are right. I tell you what. I'll pick Teke up, while Alex and you go get pizza. Explain to him that his bedtime is ten sharp. Then, we will sit down and see if I've overlooked anything."

Barbara nodded in agreement as he handed her a twenty.

"Thanks, Barbara." Bret paused, his mind drifting to another subject. "The thing about Teke is nuts, isn't it?"

"It's different, that's for sure."

"Do you disapprove?"

"I don't approve or disapprove. It's your life. I won't tell you that I would choose the same path."

"I guess they only receive equal rights to a certain point, huh?"

Barbara was taken back by not only what she had heard, but more so from whom it derived. She could not give him an answer. His words troubled her. As she watched him walk to his car she was not all that pleased with what she was forced to see inside herself.

* * *

Another long day of work was completed at the home of Dr. Rowell. The remodeling project was nearly finished. Clarence studied his son as he had much of the day. Their work time together was usually filled with chatter and much laughter, but not today. There was something weighing on his son. He refrained from prying, feeling comfortable as always that his son would talk when he was ready.

They were in the basement putting the tools away. Money sat the skill saw down on the bench. "Dad," he said before hesitating. "Could you work the last couple of days without me?"

"I could if you have a good reason."

"I want to go home and spend a couple of days with Teke before she leaves."

"Is that the only reason?"

"No."

He watched his son until it was obvious that he was not going to be offered additional information at the present time. "You don't want to tell me now."

"No, sir, I don't."

Clarence smiled as he nodded slowly. "That's okay, son. How do you plan to get home?"

"I'll fly and I'll pay for it out of my wages."

"I hate to see you spend money that you'll need at school. If it's that important to you, I'll pay for the ticket."

They were interrupted by a noise at the top of the stairs, turning they saw Dr. Rowell.

Dr. Rowell was a short thin man who was nearing sixty. He was dressed impeccably as always and he always wore a bow tie. Today's choice was a deep rich blue color, framed on a white shirt. The neatly pressed pants he wore were navy blue.

He was a driven man, a practical man. The practice he had built enabled him a nice lifestyle and time to pursue his passion, civil rights. He had dined with Dr. King and he marched the streets of the Deep South. And he still had so much to do.

"I'm sorry. I wasn't eavesdropping. I wanted to invite the two of you out for dinner tonight. It's been a long day and the two of you have worked extremely hard. I know I'm not the easiest person to work for. In fact, I'm rather demanding about everything being just right, a perfectionist, so I've been often told. Clarence, if you do indeed approve of this young man going to see his sister, and if you don't mind my intrusion I would like to pay for his airplane ticket. Consider it a little added bonus to show my appreciation of a job well done."

"There is no need for that, Dr. Rowell. You have been more than fair to us," Clarence replied.

"Oh, it's worth it. I have a lot of good things in my life, but no family. My parents died years ago, and I was an only child. My priorities didn't allow time to find a woman to share my life with. That's a fine young man you have. I'll pay for his ticket today so he can have time with his sister. One day when he sees a brother in need, he will help him. Agreed? Besides, the young man needs his money for school. Scholarships don't pay for everything a young man needs. I remember that all too well."

Money looked at his dad for approval. Clarence gave an ever so slight shake of his head.

"Go upstairs and call the airport. Go ahead, son," Dr. Rowell instructed.

"Thank you," Money said as he started up the steps passing him at the top.

Dr. Rowell smiled at the gifted carpenter below. "Thank you for allowing my help and forgive my interference."

"There is nothing to be forgiven for, Dr. Rowell. Thank you for your kindness."

The two men were sitting and chatting in the basement a few minutes later when Money appeared. "There is a flight leaving in an hour or I can wait until tomorrow afternoon. Can I go now?"

"Sure, son," Clarence answered. "We'd better get moving."

Dr. Rowell extended his hand to Money. They grasped each other's hand. "You do well in school. Place academics first, young man and basketball second. It may not seem this way at the present time but the academics will take you further in the long run of life."

"Yes, sir."

"Well, Clarence," Dr. Rowell said, "it appears that only two of us will be going to dinner. I'll pick you up in an hour and a half, if that is satisfactory?"

"That sounds fine. Thank you," Clarence said as the two men shook hands. Dr. Rowell had a slight bounce in his step as he hurried back up the stairs, still basking in the warmth that he felt from helping the son that he never had.

* * *

By seven p.m., Bret and Teke were at the Marin house much to the delight of Alex. Barbara felt a twinge of jealousy as she watched Alex gush over Teke's arrival, then quickly felt foolish for the thought.

The drive from Castle Hayne to the richest neighborhood in the city had proved interesting. In the light of day, Bret demanded that Teke ride up front. He reasoned that by the time word got back to Walker Sr. everything would be over, one way or the other. He knew he was flaunting it when they rode with the top down, but he really didn't care. It was their last weekend together and he refused to see her hide any longer.

Teke reassured him that she did not mind hiding and they argued for ten minutes in the driveway at the river house. He refused to soften his position. They stood silently by the car for what seemed minutes before he won the stalemate.

"Ms. Wilkins," he had said as if he were announcing the Miss America Pageant. "I'll have to insist that you ride in the front of the bus."

He also had an ulterior reason that he did not share with her. He knew that she wanted to remain here and forge a life together. He knew she believed that somehow they could overcome the difference in their skin color with what flowed so freely between them. He set out to prove her wrong.

The good people of the south did not let him down. There were several glances from the cars he passed. The most interesting incidents were when they were caught by a red light. People could not resist staring. Some shook their heads, distraught, as if something pure was being desecrated before their eyes, while others cast disparaging remarks.

His plan was foiled because Teke knew exactly what he was up too and when they arrived at the Marin house, she looked at him, and said evenly, "I don't care about those people. Everyone is not like that."

It was eleven o'clock. Alex was sleeping soundly in his bed. Bret, Teke, and Barbara sat at the kitchen table. Walker Sr. had called Barbara earlier in the evening. His time of arrival was estimated to be eleven o'clock Monday morning.

Bret laid out Walker Sr.'s financial papers and proceeded to share the intricate details of his plan. They listened closely.

The girls bounced questions off of him for nearly an hour, but nothing new was discovered.

It was just past midnight. Barbara was flipping through Walker Sr.'s portfolio again. "He doesn't miss anything. Why would he risk this with this Jerry that you can't find? He's got so much."

"He'll never have enough. He grew up as poor white trash, being scorned and ridiculed."

"What about his family?" Teke asked.

"His parents died in a car wreck when he was in college. He was an only child. Wealth and power is the name of the game with my old man. It is the sum of his existence."

Barbara's eyes brightened suddenly. She smacked the table with the palm of her hand. "Bret, maybe you don't need to find Jerry."

"But that's my only chance."

"What if your father has already purchased the stock?"

"That's possible, I suppose. I planned to feel Jerry out in our conversation before asking about the computer contract."

"So you were going to pretend to be your dad right?"

"Right."

"You have the number of his stock broker. Call and tell him that you need an update on his last stock purchase. Think of some reason why. And maybe..."

"And maybe he mentions one of the four computer stocks, if he's already bought it. That's the one. That might just work. I've focused all of my energy into finding Jerry. Maybe, if I'm lucky, real lucky, I don't even need him. Why didn't I think of that?"

"Because you needed a woman's brain," Barbara said mockingly.

"Let me get this straight Bret, you are going to pretend to be your father on the phone?" Teke asked.

He nodded.

"Are you sure that you can pull it off?"

He smiled as Barbara answered the question. "He's fooled me countless times. He can do it."

"Well, at the very least, it gives me another option in case I don't find Jerry." He rose from his chair. "I'm going to tuck Alex in."

* * *

Money stared out the airplane window into the darkness, seeing nothing but a small group of stars in the distance. It was three a.m. and he was exhausted. He tried to sleep but finding a comfortable position in a cramped seat with his tall frame proved fruitless. The plane departed Raleigh just minutes before. It was his third and last connecting flight to home. He continued debating on his course of action as he had all night. He wanted his suspicions to be wrong, but he was unable to convince himself. Teke didn't like Bret when he left. He practically forced his sister to stay at the river house. Now, she would turn down returning to Philly under the pretense that she wanted to spend time with his dad and him. He loved Bret like the brother that he never had. But there was one disturbing thing about Bret. He rolled through women as freely as the wind moves the leaves of a tree. What he could not shake from his mind was that Teke was his best friend's latest conquest. He would know soon enough.

It was just past seven and the sun was giving off the intense heat of summer already. A lady from the front desk shook Money slightly. "There is a cab out front."

Money slowly woke and almost fell to the floor as he tried to rise from the bed that he had made from chairs. His flight arrived at four-fifteen and every taxi-driver in the city was asleep. He debated briefly about walking the five miles to Vicky's house but exhaustion won out over that idea. At least he managed a couple of hours of rest. He looked at the middle-aged woman in front of him. "Thank you," he mumbled, as he grabbed his bag and started for the cab.

The stifling early morning heat embraced Money as he threw his bag into the back seat of the taxicab and slid in beside it. He gave the elderly black man the address and lay back against the seat.

Money endured the driver's excessive chatter along with the disgusting smell of his cigar during the ten minute ride. He instructed the cab driver to drop him off at the highway that ran in front of

Vicky's property. He gave him a five dollar bill and shut the door.

He walked down a worn path in the woods that ran a few yards off of the drive. He wanted to avoid Vicky's watchful eye and he wanted to arrive in silence. He reached the bottom of the steps to the river house, breathed deeply, and preceded silently up the steps. He noticed that the door was open, probably in an attempt to catch any breeze that the morning air was surrendering. He heard voices coming from inside.

He walked to the front door, still undetected. Bret was sitting at the kitchen table with a plate of bacon and eggs before him. There was his sister bent down behind him with her arms around his upper chest. She was wearing an over sized baseball undershirt, white with black sleeves, and orange basketball shorts. She rose smiling and walked to the other side of the table. She was sitting down when she noticed her brother now standing inside the house. Her gasp startled Bret and he quickly turned to the door. The picture in front of him was haunting. His friend's face was masked in a mixture of pain and rage.

"Well, isn't this great? The two of you playing house in the woods," Money said as he walked to the end of the table and pulled out a chair and sat down.

Bret and Teke sat stunned, speechless.

Money continued, his voice calm, his outward demeanor tranquil, camouflaging the furious turmoil from within. "Can't think of anything to say? So, little sister, this is why you wanted to remain here, to be with this lying back stabbing friend of mine." He turned his anger toward Bret. "So, I guess you slept with all the white girls at the club and now you need a little variety, or should I say some brown sugar."

"It's not like that," Bret said, finding his voice.

"Well, explain it to me then, friend. I asked you to protect my sister, not sleep with her," Money said, his voice rising slightly through his clenched teeth.

Bret knew there was no answer that he could give that would prove adequate at this moment. Besides, what could he say? He betrayed the only friend that he had. No matter how he attempted to spin it that much was true.

Money used the silence to turn back to his sister. "Do you have any idea how many girls this guy has slept with? Do you think that any of them have ever meant anything to him? He's a rich white boy who is used to getting everything. You are nothing but another conquest. How stupid can you be?"

"Wait a minute," Bret demanded. "You've got every right to be mad at me, to be disappointed, but don't come in here acting as if you are the pure white snow, untouched, unblemished. That's wrong and you know it."

"I am nothing like you."

"Maybe, but you have had your share of women. So, if I had a few more, that makes me so much worse than you?"

"No!" Money shouted, and slammed the table with the palm of his hand so hard that the dishes rattled, causing Teke to jump. "No, you are worse because this notch on your bedpost is my sister.

"And what if she is pregnant? Did either of you think of that? It's hard enough for a black person to survive in this country and you want to risk a child that would be shunned by black and white. That's pretty damn selfish."

"I was on the pill before I got here," Teke answered.

"What?" Money asked, in disbelief.

"Mom and I talked about it a few months ago. I was dating Lawrence at the time. I was in no rush but we had an open honest talk and decided that it was best for me to be safe. I want a college education and a career. I didn't want to be another unwed young mother stuck in a hole from which I could never escape. Look, big brother, I know that you want me to be this symbol of wholesomeness while you slide from one girl to the next. That's not really fair."

"It's different for guys." Money knew as soon as the words escaped his mouth that they were wrong and they reeked of shallowness and unfairness.

She smiled. "Yes, I know. If a guy has a dozen partners, he is a stud, but a girl, she's a whore if she does the same. Now, I want you to listen to me and cut the older brother crap. Fourteen months is not all that much. I asked Bret to sleep with me. He is my first and my only. He said no, but I persisted."

"Why Teke? Why him?" he asked, the exasperation clinging to his every syllable.

"I love him."

Money shook his head in disbelief. "You are seventeen years old and you are in love. Give me a break."

"Why is it impossible, because it hasn't happened to you? Well, I won't try to explain it to you. It is something that you have to experience to know how it feels. It's not about age. It's a feeling between two people."

"Oh, and I guess he loves you."

Bret said nothing as he felt the eyes of the table descend on him.

"Speak up, lover boy. Tell my sister the truth. Do you love her, or is she like all the rest with the exception that she is not white?"

Bret fought the anger that was growing inside of him as he tried to explain. "I know that you are disappointed in me. I let you down and I'm sorry. I know that is not enough. But Money, your self-righteous behavior is getting on my nerves. What difference does it make how I feel about your sister? Nothing can come from it. I know that. We can't ride off into the sunset and live happily ever after. We are different. That can't be explained away. But I'm tired of you degrading your sister. She is not like anyone else that I've been with. I care enough to send her home when she wants to stay."

"How long has this been going on? I mean, did you bag her the day we left?" Money asked callously.

"No," Bret answered angrily.

"Tell my sister how many other girls you were with during the time she has been here." Money looked at Teke, who wasn't completely sure of the answer.

"None," he responded firmly.

"None?" Money asked incredulously. His voice raised in pitch.

"I have never lied to you about anything."

Money rose from the table. "Teke, get your things. Dad will be home Tuesday and you can fly home after that."

"Are you going to tell him?" Teke asked.

"No, you are. Now get your things."

"No."

"What do you mean no?"

"That's what I said. I'll be home Monday. I'm staying the rest of the weekend here."

Money grabbed her arm tightly. "Get up now."

"Stop it. You're hurting me," Teke shouted.

Bret was up moving toward them. He shoved Money hard, knocking him back several feet. "Let go of her."

Money moved toward Bret but Teke jumped in between them. "You two are not going to do this. Money, go home. I'll be home Monday."

The two men stood a few feet apart, fists clenched, insides churning.

Money finally nodded, his eyes never leaving Bret. "Okay, I'll go home. The debt I owe you is clear. I never want to see you again. Stay away from my house and don't call my sister when she returns to Philadelphia. Just move on back to your white country club girls."

Money was half way to the door when Bret asked, "So, Money is it because she is your sister, or because I'm white? I was good enough to be your best friend but not good enough for your sister. This equality puzzles me. You seem to pick and choose it to fit the situation."

Money was at the door when he turned back. He shook his head admonishingly. "No, it's because of how you are with women."

Both men's words reached their intended target, stinging the other with their sharpness, and even more with their clarity.

CHAPTER TWENTY

The meeting

The early morning thunder woke Teke. She looked at the space beside her, feeling the emptiness. They had said their good-byes last night or more accurately early this morning, when she held him one last time.

She rose from the bed thinking of the busy morning in front of her. Vicky's car was parked by the stairs. Vicky would drive her to Castle Street after one last meal together. That was the plan. A plan she found heartbreaking.

She cast a glance to the tiny nightstand beside the bed and was dismayed to see that same white Bible resting on it. *How?* It was open and she picked it up. Her eyes drew to Psalms 20:4 *May he give you the desire of your heart and make all your plans succeed.*

She knelt down beside her bed.

"Jesus, I hope that you can really hear me right now and I pray that you take into your heart what is in my heart and that you do me the honor of really contemplating what I am asking. I need to believe that you are not this huge scowling figure writing down all we do wrong on some huge blackboard in the sky to be used against us at a later time. That seems to be what I hear when I do attend church. Sometimes I want to stand up and scream what about love, grace, compassion, and understanding, but of course, I don't. I do not believe that I will ever have a request more important than this. How strange to find this Bible beside me and such an ironic scripture. I have so many desires in my heart and I believe that you know them all. I would that you would grant Bret and me a life together but the greater desire of my heart is that you please help Bret today. Maybe what he is doing is not pure, but his motivation certainly is. He is trying to save his little brother and what could be of more importance than that? Please make sure that he and Alex remain together. They need each other desperately."

Tears began to fall on the bed below, gently at first, but escalating rapidly. She sobbed, "God, I knew that it would hurt, but it's so much worse than I thought it would be. I feel so empty inside. Is it punishment for doing wrong? Was I wrong, God, to love a white man? Are we really different because of the color of our skin? I want to believe that you look on our hearts and that you don't see color, and if you don't see color should anyone else?" Her question lingered in the air with no apparent answer.

She cried several minutes before finally regaining at least temporary control of her emotions. She placed the suitcases on the bed, opened them, and began to pack her clothes. She looked around her favorite room in the house and then she walked out into the upper hall. She looked around the house and began collecting memories that would need to endure for a lifetime.

The walls that now sectioned off the various rooms. The floor below glistened with varnish. She managed a brief chuckle at the memory of her fall with the sander and the laughter that ensued with two people she held so tightly in her heart. It was a beautiful house. An empty building waited decades for someone to occupy it and to make it a home. It proved in many ways to be a hideaway for Bret and then for her. "*The River Hideaway*," she said softly with a forced smile.

She heard thunder clap and an early morning shower descend gracefully to the earth. The thunder boomed again and she smiled faintly as she recalled the intense storm that sent Bret scurrying home to her that afternoon. She returned to packing, fighting gallantly to stave off additional tears.

* * *

Bret parked near a pay phone close to the law firm. It was almost nine o'clock. He had continued to dial the number in D.C., but with no luck. He stepped out of his car into the morning rain, walking to the phone booth. He breathed deeply and looked up into the dark gray sky. "God, I sure could use some help right about now. I have done more wrong things than I can count but trying to take care of my little brother is not one of them. I realize that I don't have a thing to bargain with. But I am asking you to help me save my little brother and maybe in the process save myself as well. Vicky says you always hear us. I sure hope you have an attentive ear at this moment." He deposited one dime and dialed the number.

A pleasant sounding lady greeted him, "Good morning, Stone Brokerage."

Bret prepared for what he hoped would be the best Walker Marin Sr. imitation of his life. He breathed deeply and thought about basketball. It was late in the game. Let others be nervous at the pace of the game while for me the game is played in slow motion.

"Jimmy Jones," he demanded.

"He's on the line with a client, sir. Could I have him call you?"

Gruffly Bret replied, "You tell him that Walker Marin is on the phone."

"Excuse me one second, sir."

Seconds later, a very anxious Jimmy Jones was on the phone. His other client quickly forgotten. "I'm sorry for the wait, Mr. Marin, how can I help you?"

"I've misplaced some records and I need the information."

Jimmy reached for the pen on his desk and proceeded to write. "Okay, what do you need?"

"My last purchase."

"That information will be in your statement that will be sent out Friday."

"Jimmy, is that what I asked of you?" he asked evenly.

"Uh, no...no sir," he stammered.

"The information now," Bret said sternly.

Panicked, Jimmy began searching his records. "Hold on, sir. I'll find it. That would be the purchase you made from Chicago," he said, trying to appease the tyrant on the other end of the phone.

Chicago, Bret thought, his hopes soaring.

"Okay, sir, you purchased one thousand shares of Gillette, DuPont, Xerox, and ten thousand shares of..."

Bret's pulse quickened as he waited on the last stock. It had to be one of the four. Everything depended on it.

Jimmy stammered slightly before releasing the final name, "And Lindell. Wait, I'll give you the prices that were paid."

He had him. My God, he had him. "Thank you, Jimmy. That's all I need for now," he said, hanging up before Jimmy had a chance to reply. He was congratulating himself for playing things so cool when he noticed the white knuckles that had not yet released their death grip on the phone.

Jimmy started to speak but stopped when he heard the dial tone. "Thank you," he said softly. Never had Walker Sr. ever said thank you to him for anything. He debated for a moment but the phone rang with the potential of another sale. He answered the phone and forgot about Bret's one mistake.

"Yes!" Bret shouted at the top of his lungs as he emerged from the glass confines of the phone booth. He thrust both arms into the air as if he had just hit the game winning shot as the buzzer exploded.

An elderly woman passing by looked very strangely at him. He smiled warmly and greeted her. "God, it is a beautiful day, isn't it?"

She muttered, "It's raining, you fool," before quickening her pace to escape him. Bret laughed loudly as he began the three block walk to his broker's office.

He arrived at Washington Securities at nine twenty. He had transferred his account from Stone Brokerage shortly after turning eighteen when his father could not legally stop him. His only reason then was to avoid doing business where his father did. The more separation from his father the better. Plus, he knew that it would anger his father and he enjoyed doing that tremendously.

He asked for Micah Brooks, a young broker who had only been in the business for a year and a half. Micah was bright, energetic, and happy to have a member of the Marin family as his client.

Bret sold all his stock when he first began to formulate his plan. The part of the plan where he would break from his father and take his brother with him, but leave with the financial security he needed as well. He needed money and he needed it now. There was the best little brother in the world banking on him. If the purchase were to be investigated at any time, which he doubted, it might look suspicious. But the way he appraised the situation, there was nothing linking him to the stock. Nothing that could be proven that is. He had not gotten illegal information from Jerry. He had simply taken a youthful gamble. He also had a pattern of buying only computer related stocks to this point. The scales tipped heavily in his favor.

A young female receptionist tried in vain to flirt with him during the brief walk as she escorted him into Micah's office. He entered the office, turned back to smile once at her, and closed the door as she stood just on the other side of it.

"Micah," he began. "You are my broker, correct?"

"Of course I am."

"I chose you and this company much against my father's wishes. He said that this was a two bit company for losers." Bret paused, waiting for his words to sink in. "I am eighteen years old and legally, if you were ever to divulge any of my transactions to anyone, including my father, I will sue you and this firm. Do we have an understanding?"

"What's the problem, Bret?" Micah asked, as he rubbed his hand nervously through his thick blonde hair.

"There is no problem. I want to know that I have your loyalty."

"You have that. I swear to you," Micah replied, as he leaned in from his seat. Sweat broke out on his forehead and Bret almost felt sorry for him.

"Very well, how much money is in my account?"

Micah looked up the account information quickly. "$18,422."

Bret pulled a certified check from the Bank of Wilmington. He had cashed in his savings account as well as his savings bonds. Everything in his name was now liquidated.

Excluding the five hundred dollars in his pocket, he was prepared to bet the ranch. "Add this to my account."

The struggling young broker in front of him choked slightly as he said, "Plus twenty-four thousand dollars." He smiled softly and his eyes lit up.

"That comes to forty two thousand, four hundred and twenty-two dollars. Now, what do you want me to do?"

"There is a computer stock that trades on the American Stock Exchange, Lindell. Their symbol is LYD."

"Let's see. The last trade Friday was a bid of nine seventy-five, with an asking price of ten."

"Bet it all."

"All of it, on one stock? With all due respect that is..."

"The move of a foolish teenager playing a hunch," Bret said, finishing his statement. "Now, how much can we buy?"

Micah punched in the numbers on the calculator, his eyes growing with his largest commission to date. "We can purchase forty two hundred shares."

Bret looked at the clock. It was nine thirty. "Do it."

Micah looked at his client. "I know about this stock. It's one of the four in the running for supplying computers to the Pentagon over the next four years. But Bret, the rumor on the street is that Maxwell is the leader to get the contract. Its stock has doubled in two months on the speculation alone. I can't know how severe the other three stocks will react when the winner is announced, but it certainly won't help."

"Are we having a problem communicating? Buy Lindell, now," Bret said evenly, leaving no room for debate.

Micah called in the order. The trade was executed within minutes as Bret sat patiently waiting.

Bret stood and shook Micah's hand. "Don't call me at my father's house or firm. I won't be there. I'll call you with a phone number later."

The next stop was his father's house. He parked the car in the drive. The rain had stopped and the skies were beginning to clear.

He entered the house seeing no one. "Alex, Barbara," he yelled.

Alex bounded down the stairs. Barbara walked to the top of the stairs to observe. Bret stood at the bottom, just below the first step and opened his arms. Alex leaped from the third step and Bret caught him, hugging him tightly. He lifted him up high in the air as easily as if he were a feather. He looked him in the eye and gave an order. "Let's get your things together. We're going home."

"Do you mean it, Bret? Do you really mean it?" he shrieked.

"You bet your skinny little behind I do," he said as he put him down, turned him around and gave an affectionate pop on his butt.

Alex ran enthusiastically to his room. Barbara, watching all of it, now moved down the stairs toward Bret. "It worked?" she asked, through her tears that emerged suddenly.

He nodded and smiled. It was a smile of satisfaction, a smile of a new life, a better life for his brother and for him. She reached him and they hugged each other tightly.

"Does your father know?"

"Not yet, but I think I have this wrapped up pretty tight. It was your idea. It paid off. I was so locked in on finding Jerry that I may have never thought of this. I owe you."

"No, you don't. Just call me when you need a baby sitter, or even when you don't. I don't want to lose touch with that little guy." She paused, before adding, "Or you."

The two friends embraced each other again. "Does Teke know?"

"No. We agreed that it would be easier if last night was our ending. Money showed up unexpectedly Saturday morning. He knows about us and he is pretty upset. I lost my only friend."

"No, you didn't. You may have lost your best friend, but you still have a friend. Heck, I actually like you now. I'll call Teke and give her the news, okay?"

"That would be good, but wait until tonight when everything is sealed."

"Tonight, aren't you going to meet your father at the office at eleven?"

"No, he's going to meet me on my home court. He just doesn't know it yet."

"Can I help?"

Bret shrugged and started to speak.

As usual, she interrupted him, "What's he going to do, fire me? My job here is finished. Besides, he paid me enough this summer that I'll be fine. School is right around the corner anyway. I need the time to study."

"Come to the old house at four-thirty."

"I'll do better than that. I'll help move Alex's stuff and help him set up his new room."

"I'm going to rent a small moving truck. I'll be back soon. I don't want to get there before one o'clock. I need to give Teke plenty of time to leave."

Barbara saw the hurt in his eyes and she knew that he wanted badly to see Teke. She also knew that he wouldn't.

"Bret, please do me one favor."

"What's that?"

"You're leaving this house and your father and brothers. Leave your hatred behind as well."

"You ask a lot of me, oh wise baby sitter," he said with a grin.

"I know, but trust me. I've been right a couple of times before. I'm right about this, too. The three of them aren't worth it. It pays them too big a compliment. Do it for Alex, if not for you."

Bret looked admirably at his friend and nodded his head. "You are pretty sharp for a baby sitter, aren't you?"

She returned his smile and replied as she walked away, "I'm not your average baby sitter."

Bret walked to the kitchen and picked up the phone. He dialed the number of the Marin Firm and was greeted by the secretary that had made his life this summer as miserable as possible.

"Ruby, this is Bret. Give my father a message when he arrives. Tell him to come to the old house by the river at five-thirty. We will discuss a proper settlement. Also, tell him that Alex is with me and that is how it will be from here on out."

Ruby started to threaten and demand that he be at the office at eleven as he was told, but Bret cut her off. "Tell him to be there, along with my two lovely brothers. Oh, be sure and tell him to bring Jerry if he wants too. See you, Ruby," and he hung up the phone.

* * *

The last of the dinner dishes were washed, dried, and put away. The car out front was packed with Teke's clothes. She had called the airport and her flight would depart at ten forty-five Thursday morning.

The young beautiful black girl and the old beautiful white woman shared a smile encased with the same sadness that is found on the beach when summer departs and its return seems so very far away.

"Vicky, I don't know where to begin to say..."

Vicky watched her as she choked on her words and felt the lump rising in her throat. "There's no need to say anything."

"Yes, there is. You saved my life and you taught me. I thought the south was full of nothing but ignorant racist white people and black people that didn't have the good sense to leave. You've treated me as a friend and helped me to grow, much the way a parent, a really good parent, would teach their own child." The tears that impeded her speech now flowed as freely as the creeks outside, replenished once again by the morning rain. "I love you, Vicky. I'll never forget you."

The two women that fate had strangely thrown together on a night intended for evil embraced each other tightly, neither wanting to let go. Vicky, as always, tried to remain strong but the hard edge worn through the most difficult times now abandoned her. Tears stored away like items in a forgotten attic began to ease out of the faded blue eyes of the woman who felt that she was watching another daughter leave, never to return. She had not shed the first tear when her daughter died, or when she watched her husband shrivel up and die. Now, she could not cease the stream of tears that flowed from her soul.

Teke was touched deeply as she held Vicky and felt the tears of a dear, dear, woman. She looked her in the eye as she had been taught, "Vicky." Their watery eyes met each other. "You have two grandsons who are coming home to you and they need you. I need to leave here knowing that I don't have to worry about them. You hear me, you tough old woman?"

Vicky nodded as she fought valiantly to regain her composure. "Teke, I wish..."

"I know," Teke said as she shook her head. "I do too."

They walked out to the car. Vicky drove steadily down the dirt road toward the main highway. Teke never once looked back. They rode in silence to Castle Street.

* * *

Vicky watched as the Cadillac rolled past her house containing Walker Sr. and his two sons. She had questioned Bret about his plan, but his only reply was, "Trust me." She would know soon enough.

The three men were dressed in their conservative gray business suits that seemed out of place here in the country. They walked up the steps to the deck and approached the door.

Before they had time to knock, Bret shouted, "Come in." He and Alex sat beside each other at the kitchen table. A stack of papers sat on the table in front of Bret.

They entered the house. Walker Sr., with his customary scowl on his face. Wally and William glared haughtily at Bret, as they walked behind him. They enjoyed watching their father defeat people and none more so than their misguided little brother.

"Win your case, Father?"

"I always win, or have you forgotten?"

"Have a seat," Bret said as he gestured with his hand to the three empty seats across the table from him. "This won't take long."

His father glared at him. "It surely won't. Alex is to come home now and you are to never see him again. You are eighteen and you are on your own."

Bret softly nodded his head. "I thought as much. He turned to Alex, who if frightened, was showing no traces of it. "Where do you want to live?"

"It doesn't matter what he wants," Wally interrupted. "Go get your things now, Alex," he demanded, his voice sharply filling the room.

Bret chuckled softly as he rose. "I think that I told you once before not to speak to him that way. Now, the business at hand is with your father. But I will take a moment if you wish to step outside," he said as he swept his hand in invitation toward the door. The offer was declined with silence and even more fear.

Bret coolly sat back down and turned to Alex. "Now, Alex, answer the question," he said, using a gentle tone of love that his father and two brothers could not comprehend.

"I want to stay with you. You love me, they don't. They're mean to me. I hate living with them."

Walker Sr. studied the situation, sure of triumph as always. "Are you crazy? You are an eighteen-year-old insubordinate boy who has blown a lifetime of riches. I'll have you arrested anytime that you go near Alex. You didn't plan this too well, did you? Have you forgotten who I am?" he roared with rage. "I'm Walker Marin Sr., the most powerful man in this state."

"No, I have not forgotten who you are," Bret replied evenly, with a dismissive shake of his head. "You are the coldest, most heartless man I have ever known, and if I could cut the blood from in my body that derives from you I would do it in a heartbeat."

Bret smiled and savored the moments passing by. His father looked at him as if he were crazy. Calmly Bret lifted the upper portion of the papers that lay in front of him and tossed them to his old man. "You have quite a gift for picking stocks, particularly defense related stocks. Now, correct me if I'm wrong, Walker, but if you receive information from a government official about who is getting a contract before the general public knows, that is illegal, isn't it? You know one thing that I couldn't find out is what you have on this Jerry. It's got to be big, really big."

"You don't know what you are talking about."

"Call my bluff then. What's the District Attorney's name, uh, Richard Simpson? Boy, how you have humiliated that man. Do you think that he might enjoy watching you sweat on the stand? Even if he failed to get a conviction it would still damage your reputation, don't you think? Think about the publicity and the whispers behind your back at your high and mighty country club." He paused and then gestured toward the documents. "Your purchases of defense stocks all so perfectly timed and never wrong. Maybe you and Jerry even got comfortable and used phones that you shouldn't have. Like the day in April when he called you at home. Remember, I came home for lunch that day? That would be when you bought Luxum, and wouldn't you know it, they were awarded the contract. How much did you make on that?"

Walker Sr. fidgeted slightly in his chair. "You're insane. You can't prove this. The records were gathered illegally."

"Prove it."

Walker Sr. searched for something to say as his sons sat motionless, their smiles slowly fading as they waited for their astute father to emerge with a scheme as he always did. Walker Sr. shook his head in disbelief. "And what reputation will you have? I know about your girl you had out here. That was quite bold Friday night driving around town with her. Was she a replacement for the girls at the club that you won't be able to get now? Those type girls don't like poor people."

The two shadows smiled and nodded as they watched dad rebound to take care of the one of them that did not belong.

"Who's poor?"

"Oh, your little bit of savings won't last long. You'll be living in a rundown trailer park, digging ditches for a living."

Bret slid the green deed to the house they were in across the table. "This house is bought and paid for. Check the name on the deed. It's mine."

Walker silently cussed Vicky under his breath before turning to Alex, "Son, you wouldn't want to stay out here and be poor. You'll miss the club and your friends."

"I want to be with Bret. I don't care about anything else."

"Young man," Walker said sharply.

"Goes for you too, Walker," Bret said evenly. "Don't use that degrading tone with him."

"You..." Walker began before Bret raised his hand in the air to interrupt him.

Bret looked at Alex and winked. "Walk to Vicky's and wait for me. Everything's okay. I promise."

Alex rose from the table and walked away.

Bret brought his focus back to the table, specifically to Wally. "I guess that it was you that sent the Klan here. You're the only one dumb enough to do that. Do you realize that was attempted rape and murder? That wasn't real wise of you. What is that called?" Bret asked, before answering his question, "Conspiracy."

"You can't prove that I sent them," Wally blurted out. "Besides, they were just supposed to scare her."

Walker Sr. closed his eyes in disgust at Wally's outburst. Bret smiled, shaking his head slightly at his oldest brother. He turned to Walker Sr. "God bless him, he never did have any common sense to go with his book sense, did he? He tries so much to be like you, but he never will. And William, he just cowers like a whipped puppy dog. Now, Walker, do you think that it just might hurt your standing in society to know that a member of your firm instructed the Klan to maim an innocent girl?"

Walker Sr. smiled confidently. "This is a nice display that you have put on, but your proof is inadequate for the courtroom."

"Maybe," Bret replied. He rose from his chair and turn behind him admiring his stereo that he had brought from Walker's house earlier in the day. "This was a nice Christmas present that you gave me last year."

"You can keep it," Walker Sr. replied, irritated at the sudden change in topic.

"What if this entire conversation was recorded? Would that bother you? The information about the financial records and not to mention Wally hiring the Klan?"

"You're bluffing," Walker Sr. responded.

"This afternoon, I removed the speaker from inside here," he said as he pulled off the speaker grill, and reached inside and pulled the recorder out. Say hello to the recorder, boys. It's still running."

Wally stood up quickly, not knowing his course of action.

"Sit back down," Bret smirked. "All three of you together couldn't get this from me."

Walker Sr. frowned before replying. "That's inadmissible."

"Well, I guess that I'll just give it to the newspaper. This kind of thing sells papers. Besides, I might have another witness, who would testify about this and more."

"Who, Alex?" Walker Sr. asked, with a derisive snort.

Bret looked under the stairs at the storage closet. The door conveniently open a few inches. "Barbara, you can come out now."

She rose from the folding chair that she had sat on, pushed open the door and walked to the table with pad and pen. "Bret, I think I wrote down about everything. And to think I balked at taking that shorthand class."

The three men sat still. The bewilderment etched in their faces.

Walker Sr. found his voice. "Young lady, you work for me. I've paid you handsomely and treated you well."

Barbara defiantly replied, "I don't work for you any longer and you never treat anyone well, especially your family. You're a disgusting, pathetic old man."

"Easy, Barbara, he's not worth hating," Bret softly said with a whisper of a chuckle. "Now, Walker."

"Stop calling me that. I'm your father."

"You were, but you disowned me."

"Maybe we can work it out."

"There is no need to work anything out."

"What do you want? Is it money? I'll give it to you." The strength in his voice dissipating.

Bret slid a document across the table. "Sign it."

Walker Sr. perused the legal document in front of him. "What is this?"

"I'm sure that you'll read it carefully but the basic of it is this. It says that you agree that giving me complete custody of Alex is in his best interests because you are unfit as a parent. I assume all care of him. Your shadows will witness it and sign where it says that they agree with the decision. Sign it and date it, gentlemen," Bret said as he tossed the ink pen across the table.

"How much money are you blackmailing me for?"

"It's not about money. The document says that Alex and I renounce all claims to the Marin fortune both now and forever more.

This is about my little brother. He's weak anyway, right? Cut him loose. He's not Marin material."

"I'll take this with me and think about it," Walker Sr. said as he rose from the chair.

"No, you'll sign it now. You don't want the court case, the publicity. It's not worth it. You got two sons that will 'toe the line.' Sign it, leave, and never go near my brother again."

"How do I know that you won't release this information anyway?"

"You have my word, and this is from a Marin who actually believes that a man's word is worth something. I just want my little brother. Sign it and you walk away. It's not like you are losing anything, right? You disowned me today and you treat Alex like he is some kind of cripple."

Walker Sr. read the document twice and signed it. The shadows did likewise.

"I guess you win, Bret, if you call this winning," he said as he motioned to the contents of the house.

Bret smiled and replied, "Oh, make no mistake. It is winning, but not in the way you ascertain winning to be."

The three men walked toward the door. One soundly defeated and the other two doing the math in their head. The estate would one day be split, not quartered.

Bret watched them walk away and a part of him felt sorry for them. "One last thing, Father," he said, invoking the name that he would never use again.

Walker Sr. turned, the rage gone from his face. The look on his face was as if he had watched a mystery movie and could not comprehend the ending. "What, son?"

"Any retaliation against anyone involved, ever, and these documents, and this tape," he said as he held it skyward, "will begin showing up at newspapers across the state. I suggest what pull that Wally has with the Klan is exercised very carefully. The Klan damn well better had made their last visit."

Walker Sr. nodded in agreement, and then looked sharply at a son dumb enough to involve the Klan. "Let's go," he said.

"Oh, one more thing for you to make sure does not happen. I also better not receive any draft notices."

"I don't..." Walker Sr. started to say.

"Never kid a kidder."

He looked at Bret and nodded. There was a look of shock and defeat in his face and his posture normally so upright now seemed to sag. It appeared he had aged ten years since he walked in the door minutes before. He walked wearily out of the house.

Vicky stood at the window and felt Alex so close to her that she could feel his breathing. She had prayed without ceasing all afternoon. She heard a car coming from the river house and prayed that it would not be stopping at her house to get the little boy that now clung tightly to her hip. There were three people in it and Walker Sr. sat slumped in the back, shaking his head slowly, as if he could not believe what had transpired. The car drove by without stopping.

She smiled through tears and shook her fist mightily toward the heavens. "Thank you, God. Thank you." She bent down and wrapped Alex up in her arms, covering him with her tears. "Bret did it, Alex." Alex cried happily with his grandmother.

* * *

It was past one a.m. Bret walked outside onto the deck. The sky was vividly clear and it seemed a million different stars were fighting for position to give off their light unobstructed.

Alex was peacefully asleep in his room, in his home, with the brother that he loved above all else in the world.

He studied the moon. It was nearing its fullness. He thought of that night on the beach with Teke. He wanted so badly to go tell her, to share this victory with her. They had built a house together and she had brought feelings out of him that he had no idea existed.

His mind drifted to his mother. He gazed up to the heavens and he wondered if she was looking down at him. Life had changed so much for him when he lost her. Nothing was ever as good. Inside of him was the joy of knowing that he and his little brother would be together, and the torment from how empty the house felt right now without Teke. He pulled the rocking chair toward him and sat down. He rocked gently as he studied the sky in its brilliance. He remembered his mom's last words. He dropped his head and then looked up again. "Mom," he said, "Alex is mine." He believed in his heart that she heard him.

CHAPTER TWENTY-ONE

Hearts without color

Barbara woke shortly after eight o'clock the next morning. She stretched her short body to its extreme limit. She smiled as she recalled the events of the previous day. Alex was with Bret, precisely where he belonged.

The three of them joined Vicky for a late supper. The meal of fried chicken, squash, and okra was prepared for a celebration of a family. Barbara saw none of the hardness in Vicky that she had heard so much about. She saw a grandmother who could not hide the twinkle in her soft blue eyes whenever she looked at the grandsons she obviously cherished.

Bret was quieter then Barbara could ever recall. She could see the glow on his face as he enjoyed the sheer bliss reflected in the peaceful eyes of his little brother. There would be no more nightmares about a little brother losing who he held sacred above all.

Still, she caught him frequently staring expressionlessly into space. She knew his thoughts were with Teke and that no matter how joyous the day had been it was not complete. It couldn't be. He never mentioned her name and Barbara knew all too well by now that it was his way. He had lived a long time closing off the unpleasantness from his life.

She left Vicky's at nine last night. She never did make the phone call to Teke. It seemed far too impersonal.

She stretched again and rolled from the bed, making her way to the kitchen for a morning glass of orange juice. Taped on the fridge was a list of errands that her mother left for her. She read the list, sighed, retrieved the orange juice container and poured juice into a glass. There was one errand more pertinent than the others. Minutes later she was driving to Castle Street.

She knocked on the door. Moments later, the door opened and Money stood before her. He appeared far different then she recalled from that spring day. The joy was gone from his face, replaced with a brooding somber look.

He looked at Barbara, saying nothing as he looked behind her to insure that she was alone.

"May I come in?" Barbara asked.

He stared at her for several moments in quietness. Finally, he nodded his head.

She entered the small living room. Clarence was seated in the corner. His face clouded with a plethora of disturbing thoughts and he seemed to be wrestling with each one without conclusion.

"Did he send you?" Money said bluntly, finding his voice.

"Did who?" she asked coarsely.

"You know who."

She shook her head tightly as if she were admonishing a small child and gave no reply, turning her attention back to Clarence. "Did you get home today?"

"Yes, I left at midnight. It was less traffic for me and that old truck to contend with."

"So, obviously you know."

"Yes, I know," Clarence answered deliberately.

"And you feel the same as this ungrateful son of yours?"

Money rose quickly from the couch. "Don't come here defending someone for whom there is no defense. So he helped me out only to repay me by dirtying my little sister, like she was some damn game. All those country club girls and that wasn't enough, he had to experience it all. The playboy of the country club and now niggertown," he said harshly.

"What a horrible word for you to use. You should be ashamed," she admonished, pointing her finger at him as if he were a third grader.

"He had no right to take advantage of my sister," he shouted.

"No, it's you that has no right," she replied sharply. "He should have left you in that alley. He put all of us in harm's way for you. You have a good time playing ball at State and each time you step on that court I want you to remember that you would not be there, if not for Bret. We can still speak his name in this house, can't we?" Any meekness that Barbara might have felt quickly left and her fury grew with each word.

"You don't know that for sure. I could have gotten away."

"They were going to break your shooting hand, or have you forgotten? After that who knows where they would have stopped or if they would have. Events such as that have a way of escalating and you could be dead at this very moment."

Clarence intervened in the youthful angers that permeated the room. "Money, sit down. Now, Barbara, what is it that you want?"

"I want to see Teke, and I want the two of you to stop acting as if someone stole something from you. You act as if Bret did this to deliberately hurt you."

"It shouldn't have happened," Clarence replied. "He was trusted to take care of her."

"Well, it did. It was unplanned, unintended, but still it happened. Nothing can change that. Do the two of you think that Bret Marin would ever do anything to hurt either of you intentionally?" She paused, before adding, "Well, I don't know what to say then," she said wearily. "Except that you are wrong, so very wrong."

"Maybe, it would be best if you leave," Clarence said.

"I came to see Teke," she replied stubbornly, her short powerful body digging into the hardwood floors beneath her.

Teke heard the voices from the bedroom that she had barely left since yesterday morning. She walked to the opening that gave access from the living room to the brief hallway that linked the three small bedrooms together. She knew that Barbara would have the news that she prayed would be good.

"Barbara," she called delicately.

Barbara looked in the direction of the voice. Teke looked as bad as someone who had been graced with such unblemished beauty could.

Her eyes were dominated by the color of dried blood and there were large dark lines below them. Her hair was tucked up under a Phillies baseball cap. She was wearing red cut off sweat shorts and a too large white tee shirt that Barbara knew belonged to Bret.

The two girls looked tenderly at each other. The men in the room sat silently. Clarence stared out the window into the street, not able to stomach the hurt in his daughter's eyes a moment longer.

Teke hesitated to ask, as if by not asking she would never hear the bad news she so feared. All she managed to get out was, "Did…"

Barbara softly shook her head yes. "He did it. Everything he set out to do. It's over. Alex is his."

Teke expected to cry, but for a day and a half that was all she had done. There were no tears left. Her heart filled with warmth that momentarily covered the hollowness that ravaged it. Barbara walked to Teke and they held each other tightly.

Barbara handed Teke a folded up piece of notebook paper. "This is my number. Call me. You hear?"

Teke nodded and said, "Stay in their life. Do what I can't."

"I will. I promise you."

Barbara turned to go.

"Barbara."

She turned. "Yes, Teke."

"Don't be too hard on those two," she said, motioning to the two grave figures. "I'm a little girl to them. They refuse to see me as a young woman. They probably never will. Deep down, they know that I mean it when I say I was the one who initiated this with Bret. It's easier for them to blame him than to allow me to grow up. The only comfort that they can find right now is in their anger."

Both men heard her comments and both wanted to reply, but neither could form an adequate response.

Barbara walked to the door. She turned to Money and Clarence. She could not resist attempting to penetrate the narrow thoughts the two men were clinging to so tightly. Besides, she had never been one to hold her tongue when there was an observation to be made.

She began softly, "You two aren't around to hear or feel the glow that comes from his words when he speaks of you. You sit here and feel sorry and betrayed all you want. But have you thought of how he feels? I know that he can't use that word love, except with Alex. It's funny. People have always been able to so easily see all that he has that it clouded their ability to see all that he has lacked. He was robbed of any decent childhood the day his mom died. He grew up so much poorer than you did, Money. He envies what you and your father have. He loves the two of you, and he loves her, too," she said as she looked across the room at Teke. "A few months ago, I would have been the last person in the world to defend Bret Marin. I would have told you that he was conceited, arrogant, selfish, and that all I could say good about him was that he loved his little brother. But Money, the two of you crossed paths for a reason. I know that since that day in the alley, he has changed into someone I am proud to call my friend. You should be too, both of you." She walked out the door, her words trailing behind her like a vapor.

* * *

It was late Wednesday afternoon. The phone rang in the river house for the first time ever. The telephone crew completed their task two hours earlier.

It was Micah Brooks. "Bret, at two o'clock this afternoon, the word came out on Wall Street that Lindell was awarded the computer contract for the Pentagon, beginning Jan. 1, of next year. The stock traded at fifteen dollars a share in the last trade of the day. Not a bad hunch for a teenager."

Bret smiled broadly and agreed, "Not bad, not bad at all."

"I expect the stock to gain more tomorrow. The word on the street is that by this time next year, it may be a sixty to seventy dollar stock."

"If it hits eighteen by the end of the week, sell one hundred shares. I need to buy a truck and I need some cash."

"I'll sell one hundred shares at eighteen. Thank you for your business."

"You're welcome, Micah."

"Can I ask one question, Bret?"

"That depends on how long you want to remain my broker."

"I'll talk to you when I have the check from the stock sale."

Bret hung the phone up. Everything was perfect, almost.

He and Alex walked to Vicky's. Alex ran along the creek bed, stopping to pick up stones and tossing them farther up the creek. Vicky was in the garden picking the last of the tomatoes and cucumbers that the garden would yield this year. They pitched in to help her.

They walked to her front porch. Alex charged inside. She stopped and turned to Bret placing her hand on his arm. "She's leaving tomorrow morning."

The news caught him off guard. He had assumed that she was already gone. It was easier that way.

"Don't you think you should go see her off?"

"And fight Money and his dad, no. Besides, we agreed that it would be easier to say our good-byes here."

"Just move on and never look back," Vicky summarized.

"I have no answers for this ,Vicky."

"Do you love her?"

He paused, that word that everyone wanted to use around him of late. "It wouldn't matter if I do. What do you want me to do, Vicky, bring her here to stay? That would make you real popular in the good old community of Castle Hayne."

"Well, I never did cotton much to what others thought of me. I don't guess that I should start now." She paused, before entering the house, and looked back at him. "Come inside. I'll say no more on the matter."

* * *

It was nine the next morning. Bret studied the layout of the kitchen and began another futile attempt at constructing the cabinets. Woodworking flowed through him as easily as a sailboat glided across a calm sea pressed by a favorable wind. It had been that way for him from the very beginning when Ralph gently coaxed the hidden artistry out of him.

He could hear his grandfather saying, "Picture it in your head, son, and then build it to fit."

He looked at the wood around him and said softly, "What do I do when all the pictures are wrong?"

He walked out to the deck where Alex sat observing the river, attempting to see all that his brother saw in it.

"Bret, why do you look at the river all the time?"

"I don't know, little man." He struggled for words that a boy of ten would understand. "You know what it is like to worry about something?"

"Sure, like a bad grade on a test."

"Well, yes, like a bad grade on a test. The river helps me not worry. It calms me. Do you understand?"

"Yes, I think so. Bret, I love our house and I'll do whatever you say. Don't worry about anything. I'll do well in school. I'll keep my room clean."

Bret touched him on top of his head and caressed his hair softly. "I know you will. I love you and you will always have a home with me. Don't you ever worry about us being apart. One day you will be an adult and you will want your own house. I will build you one on this property if you choose to live here."

"Is this where you will always want to live, Bret?"

He looked at his little brother and then gazed out at the river. "I can't imagine why I would ever choose to leave. Vicky, as tough as she is now, will get older and we will need to look after her." He laughed softly before adding, "I would not ever suggest sharing that with her."

"I'm glad it is you and me, and Vicky," he added. "I just wish Teke was here with us where she belongs."

Bret gazed curiously at his little brother. He wanted to reply, but finding no words he fixed his eyes on the river. What was it Teke said? He asked silently, trying to remember her words. It dawned on him. "Peace," he softly repeated.

The river would not grant him that peace today. He had won. Alex was his. There was money and a place to call home. Freedom from his father achieved. He looked for a few more moments and suddenly said loudly, "It's not enough. It's not enough," he repeated.

"What's not enough, Bret?" The youngster beside him asked with the most puzzled of expressions.

"Come on, I'll drop you off at Vicky's. I need to go somewhere. Come on, move," Bret urged him.

Minutes later he was speeding through Castle Hayne to Wilmington. He entered the driveway of the house on Castle Street so quickly that the wheels of his Mustang squalled slightly on the concrete at his harsh braking.

He banged on the door and when it opened, there stood Money.

"Let me in," Bret demanded, not waiting for the invitation that he felt certain that he wouldn't receive.

"No," Money stated firmly, refusing to move out of the doorway.

"I'm coming in, one way or the other. You decide."

Both men stood there, neither willing to give any ground. Clarence and Teke emerged from the back to see what the commotion was about.

Clarence spotted Bret first. His first inclination was to go pound him into the street. His second option was not much better.

"Get away from here. Her bags are packed and she's leaving for the airport. We don't have time for this."

"You'll have to make time. I'm not leaving until I see her."

Clarence replaced his son's space in front of the door. "Son, do you realize that right now, I could toss you out in that street on your head?"

"I'm aware of that. Go ahead." Bret stood in front of him frozen, unwilling, unable to move.

"Daddy, let him in, please?" Teke asked.

Clarence turned to Teke and shook his head no. "He needs to stay in his world and you need to return to yours."

She smiled softly and placed her hand on his cheek. "Daddy, that's not you. You've always been a fair man. What is this his world, my world? That's the hurt in you talking. I'm sorry that I hurt you, Daddy. You and Money blame Bret for all this but that's not right. Daddy, you are the fairest man I know. Don't stop being that because of something I've done that you don't understand. Let him inside."

Clarence slowly vacated his spot in front of the door. He walked to the couch and sat down. Money slumped down in the chair across from him. Neither would look in the direction of the intruder.

The door free from all barriers now, Bret moved quickly inside. He looked at Teke and saw the suitcases on each side of her. During his ride across town, he did not have the first thing planned to say. It showed now in his silence.

She looked compassionately at him before asking smugly, "Did you barge in here to become a typical dumb southerner, you know, your brain working even slower than your drawl?"

"You always could make someone feel right at ease with those northern manners?" He paused, studying her, her hair falling down on the sleeveless white cotton shirt. She was wearing a bright red skirt that stopped just above her knees. She was a stunning young woman from head to toe. He smiled, because he now knew what made her different. As beautiful as her physical appearance was she was even more beautiful inside.

Clarence interrupted his thoughts. "You had the nerve to show up here, so I suppose you have a reason?"

Bret answered, "I do. I want your daughter," he said, all the words coming in a rush.

"What?" Money asked, unable to believe the audacity of what he had heard. "You need to get out of here now," he said as he stood up and moved toward him.

"So help me, Money, I don't want to fight you, but I will."

Teke stepped between the two of them and faced Bret. "We've been through this. It won't work."

"You are probably right, but don't we have to try?"

Clarence spoke, "She's seventeen. You are white, she's black and this wouldn't go over well in the north, much less here. Are you going to take her to the country club boy? To your father's house? Come on Bret, who are you kidding?"

"I don't have a father," Bret replied quickly. "Alex and I are free and clear from him, but I didn't come here to talk about that. I came for you, Teke. I want you to come home with me. I've got this great house and I have a little brother to share it with. Alex is going to have a good childhood and he is never going to be anything like me. He is going to be a man so much better than I could ever dream to be. I have a generous grandmother who will do anything to help us, to support us. But none of that has kept the emptiness out of that house. There's too much life gone from it. The life of the house was you. I know that now. Let's take the suitcases and go home. I want you, Alex wants you, and Vicky wants you."

She stared at him and drank in the words that now flowed so easily from a man that held everything so tightly. But the past days away from *The River Hideaway* had brought her back to reality. "It's crazy, Bret. I admit when I was out there, isolated from the prejudice of the world, I thought it possible, but it's a dream world."

"That's her answer. Now leave," Clarence gruffly said, not wanting to give him any more time to sway his daughter.

Bret turned to the man he admired so much, even at this moment with the hostility the man had for him. He looked at Money before reverting back to Clarence. "Clarence, I respect you more than any man I know. You are the father I wish that I would have had. Money, you are my best friend.

Money answered defiantly, "You sure have a funny way of showing it, friend. I trusted you."

Bret kept his temper in check and replied, "You asked me to protect your sister. I did. I also hurt her by pushing her away when all she wanted to do was stay."

"My sister should not have been another of your conquests," he answered angrily, and took steps toward him.

Bret lost the composure he had fought so valiantly to maintain and shoved Money hard across the room. "Don't you do that to Teke. Don't you dare cheapen her. I grew up in a world where class supposedly reigns and she's got more class than anyone I've ever seen. Money, did you think I planned to fall in love with her?"

Money moved toward Bret again, but his father stepped in between them. "Not in my house."

"Well, then it will need to be in the street if you say another word to degrade her," Bret said evenly.

Clarence held each of them back. "No, not in the street either. Bret, you said all you had to say. Now leave us be."

"You told me that day I helped Money in the alley that if I ever needed anything, all I had to do was ask," he pleaded. "I'm asking you to try to understand this. I'm asking you to believe me right now," he pleaded.

"You're asking too much."

"So all of it was just talk, Clarence? All your words, and your lessons," he exclaimed exasperated. "Hey, remember this one? Sometimes something is inside of you that no one else can see, but you see it and you know that it's right. Well, this is my time. If it doesn't work out, then at least we know we tried. Teke and I don't go our separate ways always wondering, or like you, always missing the one that left."

Bret saw the last words penetrate deeply into Clarence and the pain they brought forth. He breathed deeply. "I'm sorry, Clarence. I had no right to say that." He paused, then said, "I guess you are right. I've said all I have to say."

He looked at Teke, who had not moved or spoken in minutes and smiled faintly. "I had to try. I could not let you leave without knowing how much I want you to stay."

He turned to the door and stopped as he put his hand on the glass doorknob. "Clarence, Money, I wish things could be fixed between us." He shook his head slightly before turning to Money. "Barbara was right. I made fun of her, but she was right. You and I crossed paths for a reason. Sometimes at night, I look at the river and wonder how so much of my life could have changed so very quickly. I beat my father. I got my little brother where he won't know the hell that I knew growing up. I got money. I got a house that you and Clarence made me begin and Teke helped me finish, almost," he said, softly chuckling to himself, as he recalled the kitchen cabinets. "It would have been more than enough a few months ago. Now, it's just not. I can't help that I fell in love with your sister, or your daughter," he said, turning to Clarence. "My God, look at her," he said, gesturing toward Teke with his hand. "She's beautiful, intelligent, tender and her wisdom..." His voice choked slightly. "She showed me a world that I never knew existed. You guys can't stay mad at me forever for loving someone so brilliant, so beautiful. Let her grow up. You won't lose her. Besides she's so far ahead of us that we don't have a prayer of ever catching up." The room was silent. "I won't bother any of you, ever again," he whispered as he walked through the door.

He was beside his car when he heard her voice "So, that's it! You can't do this."

"Do what?" he asked, turning toward her.

"You can't walk in here and tell me that you are in love with me and walk away."

She was to the first step now. Clarence and Money stood behind her on the porch. "Tell me again."

"Tell you what?"

"That word that only Alex gets to hear."

He dropped his head slightly. He forced a chuckle, and the humility that he had displayed in the house gave way to his more natural arrogance. "What does it matter? You are going to Philadelphia. Your father and brother are right. Why would you want to throw your life away on someone who will love you, who you can trust above anyone, who will be your best friend, and who will be the best builder in this town," he said as he eyed Clarence.

"You didn't say it. Look me in the eye and say it, or get in that car and leave," she demanded.

He walked to her. He gently grasped her elbows. "I love you, Teke."

"Since when?" she asked, refusing to soften.

"Teke, do you have to make everything so difficult?"

"I want to know."

"Would a man move the clouds out of the way just so the moon could shine if he hadn't fallen in love with her?"

Her defiance gave way to her tears. "Wait right here," she commanded, as she turned to the men on the porch.

"Here's what I want from you two. Give us until Christmas. If this is wrong, we will know it, and I'll go back to Philadelphia."

Clarence cleared his throat to speak but he did not get the chance.

"I know what you are going to say. I'm seventeen, and you and mom can make me go home. I'll be eighteen on September 14th, and I'll be right back here."

"Why not wait until then and give this some time?"

"No. I want to go home with Bret. It's where I belong."

"You'll live with him?"

"Well, he hasn't asked me to marry him yet," she joked. She took her father in one hand and her brother in the other. "If it doesn't work, at least we'll know. I know this is hard for you. You want what's best for me. I know that. I believe in this man and I believe in his love for me. God knows I can't love any more than this. It's not humanly possible. What if this is my only love in a lifetime, Daddy? Should I send him away because he is white?"

"I can't stop you, can I?" he said softly, resigned to her choice.

"No, you can't. The two of you can give us a chance."

Clarence was losing and he knew it. "I guess you want me to explain this to your mother?"

"It would be nice for you to try. She knows I've never been irrational. I'm the brain in the family. He's the jock," she said, motioning to Money.

"What about school?"

"There is a fine college here, Wilmington College. I talked to them this summer when it appeared that it might never be safe for me to return to Philly. They will bend over backwards to admit someone with my GPA."

Bret spoke up. "I'll pay for it."

"You don't need to. They will give me a full scholarship."

Clarence wanted to win the argument that began a few minutes ago. But he would not prevail and a man, a good man, needed to know when to step aside. "You're right, child, if I stop you. You'll be right back, more determined than ever."

"I want something else."

"What?"

"I want the two of you to remember that this man is someone you both care a great deal about. It's not anyone's fault and I don't want to hear that said one more time. Bret was right. It cheapens me when either of you say that. You guys love me and I know you are not making me a part of something shameful."

They dropped their heads slightly at the lecture directed their way.

"I want it resolved right here, and right now."

They both hesitated and shrugged their shoulders.

"Please. You don't have to agree, but you do need to remember, Money, that this is your best friend and they don't grow on trees. Dad, you liked him from the first day he came here. All I heard was what a great thing it is the way he looks after his brother. Maybe one day I will tell you just all that he has sacrificed for that little brother. Are you going to be mad at him for loving me? It would be easier if we both were white, or black, but we're not. Hearts have no color, Daddy. You taught me that when I was a little girl."

Her words shook them and the goodness that abounded in each of them emerged. Clarence extended his hand and Bret took it and held it firmly. They said nothing, but in their eyes was the peace they all needed to move forward.

Bret stepped toward Money. "I never even cared about friendship before you came along. You wore me down. Only man I ever met with more charm than me, or that could play basketball better. I didn't let you down on purpose. Something happened that seemed to have a mind of its own. I have won so much the past few days but you know how it is to want to win it all. I can't win it all if I leave here today without my best friend."

Money blinked back the water that wanted to escape his eyes. All he could manage to say was, "I'm sorry, Bret."

The two boys that had become men this summer embraced. Teke blinked away tears and she saw her dad fight back his own.

"I guess I got a phone call to make," Clarence said. "That is unless the two of you have any more requests."

"I do. God help me, I do have one. It's a big one," Bret replied.

Clarence stopped and stared in disbelief.

"I need some help. The house is a showpiece, but I can't for the life of me figure out how best to build the kitchen cabinets. Will you please help me?" he asked humbly.

Clarence nodded. "Okay, tomorrow morning. Would that be good?"

"That would be great. Money?"

"I'll be there."

Clarence turned once again to the door.

"Uh, one more thing."

Clarence turned slowly and spoke evenly. "You got my daughter, son. I'll start on the cabinets tomorrow. What else could you possibly want?"

"I have a little guy who has talked about pancakes at your house now for weeks."

A beaming smile broke the gruff exterior of his face. "Saturday morning, eight o'clock, and bring my daughter too." He took a step toward the door before turning back with an enlightened expression on his face. "Hey Teke, I actually get to see my daughter more than once a year for a couple of weeks."

"That's right, Daddy," she assured him. "You will see me all the time."

He turned back to Bret. "Now may I go inside and figure out just how I am going to explain all of this to her mother?"

"I'm done," Bret answered. "That's all. I'll get the suitcases."

He was putting the suitcases in the trunk. Teke sat comfortably in the passenger seat. She felt as if she were in a dream, a wonderful dream from which she never desired to wake.

He closed the trunk and walked to the door. Money called from the porch, "Hey, Bret."

"Yeah."

The smile was back where it belonged on a face naked without it. "Ball on Sunday at one."

Bret nodded. "I will absolutely be there. And don't feed me to big Willie."

"Hey," he exclaimed. "That's a thought."

"Money Wilkins," Teke called his name like a teacher would call down an unruly student.

He cackled loudly. "Just kidding, sis. Just kidding."

They backed out the drive in the direction of a life that they realized would be complex. The only thing that could possibly prove more arduous would be not to try.

CHAPTER TWENTY-TWO

Christmas

There were but a few minutes of Christmas night left. Teke and Bret sat comfortably holding hands in the swing that had been added to the porch, and gazed out in the darkness toward the river. The moon was near full and without a word being spoken they each knew the other thought about the night on the beach when clouds separated and the moon came forth in all its glory. Alex was asleep in his bed, but not before proclaiming this day as the greatest Christmas ever.

Bret reflected to earlier events in the day. Minutes after noon, family and friends sat down to the long dinner table that they purchased back in September. The people seated at the table enjoyed the finest feast that Bret ever tasted. In addition to being a chef at breakfast, Bret gained knowledge that Teke and Money already possessed. Clarence was a champion pig cooker. He towed his homemade pig cooker to *The River Hideaway* at two that morning, banged on the door, woke Bret, and told him it was time for him to learn the art of a proper pig picking. Bret had been asleep for two hours but he didn't mind. He was happy, and he truly knew that was the rarest of riches in this world.

Vicky balked at first when she heard that turkey was not on the menu but she was more agreeable these days and she relented quickly. She prepared enough cole slaw for a small army, and baked seven different pies in an attempt to make everyone's favorite. Teke made a huge pan of baked beans. Louie and Elma came, and at Louie's insistence he cooked the hush puppies, which was his specialty.

Money was present at the table also and the amount of food that he consumed led one to believe he had not eaten since he left for Raleigh. Barbara came and brought her parents, who were a little shy at first but by the end of the afternoon Barbara's dad was joking with Clarence, who agreed to come to their house and give them a price on remodeling the kitchen the following week. At Bret's insistence, Money invited Big Willie and his mama. Big Willie's mom cornered Money and talked hoops for an hour straight.

The surprise visitor was Jacky Wilkins, who flew in the day before. Money was asleep in Teke's old room, partly because he wanted to be at the river with his sister and best friend, but also in hopes that if his parents found time alone maybe something new and good would come from it.

Bret smiled again as he pictured the group at the table and he hoped that they would return each year. Louie located him on a job site one day after word reached the Club about the foolish young man who broke from the Marin family and squandered his riches for a *colored* girl. Louie knew better and each time he overheard the story he smiled and thought of his dream and felt good that he was witness to such a miracle. He told Bret how happy he was for Alex and him, before adding how proud of him that he was. Bret felt warm inside each time he recalled the words the elderly gentleman spoke that day.

He told Louie that he was the only part of the club that he would miss. Louie reminded him of where he lived and told him that he was welcome anytime.

The first time he visited Louie, they sat on the front porch and drank sweet tea that Elma made. The porch had several loose boards and quite a bit of the structure was rotten.

The next morning Louie woke to the sound of something close by being torn down. He walked to the front door where he saw Bret and Money tearing out the old porch, while Clarence and Alex were stacking the wood that Bret purchased that morning.

Bret saw Louie standing in the door way looking out the screen door, unable to comprehend what he was seeing. "You and your wife just use the back door today. I think we can finish today but if not, by tomorrow at the latest."

"But, Bret," he tried to find words to say.

"Louie, I plan on drinking a lot of sweet tea with Miss Elma and you so I consider this an investment."

Louie nodded his head and shuffled back to the bedroom and informed his wife about the origin of the sound. They held each other and cried softly and thanked Jesus for their friend, and his friends.

The week of Thanksgiving, Louie and Elma were awaken again. It seemed that several facia boards were in need of replacement that Bret had made note of earlier. Clarence and Alex were there to help again and this time Teke joined them. Louie walked back in and shared the news with his wife. They cried once again, and thanked their Savior profusely for supplying what they never could afford.

Louie's eyes grew wide upon meeting Teke. He turned to Bret, and said, "Boy, you done outdone yourself."

Teke smiled warmly and hugged him tightly. "I have heard so much about you."

It was late in the day as tools were loaded up and thank you offered a dozen times by Louie and Elma when Louie searched in Bret's eyes for some kind of reason that he could understand. "Why Bret? Why all of this for me?"

Bret placed his hand on the old man's arm, smiled slightly, and offered, "You believed in me when I did not believe in myself. You saw something good where I did not. We are coming back next weekend and we are going to paint the house now that all the rotten boards have been replaced. Sometime this week Clarence or I will drop off some paint charts. You and your wife pick a color out, okay?"

The dignified gentleman man nodded and shuffled back inside so they would not see him weep.

Bret looked at the crew that assembled each time he mentioned what he wanted to do. They never hesitated to help. "Is that good with you guys? We finish next weekend."

Clarence smiled and nodded his agreement. "Feels good, doesn't it son?"

"Yes, it does," he answered.

"You are a good man, Bret."

Teke squeezed his hand startling him from his thoughts. "Where are you?" she asked laughingly.

"What do you mean?"

"That beaming grin on your face."

"I was thinking about today and all of the people at the dinner table. Louie," he said, his voice trailing off. "I mentioned to him that we were going to start on the inside of his house. He told me no, absolutely not. You done too much for Elma and me already, Bret."

"So?" she asked.

"I told him that the floor in the bathroom was sagging and whether he liked it or not that we were going to rebuild the floor and whatever else needs doing."

"And what did he say?"

"It did not matter what he said."

"But what did he say?" she reiterated.

"No, but then I asked him, what if Jesus was sending us to do this work?"

"And what was his response?" she asked.

He reflected back on the day he watched Louie shuffle toward home after having told him about his friend with words as soft and smooth as the river in front of them. "There is no one Louie loves more than Jesus."

"Did you mean it when you said it, about Jesus sending us to help, or did you just say that to get your way?"

Bret shrugged and replied, "Maybe it is true, or at least not as far-fetched as it once might have seemed."

She studied him and said assuredly, "There is more to this story."

He looked over at her and thought of how she could read him. He knew he could never pull anything over on her, could never be dishonest with her without her knowledge, but that was good because he had no intention of being anything but a good and honest man to her. She deserved that and he was not embarrassed to know that he wanted to give her that. He wanted to always be a man that she was proud of.

"Louie had a dream or a vision as he called it." He described the dream Louie had about Alex and him at the lake with people tearing at them while his father looked on.

Teke felt as if she had goose bumps layered deeply on her body. She shook her head from the chill. "Wow," she mumbled softly. "God really did help us, didn't he, Bret?"

"I don't think there is much doubt about that," he answered.

"So, what do we do with that?"

"I don't know the answer to that yet."

"But you are working on it?"

He kissed her lightly on the cheek, ran his hand through her hair. "I look at my life and how different I view everything and I think I would have to be a fool to not believe that I had unseen help."

She leaned over and kissed him. "Could we be any happier?"

"I don't think so," he answered, as he looked at her. "You know, Louie was right that day that he met you."

"What do you mean?"

"I did outdone myself," he said.

"Great English," she cracked. They looked at each other and she said, "I did pretty well myself. I got a good man with a great heart."

"Sometimes I can't believe it."

"Believe what?"

"You were gorgeous when I met you, but I watched you grow into this woman who becomes more beautiful every day."

"Wow," she said.

He chuckled softly.

"Go ahead."

"What?" he laughed.

"You share your heart and soul with me and even now you have to make a joke so you don't get too uncomfortable."

"You know I don't get uncomfortable with you."

"Still, go ahead. Make a joke. I can take it. I mean you did just tell a woman that she gets more beautiful every day. That grants you a little bit of leeway, but I advise you to tread lightly."

"Even your chest is growing," he said before adding, "Must be a late surge."

"Why would that matter? You are a leg man."

"That's true," he said, smiling mischievously. "Still, it doesn't hurt."

She shook her head at him admonishingly, but the smile never left her face. She rose up and then sat down in his lap. Her back nestled against his chest, securely wrapped in his arms.

He chuckled louder this time.

"What?" she snapped, feigning irritation.

"This swing can only bear so much weight in one spot. I was afraid that your chest might tip us over the limit."

"If we go down, we go down together," she whispered in his ear, nestling tighter to him.

He held her closer and they became comfortable in silence as they so often did these days. Minutes later she rose and sat next to him. She snuggled as close to him as possible. Bret gazed at the sky, noticing the stars and moon were now covered by low hanging clouds. It was the most peaceful, the happiest Christmas he had ever known. He turned to Teke, taking her hand in his. "I guess it's time."

"Time for what?"

"It's Christmas. We gave it our best shot. You better pack for Philly."

She smiled at the beauty of the river that she no longer saw through Bret's eyes. "I didn't say which Christmas."

Silence ensued again before she asked, "Bret, do you really feel like God had a hand in all of this?"

"Yes."

"Vicky and I talk about a lot of subjects and that includes God and, by the way, it was she who placed that white Bible in our home."

"The morning I set out to finalize the deal to have Alex that Bible was open on the kitchen table. My eyes fell on Psalms 20:4 *May he give you the desire of your heart and make all your plans succeed.* I remember feeling encouraged.

"I know I did some deceitful things to save Alex and I guess..." his voice trailing off in doubt.

"I believe God forgives us each time we ask. Maybe even before we ask. Do you have any regrets?" she asked gently.

"No," he stated firmly. "I promised Alex that I would take care of him and I knew of no other way. The court system surely would not have been in my favor."

"Let's move forward and know you never have to do anything like that ever again. Alex is safe inside asleep and he is as happy as any kid I have ever witnessed. He has no bad dreams. He has no sense of loss. I asked him one day if he was okay with leaving the life he knew behind and he answered quickly, as long as I am with my brother I am where I want to be. You know," she said before pausing to choke back tears. "Do you know the next thing he said and did?"

Bret looked at her and wiped a tear away with his index finger as gently as a mother holds a new born baby.

"He reached over and took hold of my hand and said I did not lose anything. Look at all the good things I got. I got you, Money, your dad, and Vicky. What else could a kid want? All of you love me. I am just a kid but I know if I need anything, you guys would come running to help me."

They were silent again for several minutes. "So Bret, you placed the Bible and that scripture by the bed that morning?"

"No," he answered, with a soft shake of his head.

"Well, that same Bible with that same scripture greeted me that morning also. So how did that happen?"

"I don't know," he answered softly. "What I do know is this. I have the desires of my heart and all plans look pretty good to me."

"I don't know how, but it was probably Vicky." She smiled broadly and added, "I never really had a grandmother before. Both died when I was a toddler. I love her."

"I would not suggest you call her that regardless of how much you love her."

Teke laughed softly. "I know. None of this would have happened without her."

"I know. So you said earlier you and she talk about a lot of things. Was there something else you wanted to say?"

Teke laughed warmly again. "Yes. She thinks God answered her prayers and gave her a wonderful family. She said that her heart was closed before you showed up and now it is so full, it overflows."

"She used those words."

"Yes, those exact words. I don't make light of her the way you do so she feels safe to share. And she wanted you to know that dinner will not be at 11:30 on Sundays anymore."

"What?"

"She wants to go to church on Sundays beginning the first of the year. She said it has been too long and she has been too blessed not to attend."

"Good for her."

"Good for all of us. She expects all of us to go."

"All of us?" he asked, with a puzzled expression.

She smiled at him and nodded her hand gently. "We went to the market one day last week and this man struck up a conversation with us. It turns out that he is the minister of a small church in Rocky Point. He invited us to church and assured us that it would be fine. He believes that no church should be segregated. God's love and grace without regard to color is how he put it. He believes this to be his calling and so he has set about to open the church doors to anyone who believes."

"Not without resistance, I bet."

"No, some members left, but new people came. I like him. He is really young for minister and you know the Civil Rights March on Washington in '63?"

"Sure."

"He was part of it. There were actually thousands of white people that marched."

He nodded.

"So?" she asked.

"Okay, we will go to church with Vicky."

"You sure are easy these days and I think dad and Money when he is home will be attending with us."

"Really?"

"She already called them."

He smiled at the persuasive powers of his grandmother.

"Bret," she said before pausing, searching for words. "We talked with him a long time." She paused unsure of continuing.

"And?"

"He said that he would be honored to marry us."

Bret nodded softly.

"But you don't want to?" she asked, hesitantly.

He cupped her face in his hands and smiled. "Do you want to be my wife?"

"Yes," she whispered.

"But, you don't think that I would want that?"

"I don't know," she replied. "I know that you love me and I know that you see beauty in me that I don't see."

"You know you are not the only one who talks to Vicky."

"What do you mean?"

"She told me that a woman like you deserves everything right. And she would never want us to get married simply because we might think it is not right for us to live together. That is never the right reason according to her and she is right."

"What did you say to all of this?"

"I told her that she was right."

"It would be hard, you know, Bret?"

"There is no doubt about that, but you know I have been through some difficult days these past few months." He looked at her, smiled and asked, "Do you know what the most difficult of those times was?"

"What?" she asked.

"It was when I thought that you had gone back to Philly and I was not going to ever have you in my life again."

She smiled at him again before the corners of her mouth turned into a slight grimace. "I don't want marriage to be my idea, Bret."

He kissed her and pulled away and said softly, "Okay, I did not plan it this way."

She started to interrupt and he put his finger gently on her lips.

"I know that you are always a mile ahead of me in everything and sometimes I would just like to think I was on the same path with you, right in step." He paused and said, "Under your pillow is a box with a ring in it. I used Vicky's setting because it meant so much to her and I took that to the jeweler and had a diamond mounted."

"Did I just blow your proposal?"

"Not at all. The only way that could be is if you said no."

"Like there is a chance of that," she answered. "Wow, Bret, you are more amazing all the time. Are you sure?"

"It is not only what is right, Teke, and it is not only what a woman like you deserves, but it is certainly what I want as well. I promise you that I am going to do my best to be everything in a husband that you deserve."

"I want one thing from you and that is you never close your heart off again. You keep it open for me at all times as I will do for you and then I know we can get through anything with God's help."

"Okay. Now, do you want to go upstairs and look now?"

"There is one more thing I want to tell you."

"Wait a minute. I thought women were supposed to get all excited about this and rush to see it."

"I want to, but this is really important also, okay?"

"Go ahead," he nodded and smiled at her again.

"Mom met this very renowned specialist in Philly at a conference. She explained about Alex and the doctor was very nice and he called the doctor here to ask for a copy of the medical files. He studied all Alex's medical records and he feels confident that he can help. I did not want to tell you earlier because I did not want to get your hopes up. Mom said that we can schedule an appointment the first week of summer vacation. He said that he will check him out and if things look good he would plan on operating right away. Mom said we can stay with her as long as we need too. And if you are building a house then, which you probably will be, I will remain with Alex when you can't."

Tears streamed down Bret's face abruptly and so fiercely that he could not find his voice. She held him tightly and rubbed his back. She heard him gasp. "A good chance?"

"Yes, honey, he thinks that there is a really good chance. He thinks at the very least Alex will be able to walk without a limp and at the very best he will one day have legs as strong as yours."

"Oh, my God," Bret whispered. Teke held him as he sobbed for the little boy that he loved so much.

Minutes later when he found his composure, he said, "Teke, the questions about God. He can have anything from me he wants."

"Me too," she agreed.

Moments later they rose and walked hand in hand upstairs. She opened the box and saw the glimmering ring and there was a small note that simply stated, "Marry me."

"That is not a question," she asked, as she winked at him.

"You are too smart to pass up a man that cares for you the way I do."

"You got that right," she said as she kissed him.

He placed it on her finger and they walked back outside, hand in hand. The temperature seemed to have dropped several degrees in a few minutes. They stood on the deck in awe as it began to snow. A few intermittent flakes at first and then it began snowing so much that you could not see the river. They stood there and laughed for several minutes.

Bret smiled and breathed in deeply. "It does not snow here often and I have never heard of it on Christmas. I think God is just showing off for us right now."

She hugged him tightly and said, "I am going to wake Alex and Money."

"Go ahead," he said.

Teke stirred Money first and told him it was snowing. He tried to roll back over and resume sleeping but she grabbed him in the rib cage where she knew his most vulnerable tickle spot lay. "Okay, okay. I will get up. Just please stop," he said, laughing.

Next she walked to Alex's room. He was soundly asleep. She kissed his head gently and thought of how much she loved the little boy. She shook him gently. "Alex, wake up, honey. Wake up."

It took a few moments but he stirred and opened his eyes and saw Teke smiling at him. "What?" he asked, in a groggy daze.

"You will never guess what is happening."

He was more awake now and it showed in his smile. "You and Bret are getting married and you are never going to leave us."

"How did you know that?"

"He asked me what I thought about it."

"And what did you say?"

He smiled mischievously. "I said I was not too keen on the idea."

She grabbed yet another person in their tickle spot.

"Stop, stop," he pleaded through breathless laughter.

"Just for that I am not going to tell you the other surprise."

"Why would you be mean to me, Teke? I am such a sweet little boy."

She shook her head, smiling.

"I always wanted you guys to get married."

She hugged him tightly. "Now put some clothes on. We are going outside."

"Why?" he asked curiously.

"Because it is snowing."

He sat up quickly. "No way," he exclaimed.

"Yes, way," she answered. "Dress properly and don't forget a cap and gloves."

Minutes later the four of them stood out on the deck. The snow was beginning to cover the ground. Bret looked at the rest of the group naughtily.

"What?" the three of them asked in unison.

"Let's go wake Vicky."

Money spoke first, "Uh, no. I know she is a lot nicer these days but she still scares me a bit."

Alex shook his head admonishingly. "Big basketball player like you afraid of a little old lady."

Bret was already walking toward her house and the rest of the group followed. As they neared her house the ground now was mostly white. Bret worked diligently to garner enough snow for a snowball.

He formed one into the size of a baseball and eyed Vicky's house. Teke looked at him and said, "Have you forgotten she has a gun?"

He just chuckled like a wayward child. He threw a strike at her bedroom window. Immediately the kitchen light went on and the door opened. Vicky stepped out on the stoop, dressed fully with coat, scarf, gloves, toboggan, and boots.

"I was wondering if all of you were going to sleep when this is the first trace of snow on Christmas since '48. I thought I might have to wake all of you."

Bret, slightly discouraged that he did not achieve the desired result of waking her with a snowball shot, said, "But you did not have any lights on."

"I did earlier but you four made so much noise I figure one of you would get cute. I also figured the one to do that would be you," she said with a winning smile. "So I turned the lights off and sat at the kitchen table waiting."

She walked toward them and took Alex by the hand. "What do you say we walk down to the river and watch the snow over the water?"

He clutched her hand firmly and said, "Let's go."

They were standing at the river now enjoying the tranquility of the scene laid out before them. Silently each one of them was thanking God.

EPILOGUE

So much had transpired since the day Bret made the wise choice to drive to Castle Street and bring Teke home. Alex received two report cards so far and was yet to bring home anything lower than an A. Teke taught him daily and he was the most prepared kid in school. Best of all, Alex was happy and secure.

Teke's first semester was complete and she made the dean's list. Money was doing well in school also, and was averaging twenty-three points per game to lead the freshman team at NC State in scoring. Bret was nearly finished with the first house in his proper career as a contractor. He hired a crew of two and completed all of the work except for the cabinets, which he subbed out to Clarence. The next house they would build together.

Lindell was selling at twenty-eight dollars a share. Bret still owned all that he purchased that morning, except for the one hundred shares sold at eighteen dollars per share. Clarence, in the past months had discovered the daughter he once felt so distant from. She was the apple of his eye, and he was a dad that she treasured. Vicky, well, she doesn't even try to be tough these days. Each night on bended knee beside her bed she thanked God for the people that had been brought into her life, casting away the emptiness that reigned before. Each day she set the food on the dinner table at 11:30 as always, but there was a change. Bret made certain that she never sat at the table alone. Many days he came and brought Clarence if they were working together. Teke was present anytime that she did not have class. Alex was there every day that he was not in school and no one had to inform him to go. Often he sprinted up the road the best he could to be with his grandmother. After dinner they would frequently go for a walk and she would explain nature to him. Alex would reach over and take her hand as they walked.

The week after their engagement Teke decided that she would live with Vicky until Bret and she were married. She explained to him that she had no remorse but wanted to give herself all over to him for the first time as his wife. He knew the determined look by now well enough to agree. Besides they had a lifetime together in front of them and their love was one that would not fade in time but grow stronger with each passing day.

There was no contact for Bret and Alex with the rest of the Marin family. There never would be. After the day of his defeat his father never mentioned the two sons that abandoned him. He did rewrite his will leaving them each the sum of one dollar. He was not a man able to see how rich the sons that left him behind truly were.

The following spring on the anniversary date that Bret and Alex lost their mother, Bret and Teke were married by their minister from the church they had joined and attended almost every Sunday. It was a small gathering of family and friends. The Wilkins family was present and Clarence wept as he gave away the bride. Vicky stood watching proudly. Barbara was Teke's maid of honor.

Louie and his bride were present. Bret, regardless of schedule went by their house weekly to enjoy sweet tea, or coffee, if it was the early morning. Mostly he enjoyed their company. He continued to do work at their house to the point now that it was better than the day it was constructed. Louie never knew that the day he was asked to help Bret that he would be on the blessing end of so much. He was thankful but he never did it to receive. He did it to please his Lord.

The simple intimate ceremony took place in front of *The River Hideaway*, on the shore of the river. The faultless sky rich with the color of cobalt. Alex served as best man.

Acknowledgements

With special thanks to the following:

Robbie Johnson, fellow Carolina Beach lover and Duke fan, for the beautiful book cover photos. Nathan Reynolds, for the author photo. Micah, who believed in this story before the first word was written. Julie, I never had a chance. You are my gift from God. Jack and Kelly. Life is easier with friends like you. Jack, remember at the end of *Tombstone,* when Wyatt thanks Doc for always being there? Pretty much sums it up. My family, for your excitement and support. The Olivolo family, for taking me into your wonderful family. The team at Oak Tree Press that provided the means for a dream to come true.

About the Author

Billy Beasley resides in Carolina Beach, NC with his wife Julie, and one spoiled rotten black Chihuahua mix, Sydny. He has lived in southeastern North Carolina his entire life and many years ago was among the very first students to be bused to another school to achieve real integration.

CPSIA information can be obtained at www.ICGtesting.com
Printed in the USA
BVOW04s1900140115

383353BV00003B/187/P